Grasshopper Flats

GRASSHOPPER FLATS

ROBERT OLIVER BERNHAGEN

MILL CITY PRESS
MINNEAPOLIS, MN

Mill City Press, Inc.
212 3rd Avenue North, Suite 290
Minneapolis, MN 55401
612.455.2294
www.millcitypublishing.com

ISBN - 978-1-936107-64-3
ISBN - 1-936107-64-3
LCCN - 2010921518

Cover Design and Typeset by Nate Meyers

Printed in the United States of America

Thanks to my cousin Andy

He provided the spark that lit my fire.

Prologue

On Friday, March 4, 1881, in a snow covered Washington D.C., newly elected President James A. Garfield gave his first and only inaugural address to the country. It was a day of gala festivities and jubilant celebrations in our nation's capital. Thousands lined Pennsylvania Avenue to watch the big parade. The famous John Philip Sousa and his Marine Corps Band provided the musical entertainment. While folks in D.C. were celebrating and enjoying a day off work, it was a day of sadness and somber reflection at the Box H ranch in northern Arizona. They were attending a funeral.

The Box H ranch was a middling-sized ranch of about six thousand acres located some thirty miles west of Flagstaff. It was nestled at the foot of Bill Williams Mountain, at an elevation of seven thousand feet midway between Kaibab Lake and Dogtown Lake. The mountain was named for the famed trapper, western guide and renowned recluse, William Sherley Williams. Old Solitaire, as he was known, was killed by the Utes in 1849 and the mountain was named for him in 1852.

The ranch was heavy in tall pine trees, short junipers and grassy meadows. The land was flat to gently rolling and at most times of the year, held ample water for the local wildlife and some two hundred head of livestock. Deer and elk were plentiful as were the wolves, bears, coyotes and mountain lions that fed on them. Migrating geese and ducks stopped by the seasonal ponds on their journeys to and fro. The skies were blue and sunny most of the year although the winters could be brutal. It was great cattle country and all things considered, a right fine place to live.

There were no parades or marching bands at the Box H on that drizzly Friday morning. Another member of the Porter Henry family was being laid to rest in the burial mound behind the ranch house. His name was John Adams Henry and he was barely twenty-two years old when he was shot to death by his twin brother, Thomas. The two of them fought over the affections of a young woman. It was a needless and senseless tragedy that never should have happened. For his part, Thomas was not allowed back on the ranch and would bear the mark of Cain for the rest of his life.

Life on the frontier could be harsh and cruel. Blood, sweat and tears were the currency of the Old West. Porter Henry had already lost his wife, Miriam, and two young sons. Now he was left to run the ranch with only his eldest son, G.W., and his daughter, Taylor by his side. His youngest son, Monroe, left the ranch three years earlier and had not been heard from since. No one had any idea of where he was or how he was. They didn't even have a way to contact him.

The solemn gathering at the funeral made them all wonder about Monroe. Was he still alive? Where could he be? How could they tell him about the awful tragedy that had befallen the family? Would he ever come back home?

Courtesy of Sedona Historical Society/Sedona Heritage Museum, Sedona, AZ

"Towns like the Flats sprung from nowhere, dried up and blew away like dust in the wind."

Chapter I

"Headin' to the Flats"

SPRING 1882

After ever'thing that happened, I was sure-fire certain that I could never return to Grasshopper Flats. In fact, I figured to walk 'cross the burning coals of hell in my sock feet before I'd go back there. Yet here I was, James Monroe Henry, in the spring of 1882, heading slowly but steadily in that direction.

The first time I rode into the "Flats" was almost four years ago on April 7, 1878. I remember the exact date cuz it was my very own personal Independence Day. When I lit out from our ranch that morning, I left a note for my pa saying I was off to see the world and seek my fortune. It sounds kinda silly now but I surely meant it back then.

APRIL 7, 1878

As I recall, it was a great day for going off and seeing the world. What with cotton ball clouds in a bright blue sky, the fresh smell of springtime in the air and just a hint of winter on the wind, the day was darn near perfect. Oak Creek Canyon, south of Flagstaff, was truly a beautiful sight to behold. The crimson cliffs plummeted hundreds of feet from the rim to the canyon floor. Oak Creek was running bank-full and the canyon was alive with critters. I spied small groups of elk and deer, a large herd of the wild pigs we called javelina, a few meandering coyotes and one big old brown bear fresh from hibernation. When I finally reached Grasshopper Flats, it was late afternoon and I had been in the saddle since before dawn. I was bone-dry, dog-tired and just plumb tuckered.

The Flats wasn't much as towns go. Located on a plateau betwixt the beautiful red rock formations south of the Mogollon Rim, it had only one short street with several false-front buildings on each side. Out front, there were board sidewalks with a couple of hitching rails and watering troughs for the horses. Here and there, behind the buildings, were the shacks and tents folks lived in. Nothing looked too fancy or too permanent. One big sneeze might have blown 'em all away. In the West, towns like the Flats sprung from nowhere, dried up and blew away like dust in the wind.

While riding in, I spied a dry goods store with boarding rooms above, a tack and leather shop next to a small café, a doc's office, three saloons and a small blacksmith's forge, set up beside the livery stable. I tied my horse, Goner, to the hitching rail and picked out a saloon. Of course, I chose the nearest one. The big overhead sign spelled out the name: "The Rainbow's End."

I busted right through the bat-wing doors like I knew what I was doin' and ordered, "Whiskey."

I must have been quite a sight. Not yet seventeen but cocksure I knew it all. The bartender was tall, hoe-handle thin and pale as a week-old corpse. He turned as I walked in and gave me a long hard look. He was so damn walleyed, it made my skin crawl to return his look. His right eye was fixed on me but his left kinda wandered about on its own. He had a few stray hairs on his bald head and even fewer teeth showing in his thin smile. After a moment of consideration, he fetched a bottle of "Injun whiskey" from under the bar and a shot glass, which he cleaned with his shirt sleeve and spittle.

This "Injun whiskey" was something new to me. Folks from the East would have called it "moonshine" or "hooch". I found out later, most saloons in the West made and sold some version of it. They usually started with river or rainwater and then added about two gallons of grain alcohol per barrel. Next, they threw in three plugs of chewing tobacco, four bars of soap, about a half-pound of red peppers, some sagebrush or other leaves and two ounces of strychnine. The recipes varied by available ingredients but they were all pretty much the same. One thing they had in common was they all tasted worse than panther piss, kicked like a Missouri mule and gave gawdawful hangovers. Some Injun whiskey was said to raise the dead but I figured it was more likely to create the condition than cure it.

The barkeep pushed the bottle and glass toward me so I could serve myself so naturally I filled the glass to the brim. The murky liquid had some little "floaters" dancin' on the top but after a moment's hesitation, I gulped down that awful coffin varnish without losing a drop. It burned all the way down and hit my stomach like a big flat rock splashin' in a small pond. I looked up and noticed several of the customers had stopped what they were doing to watch me as I rushed headlong into my first taste of sin.

Thinking back, I don't rightly know what started all the ruckus. Guess it was me being young and dumb and them knowing it. After I downed that first glass, I slapped a ten-dollar gold piece on the bar so the barkeep would know I was ready and able to pay for more. After seeing the color of my money, someone asked if I would like to fill the empty seat over at the poker table, so I joined 'em. I was right flattered those older gents would invite a young buck like me to sit in the game. I should of known better. I sat in on the next few hands and won ever' one. That ought'a set off warning bells in my head but it didn't.

One of the five players at the table had the look of a professional gambler. My Pa would have called him a "green-felt rider." This gambler fella, think he said his name was "Slick", was real easy-goin' and friendly. He asked my name, so I stood up straight and told him ever bit of it: "James Monroe Henry."

Slick didn't laugh like ever'body else but waited till the laughter died down. I took my seat and then he leaned over the table and jabbed his finger at my chest.

"You got a real proud name, boy. I reckon your folks were right smart to give you that name. And a young man with such a fancy name deserves another drink, right, boys?" Everyone in the bar shouted their approval.

"And I'm buyin' the first one." Deke the barkeep grinned at me and refilled my glass. Quick as a wink, a couple of other players did the same and jus' like that, I had a line of jiggers beside my stack of chips, all of 'em full of that amber-colored joy juice. I figured they were just funnin' with me but before I knew it, I got downright stupid.

I remember doing real well with the poker playing right off, as I did know the game. I used to play with my brothers when we went on our short cattle drives to Flagstaff or "Flag" as we called it. We never dared play cards around the ranch since Pa was death on any sort of gambling or hard-liquor drinking. There was never no cursing around Pa, neither.

That gambler fella, Slick, was really something. With his black store-bought broadcloth suit, white lacy-front silk shirt and black flat-crowned hat, he looked like he'd just stepped off a Mississippi River boat. He had a smooth way about him and could talk up a storm. He was always smiling, laughing and telling stories. Slick said I was blessed with beginner's luck since I started out by winning so regular. I thought I was gonna find the pot o' gold at the Rainbow's End but the rest of the hands didn't play out that way.

All of a sudden, I couldn't win a damn thing. No matter how good my cards were, one of the other players always held better. Seemed like they just took turns pickin' my pocket. Right about the time I ran out of all my saved-up money, my head commenced to spinnin' and my stomach started to buck like a horse with a cocklebur 'neath its saddle. I 'scused myself and headed as fast as I could for the front doors. I barely made it.

All of that whiskey and most of my breakfast came back up and left me on my knees in the street in front of the saloon. I'd never been that sick in all my life and hope never to be again. I was truly wishin' to die right then and there.

It sure didn't take long to draw a crowd. I could hear folks joking and laughing. In the middle of the throng, I caught a glimpse of a right pretty girl who was just passing by. She was wearing a pure white dress and had long red hair. Actually, I mostly saw her little red riding boots as she walked by but I'm sure she must have seen me retchin' in the street.

I couldn't believe I'd only been in town two hours and I'd already managed to lose ever' bit of my hard-earned savings, not to mention getting stinkin' drunk and deathly sick on that damned rotgut whiskey. I couldn't imagine things getting worse, but they were about to. 'Fore I got shut of that place, I was hard-slapped by that pretty girl, beat up by an old man and shot at by the town drunk.

SPRING 1882

Thinking back, it was a miracle I got out of Grasshopper Flats in one piece. I ran long and hard to get away from there but could never outrun the memories. The Flats left me broke, sick, hurt and embarrassed. Long after I got over being broke, sick and hurt, the embarrassment stayed with me. I even dreamt about it. I'd wake up in a cold sweat with my heart pounding something fierce. Somehow, every sordid detail of what happened that day came back to haunt me.

Now, after 'bout four years of stewing on it, I finally figured out that going back and facing up might be the only cure for what ailed me. I sure didn't want to spend the rest of my life worrying about being recognized as the storied "Kid from Grasshopper Flats."

Yep, that story had been told and retold all over the West. Like any other juicy piece of gossip, it traveled on the wind. Folks were hungry for news of any sort, good or bad didn't matter and a funny story was always welcome. From campfires and stagecoaches to saloons, hotel lobbies and small cafes, everybody knew some version of what happened. Luckily, very few of the stories included my full name or what I looked like.

As it stood now, Grasshopper Flats was close to home and I longed to see my family again. My horse, Goner, seemed to know how I felt. He was happy to be out on the trail and stretching his legs once again but he sensed I wasn't too keen about the direction we were taking. A feller and his horse got like that after awhile, knowing each other's moods.

I found that buckskin mustang almost seven years ago. He was a scairt colt that got stuck in a snow bank in the midst of a blizzard. When I drug him out, he was exhausted and half froze. Pa said he would've been a goner without my savin' him and that's how he got his name. We've been together ever since.

My folks have a ranch in the high country, some thirty miles due west of Flagstaff in the Arizona Territory. Back in the fall of '61, their covered wagons broke down on the way to California. Like a bunch of folks back then, they had headed west to start a new life and get as far as they could from the Civil War. Broke down like they were, I reckon they figured what with winter coming and all, they'd gone far enough.

The winter of '61-'62, came early and stayed late. It was packin' bitter cold and heavy snow. What started out as a temporary shelter made from dead falls eventually became our ranch house and the wooden parts of the broke-down wagons fueled the first fires in that shelter. They tell me I was born in that ranch house that first winter. I was much too young to remember, of course, but those next few years must've been brutal. My folks and three older brothers sure had a time of it. When the folks started building the ranch, my oldest brother, G.W., was just five years old, and the twins, John and Thomas, were only three. They battled the harsh weather, marauding Injuns, and thieving rustlers as well as cholera to build a right respectable ranch in the Kaibab wilderness.

Funny thing about our names. Our folks, Miriam and Porter Henry, were right partial to dead presidents so we all got famous names. "G.W." was short for George Washington. John was named for John Adams, and Thomas, of course, for Thomas Jefferson. As I said, I was christened James Monroe Henry. I had another brother, James Madison, but he died on the trip west. Ma and Pa called me Monroe since they still had another "James" in their hearts.

After me came my little sister, Taylor Henry. The folks only gave her two names figuring she'd latch onto another one later on. I had one younger brother, "A.J.", who was named for "Old Hickory", Andrew Jackson, but he died from cholera when he was only a month old. I reckon Ma caught the fever from him, since she died not long after. I have only slight memories of her but they sure are warm ones.

So there I was heading home again. I figured to be near the Indian Trail Ridge in the San Juan Mountains of southwest Colorado at an altitude of about ten thousand feet. I had been meandering south and west for a couple of weeks. Sometimes I found an old trail and sometimes I made my own. I was basically heading for the Animas Valley, which was just east of the La Plata Mountains. The early Spanish explorers must have figured those mountains were made of pure silver.

I'd spent the winter nurse-maidin' a herd of cattle on the Circle K Ranch, which was just a few miles south of Leadville, Colorado. Times were tough on the ranch and they needed to cull the outfit a mite, so I volunteered to drift now that spring had finally arrived. I'd about used up my welcome there anyhow. I left few friends 'cept for the boss' daughter, "Sissy", and my saddle partner, "Banjo Billy". I sure miss his pickin' and grinnin'.

It was a beautiful day for riding. I could see the snow-capped Rocky Mountains off to the east. The air was thin in the high country but it was also crisp, cool and clean. Blue skies and sunshine ever'where I looked. Mother Nature was awakening from a long winter's hibernation. Birds were singing and wild flowers were blooming. As the sun rose higher in the sky, its warmth seemed to heal all the wounds of yet another cold, cruel winter. Small patches of snow here and there were the only reminders of earlier snowfalls.

I wasn't in any hurry to get where I was going, so I let Goner have his head and set his own pace. We spooked a small herd of elk that ran off a short distance then just ignored us and went back to grazing. A covey of quail took off as we passed and I noticed a turkey vulture gliding overhead. I was lost in thoughts of home, family and of course, Grasshopper Flats. That lack of attention could be a fatal mistake in Injun country. I knew better but was careless.

Suddenly, I felt Goner's muscles tighten and saw his ears prick as he shied from a clump of scrub oak. Then I heard a deep, gravelly voice whisper, "Don't move or make a sound, Pilgrim. You'll git us both kilt."

All at once, I was very aware of sounds and movement on the trail ahead. I didn't relish being thought a pilgrim but I sure had acted like one. Daydreaming like a greenhorn fool, I'd rode smack into a hornet's nest and figured to be in big trouble. I tried to remain motionless, barely breathing, while I slowly stroked Goner's neck to keep him calm. With my right hand, I carefully removed the leather thong that secured my six-gun.

As the sound of horses and men got closer, the whoopin' and hollarin' made it clear they were Injuns. As the war party passed us by and rode off to the north, the gravelly voice ordered, "Now get down real easy-like and lead your cayuse over here."

I did as I was told. Goner seemed to sense the danger and followed close behind as I led him by the reins. I caught only a glimpse of a man leading us through the brush. He was covered with animal skins so all I could make out was a whiskered face and bright blue eyes when he glanced back to see if I was followin'. Hurriedly, he led us away from the trail and into the tangled underbrush.

The Injuns were more'n likely Utes and they sounded like a good-sized war party of a dozen or more. They seemed in an almighty hurry to get somewhere or catch up with someone. From the tone of their hollering, they were mighty agitated and on the warpath. I wanted no part of 'em and was relieved they were headed away from where we were holed-up.

We remained still for several minutes and then the raspy voice spoke again. This time, the man was much closer but he was still hidden from my view. He spoke slowly and deliberately.

"Them Utes are after me, Pilgrim. They figger to double back when they can't find my trail. A body can only fool 'em for jes' so long."

"Do we run or fight?"

After a moment of silence he answered. "I'd rather hightail it but I'm afeared we'll have to fight 'em. You much of a fighting man, Pilgrim?"

"I'll stand if I have to.... but I sure don't like our chances here."

"Me neither. Reckon we'd best find a better place to fort-up."

I heard him moving away rapidly, going deeper into the brush. I pulled my Winchester from its scabbard and tried to stay close. We came upon an old game trail and followed it down a steep slope into a wash. It was too early in the spring for much melt-off so the wash was running low. We stayed in the wash and headed upstream as we climbed higher into the hills.

The old mountain man was moving well ahead of me but I could see how he picked his way along the wash leaving as little sign as possible. He knew what he was about and was pretty spry for an old-timer. I struggled some to keep up since he was wearing moccasins while I wore high-heeled riding boots. Being a normal cowhand, I was never much for walking when I could ride. 'Specially at that altitude.

My new "trail partner" was a short, stocky feller. I figured he was a trapper or hunter of some sort. Since he was wearing a coat made of bearskins, he kinda favored a small griz from the back. I noticed right off he was toting a long rifle that looked to be .50 caliber. Most likely an old Sharps buffalo gun.

He scrambled up a rockslide and lit behind an outcropping of large moss-grown boulders. They formed a natural waterfall that rose some twenty feet above the level of the wash. His position made for a great field of fire and afforded us plenty of good cover, too.

He waved me on with a sense of urgency. "Come on, Pilgrim, they're right behind."

I took the hide-hunter at his word and led Goner up past the rocks and through a small stand of quaking aspen as quickly as I could. I picketed him behind a large ponderosa pine so he would be as safe as possible. With rifle in hand, I hurried back and took a spot beside the old-timer as the first Ute warrior made his way along the wash below us. The Injun was painted for war and moved like a catamount hopping from rock to rock. The rest of the braves were spread out behind him on both sides of the wash looking for sign of our passing.

The next thing I knew, an almighty loud concussion went off next to my head and was followed by a triumphant shout. "Got yah, yah red devil."

That first warrior never knew what hit him. He went to the happy hunting ground faster than sunlight 'cross a meadow. At that range, the slug from that buffalo gun liked to split him in two. He had a hole in his chest big enough to sink a fist in. The other warriors quickly slipped into the underbrush and all was silent 'cept for the lonely echo of that Sharps bouncin' off the mountains.

My furry friend spoke tentatively as he started to reload his rifle. "That might just stop 'em."

I was desperately searching for any movement down in the wash. "I've never known Injuns to give up that easy."

"Yeah, but old Red Dog was leading 'em and now he's deader'n this old coonskin cap."

He waved the cap around to make his point. Out of the corner of my eye I could see a huge grin on his fuzzy face. His bright blue eyes were twinkling and he looked like he was about to bust out laughing.

"You knew that one?"

"Guess you could say so. We were kin, sort of."

"You're an Injun?"

He chuckled. "Nah, but I've been laying-up with his sister. I suppose that makes us.... brothers-in-law."

Suddenly, several war cries were followed by a half dozen Utes coming up at us from out of the wash. I only saw one with a rifle, but the rest were well armed with lances, tomahawks, war clubs and knives.

Without giving it much thought, I stood up, drew my six-gun and fired three quick shots at the advancing warriors. I managed to stop the first two dead in their tracks. The first Injun took two hits in the chest, spun full round and collapsed. The second caught one in the neck, stumbled to one knee and then fell flat on his face. They both died where they lay. That Sharps boomed in my ear again and the Ute with the rifle was blown backward off the rocks and tumbled down into the wash, which ran red with his blood.

With the momentum of the attack stopped, the other three Utes scattered every whichaway and faded into the underbrush once again. I sent a couple of quick shots after 'em just to hurry their movin'.

The old-timer slapped my back and shouted, "Right smart shooting, Pilgrim. Yessiree-bob, we showed 'em. Yeehaw."

I was busy shucking my empties and reloading my Colt as fast as I could. I still had my Winchester handy but I wasn't about to take any chances since this scrap looked to become close-up and personal. When they came at us again, they'd apt to be a sight more careful since Injuns seldom made the same mistake twice.

We watched and waited without saying much for a few minutes. I was half afraid they'd come at us right away and half afraid they'd spread out and encircle us. Injuns were notional and a man just never knew. Finally, I just had to ask.

"You were living with a squaw?"

"Been sharing her wickiup for almost two years now," he replied. "Good woman, mostly."

"Then why are they after your hair?"

He sighed and rolled his eyes at me. "They caught me laid-up with another squaw. She was a lot younger and a real looker. You gotta understand, these here Tabawatshi Utes have been fighting with white men and red men alike for years. Old Chief Ouray took most of 'em to the reservation with him a while back but Red Dog wouldn't hear of it. Now, they're getting mighty short of men-folks so I sort of took it on m'self to service as many of their women-folk as I could." He paused, looking around and chuckled. "Mebbe start my own tribe of blue-eyed redskins. Whaddaya think, Pilgrim? With blue eyes like your'n, you could help me out."

While I considered his offer, he sighed again. "Old Red Dog didn't see it thataway. Right prideful he was. I barely got out of the village 'fore they give me an Apache haircut."

I'd never heard that term but figured he meant a scalpin'. Keeping a watchful eye I asked, "Do you really think they'd give up and quit?"

"Mebbe. Like I said, they can't rightly afford to lose many more young men. 'Specially dogging crow-bait like me. Red Dog was their chief so they'll have to pow-wow a new one. Mebbe they'll figger their medicine's no good here and leave us be."

I rose up slow and careful-like. "Well, I'd like to thank you, Mister?"

He offered his hand. "Dunbar, Cleetis Dunbar. The Utes say I'm half-mountain man and half-mountain goat, but when it comes to fightin' or courtin', I'm a one hundred percent, fire-breathin', pole-cat. Yessiree-bob. Now who'd you be, Pilgrim?"

I shook his hand and replied, "Monroe.... Henry Monroe"

I thought back to the first time I'd used that name. It was after I got done running from Grasshopper Flats. I joined up with a cattle drive that was heading to the Nevada goldfields near Virginia City. I figured to be the first of my family to make it all the way to California. When Sherman Goddard, the trail boss, asked for my name, I started to say "Monroe Henry", but I sorta stalled and stammered and said, "Monroe, Henry Monroe". Guess I was afraid someone would start funnin' with my name or somehow connect me to what happened in Grasshopper Flats.

Cleetis looked hard into my eyes like he was measuring me. "Well there, Mister Henry Monroe, I'm right proud to know ya. Let's light a shuck and git."

Up close and head on, Cleetis really favored an old he-coon with his whiskered face, chubby cheeks, coonskin cap and all. He was no more'n five foot seven and had to carry at least two hundred fifty pounds easy. He might be pushing sixty, but there was no mistaking the power of his handshake. That canny old man had been over the snowy mountains and down the raging rivers a time or two.

I could tell he was taking a hard look at me at the same time. He was probably wondering about a young pilgrim with a quick six-gun. I'd just passed twenty years and stood two inches over six feet. I had fair hair and sharp features with deep blue eyes and a mouthful of pearly white teeth. Folks saw the face of a boy that masked the heart and soul of a grown man.

I'd gotten some late growth after leaving home four years ago. At only five feet ten and one-fifty, I figured to be the runt of our litter. Now I weighed some two hundred pounds, which was mostly muscle and bone. I'd been getting by with gristle and grits all winter long on the Circle K and could certainly stand a few home cooked meals.

I was rigged like most cowpunchers 'cept for my boots, saddle and shootin' iron. My black boots were custom made with silver spurs that had the big Mexican rowels. I always tried to keep'm shined like new. My saddle was a hand-tooled beauty with all the trappings. On my hip, I wore a fancy Silver Star gun belt and an even fancier Colt .44 pistol. The revolver was fully engraved and had gold inlays on the cylinder.

Cleetis must'a figured his questions would keep. "Suppose we go back 'round and pick up old Stumpy 'fore them Utes come back and make a liar outta me."

"Stumpy?"

"Oh, he's my old mule. Stubborn as a stump when he's of a mind to be. All my traveling gear is with him. He'll be waiting on us back yonder."

I gathered up Goner's reins and we picked our way through the thick underbrush. It was hard work cutting the brush and slow going but a lot safer than going back down the wash. A savvy man never doubled back on the same trail if he could help it.

True to his name, Stumpy had not moved and was patiently awaiting our return. He let loose with a long bray and a short honk as we approached. Stumpy was certainly no scruffy pack-ass. He was a huge black critter, at least sixteen hands. I reckoned he could be salty as all get out but he sure loved Cleetis. They nuzzled each other like a couple of courtin' chipmunks. Guess they shared some tough miles together like Goner and me. For his part, Stumpy was loaded for the road and seemed eager to get on it.

With some effort, Cleetis climbed aboard and took control, sort of.

"Which way you headed, Pilgrim?"

Looking around at my choices I replied. "Whichever way them Utes ain't."

Cleetis took a moment to get his bearings. "Well, their village is about ten miles south of here." He pointed in the general direction. "Over thataway."

"Figures. That's the way I was going. Since I'm heading for the Animas Valley, I reckon I'll just swing to the west a mite and give 'em a wide berth."

He considered his situation. "Mind if I ride along?"

"Suits me, if you're of a mind to. You know any of the trails?"

"Ain't been there but I've heard some talk and I reckon I can recall. Although, my memory's been kinda leaky lately."

As he spoke, a shot rang out and dust flew off his saddle packs. Stumpy honked, snorted, and leapt all at the same time. Cleetis had all he could do to hang on. I stuck my spurs to Goner and he lit out like a scalded dog as more shots echoed in my ears and whizzed over our heads. Well, it was a sure thing a couple of them Utes still had rifles.

Old Stumpy was a good mover but with his load, he was no match for Goner. We were quite a ways ahead when more shots rang out and I heard Cleetis cry for help. "Pilgrim, I'm hit!"

I reined-in Goner so Cleetis could catch up. He was pitched forward in his saddle and hanging on for dear life. He had a spreading bloodstain on his left shoulder. I checked our back trail and saw a dust cloud. Sure enough, them Utes were still a'comin'.

I nudged Goner closer to Stumpy and Cleetis. "Can you hang on? We need to keep some distance 'tween them and us."

He coughed and said, "I'll make it. My hair ain't fit for no scalp-tree."

I took out a rawhide piggin' strip and tied his hands to the pommel. After taking up his reins, we lit out again. That old man had better be tough cause this didn't figure to be no buggy ride in the park.

We rode southwest at a steady pace but that dust cloud kept gaining on us. Since we couldn't out run 'em, we'd have to fort-up and try to out-fight 'em again.

I spotted a heavily wooded flattop mesa and headed right for it. We climbed almost to the top and then dug in amongst the pines, spruce and aspens. The trees offered some cover and the steep slope was sure to slow 'em down a mite. It was the best spot I could find on such short notice. I untied Cleetis' hands and helped him off old Stumpy. He'd lost some blood but didn't seem any worse for wear. I could see he'd been hit high on the left side in the upper arm or shoulder.

Being ground-hitched like they were, I left Goner and Stumpy to get acquainted. They didn't figure to wander too far and were reasonably safe behind two huge old alligator junipers.

"Come on old-timer, get ready for another turkey shoot."

"Yeah, but which of us are the turkeys?"

As I propped him up behind a lightning-struck stump, I replied, "Guess we're about to find out."

I fetched his Sharps and his ammunition sack. When I dumped the sack in front of him, I counted only seven rounds. "At this distance you'll get the first shot so make it count."

His face was pale and he was sweating buckets but he was still full of fight. "This ain't my first rodeo, Pilgrim. I'll do my part. See you do your'n."

The slope was steeper to our left so I took up a position on the right flank and hunkered down behind some small boulders. I gathered some old deadfalls to give me more cover and protection. I had my rifle and my six-shooter but not an overabundance of ammunition. I'd have to make my shots count, too.

I counted seven Utes riding abreast as they bore down on us. They knew better than to ride all bunched up. As far as I could tell, only two had rifles. As I sighted-in the Winchester, I yelled over to Cleetis.

"Start from the left and work towards the middle. I'll do the same from the right."

He looked my way and gave me a "thumbs-up" as he sighted-in that big ol' buffalo gun. When it boomed, an Injun pony went down throwing its rider headfirst. Barely shaken, the Ute came up running and veered off to our left.

As the rest of the Utes rode closer, I fired at 'em with my rifle but they scattered after the first shot and were much harder to hit. I thought I might have winged one in the shoulder but if I did, it was pure luck.

Cleetis' second shot was right on the mark and a Ute was blown ass over teakettle off the back of his pony.

"Yeehaw, Pilgrim. That's how it's done."

The rest of the warriors dismounted and faded into the trees. It would be a dogfight from now on. No more shooting turkeys.

We exchanged a few shots with no effect and then things got deadly quiet. I was thankful they were short on rifles as well as warriors, but the quiet meant they were going to ground so they could "Injun-up" on us. It's uncanny how an Injun can make his way without being seen. I noticed Cleetis pull out his Bowie knife and stick it in the ground next to him. It looked to be sharp enough to shave with, not that he ever had. Reckon this fight would be tooth and claw from here on out.

The slope below us seemed to be alive with Injuns. Moving as if in formation, they appeared and disappeared behind trees, rocks and bushes. There was nothing to shoot at and I couldn't afford to waste any more ammunition so I jus' sat there and waited. There could be no more than six and maybe only five but it seemed like there were at least a dozen.

Lookin' across, I had a pretty good angle on an Injun that was edging up on Cleetis. When the Ute stood up to take aim with his rifle, I was waiting for him with mine. My first shot burned his hip and spun him around. I levered my rifle as quick as I could and my second shot hit him in the chest and he was done for. His rifle flew off in the tall grass behind him as he fell backward.

Suddenly, I drew a heap of attention from that second rifle. I was tucked behind a a good-sized boulder but my Winchester was exposed and got shot out of my hands. It fell a few feet away with a bullet lodged in the loading ramp. Another shot ricocheted off the rock, hit the rifle's stock, and split it in two. I hugged the ground as two more shots screamed overhead. The next shot nicked a juniper tree just above my head and showered me with splinters, bark and little blue berries.

Cleetis was waiting for 'em to rush me so he could get 'em in a crossfire. When one did, his Sharps rifle thundered once again and the Injuns' head seemed to explode like a ripe melon. The bullet must 'a hit him somewhere near his right eye and it was a gawd-awful sight. If I hadn't been so scairt and excited, I might have been sick to my stomach.

After that, things got deathly quiet and we waited once again. No one has patience like an Injun. We had the better position but they still had us out numbered. Cleetis was reloading his single shot Sharps and singing to himself.

"One little, two little, three little Injuns...."

A Ute came up out of nowhere, leaped over some rocks and dead falls and lit right next to Cleetis. Without hesitatin', Cleetis dropped his rifle and grabbed for his knife. I saw the bright sunlight flicker off it as he went into action. They rolled over and over with a death grip on each other.

Since my attention had been on Cleetis, I was surprised when I turned around and saw two Utes coming hard at me. One was lever-ing his rifle from the hip and I saw the flash of his bullets as he fired at me. Since they were charging uphill, his shots were low and hit the ground around me. Bits of dirt, rock and bark flew in my face. I looked up just in time to see the second one poised to throw his lance. Instinctively, I rolled away and drew my Colt. His spear lit twixt my legs and he rushed me with his knife held high. I took good aim and shot him three times in the chest before he quit comin' at me. He fell on his back and rolled down the slope.

I twisted and turned over as the first warrior tried to shoot but found his rifle was empty. Enraged, he grabbed the rifle by the barrel and swung it at me. The butt just missed my head but hit me hard on the right shoulder. I lost all feeling in my right hand and dropped my pistol. As he prepared to swing again, I lunged for the Colt with my left hand, rolled out of his way and quickly fired the remaining three rounds from my revolver into him at point blank range.

He staggered a bit and stared down at his wounds, unsure of what had happened. He tried to swing his rifle at me again but found he couldn't lift it. He tried to pull the lance out of the ground but lost his balance and fell atop me. He died with his face pressin' agin' mine. I'll never forget the fierce look of hatred in his dead eyes.

I could barely breathe and struggled to push him off. With only one good arm, it was all I could do to move him as he was truly dead weight. I tried to get up but lost my balance and fell to my knees. My right arm was useless and I was covered with blood. Luckily, it was the Injuns' blood and not mine.

Gasping for air, I turned and looked for Cleetis but he was no-where to be seen. I called out, "Cleetis?"

I saw a bloody Bowie knife waving at me from behind the black-ened stump.

"Over here, Pilgrim. Counting coups like a 'Pache."

Then I saw the Ute warrior I must have wounded earlier. He'd been hit in the shoulder and was staggering around behind Cleetis with his knife held high in his right hand. He was badly wounded but there was no quit in him. Instinctively I aimed the Colt with my left hand but the hammer fell with a loud "click". It was empty.

As I screamed out a warning, a shot rang out and the wound-ed warrior stopped mid-stride, turned half way 'round and fell in a heap.

I must'a passed out cause the next thing I recall, I was staring at dirt. My heart was pounding and my shoulder felt like it was afire. I still couldn't move my right arm. I tried to focus but my mind was addled. I couldn't recall what had happened. As I struggled to move, I heard Cleetis calling to me through the haze.

"Are you all right Pilgrim? I won't take it kindly if ya' up and die on me. Not after all we've been through today. No sirree."

Painfully, I rolled over to see Cleetis grinning at me. He was leaning against that burnt stump once again. He held his bloody Bowie knife in one hand and two fresh scalps in the other. Kneeling beside him was an old squaw. She was fussing over his wounds. He had dried blood on the side of his face from a scalp wound and a dark stain on his upper chest near the left shoulder. His face was pale and his breathing seemed labored. Then things got a little fuzzy and I must have blacked out again.

The next time I came to, it must have been late afternoon. The sun was settling in the west and the air was getting chilly. I was lying on a bed of pine needles and juniper berries under a blanket next to a roaring fire. There was some kind of clay poultice strapped on my right shoulder and there must have been some fixings in the clay cause it smelled like something four days dead. Cleetis was snoozing against that same blackened stump while the old squaw seemed to be taking care of things. When she noticed I was awake, she brought me a cup of coffee and indicated that I should drink. It was hot and cast iron strong but it tasted mighty good. Old cowhands figured coffee should be strong enough to float a horseshoe and her coffee might have done the trick.

The squaw took bandages out of a pot of boiling water and placed them over the poultice. Cooking like that, my shoulder felt some better but my right hand and arm were still tingling like crazy and I had little or no movement.

I watched her tending to the fire. She was getting on in years and was a mite overweight but still moved smoothly and surely. Her weather-beaten face bore the sorrows of all the Injun nations. The world she knew was no more and yet she lived on. She simply did what was needed when it was needed without thought or complaint. It was the only way she knew and the surest way for her to survive.

Slowly, bit-by-bit, I began to recollect. She must be the squaw Cleetis had told me about. She could've followed the war party. Since my pistol was empty and Cleetis' back was turned, she must have shot that wounded Ute. I wondered why she'd do that.

As I looked around, I saw Goner and Stumpy cropping grass. They seemed to get along although I'll never know why. That feisty mustang stallion and the old black mule sure made for an odd pair. Kinda like Cleetis and me. A little farther away I saw there were six Injun ponies hitched to a dragline.

The old squaw was fussing with something in a well-used pottery crock. She chopped up what looked like herbs or roots and stirred them in the boiling water. It figured to be some sort of Injun concoction to help with our wounds. Folks held that Injuns could cure damn near anything with one potion or another.

Cleetis awoke with a start and grabbed for the Bowie knife that had fallen from his hand. As he looked around, his fears subsided and he relaxed a bit. The loss of blood had weakened him and he looked to be fit for skinning. He smiled at his squaw and then looked over at me.

"Well, what do you know, Pilgrim? Looks like we made out." He coughed and fought for breath. "How's the arm?"

I made a feeble attempt to move my right hand and arm. It felt like dead weight but it didn't hurt too much. "It feels better but ain't working so good. Guess it'll take some time to get it moving again. How about you?"

Cleetis looked at his bandaged shoulder and gently fingered his scalp wound. "I'm as weak as a new born kitten but I figger to mend. Lost a chunk of my skull but gained a chunk of lead in my shoulder, so I reckon I came out about even."

"That bullet should come out."

He agreed grudgingly. "Yeah, I know. But up here in the mountains, we just plug up the bullet holes with pinesap and go on about our business. Wounds heal without infections this high up. Hell, meat don't even spoil. I've been carrying a musket ball in the back of this here leg for almost forty years."

He was pointing to his left leg. "I got it fighting over a beaver pelt, of all things." He thought for a minute. "Should'a just let Wheezer have it."

"Wheezer?"

"My partner, Ab Huckaby. We come west in '37. We were a couple of wet-nosed greenhorns. Met up with Jim Bridger, Christopher Carson and all of them famous trappers at the big fur rendezvous. We were fixing to trap ever' critter in the Rockies and sell the pelts. We got beaver, otter, coon, fox, wolf, muskrat and even a polecat or two. Figgered to hightail it to San Francisco and make our fortunes. Too damn bad we never made it."

"Where'd he get the name Wheezer?"

"He had a broke nose and it made a funny wheezing noise ever'time he sucked air."

"Who gave it to him?"

Cleetis chuckled. "Nobody give it to him.... he had to fight for it."

He seemed flooded with memories and paused a bit. The old squaw took him another cup of coffee, which he gratefully accepted. He said something to her I couldn't get and she smiled happily.

She washed his wounds and tried to fuss with his bandages but he gently stopped her. There was no mistaken' the feeling between 'em. Guess it was plain why she'd followed us and shot that wounded Ute. Blood or no, when it came down to it, Cleetis was her man.

Cleetis saw me watching her and commented. "Her Ute name means little water lily or some such. I just call her "Lil". Reckon we're stuck with each other now. We're all we've got."

He chuckled and with some effort, managed to drink some of his coffee.

I just had to ask, "How did you come to lay-up with her?"

He broke into a large grin. "I saved old Red Dog's bacon.... by accident. He was scrappin' with a couple of them Jicarilla Apaches and they ran smack across my trail. At the time, I was minding my own business just tracking a griz bear. I figgered they was after my hair so naturally, I let 'em have what for. Red Dog was down and wounded, so he supposed I saved his life a-purpose. Since he felt beholden to me, he give me his sister. She'd been alone since her man was killed by the Navajos. Like I said before, them Utes were awful short on men folks."

I looked over at Lil who seemed to be paying us no mind. "Does she understand what we're saying?"

He shook his head. "Not a word and I keep it thataway. My business stays my business. Yes, sir."

"Then how do you?"

"Sign mostly. Oh, I know some Ute and a few words of Spanish so we get by. Talkin' betwixt a man and his woman don't need to be with words. Iffin you get my drift."

I nodded in agreement.

For the next few minutes we just enjoyed the afternoon sun with our hot coffee and warm memories. He was probably recalling women he'd had while I was thinking 'bout those I hadn't. The name "Sissy" came to mind once again.

Lil got more wood for the fire. Our beautiful warm spring day was rapidly becoming a chilly winter's eve. The wind had picked up and the temperature was goin' down with the sun. A coyote was mournfully calling out to no one in particular and an white-faced owl was constantly asking, "Who? Who?"

Lil rinsed out our coffee cups and brought us some of her potion. It smelled gawd-awful and tasted worse than H. J. Baker & Brothers Castor Oil but figured to help with our mending.

Cleetis seemed to be enjoying the potion and my discomfort with it. He stared at the cup and then commented. "Injuns eat and drink lotsa things white folks can't stomach. Guess a body can get used to damn near anything after awhile."

I nodded towards Lil. "Does she know about Red Dog?"

He shrugged. "Reckon so. No matter. Wherever I go, she'll follow. It's her way."

"Well, it's a good thing for us she followed today. She saved your life and mine, too. Considering you just killed her brother, that was a right neighborly thing to do."

"Like I said afore, most of them Utes are peaceful, nowadays. Old Red Dog just couldn't or wouldn't quit the warpath so he got some young hotheads to join up with him. She knows he died in battle like a warrior. That's all that matters to her. Injuns see things different than we do. They believe in the circle of life. A thing is born, lives its life, then dies and another is born to take its' place. Thinking like that keeps life simple. Injuns are well suited for this country."

Lil had taken some fixings from Cleetis' saddle packs and was rustling up some grub for supper. I was getting plumb spoiled what with all that attention. My arm was still numb but I was able to move my fingers a little. I took that as a sign I was going to get better.

Cleetis was strollin' down memory lane again as he stared into the fire. "It's been a real pleasure to talk with a white man again. Been a while, yessiree-bob."

Trying to be friendly, I asked, "So you knew Bridger and Carson?"

"Sure thing. I knew "Old Gabe" the best. Did you know Bridger was given that name by old Jedediah Smith hisself? He said Bridger brought to mind the Angel Gabriel as he went out and spread the word. The Injuns took to calling him the Blanket Chief cause of the red and blue robe he wore all the time. Bet you didn't know his Injun wife made it for him. Yessir, those were the days.... me and Wheezer...."

"Whatever happened to Wheezer? Is he still around?"

Cleetis' face tightened some but I could see he wanted to talk about it. He was just searching for a place to start. He got out his rolling paper and pouch of Bull Durham and started making a smoke. He offered some to me but I waved him off. I never learnt to smoke.

He indicated the tobacco. "It's the only good thing I ever got from the 'Paches. Now, where was I?"

I hoisted my cup of potion. "Wheezer. I was asking if he was still around."

"Nah, he ain't." He finished off his potion and tossed a few sticks at the fire.

"Wheezer and me were partners, real partners, close as brothers. Closer mebbe. We came west when trapping varmints was easy and the price of pelts was high. We had us a great load of skins back in the spring of '42. When we were dividin' 'em up, we started fussing, like brothers will, over one special beaver pelt. What with all our scrapping, we didn't keep a watchful eye."

"What happened?"

"The first shot hit me hard in the back of this here leg and I fell flat on my face and must have blacked out from the shock of it. The second shot hit Wheezer head on and kilt him on the spot. He fell right across me. What with all the blood and such, them bushwhackers must of figgered we was both dead. They just stole our pelts and skedaddled."

"Injuns?"

He glared at me and growled. "I still got my hair, ain't I? They had to be white men. Them that would rather steal skins from honest men than trap 'em themselves. They'd be the reason I lit out for the wilderness in the first place. There's a heap of folks in this world that ain't worth the powder it'd take to blow 'em straight to hell, Pilgrim."

He paused to catch his breath and sort out his memories. "I was laid up with that leg for weeks and their trail got mighty cold. Reckon they headed for Denver, or Santa Fe. Bet they sure were disappointed. You see, the fur market bottomed out that spring. Folks in Europe got their fill of fur hats and all them pelts were damn near worthless."

"Wish I could have found 'em... just to get back that silver-tip beaver pelt."

"Silver-tip?"

"Yah, that's what we were scrappin' over. The purtiest thing I ever saw, Pilgrim. All the hairs were silver tipped. Would have made a be-u-tee-ful hat, yessiree-bob."

We sat quiet-like for some minutes and watched as Lil continued with her cooking. I finally finished my potion and was ready for supper. Whatever she was fixing sure smelled invitin'. What with all the excitement, I had worked up a fierce hunger.

When she started to serve us, Cleetis added, "When you find one of the few good people, man or woman, whatever color, young or old, you best hang on to 'em, Pilgrim. If you have a handful of true friends when you meet your maker, you're a lucky man."

Whatever I was eating tasted even better than it smelled. I started to ask what it was but remembered the dead Injun pony and thought better of it. Some things are better left alone. Cleetis and Lil talked some back and forth till he drifted off to sleep and she went back to her fussing around the camp. When I finished eating, I felt tired again and was about to go to sleep myself when I noticed it was getting chilly on my backside so I reached for a blanket. Underneath the blanket was my gun belt and Colt pistol. Those silver stars on the black gun belt always brought back memories.

Chapter II
"Alias Henry James"

SUMMER 1878

I was mindful of my first partner, or partners, really. We spent three months together on a cattle drive. They were brothers; Malachi and Joshua James. Unlike my parents, their folks seemed to favor the Old Testament when it came to naming their young-uns. They told me they had an older brother named Zachariah, and a younger sister, Esther.

It was kinda surprising, but Mal and Josh had more trouble with their surname than their given names. The trail hands referred to them as the "James Boys" and that was a fighting name to some folks. Ol' Frank and Jessie were hated by most of the Yankees but were honored as heroes by Southern sympathizers. Everyone seemed to have a strong opinion about them, either for or agin'.

Mal and Josh were fresh from the farm when they joined up with the cattle drive. Jus' like me, they hightailed it from their folks' ranch and were itching to see the world. We became friends right off and hung together like new-born pups in a basket.

At twenty-one, Mal was older and a whole lot bigger than Josh. He stood six foot two and weighed two hundred twenty pounds while Josh was about four inches shorter and at least fifty pounds lighter

Mal was a good-natured, friendly cuss with a big smile. He lacked a formal education but had good common sense. He was an eager and able cowhand who always did his share of the work and then some. The trailhands took to him right away.

Josh was about my age, seventeen. He was quiet and rather shy. He stood in the shadow of his big brother and stayed pretty much to hisself, until we became friends. He wasn't as good a hand as Mal but he always did the best he could. For the first few weeks, Josh was mighty homesick but he finally got over it. He must'a wrote a letter to his folks most ever' night and had a whole stack of 'em in his saddlebags when we got to the end of the trail.

Together, the three of us went to cowhand school. We spent as much as eighteen hours a day in the saddle fighting the miserable heat and cold, sand storms, stampedes, rustlers and maraudin' Injuns. At times, some of our very own longhorns were the most dangerous part of the drive. Those old mossy-horns could be as contrary and treacherous as a lit stick of dynamite.

Along the way, several of the older hands took pity on us youngsters and took the time to teach us the western skills we should've already had. Even though we'd worked with cattle at home, we lacked experience and were "wet behind the ears" as far as the old timers were concerned.

Some of the older hands made sport of us and only offered western wisdom such as, "never squat with your spurs on" and "always drink upstream from the herd". When we entered Injun territory, they cautioned, "a fool and his hair are soon parted". We tried to take the joking in stride. My favorite line was, "the only way to move cattle fast is slowly".

Carlos Delgado, the *Californio*, tried his best to teach us all about ropin' and fancy trick ridin'. He was a true *vaquero* and a master with a *riata*. Carlos rode with a style and grace I'd never seen before. He wasn't just getting the job done. To him, riding was an art form. It seemed like he became one with his horse. He carried a limber rope that was twice as long as any of ours and he could really sling it. I never saw him miss a single critter, not once. We did our best but were never able to match his skills or his style

Big Gideon Brown was a retired Buffalo Soldier and the first Negro I'd ever known. He'd been a plantation slave down in Mississippi before he ran off to join the Union Army during the War. After ten years of chasing Apaches, he decided to chase longhorns instead and became a trail hand. Gideon was an artist who created his art with a running iron. He showed us all about branding cattle and re-branding 'em. Using a cinch ring, he could alter almost any brand into some other. First, he taught us what ever' rustler knew about alterin' brands. Then he strongly advised us against it. Getting caught changing brands was a surefire way to get your neck hemp-stretched. As a former runaway slave, Gideon was very wary of any kind of lynchin' parties.

Life on the cattle trail could vary from monotonous and boring to terribly exciting but sometimes it was just downright dangerous. I'll always be beholdin' to our cook, Cactus Charley, for fetching me out from under my first stampede and to Gustav (Gus) Johannson for shooting a Paiute off my backside during an attack. We were like a large family of brothers and I felt right at home.

One way or another, we lost five cowhands during those three months. Two were killed by redskins, one by herd-cutters and one got hisself stampeded flat. The fifth, Jody Mack, just rode out on midnight watch one night and never came back. Neither hide nor hair of him was ever found and we spent most all the next day lookin'. He was a good hand and had wages coming so it didn't figure he'd drift off on his own. Something out there on the trail just swallered him up. It happened like that a lot in the West. Men disappeared and no one ever knew the why or wherefore of it.

All things considered, I do believe we earned ever' bit of our twenty-five dollars a month. That was the going wage for green-horns while top hands got "forty and found" which meant they got year-round room and board in addition to wages.

Besides Mal and Josh, I really took a liking to Major John Wilkes. He was the brains of the outfit and wiser than a tree full of owls. His military rank became his nickname, as he was known by one and all as "the Major". Seems he'd been a Major with the South during the

Civil War. He served under General Stonewall Jackson and was by his side when old Stonewall died after the Battle of Chancellorsville. The way the Major told it, the general was accidentally shot by one of his own. When the doctors had to remove Jackson's left arm, folks said General Robert E. Lee lost his right arm the same time. The Major told us that old Stonewall survived the amputation but died of pneumonia eight days later.

Besides punching cows with us, the Major did most of the hunting and kept Cactus Charley supplied with fresh meat. He also kept the three of us greenhorns supplied with hair-raisin' stories. We sat around the campfire at night and listened to him go on about Civil War battles, cattle drives, Injun raids, gun fighters, you name it. As far as I could tell, he'd been ever'where and done most ever'thing there was for a fella to do, at least once.

The Major was a big man around six foot four and probably two hundred fifty pounds. Not an ounce of it was fat, neither. His hair was showing white but his spirit was young and strong. He used to fuss with the waxed tips of his handlebar mustache as he told his stories. He called them his "longhairs" since they resembled a set of longhorns. Campfire stories were jus' about our only entertainment and educated us about the West. Like in any schoolhouse, the more we listened, the more we learned. The Major wanted us to benefit from his mistakes although he reasoned that some mistakes were so much fun that they should be made more than once.

And like so many other soldiers, both blue and gray, the Major drifted west after the war. He'd hunted buffalo, rode a few cattle trails, scouted for the army, wrangled mustangs and even prospected a little. The man loved to talk as much as we loved to listen. Some of the older hands would listen in on occasion and as Cactus Charley put it, the Major never told the same story the same way twice.

Since none of the three of us had ever carried a six-shooter, Major Wilkes decided we best learn if we were to survive on our own in the "wild and wooly West". As he set out to teach us the basics, he gave us a very strict code of behavior regarding pistols.

"Never draw on a man unless you intend to shoot and never shoot unless you mean to kill". That was his main rule and number one priority. Guns were serious business and never to be taken lightly. We practiced on rocks and bottles and some of the other wranglers took to cheering us on. That really made the learnin' fun.

The Major was mighty good at teaching by example. He was right quick on the draw and generally hit what he had a mind to. He was forever reminding us shooting was easy until the target shot back.

It turned out Mal could shoot pretty straight but was really slow on the draw. The Major said it was just a matter of coordination and repetition but Mal couldn't get the hang of it. Whenever he tried a quick-draw, he was more apt to drop the pistol than shoot it.

Josh wanted no truck with a pistol. He never got his heart in it cause he felt pistols were only for killing and that seemed to bother him. He figured if a fella wore a six-gun, sooner or later he'd be forced to kill or be kilt just for the havin' of it.

On the other hand, I took to the six-shooter like a duck to water. I think I even surprised the Major with my speed and accuracy. He had me practice with both hands just because "you never know". I was almost as quick and accurate with my left hand as I was with my right. This surprised us both. He cautioned I might even be too good for my own good.

I can still hear him sayin' getting a reputation as a gunslinger would be the death of me. Being young and cocky, I figured the faster the better. It didn't take long before I was to find out just what the Major meant.

Sean, "Chip", O'Leary taught us how to scrap. He was a short, redheaded Irishman that stood a shade under five foot tall but weighed all of a hundred and ninety-five pounds. He looked like a cannon ball perched on two pipe stems and was as bowlegged as a barrel hoop. The little Irishman was also hard as a rock and twice as stubborn. His nickname came from the chip that seemed to be on his shoulder all the time. The Major said he suffered from "short-man's disease" and tried to whittle everyone else down to his size.

Chip would slug it out if he had to but he never saw any percentage in tradin' punches when he could just duck and cover. This was possible because he moved like a jackrabbit and hit like a pint-sized Brahma bull. His feints and footwork were stuff of legend. It was said bigger men spent all of their energy just chasin' and swingin'. Chip could just dance around till they lost their wind and fell of their own accord. He didn't always win but he never lost cuz many fights ended in a draw when the bigger men ran out of steam and jus' up and quit.

Chip did his best to teach us the finer points of boxing. His training kinda felt like dance lessons but I got the idea after a bit and did all right. Mal found out he had two left feet and stopped trying but Josh hung in there with me and we sparred for hours. Chip always cautioned us not to corner anything meaner than we were.

Back in '80 or '81, I heard tell one of them big fellas finally had enough chasing and shot "Chip" in both knees just to slow him down. Always wondered if it worked.

It seemed to take forever but we finally made it to the Flowery Mountains of southwestern Nevada and headed through Gold Canyon. We passed by Silver City and Gold Hill before finally bedding the herd down outside of Virginia City.

The "Big Bonanza" days that started in 1873 were past but the mining still continued and the miners were always in need of fresh beef. Knowing that, "Sherm", our tough old *segundo*, dickered with the cattle buyers till he got top dollar for our herd. He was a stern trail boss but a fair man and he'd forgotten more about trails and cattle than I'll ever know. When he settled up with us, we got our three months wages plus a fifty-dollar bonus. We were in hog heaven what with all that extra money burning holes in our britches.

Mal, Josh and I had so much youthful spirit; we raced each other into town. Goner and I won, of course. After three months of pushing cows around, Goner wanted to run worse'n I did. We boarded the horses at the livery and set out to look around on foot.

Virginia City was the biggest town any of us had ever seen. It supposedly got its' name from a Virginian, James Finney, one of the original founders of the famous Comstock mine. Not wishing to waste a dropped bottle of whiskey, he used the accident as an excuse to christen the ground "Virginia" in honor of his home state.

When we arrived, Virginia City had almost a hundred saloons but only three undertakers and four churches. With streets built up and down the hills, they figured to have some of ever'thing. The six-story International Hotel, on "C" street, was the biggest sight around but we just gawked at all the buildings, the railroad tracks, and the many different kinds of people we ran into. Some said twenty thousand folks lived in the city but we couldn't believe it. Not all in one place, no way.

Immigrants from all over the world flocked to the Comstock. Three fourths of all the miners were foreigners. As we walked around, we rarely heard English spoken. There were mines and miners all over the city. Huge scrap-rock piles were ever'where. From huge operations to little one-man "holes in the ground", all of the miners were chasing gold and silver dreams. It was my first encounter with gold and silver fever but certainly not my last.

First on my list of things to do was to get a bath. Three months on the trail wearing the same clothes day after day was more than I'd bargained for. We took rooms at "Sadie's Boarding House" and hustled to the bath barrels. Sadie and her girls took good care of us and kept the hot water a'coming. We left there smellin' of bear grease and lavender soap.

Our next stop was "Anderson's Dry Goods Store". I'd never seen such a fine selection of wares. They had clothes, boots, hats, saddles, leather trappings, firearms, foodstuffs, books and anythin' else you could think of. We all bought new shirts, jeans and underwear right off. Rather than washing our stinkin' trail clothes, we just burned 'em.

Mal spent his entire bonus money on a brand spankin' new Colt Peacemaker. It had the "gunfighters barrel" of four and three quarter inches and real elephant-ivory grips. It was engraved all over but the cylinder had gold inlays that really stood out. It came with a Silver Star hand-tooled gun belt that had silver stars about the size of a ten-cent piece all around the belt and a dollar-sized star on the holster. It was fancy as all get out and so showy you couldn't miss it.

I used some of my bonus money to buy my first pair of store-bought custom-made cowboy boots. They cost me over fifteen dollars and were made by a man called Big Daddy Joe Justin from Spanish Fort, Texas. The boots had a white leather buffalo skull inlaid on the front, eight rows of fancy stitching, pointy toes and two-inch riding heels.

Josh, being Josh, went right over to the Western Union office and wired his bonus money back home to his folks. He also mailed all the letters he'd written along the trail.

After our shopping, we ended up at the "Gold Hill Café" for supper. It was a small place with just a few tables but it felt like home to us. The aroma from the kitchen was like heaven itself. After three months of beef and beans, even beans and beef would have been welcome but the food at Gold Hill was real good. We ate like wolves in a hen house.

Jenny Carpenter, the owner, cooked and served all by herself since business had been slow. Most of the trail riders ate at the big hotels or the saloons and cafes downtown.

Jenny wasn't old but she looked it. Life was not easy for a single woman in a mining town and it was clear she'd been through some hard times. She'd grown a hard shell but still had a soft center. After we talked awhile, she took a real liking to us and we each got an extra piece of her special strawberry rhubarb pie. We were so stuffed it was hard to move.

Josh and I wanted to hang around and talk with Jenny but Mal had an itch to try the local saloons. After Grasshopper Flats, I wasn't too keen on saloons or drinking in general and neither was Josh. Since Mal was older, he figured somehow he knew better and headed downtown.

When Jenny finally closed up, we went hunting for Mal. It was a clear night with a full moon and lots of stars. We could hear the boisterous sounds coming from the saloons on Broad Street but the rest of town was shut down and quiet. We went from building to building along the way to see what was inside. I remember we laughed at the sign at the Justice of the Peace who was also an Undertaker. It read, "We marry 'em and bury 'em at reasonable rates."

While we were having a hoot just looking around, Mal was nudgin' trouble over in the "Landslide Saloon." As we neared the "Landslide", we heard a loud drunken voice over the din.

"I said, what's your name, boy?"

All of a sudden-like, things got real quiet and then we heard Mal's stammer. "Malachi, Malachi James, sir."

Then the drunken voice challenged again. "Who are your people? Are you from Missouri, boy?"

"No sir." Mal was being real polite. "My folks hail from Alabama but we have a small ranch in the Arizona Territory.... down 'round Fort Yuma."

The drunken voice challenged him. "Well. I say you're one of them gray-bellied bastards from Missouri.... the James Boys."

Josh and I knew the sound of trouble so we raced to the swinging doors and looked in.

There was a long bar down the right side of the "Landslide" and tables spread throughout. I could see a player piano and a couple of faro tables against the wall in the back. There must have been twenty or thirty men in the crowd. Cowboys and miners, mostly. Some had been playing cards but now everyone was just watchin' and waitin'. You could almost taste the tension building in the room.

Mal was leaning against the bar with a whiskey glass in his right hand. At the far end of the bar was a swaggerin', staggerin' hulk of a man wearing a worn army jacket over his long johns and jeans. With his filthy clothes, unshaven face and bloodshot eyes, he figured to be a down and out miner. He carried a worn-lookin' Starr Double-Action Army .44 in the left side of his waistband and looked eager to use it. As my Pa used to say, he looked like a stick of dynamite with a half-inch fuse in the middle of a prairie fire,

Mal cleared his throat and spoke extra polite. "That would be Jesse and Frank, sir. We ain't no kin to them that I know of."

The drunk stepped closer and roared. "You calling me a liar?"

"Uh, no, no sir, not at all .... wouldn't think of it."

All at once, the crowd stepped back from around the bar. The fat old bartender looked from the miner to Mal and retreated to the far end of the bar. Several well- dressed customers finished their drinks in a hurry and rushed past us through the swinging doors. They figured to be businessmen and drummers who wanted no part of what was comin'. The tension kept buildin'.

The drunken miner was fully primed. He had a beer in his left hand and a fist in his right. His face bore the scars of cruelty and pain. He'd probably given and received more than his fair share of both.

The drunk came closer. "Stop calling me 'sir'. I ain't no gawd-damned officer. I'm a three-striper, see?" He pointed at the faded hash marks on his tattered jacket sleeve.

"I'm Sergeant Ezra Collins.... and I hate all gray-bellies. Grant and Sherman should'a let us kill 'em all after what they did to poor old Mr. Lincoln."

Collins was edging ever closer to Mal who looked at his feet and muttered, "Yes... sir."

Collins slammed his beer on the bar and screamed. "You funning with me, boy? I just told you.... I ain't never been no 'sir'."

Again, I was reminded of my Pa. He always warned us to never argue with a drunk cuz it was just like mud-wrestlin' with a pig. Try as you might, you cain't win so you jus' get muddy for nothing and all the while, the pig likes it.

Meanwhile, Mal was frozen scairt and couldn't shake his good manners. He'd been raised to speak respectful-like and couldn't help hisself. In the West, such manners were often mistaken for weakness.

"No sir, I mean, uh.... no...."

Collins lunged forward and swung a meaty right backhand at Mal that connected high and hard. Mal dropped his glass and it shattered on the floor. He staggered a bit but was able to cling to the edge of the bar to keep from going down. His lip was split and he was spitting blood.

"That cuts it, boy. I see you're wearing a mighty fancy shootin' iron. Do you have the guts to use it?"

Josh pushed open the swinging doors and pleaded. "Mal, don't."

Mal looked our way but didn't seem to hear. He must have still been a'buzzin' from the backhand. The smart thing for him to do would'a been to walk away but Mal wasn't thinkin' smart. He seemed afraid to draw and afraid not to. He was stuck, half in and half out of a mess with nowhere to hide.

Collins waited like a coiled snake. All eyes were on Mal and it felt like someone sucked all the air out of the room. Mal was still clinging to the edge of the bar with both knees bent. As he tried to stand up straight, his right hand came off the bar and dropped to his side.

I'll never know if Mal intended to draw or not. His movement was all the excuse Collins needed. There was no missing at six feet so the drunken miner cross-drew his pistol and plugged Mal dead center in the chest. After being shot, Mal tried to draw but barely cleared leather. He just stood there, pitching back and forth, staring at the flowering bloodstain on his chest like he couldn't believe his own eyes.

Josh pushed on through the swingin' doors and rushed to him but Mal collapsed at his feet. I heard Mal gasp, "Don't tell Ma 'bout the drinking."

He coughed a bit, choked and tried to speak but nothing came out 'cept blood and foam. As Josh knelt over him, Mal took his last breath. You could've heard a pin drop in that saloon.

Collins was grinning like a mouse-fed alley cat. He retrieved his beer from the bar and took a long swallow. When he finished, he turned to boast to the crowd.

"Well, whaddaya know? Old Ezra Collins whipped one of the no-tor-ee-us James Boys."

A few men in the crowd cheered half-heartedly but the rest edged up the bar to get fresh drinks and gawk. I pushed through the doors and joined Josh alongside Mal's body. I just didn't know what to do. Guess I was in shock or just frightened half to death.

Both Josh and I were dumb-stuck by what we saw. Mal's cold dead eyes staring up at nothing at all and his blood spreading all over him and onto the floor. All I could think of was to get away from there as fast as I could. I bent down to help Josh move Mal's body. As we started to lift him, his fancy Colt slipped from his dead fingers and "clunked" on the floor.

Josh bent over to pick up the gun and looked at it as if he didn't know what it was. I continued to drag Mal's body toward the door but Josh just stood there staring at that damn pistol. Then he carefully picked it up.

Collins had gone back down the bar and was leading the crowd in a twisted celebration of sorts. When he glanced back and noticed Josh just standing there holding that Colt, he said casually, "You wouldn't be kin to that gray-belly, would ya, boy?"

Josh was in shock and beyond hearing anything. I could sense what was about to happen and urged him, "Josh, come on."

That seemed to snap him out of his trance and he looked at me. I motioned for him to help me with Mal's body and he seemed to understand. He started toward me when Collins' guttural snarl filled the air.

"Don't you walk away from me, boy."

This time, Josh heard him and turned his head. Collins was stalking him with fire in his eyes and beer foam dripping down his chin. It was like looking at the face of a hydrophobic bulldog.

Josh stammered, "What?"

Collins stepped closer. "I said, are you kin to that gray-belly?"

Josh looked at Mal's body and then back toward Collins.

"Yes.... sir.... he.... was.... my.... my brother."

Collins grinned widely and played to the crowd. Few men in that crowd agreed with what he was doing but none chose to raise a hand to stop him. They stood by and grimly watched the scene play out. The drunken miner was collecting souls like old "scratch" hisself.

Collins continued to speak slowly like he was funnin' with Josh. "And what's your name little gray- belly?"

Josh hesitated a mite. "Joshua.... Joshua James.... sir."

Scared and shocked as he was, Josh was afflicted with the same good manners as his brother and drew the same outrage from Collins. "Now you're making fun of me, ain't ya' boy?"

Josh answered, "No....." he swallered the "sir" that was trying to escape his lips. He looked at the floor as Collins took another step closer.

Josh was looking at Collins over his left shoulder with the Colt in his right hand by his side.

Collins asked. "You plannin' to use that fancy smoke pole, boy? If not, you can give it to me. Something to recollect tonight by." He laughed aloud at his pathetic attempt at humor.

I reached out to Josh and whispered, "Toss the gun to me.... now."

Josh started to hand the Colt to me but Collins shouted, "I said gimme that there pistol."

Josh turned at the sound of the loud voice and the gun in his right hand turned with him. I know he didn't realize, but it did look like he was turning it toward Collins and that was exactly what Collins had been waiting on. He drew again and shot Josh right in the heart. Josh's body was jolted backward by the impact and collapsed at my feet. He was dead before he hit the floor and never knew what hit him.

Collins cheered. "Hot damn, got me another." He did a little dance before he faced the crowd and boasted, "Looks like I'm going to wipe out the whole damn James gang in one night." This time there was even less cheering from the crowd as several more patrons headed for the doors.

Suddenly everything seemed to slow down as I was intent on what I was doing and moved with a firm conviction. I unbuckled Mal's gun belt, yanked it out from under his body and strapped it on. Then I bent down and picked up that fancy Colt from Josh's dead hand, spun the cylinder a couple of times to check the load and let 'er drop back in the holster. Then I stepped over Josh's body and squared-up, facing Collins.

Collins had his back to me as he confronted his less than enthusiastic audience. He just couldn't grasp why so few seemed excited by his great deeds. Then, some of the crowd took heed of my stance and started edging away. Collins wore a look of confusion as he turned around and saw me. When he noticed my hand stretched out over the Colt, he smiled viciously and wet his lips. Holding back a laugh, he blurted out. "Well, there's always room for one more up there in the bone yard."

He held a beer in his left hand and his gun in his right. The pistol was by his side and ready for action so when he raised it to shoot, I was ready for him. To me, it was just like shooting at rocks and bottles. My draw was smooth and quick. I felt the Colt buck in my hand and saw the bullet punch a hole in Collins' chest. He reeled from that first impact and the downward shot from his pistol took a piece of his foot along with it as it bored into the floor.

Collins tried to speak. "What.... happened?"

Now he was really confused. There was a dark bloodstain spreading on his chest and he couldn't raise his six-gun for another shot. Again and again I fired as he refused to go down. After five shots, I finally clicked on an empty chamber and stopped pulling the trigger as Collins slowly crumbled to the floor.

As things returned to a normal pace, the pungent smell of gun smoke hung in the air. The crowd had taken cover behind overturned tables and chairs when the shooting started. The barroom was littered with broken glasses, scattered playing cards and spilled drinks. For a moment or two nobody moved or said a word. Collins lay in a widenin' pool of his own blood. He had five bullet holes through his upper chest. One silver dollar could've covered 'em all. His body jerked and gurgled but there was no life in it.

I was frozen in place, gun in hand, staring down at him, until some of the crowd started to react. The fat old bartender peered cautiously over the bar to look down at Collins and he didn't seem too disappointed.

"Would ya' look at that? All five shots in the heart. That's some shootin' young fella."

The others rose slowly and walked over to confirm his claim. They looked up at me with a combination of awe and fear. I'd never seen that look before. I wasn't certain what to do so I just spun the Colt a couple of times and let it slip back into my holster.

I heard one of 'em say. "I've seen 'em all and there's none faster. That includes Hardin, Holliday or Wyatt Earp."

Suddenly folks were all around me, slappin' my back and givin' me congratulations. These were the same men who were cheerin' for Collins just minutes before and now they were cheerin' for me. Several offered to buy me a drink but I thought better of it.

All of a sudden, I felt a strong hand grip my shoulder and heard a familiar voice behind me. It was "the Major".

"I figure it's about time to fetch those boys outta here. What do you figure, Henry?"

I turned to face him and suddenly felt like crying. My eyes teared up and my throat was as dry as an old burro bone. The Major read my look and draped an arm over my shoulder and said, "It's over, Henry. You did what had to be done. Now let's get the boys outta here and see they get a decent burial."

Cactus Charley, "Chip" O'Leary and some of the other wranglers pushed through the doors to help. Like ever'one else in town, they'd come to the "Landslide" to see what the shooting was all about. The street was packed with on-lookers cranin' their necks to get a better view.

As we were leaving, the bar really sprung back to life. I heard the bartender calling, "Come on boys, show's over. Drinks on the house. 'Smitty', get Collins out of here. Truck him over to Potter's Field. They can plant him tomorrow."

The crowd released it's tension by babblin' all at once.

"Did you see that shootin'?"

"Yep, never seen the like of it."

"What did he say his name was?"

"Didn't say, but that big fella called him Henry."

"Then that's it.... he must be another brother, Henry James."

"Do you suppose they're actually kin to Frank and Jessie?"

"He sure enough shoots like 'em."

"Amen. Hey, get me another beer, will ya?"

Their voices faded away as we reached the undertaker with the funny sign. We only knocked once and the door opened. The undertaker was dressed in his nightshirt and cap but he was holdin' an oil lantern and motioned for us to come in. He must'a been a light sleeper and knew gunshots in the middle of the night were the sounds of business.

SPRING 1882

So there I was, listening to Cleetis snorin' and staring at that Colt six-shooter with the Silver Star gun belt, when it suddenly occurred to me that it was in need of cleaning and reloading. Lil had placed it atop my saddlebags within easy reach. I fumbled in the bags and got my gun cleaning supplies and extra ammunition. With only one good hand, it took awhile but I finally got it cleaned. It took a bunch of .44s to fill the Colt and the empty loops on my cartridge belt. Sure was glad I had 'em.

I couldn't help but recall Mal and Josh whenever I fussed with that gun. Just thinkin' about the message I sent to their folks made me feel sad all over again. I wanted them to know what happened and how truly sorry I was. I made it clear there had been a full measure of justice given. I just signed it "Henry." I figured Josh must have mentioned his friend "Henry" in one of his letters and that would be enough.

FALL 1878

We buried the boys the next day with a proper ceremony and hastily carved marble headstones. It was cold and cloudy and threatened rain. Most of the trail hands were there as well as Jenny from the "Gold Hill Café." When the cloudburst finally came, we went back to the café where Jenny served us hot coffee and potato cakes. We talked for awhile and then said our good-byes. Jenny and the Major seemed to hit it off so he stayed around to help clean-up. I think the boys would have approved of them getting together. Maybe some good would come of all that tragedy.

I planned to leave Virginia City the following morning since the name-makers had started to roll in. They were wanna-be gun fighters who were looking to make a reputation for themselves by killing the suddenly famous "Henry James."

The local newspaper, "The Territorial Enterprise", ran a big article on the shootings. The editor, Dan de Quill, who wrote the book "Big Bonanza", reported greatly exaggerated versions of my shooting ability and they were spread all over the territory like wildfire. The Major had warned me, and now I knew.

When I went back to "Sadie's", the sky was clear and the storm was over but the night held other challenges for me. Two young fools not much older than I were waiting on me. One was tall and lean with a face like a cross-eyed weasel. He had a thin mustache and really yellow-looking teeth. His partner was short and thick with no noticeable neck and only one eyebrow. Neither one measured-up to be a real gunfighter. They were nothing but young cowhands chasing a crooked dream. They'd ridden over from Reno as soon as they heard all the stories.

I tried to walk past 'em but they blocked my way. I tried to tell 'em I was nobody and killing me wouldn't make 'em famous. When that didn't work, I even tried threatening 'em but they would have none of that, either. By then, quite a crowd had gathered and we were caught in the middle of a Mexican stand-off.

In a panic, those two young fools braced me and slapped leather. I plugged 'em both before either one could get off a shot. Tall and lean got it in the right shoulder and spun to the ground. Short and thick got it in the right elbow and fell to one knee. Simple as that, both men dropped their guns and it was over. They both knew they were lucky to be alive. Never did get their names. That rowdy crowd cheered like I'd just won a big horse race.

Since they'd called me out and asked for it, there would be no trouble with the law but I knew trouble was coming after me anyway. Shooting both of them like that was really gonna get around. I went into "Sadie's" and hid out in my room all night with my back against the wall and a chair wedged under the doorknob. The Major always said there was no rest for a gun fighter short of the grave and now I believed him.

The final chapter in the Henry James saga occurred the next morning. I lit out just after sun up. Goner rolled his eyes and nickered at me as I saddled him. He seemed as anxious to be out of the stable and on the road as I was. The weather was cool and the air smelled like it was fixin' to rain once again. The rising sun was playing peekaboo with the dark clouds and the wind was brisk.

All I wanted was to get away as quickly as I could. Sadie told me that rumor had it there were at least a half dozen gunmen already in town or on their way and they'd all be hunting for "Henry James."

Since I wished to head west for California, I naturally left town heading east. I figured to circle around after I shed anyone that was following me but it didn't work out thataway.

The first thing you know, I passed three riders on the trail as I was leaving town. I tipped my hat so I didn't have to meet their eyes. Sometimes all it took was a "look" to start a ruckus. As we rode past each other, I could hear 'em talkin'.

"That's gotta be him, did you see those silver stars on his belt?"

I cringed and held my breath. Goner and I continued down the road.

I heard another voice call out. "Hey mister, hold up. I'd like a word with you."

I pretended not to hear and kept on riding in the hope they'd let it be but of course, they wouldn't. I heard them turn their horses around and start after me. I considered trying to outrun 'em but thought better of it. They would only follow and we'd have to do this somewheres else. I reined-in Goner and waited for 'em.

Right off I could tell who was at the head and who was the tail of this herd. Two of them looked like trail riders but the fella in the middle was no cowboy. He wore a black gambler's outfit with a flat-crowned hat, a white silk shirt and a coal black tie. I couldn't help but notice a bright red handkerchief tucked in his left breast pocket. The morning sun was still playing peekaboo through the clouds behind me and flashed off his gold-plated belt buckle, which made it a right smart target. Then I saw the left handed cross draw rig on his right hip with an ivory-handled pistol sticking out from under his coat.

He rode a fine looking black Morgan mare with a fancy black and silver saddle. He looked to be tall, well built and confident in his ability as a gunfighter. There certainly was no mistakin' what he had in mind.

The other two seemed to be along for the ride. They were a couple of two-bit drifters there to watch and wait like buzzards at a dried-up water hole.

He reined-in about twenty yards off and sat there sizing me up. As he slowly walked his horse toward me, I could feel the cold stare of his gray eyes. I tried to remain calm but my stomach was flipping like flap jacks on Sunday morning. His mare was blowin' and snortin' and it was clear to me she was excited by Goner, who was still a stallion. I'd never got around to geldin' him.

The gunman was all business. No emotion showed in his face. He advanced cautiously at a measured pace. I guess he was trying to figure me out before he went any farther. I continued to look back at him over my left shoulder as I slipped the rawhide thong off the Colt and let my right hand rest on its grip.

"Sorry, I mistook you for Henry James, the gunfighter. Now I see I might be mistaken. Henry James is a known gunman and you're nothing but a boy."

"Yes sir, reckon that's right."

He hesitated again and then started his horse forward. "Well then, tell me.... boy.... why are you wearing his fancy gun belt?"

With the reins in his left hand, he pulled his coat back with his right to fully expose his pistol. If he was trying to frighten me, he was doing a pretty fair job of it. His mare was still twitching all over and fighting the reins. He dug in his spurs to settle her down but it did little good.

"He left it behind when he lit out, yesterday. I swear to you sir, my name is not Henry James. You've got the wrong fella."

He reined-in again, about fifteen feet away. His partners stayed back but they edged their horses out of my line of fire.

The gunman figured to rile me and was wary of my calm manner. His horse was still skittish and that distracted him. The sun must have been peeping in and out of the clouds again because it came and went across his face. He carefully switched the reins from his left hand to his right while keeping a watchful eye on me.

Then he upped the ante. "That's a man's pistol and a man should be wearing it. Why don't you just toss it to me? You can keep the fancy gun belt since I'm left handed and won't have a need for it. If you give me the gun, maybe.... just maybe, I'll let you be on your way."

I nudged Goner around so we were lined up straight on. Like two knights on a jousting field, we faced each other across a field of honor. My heart was pounding and my hands were sweatin' but his arrogance rankled and suddenly, I was ready for a fight. It never once occurred to me I could lose that shootout and die right there, right then, over nothin' at all.

"Well, I fancy this gun so I don't figure I'm gonna do that."

He was still fighting his fidgety mare and was having some trouble controlling her with his right hand. The more he fought for control, the more she resisted. Pulling on the reins was getting in the way of his drawing his gun. I could tell that bothered him but he had gone too far to back off.

"Then you better use it."

With that, he made his move and was real quick about it. I matched his draw and we shot as one. I'll never know if it was his horse jumping around, the sun peeking through or what, but he missed with his first shot while I didn't. His bullet whistled past my ear and I felt the heat but he was gut-shot, right above that shiny belt buckle.

Though he was doubled over in agony, he was still full of fight and tried to get off another shot but his horse was buckin' and jerkin' him all about. I waited till he was able to take aim and then shot him again. This time he took it high in the left chest. Right through his bright red handkerchief. He slid down the side of his horse, fell to the ground and stayed put.

I leveled my gun on his partners but they kept their hands free as they rode slowly toward me. The two of them just stared at his body, not believing their own eyes. One of 'em dismounted and turned the body over. His eyes were wide white and he seemed to have a hard time with his words. In a hollow voice, he muttered to his partner.

"There'll be hell to pay when the Deacon gets wind of this."

His partner never budged from his saddle but looked at me with a mixture of shock and awe and stammered as best he could."

"I saw it, but I don't.... I don't believe it.... do you know who that is?"

"We were never formally introduced."

"That there's.... uh.... Preacher Daniels. He's kilt ten men that I know of. Nobody's faster than the Preacher.....'cept for the Deacon, of course."

"Hmm. Guess I must'a got lucky." I motioned the other one to get back on his horse. "Unless you want cards in this game, I suggest you load up his body and git."

He bent down and picked up the ivory-handled, silver-plated Smith and Wesson Schofield .45. "Iffin you don't have a need, mister, I sure would fancy to have this fine shootin' iron.... to remember him by."

I started to say "no" and then thought better of it. One fancy gun was more'n enough. I offered him a trade. Preacher's pistol for his. He couldn't believe his ears or move fast enough as he tossed me his beat up old Colt Dragoon, along with two loaded cylinders and a small pouch of cap and ball. It was a heavy, well-worn old percussion pistol but seemed to be in good working order.

He holstered his new pistol, grabbed up the mares' reins and mounted his horse. They took one last look at Preacher's body and then the two of 'em rode off toward Virginia City. Guess they figured to fetch his body later. They rode like the devil hisself was chasing 'em. Bet they couldn't wait to spread the news.

The Major's words were echoing in my mind and so were the Preacher's. Why was I still wearing that damn gun belt? It was like wavin' a red flag in front of a bunch of gun-fighting bulls. I got off Goner and unbuckled Preacher's gun belt with the left handed cross-draw holster. The other fellas' Dragoon fit a little snug but it did fit. I switched gun belts, rolled up Mal's fancy rig and put it in my saddlebags where it was to remain for almost two years.

Now I had to try to outrun the legend of "Henry James."

Chapter III
"The Farley House of pleasure"

SPRING 1882

I must'a slept like a rock. I finally woke to the smell of brewin' coffee and the sound of a cracklin' fire. It was half past my risin' time. Dawn was peaking through the mountains to the east, the sky was still gray and the wind was blowing cold from the north. I could hear the chirpin' of early birds chasing worms.

Thinking back to the events of the day before, I hoped today would be uneventful. As I looked about, Lil was busy fixing breakfast. Cleetis was having a tough time moving about but kept busy by tossing sticks at the fire as best he could. I was relieved to find my shoulder felt better and I had some movement in my right hand.

Seeing me awake, Lil brought me a cup of coffee and fussed with my shoulder. She saw me testing my right hand so she removed the poultice with a look of satisfaction. Her medicine was working its' magic.

"Thought you were gonna sleep all day, Pilgrim. I figger it to be almost seven o'clock. How's the hand?"

My right arm was still dead weight so I shook loose from the blanket and reached for my boots with my left hand. "I reckon it's gonna be all right, after a time. What about your head and shoulder?"

He shrugged and fingered his head wound tenderly. "The shoulder hole is plugged up fine but my head sure hurts. Cain't believe I plumb forgot to duck. Must be getting senile."

Lil motioned for me to sit as she served breakfast. Like the night before, ever'thing smelled great and I was hungry enough to eat a horse blanket. Along with the rice, beans and hard tack biscuits, she'd cooked us another kind of "mystery" meat. I poked at it and it didn't poke back so I ate it. It sure was tasty but I couldn't help wondering what it was before it landed on my plate. Once again, I chose not to ask.

I finally got to moving about and stretching my legs. From the top of the mesa, everything looked natural enough. No dust trails or movement I could detect. After I fed and watered the stock, I gave Goner a rubdown, which he seemed to enjoy. My right arm still hurt and wasn't much use but I got it done with my left. Stumpy was as wary of me as I was of him so I left well enough alone and was content just to feed him.

As I walked back into camp, two yellow-bellied marmots rushed past playing a game of race and chase and paid me no mind. I also watched a gray squirrel scamper up the side of a pine tree and that's when I noticed the sunlight reflecting off the brass receiver of a rifle leaning agin' the tree.

Cleetis saw me looking at the rifle and grinned. "That there's a gin-u-wine Henry rifle. Purty thang, ain't it? Yesterday, I lit out in such an all fired hurry that I forgot it but Lil brung it to me. Guess it came in mighty handy." He chuckled recalling our narrow escape. "Yessiree bob, mighty handy."

I rolled my bed and "gophered" through my saddlebags for my shaving gear. Divorcing my beard ever' morning was one habit I just couldn't shake. It was hard to do with my left hand but somehow I managed. When I finished, Lil handed me a small sack of fixings and pointed to my shoulder. I gratefully accepted whatever it was and started to stick the sack and my shaving kit back in the bags, which were getting kinda full. To make more room, I pulled out that old left-handed cross draw gun belt and the old Colt Dragoon.

Then it occurred to me it might be a good time to switch back to that rig while my right arm was on the mend. I buckled it on and tried my left-hand cross draw a couple of times. I was a little rusty and the Dragoon was heavy but the speed and the confidence were still there. Mal's fancy rig would have to ride in the saddlebags once again.

Never missing a trick, Cleetis just smiled and shook his head. "You seem mighty handy with your left hand, Pilgrim."

He was right; I was really good with my left hand. For almost two years, I wore that cross draw holster to distance myself from the reputation of "Henry James". Along the way, however, I created yet another alias, "Jim Monroe". He was a hard-rock miner and tin-pan prospector and it all got started at the very same place, Virginia City

FALL 1878

After my shoot out with Preacher Daniels, I headed due east for a few miles and found a shallow running creek I followed for another mile or so. I figured that would discourage anyone trying to track me so I swung wide to make my way south and west toward Carson City. I wasn't bound for anywhere special and was just heading in the general direction of California. That's when I ran into "Cousin Jack" and "Cousin Jennie".

Actually, "Cousins Jack and Jennie" were names given to all recent immigrants from Cornwall, England. For centuries, Cornishmen had been digging for tin in Cornwall and were thought to know all there was to know about hard-rock mining. Their knowledge of underground mineral formations was highly prized on the Comstock.

Following the California Gold Rush, most American miners knew all about placer mining but had little experience with hard-rock mining, which the Comstock demanded. The rich veins of gold and silver ran deep into the mountains but the veins drifted and crisscrossed underground. Some veins played out as fast as they were located. For this reason, Cornishmen were in great demand in all the large gold and silver mines of the Comstock Lode.

For the most part, the "Jacks" and "Jennies" were a hard working and a hard-drinking lot. They spoke their own flavorsome version of English and brought their unique customs with them when they came to the West. Being friendly and fun loving, they seemed to get along well with most folks. Most, but not all.

I met my first "Cousin Jack" on the way from Virginia City to Carson City. Folks that could afford the fare preferred to take the new railroad coaches up and down the mountain but those who couldn't, crowded the old mountain trail with their comin' and goin'.

This Cousin Jack's real name was Albie Penrose and his wife's was Priscilla. They were bound for the Comstock but got held up on the trail by their contrary mules. Albie's wagon was blocking the trail and those behind were getting mighty edgy while he rasseled with those cantankerous long-eared critters.

My way south was also blocked so Goner and I pulled up to watch the show. It was kinda funny, really. Albie was cursing as loud as the mules were snortin' and hee-hawin'. The more he cursed and threatened, the more they stubbornly refused to budge. The folks behind them were hollerin' at all of 'em. It was quite a spectacle.

Finally, a big teamster came up from behind with a shotgun. He made it clear the mules had better get moving or get shot. Albie took offense and the two of them went right after each other, skull and knuckles. Both men were tough and it was a right even scrap until two more teamsters joined in. They held Albie's arms and the first teamster was fixin' to beat him into ground meat.

It was none of my affair but it wasn't in me to let them gang up on him thataway. I drug out that big old Dragoon with my left hand and casually fired into the air. That .44 sure got their attention and the sound of the shot echoed forever down the mountain. Even those contrary old mules seemed ready to get back to pullin'.

Priscilla got down off the wagon and helped Albie to his feet. The teamsters backed off but kept watchful eyes on me and my Dragoon. They were still spoiling for a fight but were willing to wait for another chance. Beaten up as he was, there was still fire in that "Cousin Jack". He hauled off and hit both of the teamsters that had held him. I had to fire once again to stop the scrappin' although if given a fair chance, Albie might have whupped all three of 'em.

Albie and Priscilla climbed back in the wagon and got the mules moving. The teamsters went to their wagons and followed right along behind. I knew they were just bidin' their time, waiting for me to back off, so they could finish what they'd started. It made little sense but I turned Goner about and rode beside the "Cousins" back to Virginia City.

After we finally arrived in Virginia City and got them settled in, Albie insisted I have a drink with him and a few of his fellow Cornishmen before heading back to Carson City. His old friends and my new friends turned out to be a great bunch of guys. Davy Trenoweth, Alf Polglase and Little John Fenno treated me like a member of their Cornish family. I said "yes" to one drink and ended up staying with them for more than six months.

A whole group of Cornishmen and women lived in three old boarding houses on "C" street, across from the 4th Ward School. They lived like one big family and I felt right at home. Since I didn't have any fixed plans, they convinced me to join 'em in the mines and learn about hard-rock mining the Cornish way.

I told them my name was James Monroe but Albie changed it to "Jimmy" right off and it stuck although Priscilla continued to call me "my 'andsome". Soon enough I was working, drinking, fighting and singing with 'em. Now those folks truly loved to sing and were real good at it. I never got the hang of the singing but I joined in once I knew most the words of "Trafalgar's Boy" or "The Wreck of the Arethusa".

I pretty much stayed put with my new Cornish family. There weren't too many young single girls thereabouts but Virginia City was nearly overrun with "sportin'" ladies. One by the name of Julia Bulette was considered the "Courtesan of the Comstock". Miners who struck it rich reportedly paid up to a thousand dollars a night for her company. I could not imagine how any one night, anywhere, with anyone could be worth that kind of money.

The hard-rock mining was hard work and I seldom felt like wandering around. Oh, I wished to see Jenny at the Gold Hill Café and wondered if the Major had stuck with her but thought it was better for all if I didn't. Changin' my name, my job and that fancy gun and gun belt had done the trick so far and I was content to let things stay that way. I did, however, go to the cemetery to visit with Mal and Josh from time to time.

"Henry James" was still the talk of the Comstock for several more months. The shootout with Preacher Daniels was talked about with little care given to actual fact. As I figured, the mines of Virginia City were the last place anyone would think to look for a suddenly famous gunfighter. The first rumors had it that "Henry James" had fought with some well-known gunfighter and had been shot to death. Next, I heard he'd been hung for murder in San Francisco and then came my personal favorite; many were convinced he had drifted south and crossed the border into old Mexico.

We all labored in the Ophir mine. It was named after the source of King Solomon's gold mentioned in the Old Testament. It was one of the Bonanza mines like the Gould & Curry or the Savage. The Ophir started as a great place to hide but turned out to be a decent place to work. Thanks to the newly formed miners' union, we got paid four dollars a day for only eight hours of work. That was big money for the time although the work was brutal. Alfred Nobel's dynamite had replaced the risky blasting powder but danger and death rode with a man ever'time he went down in that mine.

I took to working the single jack. That meant smashing a steel drill into solid rock with a four-pound sledgehammer all day long. Sometimes I'd team up with another miner and work what they called the double jack. One of us held the drill in place while the other hit it with an eight-pound sledge. When a miner got tired of wielding the hammer, you just swapped places. A person had to be trusting of the other fella. One miss could cost you a finger or even a hand. It was hard work but swinging the four and eight pound sledges sure made a man strong. I got so I could crush walnuts with my bare hands.

Philip Deidesheimer created a square-set shoring system for supporting mine shafts for the Ophir mine in 1860. His amazing "cube" system allowed the mines to extend deeper and deeper into the mountains. Some shafts went over two thousand feet down. The temperature at that depth could get over one hundred thirty degrees. In that heat, a miner could work only a short time or he'd die from it.

I had the misfortune to watch several men die from that heat. I also saw accidents of all sorts. One time a dog fell down a shaft, more than a thousand feet, and killed two miners who were just waiting to come up. Sometimes charges went off too soon or too late. There were cave-ins and choking dust that ate a man from the inside out. One miner mixed a small blasting cap with his tobacco and stuffed it in his pipe. He blew up the pipe and the end of his nose but lived to tell of it.

After about six months, I had enough of the mines. I'll always miss the Cornish miners and their families but I'd been bitten by the gold bug and wished to try prospecting for myself. I figured that I'd learned enough from them to strike it rich on my own. Looking back, I can see that life is a continuing education and I still had much to learn.

SPRING 1882

Cleetis sighed and looked to the fire. "Reckon I'll be laid up for awhile. You best head out without us, Pilgrim."

"I figured as much. Guess I'll get going while the going is good. I figure you're in pretty good hands. Where will you go?"

"Haven't got that worked out, but.... mebbe.... we'll just head south and west over to Arizona Territory. Heard of a place there called Oak Creek Canyon. Supposed to have mild winters, with plenty of water and game. I have an older brother that used to squat thereabouts. Think he was bear-hunting. His name's Rufus, but as kids we always called him "Roof " 'cause he was so damned tall. Been wondering if he's still alive. Mebbe I'll go see."

"I know the area and you should do well there. It's near my home. Maybe we'll run into each other again."

Cleetis smiled a knowin' smile. "I'd like that, Pilgrim."

As I secured my bedroll and saddlebags on Goner, I noticed my empty scabbard and walked over to my broken Winchester. It had been shot up beyond repair. The stock was split and a slug was lodged in the feed ramp. Back home, Pa would have thrown it in the shed to use for spare parts. He seldom threw anything away or let it go to waste.

Next, I picked up the Injuns' Winchester rifle. Its stock was also cracked and most of the metal was badly rusted. He must've split the stock on my shoulder. I looked around for the other Injun rifle but it turned out to be an old single shot Springfield. It was out of date and ammunition so was of little use to anyone. It seemed like my only choice was to do without until I could afford to buy another Winchester.

As I walked back to Goner, Cleetis was watching me and considering. Then he pointed at the Henry rifle.

"Why don't you take that shiny rifle with you. I always figgered it was too purty for me to shoot." He paused a bit and looked to Lil. "Anyway, I won't be needing it and you prob'ly will. It'll go right along with your fancy shootin' iron and saddle."

Ever'one noticed my fancy saddle. It'd been given to me and was way beyond the budget of the working cowboy. Seems like having nice things like that just got a body in trouble.

I started to object but I knew he was right. I truly needed another rifle and that Henry was a great rifle. All Cleetis would ever need was his old Sharps buffalo gun. He'd hunted and trapped the mountains for more'n forty years and that old rifle kept him alive and fed.

I remembered my pa being so proud of his old Henry rifle. He always boasted we were kin to the maker of that fine weapon, Tyler Henry. Come to think of it, his name would have fit right in with our family of dead presidents. Maybe that's why the folks skipped John Tyler when picking out our names. Anyway, I always wondered if we were kin to the hero of the American Revolution, Patrick Henry.

Pa planned to buy a Henry rifle for each of us boys but cash money was usually our short crop. By the time I'd saved up enough, I couldn't buy a new Henry anymore since they stopped making 'em around '65 and they had all been sold. I had to settle for my '73 Winchester instead.

I picked up the Henry and looked at the floral pattern engraved on both sides of the receiver. The brass was tarnished and needed polish but I could make out some initials in the center of the pattern, scrolled so fancy they were hard to read. There was a woven rawhide sling attached with some feathers and beadwork that looked like a Navajo design. The entire rifle was a pure-dee work of art and in prime working condition. Some master engraver sweated a long time over that gun and some other fella spent top dollar to own it.

As I admired the rifle I couldn't help but wonder why Tyler Henry didn't put a wooden fore grip on it like Oliver Winchester did with his later rifles. Then I noticed the feeding tube spring mechanism was in the way. Guess Winchester solved that problem by putting a loading ramp on the side of the receiver. That allowed for the wooden fore grip and made good sense.

"This is a beautiful rifle, Cleetis. I've never seen the like of it. I'm much obliged."

Looking again at the initials, I had to ask. "Where'd ya get this? Do you know who's rifle this is.... or.... was?"

"Couldn't say. Old Red Dog give it to me. Sort of a wedding present, I guess. He took it off a dead 'Pache but judging by the trappings, the 'Pache probably fetched it off some poor Navajo. No telling how far it's come or how long ago. Funny how a good gun like that can get passed around."

He pointed at a colorful beaded leather bag. "There's some extra rounds for it in that there Navajo bead bag. It won't handle those .44 centerfires like a Winchester. That Henry takes 215-grain rimfire .44 and holds sixteen of 'em. They say you can load it on Sunday and shoot for a whole week."

I checked the load and found it one shy and that figured. I got another round from the bag and tried to fill 'er up. That was easier said than done with only my left hand. Loading a Henry was really different from loading any other rifle I'd ever seen. The feed tube spring had to be fully compressed and the feed tube itself had to be rotated away from the barrel about four inches from the end of the rifle. It was a tricky little maneuver I decided I would surely have to practice. When I finally got the last cartridge loaded, I walked over to Goner and "snaked" the Henry in my scabbard. There was barely enough room for the beaded bag in my over stuffed saddlebags.

Cleetis was swiggin' the last of his coffee and Lil was preparing to break camp. Guess she figured to move him to a safer location. Probably some place closer to water. It would surely be weeks before he'd be back to normal. I was trying to find a way to say a proper good-bye and then Cleetis spoke up.

"Kinda makes sense, you being a Henry and all."

"What's that?"

He looked up at me with a twinkle in his eyes. "Well, a Henry should have a Henry rifle, I figger." He laughed to hisself. "That is your name ain't it, Henry?"

I tried to sound as truthful as I could but did a poor job of it. "Sure enough. I've always been a Henry."

"Well.... Henry Monroe.... or whatever your name is.... you sure ain't no 'Pilgrim' so I figger you'll make out all right without me to back your play. Good luck to you."

"And to you, too."

We shook hands with feelin'. Ailing as he was, he still had power in his grip. I knew he'd make out somehow. I did my best to thank Lil for all her help and care. I hoped she understood the feelin's if not the words.

Carefully, I even said good-bye to Stumpy as I mounted up and headed Goner back down the mesa. Being alert to any movement, I saw something or someone coming up through the trees. I pulled out my new Henry rifle and ducked behind a stand of ponderosa pines and waited. It was an Injun all right, riding a pinto pony and leading another. The second pony had traveling packs strapped on. They looked to be stuffed full of supplies. As they got closer, I could see it was a squaw, and a young one at that. She was tracking our sign from yesterday. She barely seemed to notice me as she passed but I'll bet she was well aware.

It suddenly occurred to me she was probably the young squaw that Cleetis had mentioned. Seems she was a'followin' him, too. Well, I'll be damned if that old man wasn't gonna make out real good. He might just start that tribe of blue-eyed redskins.

Goner and I lit out west by southwest and spent four days ridin' by day and campin' out under the stars at night. The weather was mild and the traveling easy. From all the run-off, there was plenty of water around and sweet young grass for Goner.

My new Henry rifle worked out just fine. It wasn't good for much over a hundred yards but I was pretty good at sneakin' up so it didn't matter much. I got a small mule deer and a couple of antelope to add to my grub line and I set most of the meat to jerky. My right arm was still weak and shaky but somehow I managed.

I saw lots of critters but nothing with only two legs. There was plenty of time to ponder but I kept my attention keen. The La Plata Mountains loomed ahead with their snow-capped peaks pushing up agin' the sky. I saw the peak folks called the sleeping Ute. It kinda favored a Ute warrior lying down with his arms crossed. I was happy to see no other Utes, sleeping or otherwise.

When we finally made it to the Animas River, it was running high and wide at full speed. I was thankful I didn't have to cross it. For some reason, the Spaniards called it the "river of lost souls" and I thought about that as I followed it south toward Animas City. Since it was late in the afternoon, the sun was going down and long shadows were spreading out across the valley. It was a beautiful, peaceful place. The sort of place that makes a man take note of and wish to return to someday.

Animas City had the look of a dying town with boarded up stores and almost empty streets. I heard tell land speculators bought up all the property around town and held out for high prices from the Denver and Rìo Grande Railroad. Well, the railroad out-foxed 'em and changed the route. The tracks went a couple of miles south of Animas City where they built a town of their own that they called Durango. Now all the businesses in Animas were closing up or relocating. The speculators lost everything because of their greed.

The livery stable was empty 'cept for a big gray bedded in the last stall. There was something familiar about that horse but I paid it little mind as I took care of Goner. I relieved him of his bridle and saddle and rubbed him down with a hand full of hay. I forked more hay into the feed bin and found a half bag of oats so we just naturally helped ourselves. With my saddlebags and Henry rifle in hand, I set out to find a room with a real bed. I also wished for a bath. It had been a long while since I'd had either.

I passed several closed-up businesses, including Atkin's General Store, the Rocky Mountain Café, and the Western Union office. The only place doing any business this time of day was a fancy saloon called "The Farley House". About a dozen horses were hitched outside and music was coming from a tin-panny piano. I could hear the voices of men and women having a time. What with the town shutting down, I wondered what they could be celebrating.

Next door to the saloon was a broken down hotel called the "Colorado Inn". It looked like it was closed until I nudged the door, which slowly opened with the squeak of a creaky hinge. Something stirred behind the counter and was followed by a loud thump and muttered cursing. A drunken and half-awake hotel clerk rose unsteadily from the floor and tried to get hisself together. He wore a sat-on cap and a rumpled coat at least two sizes too small for him that looked like it had been slept in before.

"Can.... ah... I help you.... sir?" He raised his hand to cover a belch.

I was amused by his attempt to be polite. "I'd like a room and a bath if you got 'em."

He struggled to straighten his clothing. "We got all kinds of rooms, sir. You can take your pick. Any of 'em 'cept...."

He almost fell over while turning around but managed to cling to the counter for support. He was staring at the empty slot in the key rack on the wall.

"Number four. Yes, sir, number four's took. This afternoon.... a nice young woman, she was real young and real pretty. Yes, sir."

The clerk turned back 'round and I got a full blast of his stale whiskey breath. It was enough to cross your eyes and keep 'em that way.

"But you'd have to go over to the river if you want a bath and it's still mighty cold this time of year. The towns' water pump broke and there's nobody left around to fix it. Only place with their own well water here 'bouts is The Farley House and they ain't ones for sharin'."

He opened the guest book with shaky hands and offered me a fresh dipped pen. "Sign, if you're of a mind to."

I continued to be tickled at his feeble attempts to act in a business-like manner. I also noticed no one else had signed the book for several days. Reckon that young woman in room number four wasn't of a mind to give a name. I took the pen and signed real slow with my left hand.

"Jim Monroe." No one knew better than I how flexible names could be in the West. Some folks changed 'em like they changed shirts. Somehow, today, that name suited me and the old left hand gun rig I was sportin'.

He looked at my signature and said. "Well.... Mister.... Monroe, my name's Doby and I'll usually be here iffin you need anything."

I picked up my bags and went up to room number two at the top of the stairs. I took notice of room number four being right next-door.

My room wasn't much but it did have a real bed and was reasonably clean. That cold river bath would have to wait. I struggled to get my clothes and boots off and flopped on the bed. What with all the hollering and music from next door, I figured it might be a while before I fell asleep but I was wrong.

I must have slept for a couple of hours when I was woke up by the sound of gunfire from the saloon next door. I heard three quick shots from the same gun and then silence. After a minute or so, the music and hollering started up again. I could guess what that meant. An argument was settled with hot lead and somene probably paid with his life.

I got to wondering if the girl in room number four was over at the Farley House or in her room and wide awake as I was. I wished to know but not bad enough to find out.

After tossing and turning for a half hour or so, I finally gave in to my curiosity and got dressed to go to the saloon. The music and laughter had quieted down some and that usually meant they were nearing closing time. I buckled on that old left-handed gun belt out of habit but I had no reason to expect trouble. As I shut my door and headed down stairs, I caught a glimpse of the door of room number four open a crack and then close. Guess she was next door all along.

The Farley House was the tallest building in town. Three stories high and decked out for the pleasure business. The second and third floors had interior balconies that overlooked the main floor. Someone must of spent a lot of money furnishing the whole place with the latest decorations from back East. There was a big chandelier hanging down from the middle of the ceiling and shiny new gaming tables all about. I saw faro and blackjack set-ups, a couple of roulette wheels and a dozen poker tables. They had a player piano in the back and a large painting on the wall of some rich fella all dressed-up for posin'.

There were two dressed-up bartenders behind a beautiful oak bar that ran the length of the building. Huge mirrors hung behind the bar with fancy liquor bottles displayed in front of 'em. It was a far cry from the run of the mill western saloons I was used to. Most taverns started out with a wooden plank resting on two empty whiskey barrels and never ventured much beyond. The Farley House seemed more like the El Dorado or the Bella Union in San Francisco. I'd never seen 'em but I'd heard plenty. It was almost as plush as the

International Hotel in Virginia City that I had seen. Either way, it was way more saloon than Animas City could currently support.

There was a pretty good-sized crowd and there was some serious gamblin' going on. There were a lot of miners "bucking the tiger" at the faro tables as they favored that game. Most businessmen favored poker or blackjack while cowboys could be found almost anywhere.

You could always tell where the big money was roosting by counting the number of watchers around the table. Like buzzards circling carrion, the drunks and losers loitered nearby and waited for the pots to get heavy. I reckon they were hoping some big winner would spring for a round on the house.

I found an open spot at the bar and ordered a beer. The bartender was dressed like a dandy in a stiff white shirt, black bow tie, bright red vest and slicked back gray hair. Even had a name tag that read "Bud". He got me a beer, changed my money but never said a word. Real professional like.

I started to look around and right off, I noticed a rather large section of the wood floor in the middle of the room had recently been swamped down and was pretty damp. Since the haze and smell of gun smoke still hung in the air, I couldn't help but wonder so I decided to ask Bud, the bartender.

"You have a shooting in here tonight?"

Bud didn't say a word but then he didn't have to. His face was a road map of a hundred saloons in a hundred different towns and it spoke loud and clear. He glanced over to that same poker table with the large crowd around and kept at his cleaning and polishing of the glasses.

Just then, I happened to look up and take notice of several saloon gals on the second and third floors. They were parading around on the balconies and watching the games below. I also noticed an older woman that looked to be a madam. She was busy talking with the other bartender at the far end of the bar.

You would expect to see cowhands, miners and railroaders here but there were also cattlemen, gamblers, drummers and businessmen in the crowd. Had to be close to fifty or sixty men still in the place. It was clear the saloons in Durango didn't measure up to the Farley House but I was dead wrong about it being close to closing time. Closing time at this sportin' house was when they ran shy of customers.

I edged my way down the bar a bit to get a better look at the poker table in the middle with all the onlookers. I noticed right off there were five players rather than the usual six. As I struggled to get a look at their faces, I suddenly felt lightning-struck. Sitting there big as life, in his black coat and hat, was Slick, that gambler fella from Grasshopper Flats. He hadn't changed even a little bit. Seeing him again took me right back to that awful day.

APRIL 7, 1878

After I got through heaving up my guts in the street, I stumbled back to the bar to clean myself up. First thing you know, good old Slick came over to console me and get me yet another drink. He said it would clear out that bad taste in my mouth. Well, he was right about that. It also got me back on that whiskey-bronc and I tried to ride it again. Soon enough, I was staggering all over and pretty much acting the drunken fool.

A grizzled old bear hunter came through the swinging doors and I ran smack into him. The old man was really tall and thin with coal-dark eyes and a full beard covering most of his chest. He was wearing old skins and smelt like a polecat dipped in sheep shit. As he glared at me, I tried to apologize but he showed no patience for a young drunk and knocked me to the floor with a sudden forearm. Now for some strange reason, the crowd thought that was the funniest thing they'd ever seen. I, on the other hand, was embarrassed and angry. Who the hell did he think he was?

Well, I was about to find out what he was if not who. I got to my feet and cursed him up one side and down the other. He stood at the bar with his back to me and wasn't impressed one whit with my ability to swear. The crowd egged me on so I swaggered over and crowded him. When he finally had enough of my mouth, he drug me outside by my ear, down the alley, and slapped the snot out of me. Didn't break anything but my high spirits and he damned near smacked me sober.

He called it "learning time" and what I learned was he was one tough old blister and I never wished to cross his path again.

Half of the bar crowd had followed us out to the alley. When that old man finally quit thumping on me, they helped me to my feet and took me back to the bar to treat my wounds and ease my pain. With Deke's encouragement, they started setting up more drinks for me and soon enough I was really feelin' no pain.

SPRING 1882

Now here he was, sitting right in front of me. It's funny, but watching Slick playing poker was almost like being back in the Flats. Although he looked the same, I had changed considerable and I was mighty curious to see if he would recognize me after all these years. Maybe when the game broke up I'd find out. As it turned out, the night was still young.

After an hour or so, I got to wonderin' if that big game would ever break up. One player had dropped out but Slick and the other three were still at it. From the cheering and hollering, I could tell the pot was boiling. Men were leaving other tables just to watch. A bunch of the girls came down the stairs and were making sure everybody had enough to drink. Wasn't a single customer gonna die of thirst if those girls could help it.

The madam paced up and down the floor with an eye to all things, large and small. Little escaped her attention. I heard one of the men address her as "Miss Victoria". She had the look of a lady who had been around a lot but wasn't any the worse for wear. She seemed to have aged like a fine vintage wine. Her alabaster skin and hazel eyes were framed by carefully done-up auburn hair. Her body still curved in hourglass proportions and moved like she knew how best to use it.

"Miss Victoria" carried herself with an air of self-confidence and assurance of who she was and what she was about. It was a good bet that underneath all the satin, frills, and lace, she was a feisty old broad who surely knew the score.

Bud, the barkeep, had been nipping from a flask he carried in his vest pocket and started to get talky. When I asked about the madam, he quietly confirmed she was indeed Victoria Bellemont Farley, owner of "The Farley House". She had come west from Chicago with the bartenders and most of the girls about three years earlier. They brought all the fancy furnishings with 'em and built the saloon and gamblin' hall in anticipation of the Denver and Rio Grande railroad coming to town. Now she was facing financial trouble like everyone else in Animas City.

I asked about the man in the painting and found out he was her deceased husband, Charles Upton Farley. Seems Charles came out west some twenty years before and was killed by Injuns. They still owned this piece of land in Animas City and after all those years, Victoria came to claim it. She had owned a big gambling hall and whorehouse in South Chicago but was forced to relocate her business after a political shake up left her without influential friends in the Windy City.

Once I got Bud talking, he was like a boulder running downhill that couldn't stop. I found out Victoria hired Slick to take over the gambling operations. She made the rules but he enforced 'em. He was to keep one eye on the dealers and the other on the customers. That was no mean trick. He also played the house hand in any big stakes games like tonight.

Old Bud was turning into a fountain of information so I brought up the shooting again. He looked all around before he leaned toward me and whispered.

"Sore loser bought trouble and had to pay for it."

"Slick?"

"You betcha. He's got a short fuse and a quick sleeve-gun. Poor drunk cowboy never even saw it coming."

Come to think of it, I'd never noticed Slick with a gun. A sleeve-gun made a lot of sense and was something to remember. He probably had some kind of derringer on a forearm rig that slid into his hand when needed. Slick was living up to his nickname.

Suddenly, the batwing doors were slammed open with a loud bang. Three gunmen walked in with purpose and fanned out. They were on the hunt and had the look of wolves stalking a herd of sheep.

The bar went stone silent and folks started backing off slow an' easy as if a skunk had just walked in. Everyone wished to get as far as they could from that center poker table. Three of the players at the table dropped their cards, picked up their chips and quickly stepped back from the table, leaving Slick sittin' with his back toward the gunmen. I was willing to bet that, given a chance, he would never sit with his back to those doors again. The tension in the room felt like an overfilled balloon.

Victoria immediately took the bull by the horns and ambled over toward the gunman in the middle. He was a powerful built old man, short and stocky, and looked to be the leader of the pack. His face was red with rage like he was right on the edge of explosion. His right hand was poised to draw his gun and he looked to be ready. The other two were younger and a bit taller than he was but they were cut from the same cloth. It figured that this was a family affair.

Slick remained at the table and casually lit a cigar as if nothing was wrong. The old man spoke out loud and clear.

"Turn around, gamblin' man. You shot my boy and now you're gonna die for it."

As bold as brass, Victoria continued to walk until she was right in the line of fire and confronted him.

"Colin got what he asked for, Angus.... no more, no less. He left Slick no other way out. You know what he was like when...."

Angus was beyond hearing. "Git out of the way! I don't want to shoot no woman but I will."

The gunman on his right took two quick steps farther to the right and drew his gun casually. "I kin nail him from here, Pa."

Angus raised his hand as if to stop his son. "Hold your water, Sean, this here is my fight."

He looked to his left. "That goes for you too, Mack."

"But Pa.... "

"Shut-up and stand down. I mean it."

Sean reluctantly holstered his gun and looked over to his brother, Mack, on the left. Angus turned back to Victoria. "I said get outta my way, dammit!"

Victoria was cool as a cucumber in a snowstorm. She knew most western men were loath to shoot a woman and Angus was nothing if not a true westerner. "Or what, Angus. Would you really shoot a woman?"

She walked even closer to him, deliberately measuring the man and his anger. She had her left hand extended but her right was hidden in the folds of her dress. Made me wonder what she might have hidden up her skirt.

No one in the bar dared move or even breathe. The silence seemed as brittle as cut glass. Sweat was dripping down Angus' cheeks and his breathing was labored. His face betrayed his indecision. He looked fit for a stroke.

Angus blurted out. "He shot Colin.... he killed my son."

Victoria continued to try talking sense. "And killing Slick won't bring him back. You or one of your other boys might die in the trying. Slick has friends here.... think about it, Angus."

She was only a few feet from him now and Angus was tied in knots. He looked around the crowd to see if anyone was going to back Slick but no one moved. His sons were frozen in place awaiting his lead.

She softened her voice a bit. "There's been enough killing tonight. Go home, Angus."

Angus kept ever'one waitin' and wonderin' until he finally broke down and fell to his knees. His eyes filled with tears and he seemed unable to speak.

Sean cried out. "No Pa, no!" and went for his gun. Victoria screamed and Slick whirled around and fired his derringer. A derringer is meant for close-up shooting and they were more than twenty feet apart but his aim was true. His shot hit Sean's shooting arm in the biceps just above the elbow. Sean's unfired pistol fell to the floor as he recoiled in agony. His brother, Mack, started to draw but was stopped by the sound of a old Colt Dragoon hammer being cocked.

I had drawn unconsciously and was actually surprised at it. I must'a gotten so caught up in the action that I reacted by instinct. Seeing I had him dead to rights, Mack backed down and raised his right hand away from his gun. Slick looked from him to me and back again, with a face full of questions.

Angus, still on his knees, looked to each of his sons and knew it was over. "She's right. There's been enough killing tonight. Mack, help your brother over to the docs'. I reckon we'll be going back home now."

Mack and Sean left the bar and Angus stood up to face Victoria and Slick, who was now by her side. "It might be over for now, but it ain't finished. We'll be back."

He turned to look me up and down, trying to figure my part in all this. Finally, he walked out the front door a beaten down old man. He had lost a son and found there was no undoing it. It was a terrible lesson for any man to learn.

I holstered my gun and turned around to face the bar. The crowd came back to life and Victoria called for a round of drinks on the house. Conversations flowered everywhere. Seemed like everyone started talking at once. Next thing, someone started the piano playing and the crowd went to celebrating again.

Bud placed another beer in front of me as I heard Slick's voice. "I'd like to thank you, mister?"

I turned to face Slick and Victoria. He was trying to figure where he knew me from while she was measuring what kind of man I was. I considered my options and then replied kinda matter of fact. "Jim.... Jim Monroe."

We shook hands as he continued to search my face for clues. "Well, my name's Slick and this here is..."

Victoria interrupted. " Victoria Bellemont Farley, owner of this fine establishment and forever in your debt, sir." She held out her hand so I could kiss it but I just shook it instead and my obvious embarrassment seemed to delight her.

Victoria had a Southern way of talking that just turned my mind to mush. Her eyes took in ever' inch of my body and made me feel like I was standing there buck naked. I felt limp all over like I'd been deboned. My face felt hot and flushed as if I had the damned prairie fever. I babbled something about how I'd done little enough and she, or they, owed me nothing

Slick seemed amused by my reaction to Victoria. No doubt he had seen it before. She was a special breed of pussycat.

"Don't I know you from.... somewhere?" Slick kept looking me over. He was obviously puzzled and curious.

My mind started to clear of the "Victorian" fog. "I don't reckon. I've never been through here before."

Slick accepted my answer but I could see he continued to search his memory. Being a professional gambler, he was a student of human nature and could tell I wasn't offering the whole truth.

"You know, when Victoria said I had friends in here, I wasn't so sure. Most men around here would be afraid to buck the MacDonald clan. I'm mighty glad to be wrong about that. Mack would have had me for certain." He was still toting the derringer and raised it up for me to see. It was a Colt Cloverleaf, four shot, .41 caliber derringer. "My derringer was empty. I foolishly neglected to reload after the earlier shooting."

Victoria raised her right hand from the folds in her dress. She held a Baby Patterson pistol in her hand. "I might have had to use this and I hate to shoot a man on such a lovely evening."

I looked from the gun to her face and saw those eyes again. She sure made me nervous. I stammered through another explanation. "Like you said.... there's been enough killin' here.... tonight. I figured Mack was looking for a reason not to draw so I gave him one."

Slick was impressed. "You surely did. That pistol came from nowhere mighty quick-like."

I downplayed my draw. "Jus' natural reaction is all."

We sat down at an empty table and continued to share polite conversation over our drinks. Slick lit another cigar and relaxed by blowing smoke rings in the air.

The two of them were fishing but I wasn't biting. Slick was just like I'd remembered him. He was laughing and joking while Victoria said little but continued to devour me with her eyes. We discussed their railroad problems, cattle prices, the weather, and current hostilities with the Injuns. I told 'em of my run-in with the renegade Utes and my injured right arm. Slick commented it was lucky I was left-handed but he said it with a question in his voice.

I could feel their intense interest in me and my background but they were hesitant to pry too much as was the western custom. Whatever a man offered by way of personal history was generally accepted as many came west to escape at least part of their past. We parted on a friendly note.

"I best be going. I plan to get back to drifting tomorrow."

Slick was still grasping for something he couldn't quite get a handle on, "Why not stay around awhile. We can use a good man around here.... ain't that right?"

He looked to Victoria for agreement and she did not let him down.

She started looking me over with those eyes again. "I can always use a good man."

I'll be damned if that didn't make me blush like a ripe tomato and my tongue refused to work properly. "Let me...ah... sleep on it."

I hurried out into the fresh night air to clear my thoughts and it didn't take long to decide I should stay as far as possible from Miss Victoria. Pa always said a man has to learn what he can handle in this world and stay away from what he cain't. Whiskey and women like Victoria were two things I was never gonna be able to handle.

I had no personal experience with famous madams but Victoria Bellemont Farley was no "Slanting-Annie", the madam with one short leg, or "Madam Bulldog", the tough old broad who favored a mutt. Victoria was a beautiful first-rate seductress and well she knew it.

Back at the hotel, I paused before I entered my room. I thought I heard some movement next door but couldn't be sure. Despite my usual caution, I hit the bed and slept like a rock.

It was almost full daylight before I awoke. Usually I was up and gone by dawn but I had had a late night and more than my usual share of beer.

I stayed still and listened for a while. The sounds from the street were normal and common enough. Folks and animals were out and moving about. I could hear casual conversations and other normal sounds of the town coming to life. It seemed a good time to take stock of where I was and what I was doing. I thought back to the events of the past evening and had to laugh at myself. What the hell was I thinking? That was none of my affair and I certainly didn't owe Slick anything from that day in Grasshopper Flats.

Come to think of it, seeing Slick was exactly like returning to the Flats. All my fears and doubts about that day came rushing back at me. There was a bright side, however. If he didn't recognize me, then few would. That was some comfort and made the trip back, if I continued, seem easier. Right now, however, I had other things to think about. I was in Animas City and had to deal with that woman.

Victoria surely worried my mind. She was too old for me to be interested in and too young for me to ignore. No matter how you spelled it, she was trouble. I figured to turn down her offer and get out of Animas City as quick as I could. Damn that woman for her power to affect me.

Next thing I had to consider was that young girl next door. I wished to know who she was and why she was here. It felt, some-how, like we had some kind of connection. Maybe it was because we were the only folks staying in this hotel, but it did seem strange for a young girl to be all alone in a town like this. What could she be thinking?

I cleaned up and shaved as best I could. My right arm was still stiff but getting less so all the time. I changed clothes, combed my hair and hitched up my cross draw rig. I left my room and hurried down the stairs as coyote hunger was once again upon me. I did not fail to notice that the door of room number four was slightly ajar. Maybe she was curious too.

Doby was erect but only semiconscious as I passed the counter. I mumbled a greeting and he replied in a deadpan manner. "Think you have a twin, Mister Monroe?"

The mention of "twin" made me think of my brothers, John and Thomas. I considered what he said and turned back to ask him. "What do you mean, a twin?"

Doby grinned like a cat with a canary in his mouth. "There was a grim old man here this morning on the lookout for a gunfighter that shaped up to be you. Only thing was, that feller he's hunting was right handed, wore a gun belt with silver stars and carried a fancy Colt Peacemaker. The old man said the feller he was looking for was the gunfighter, Henry James."

Doby was trying to read my face and I was trying to remain calm. Then he went on.

"Some folks say we all have a twin somewhere. Maybe that "James" feller is your'n."

Then it hit him. "Hey, I wonder if he's kin to the James boys from Missouri? Being a gunfighter, I'll bet he is."

I leaned closer to Doby.... "What'dja' tell him?"

Doby looked surprised and hurt. "Nothing, jus' nothing at all. None of my affair." He gave me a look that suggested we shared a secret.

I judged him to be truthful and fished in my pocket for a silver dollar and put it on the counter. "What did this old man look like?"

Doby grinned at the dollar like a kid in a candy store. "Like the Angel of Death riding a black steed on Judgment Day. He was big, Mister Monroe, bigger than you. Hard gray eyes that looked right through a feller. Dressed all in black and riding a big black gelding with a white blaze. Carried one of those big old Walker Colts. If that old gun had a set of wheels it could pass for a cannon. Oh, and he was toting the good book like he wrote it."

He paused and looked around real nervous-like. "No hello or how are ya.... all business. That old man just looked at the guest book and then asked about you. Said you could be the man he was chasing if you weren't left-handed. I told him you were and he walked out without another word. Come and gone in couple of minutes."

I headed out the front door with something new to consider. Who the hell could that old man be? I thought "Henry James" had been put to rest three years ago. But no matter, the old man in black was gone and I was still starvin'.

The bright sunshine and blue skies promised another beautiful day ahead. There were scattered clouds to the west over the La Plata mountains and a little breeze to push 'em along. There were more folks around but the town still had a sorry look about it. Only three businesses looked open. "The Farley House" of course, the Assay Office and thankfully, the Rocky Mountain Café. It had looked to be shut down last night but was open this morning.

As I passed "The Farley House", Bud came out to toss a bucket of swampin' water. We exchanged greetings like total strangers. Guess he couldn't place me from last night, or didn't wish to.

The assay office was doing a brisk business with several miners coming and going. I flashed back on my mining days and wondered about the prospecting hereabouts. I could guess the answer by the condition and the mood of the miners. They were just scraping by and none of 'em were celebrating. Gold chasers were a sorry lot and looked the same ever'where.

The café was open, but just barely. There were two cowhands at one table and a scruffy looking old coot at the counter. I held the door for a group of miners who walked out as I walked in. A young boy who looked to be about twelve came from the kitchen with plates of food for the men at the table. The old coot was nursing an empty coffee cup as I straddled a stool at the counter and waited to order. Like most small cafes, it had the smell of home coming from the kitchen.

The old coot, unwashed and unkempt, kept staring frog-eyed at the dregs in his coffee cup. He looked to be about a hundred years old but was probably less. He was decked out in an old Confederate cap, red long johns and blue bib coveralls. I was amused by his strawberry nose and coffee colored teeth when I suddenly noticed he was missing his left arm. Somehow it didn't look unnatural.

The young waiter finished serving the cowboys and scurried back behind the counter. "Your food's a'coming mister.... scrambled eggs, side meat, biscuits and gravy. Ma's cooking as fast as she can."

Without asking, he filled a fresh coffee cup and brought it to me. I noted the old man watching with interest. "Fill that cup for my friend here, would ya?"

The boy looked from him to me and back again before filling the cup. He wanted to say something but held his peace. The old man eagerly sipped at the coffee but it was too hot to drink. He smiled with half a mouthful of rotten teeth and held out a gnarly right hand.

"Reb Hopkins, Corporal, Confederate States of America, retired.... At your service."

Reluctantly I shook his hand and wondered where a fella could wash up before breakfast. "Jim Monroe, glad to know ya."

Without reason or rhyme he just started yarning. "Lost my arm the same day and in the same hospital tent as old Stonewall Jackson. I figger they buried my arm right along with his. Yessir, they had one big grave for the lopped-off parts. I was still there in that hospital eight days later when he died. Let's see, it was back in '63, if I remember...."

The young waiter had heard it a thousand times and just had to interrupt. "We've all heard about the war, Reb, let the fella be." He looked at me and sighed. "Sorry mister, he gets to ramblin' sometimes."

"That's all right, I don't mind a little company with my eggs."

The boy suddenly remembered. "Your eggs, yes sir, comin' right up." and he hurried back to the kitchen.

I was thinking of my old friend, Major Wilkes. "Tell me Reb, do you remember an officer name of Wilkes? I believe he was part of the general's staff."

Reb tried to recall and I could see it wasn't easy for him. "Let's see now.... Wilkes, ya say?" He seemed lost in thought and for a while, I wasn't sure if he was still conscious or not. "Yessir, Major Wilkes, big fella, from Tennessee, I believe. Remember him well. Is he a friend of your'n?"

I had to smile a little. "Yup, he was a good friend when I really needed one. We rode a cattle trail together."

We both took to our coffee and then my breakfast was served. The boy was out of breath from running back and forth. "What's your name, boy?"

"Bobby Maxwell, sir. My ma does the cooking and I help out."

"Well you do a fine job of it and the food looks great. Thanks, Bobby."

Bobby continued. "My ma's a widow woman. Pa died of the fever last winter. But we get by, Ma and me."

"Good for you. You've a right to be proud. A boy has to become a man when his pa dies." It felt like Bobby was casting around for a new pa but I only wished to eat so I started wolfin' down my breakfast. I was way beyond hungry by that time.

I noticed Reb staring at my plate now and again so I ordered a side of biscuits and gravy and slid it over to him. This breakfast was liable to cost me half a dollar if I didn't stop ordering for two.

The cowhands finished before I did and got up to leave. They took notice of me for the first time as they were walking out. The taller of the two stopped behind me. "Last night ain't over Mister. If I was you, I'd lite out before old man MacDonald comes back here. He's got more than twenty riders and he's apt to tree this sorry town".

I answered without turning around. "Sounds like good advice."

They left without further comment and then I turned toward Reb. "Suppose he means Angus MacDonald?"

Reb was suddenly in a hurry to finish his biscuits and gravy. "Yup, that was his son Colin that got hisself kilt last night. Heard his boy Sean took one in the arm too. Angus figures to wake up madder than a bobcat in a 'tater sack this morning. I hear he's from one of them feudin' clans back in Scotland. That reminds me, I gotta go."

Reb got up and left without finishing his coffee and was moving pretty spry for such an old codger. Bobby bussed the table and made himself busy in the kitchen. I finished up my eggs and savored the coffee. It was real coffee and much better than I was used to. When times were tough, most trail coffee just tasted like water that had been scalded to death.

Now I had something else to consider. What about Angus MacDonald and his riders? Would they try to tree the town? Would that young one, Mack, come looking for me? I started to wonder what else could happen when the café door opened and my worst nightmare came to life. Right there in front of me stood "Sissy" Kaufman.

She was quite a sight. Fifteen going on twenty with long blond hair, pale green eyes and a figure built for comfort. She wore a grey riding skirt, a red blouse, white scarf and fancy white high-heeled boots. I couldn't believe she was here in Animas City.

Right then, I remembered that big gray I'd seen in the livery. That was her horse, Casey, and I should'a knowed it. His name, Casey, was short for Kaufman Colt. He was the first bred and born on their ranch. He was more of a pet than a working horse but a striking animal just the same. "Sissy" figured to be the nice young girl in room number four.

Banjo Billy and I signed on to work for her father, Karl, during their gather last summer. The Circle K was a small ranch and just starting to show a profit. They needed an extra hand or two at the same time Billy and I needed jobs so we were a perfect fit.

Being that I was easily the youngest hand on the ranch, Sissy and me naturally hit it off. Her given name was Sarah but she was always ever'body's little sister so she became "Sissy". Even I thought of her as my little sister. Well, most of the time that is.

We rode out together and talked some. Her ma had died some years before and she was stuck doing for her pa and older brother, "Hoss". His real name was Horst but as a child, Sissy could only say "horse". Soon enough "horse" became "Hoss" and it stuck. He was foreman of the ranch and real protective of his baby sister.

Old Karl just liked having a woman around to cook, clean and fetch. Sissy was primed to run off and figured at fifteen she was already woman enough to pull it off. She had told me as much several times.

Being that I was the new hand, I got stuck staying at the line shack when winter set in.

Sissy would bring me supplies once or twice a week, weather permitting, and her mama had taught her how to bake doughnuts, or as we called 'em, "bear sign." They were mighty tasty and I was always glad to see her riding my way.

The last time Sissy visited me at the line shack, we had more time to talk and get to know each other a little better. That was good and bad. With her mama gone, she knew little of a woman's ways with men so she set out to practice on me. It was a good thing that Banjo Billy came along just in the nick of time or.... well.... her father and brother might have skinned me alive and roasted me over the barbeque pit. A man, specially a young man, can only stand so much temptation. Sissy was the main reason I volunteered to drift this spring.

Seeing her again made me feel good and bad all at the same time. What the hell was she doing here?

Sissy paraded around the café a bit and then straddled the stool next to mine. She tossed her hair back and placed her hand on my shoulder. "I just knew I would find you here, Henry. Banjo Billy let it slip you were drifting toward Animas City."

I flushed to my ears and felt like a fool. "How did you git here?"

She continued teasing. "I can go wherever I want. I rode over to Silverton and took the new railroad coach down here to Durango. They even made room for Casey in the stock car."

She started fussin' the hair around my ears with her fingers. She was also battin' those innocent green eyes like an owl in a hailstorm. "I've been waiting for you to get here so we could be together."

Bobby came out of the kitchen to see if Sissy wanted anything but got embarrassed by her words and turned back.

"Together? How was I to know you were even here?"

She pretended to be a little girl hurt. "Don't pretend we didn't speak of it. You said you wished to run off with me.... just like we planned."

I brushed her hand off my hair and stood up with a jolt. "We didn't plan any such thing and well you know it. If you're running away from home you'll do it by yourself." I turned and started to walk to the door.

"What happened to your fancy gun, Henry? Or is your name really Jim...? Funny, but I always thought you were right handed."

She had me there. What could I say? I was using a left-handed gun setup and a different first name. Doby must have let her see that damn hotel register. Answering all of her questions called for a lot more explaining than I was up to. My only thoughts were to get shed of her and this town as fast as I could. I walked out of the café and headed straight for the hotel.

Sissy called out for me and started to follow but stopped when she got to the door and went back inside. It wasn't like her to give up so I was puzzled until I looked across the street. She had seen what I was facing. A rider had just hitched his horse in front of The Farley House and was going through the swinging doors.

Even from behind, that big and that ugly could only be one person, her brother "Hoss". He stood six foot five inches tall with stoop shoulders and weighed well over three hundred pounds. Under his droopy hat, he had a long and narrow unshaven face, which made him truly favor his nickname. His disposition was more like that of a big old draft horse rather than a thoroughbred. He was a born foreman but worked as hard as any of the hands. Everyone accepted him as a proven man without the need to impress. He was normally easy going and slow to rile as long as a man did his work and stayed shy of trouble. His baby sister was trouble.

"Hoss" was surely tracking her down and would have no business with me unless he figured I was part of her runnin'. There would be no reason for him to think that unless Sissy....I didn't want to think what she might have said about me. I hustled toward the hotel as fast as I could.

I rushed past the front desk without a word to the startled Doby and sped up the stairs two at a time. I fetched my gear as best I could and opened the door to leave.

Then from downstairs, I caught a wisp of cigar smoke and heard Slick's voice. "Good morning Doby, is Jim Monroe in his room?"

Doby replied. "Yes sir, just came back from breakfast and seemed in an almighty hurry. He's right at the top of the stairs, room number two."

I had no time for Slick so I quietly closed the door and headed down the back stairs. Cautiously I walked behind the old buildings and over to the livery. Upon hearing voices, I paused outside the rear entrance to listen. It was Hoss, asking about the big gray horse, Casey. The stable hand told him about Sissy coming to town yesterday. He said she had come to town alone and was staying at the "Colorado Inn". I was relieved to hear him say that. Hoss thanked him and headed off in the direction of the hotel.

Things were really getting out of hand. I really wished to get out of that town. I snuck through the back door of the livery and into Goner's stall. He nickered at me and stomped around a bit but seemed happy to see me. I stroked him and talked quietly to him to keep him calm while I saddled up. I noticed that the silver trimming on my saddle was badly in need of polishing. I vowed to restore the saddle to its original condition as soon as I could.

Suddenly I heard Victoria's voice from out front questioning the stable hand. "Have you, by chance, seen Mister Monroe this morning?"

The stable hand was flustered as I had been and found it hard to speak. "Well.... ah.... sorry Miss....Victoria, but I don't know any Mister.... Monroe, is it? All's I know is someone stabled that buckskin mustang back there last night while I was having supper. Fine looking horse."

Sweet as pecan pie, Victoria gave him instructions. "Well, if you see Mister Monroe, be sure to tell him we would like to see him over at The Farley House." She turned and walked away leaving the poor stable hand speechless.

Victoria, of all people, why the hell was she hunting me? What else could happen? I felt like I was chin-deep in quick sand. As it stood now, I had to fret over Sissy, her brother Hoss, my old friend Slick and Victoria. Not to mention Angus McDonald and his riders and that crazy old man dressed in black. Ya know, for a dying town, Animas City sure was getting crowded.

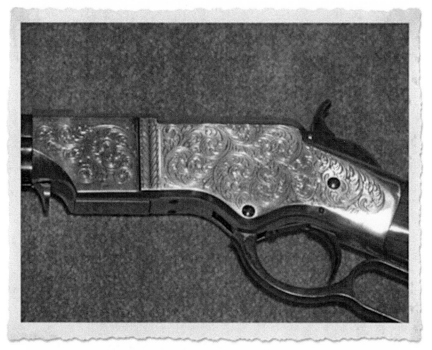

"The Henry rifle had a floral pattern engraved on both sides of the receiver."

Courtesy of Sedona Historical Society
Sedona Heritage Museum, Sedona, AZ

Bear hunter and friends circa 1880

Courtesy of Sedona Historical Society/Sedona Heritage Museum, Sedona, AZ

Jim Thompson's cabin in Oak Creek Canyon circa 1880

Chapter IV

"Hot time in the old town"

Now more than ever, I had the strong urge to saddle-up and leave Animas City far behind. I tightened the cinch and tied on my bedroll. Goner was eager, as always, to be off and running. As I positioned my saddlebags, I heard the sound of boots on gravel like someone was coming to the back entrance of the livery. From the cigar smell, I figured Slick must have followed me around the back way from the hotel. He came in the livery and ambled over to Goners' stall.

"Where ya headed in such an almighty hurry? I thought you were gonna stop by 'fore you left."

I tried to act like everything was normal. "Planned on it. I'll be along in a minute or two. I have to settle up with the hostler."

Slick wasn't sure he believed me. He thought about it as he blew another smoke ring. "I'll wait outside and we can walk over together. Sure is a nice day."

I continued fussin' over the saddlebags. "That it is."

Slick started for the front entrance and then turned back. Something was nibblin' on his memory and he could feel the tugs. "I'm sure I know you from somewhere and I'm pretty sure you know where. What are you hiding?"

I tried to act surprised. "Me? I ain't hiding nothing, nothing at all."

Slick didn't look convinced but he shrugged it off and went out the front entrance of the livery into the morning sunlight.

The hostler was a short, thin, fidgety sort of feller with a bald-head and spectacles that slid down his nose. I could see him perched in his office so I walked in to settle up. Slick was waiting by the hitching rail out front so when I'd paid my bill, I walked out to join him.

Just then, Sissy burst out of the café door and made a beeline for the livery. She was bouncin' straight toward Slick and he surely took notice. He was more than twice her age but at that moment, her age was the farthest thing from his mind.

Suddenly, Hoss charged out of the Colorado Inn and spied Sissy heading across the street. He yelled. "Sarah.... Stop." That was the first time I'd ever heard him call her Sarah.

Sissy, of course, did no such thing. She turned at the sound of his voice and then started to run faster until she ran head on into Slick. He staggered and dropped his cigar as he grabbed the hitching rail to keep from falling. In a panic, Sissy clung onto him to stay on her feet.

Hoss was closing in and shaking his fist. "Stay right there, you're coming with me."

Sissy grabbed Slick's arm and pleaded. "Don't let him take me, Mister, he'll kill me sure."

Slick reassured her. "Take it easy, Miss, no one's gonna kill you."

Doors were opening and closing as the town came out to see what all the ruckus was about. The hostler rushed out of his office and even the stable hand came down from the loft with his pitchfork still in his hand.

Sissy tried to slide around behind Slick but Hoss reached out and caught her by the wrist. She screamed and Slick tried to break his grip but Hoss responded with a wicked backhand that sent Slick sprawling in the dirt. As big as Hoss was, his backhand was kin to the swat from a full-grown griz-bear and Slick lay stunned and motionless. Sissy slipped his grip by duckin' under the hitching rail and wouldn't ya know she came running straight at me.

"Henry, please.... don't let him take me back."

In hot pursuit, Hoss paused at the sound of my name and suddenly recognized me. "Henry, what the hell?"

Sissy shrieked. "Henry and I are in love. We're fixin' to get hitched as soon as we can find a sky pilot." She stumbled and fell into my outstretched arms.

I helped her regain her balance and she clung to me for dear life. How I wished for a sock to stick in her mouth. Desperately, I tried to explain. "Wait, Hoss, that ain't no part of the truth. I didn't...."

Hoss roared like a wounded catamount. "You and little Sarah... are you crazy?"

He lunged out and grabbed Sissy by the wrist again and pulled her toward his side. While struggling to hold her steady, he took an off-balance swing at my head. I slipped his wild punch and backed off beyond his reach. Sissy was screaming and kicking his shins while he was yelling at both of us. Then, I said something I was certain to regret.

"Let her go, Hoss."

I can't imagine what I was thinking as I unbuckled my gun belt and stood straight up before him. All I could think of was the biblical story of David and Goliath and I felt the urgent need of a slingshot.

Hoss looked to the crowd and found encouragement aplenty. Western folks were always starved for entertainment and this fight figured to be the highlight of their day. Slick was still on the ground and slowly coming out of the fog. I heard bets going down. "Five to one on the big fella."

Hoss released his grip on Sissy, dropped his own gun belt, waved to the crowd and lunged at me all in the same motion. He was a lot faster than I figured but thankfully, I was ready and slipped out of his grasp.

All that sparing with Chip and Josh was about to pay off again. I ducked, feinted, sidestepped and back peddled as Hoss tried desperately to catch me. I popped him on the beak with a straight left jab ever so often just to keep him off balance. My right arm felt pretty good so I tried a right cross which caught him in the teeth and gave him a taste of his own blood. Wouldn't ya know he seemed to like it? The crowd was really getting into it as more folks came over to watch and cheer.

Hoss was basically a brawler and showed no fighting skills at all. His mammoth size and strength had won him many fights without much effort on his part. As I danced around, he swung wildly and tried to bull-rush me. While catching his breath, he accused me of being a dancer and not a fighter so I responded with a short version of an Irish jig that Chip had shown us. The crowd roared its approval and Hoss fumed.

As his anger and frustration grew, I got overconfident and tried to get fancy with him. My one-two combination that should'a worked perfect.... didn't. I could'a got the same results by punching out a side of beef. Hoss took my best shots without flinchin' and then just wrapped his huge arms around me and tossed me into the air. I blasted through the hitching rail and hit the ground like a sack of manure. He tried to "pancake" me but I was able to roll out of his way just in time.

I went back to duckin', weavin' and jabbin' as that seemed the safest course. I wasn't really hurting Hoss any, but he was getting winded. He was able to grab my left wrist and pull me in but I came headfirst and gave him a "Liverpool kiss" with a head butt under his chin. Little Chip would'a been right proud of that move.

What with all the yelling and encouragement from the crowd, neither of us figured to ease up or back off. My right arm still felt strong but both of my hands were hurtin'. When Hoss came at me down low, I saw the opening I'd been waiting for. I hit him with a left upper cut just above his breakfast and a solid right hook to his left ear.

Hoss gasped for breath and went to one knee. It was probably out of exhaustion rather than being hurt but it made me feel good. His right eye was closing up due to my left jab and he had blood on his shirt from his busted lips. Even his left ear was puffy and red while all I had to show from this scrap was some dust on my back-side. Maybe he wasn't so tough after all.

The crowd urged me on so naturally I moved in closer and got stupid again. I was so glad to have my right arm in working order I wanted to give Hoss another taste of it. I figured to jab first with my left hand to set up my right hook but quicker that a wink; Hoss threw a wild right from his knees and caught me on the end of my chin.

I spun all the way around and bounced about six feet before I skidded to a stop in the dirt. My hat flew even farther. Stars and moons were whirling in my head and I couldn't make sense of any-thing. When I could finally focus, there was Hoss, standing over me and grinning like a jackass on locoweed. He muttered something I didn't get and then wood splinters were ever'where and Hoss went down hard. He raised a major dust cloud as he impacted the dirt beside me.

I found out later that Hoss had said he was gonna stomp me flat before Slick rose up from the street and parted his hair with a piece of the broken hitching rail. No matter how it happened, I was thankful.

There was a lot of cheering and arguing over bets but all I re-ally remember was Slick and me heading arm in arm for the Farley House. I saw Sissy fussing over Hoss and the hostler dowsing him in a pail of trough water and I recall hoping he wasn't hurt too bad. At the end of the day, he was just a big brother trying to protect his little sister and fetch her back home.

Slick and I staggered into the saloon and sought out a table. The place was damn near empty so we had our choice of tables and sat near the bar. Bud brought us a couple of beers as Victoria directed two of her girls to tend to our injuries. A young Mexican girl with large brown eyes and long black hair tried her best to help me while a tall, buxom blond girl fussed over Slick. He only had a bloody nose and a swole-up eye but she gave him lots of attention. Maybe a little too much attention if I read Victoria right.

I suffered mostly from an unhinged jaw and scuffed knuckles. My head was still buzzing like a bee in a bonnet and I was unsure of just what all had happened. "Conchita", as I heard her called, bathed my hands with hot salt water and cleaned up the dried blood around my mouth and chin. I do remember her tender touch and thinking she smelt better than any girl I'd ever been close to. I reckon Miss Victoria was a shrewd judge of women as well as men.

I tried drinking my beer but my poor jaw wasn't working too well and I spilt more than I drank. Slick was recovering quicker than I was but the tall blonde, I think he called her "Goldie", was still fussin' over him. He was trying to tell me what a tussle we'd been in but was clearly distracted. "Goldie" was wearing little in the way of clothes and there was a lot of her to cover. Slick noticed Victoria watching them and impatiently brushed Goldie away but she didn't brush-off easy. More folks were coming in from the street and they were all going on about the big fight.

Next thing you know, them damn batwing doors slammed open like they'd been hit by a runaway locomotive and the bar got church-sermon quiet. I turned toward the doors and wouldn't you know it? Hoss was filling the whole doorway all by hisself.

He was packing his shoot-in' iron again and held my gun belt in his left hand. He'd lost his hat somewhere and I could see matted blood on the right side of his head. His right eye was almost closed shut and his lips were split and bloody. There was drying blood all over his shirt and pants. Like a statue, Hoss just stood there without saying a word. Guess he was trying to make up his mind about something.

Cautiously, Sissy squeezed by him and tippy-toed into the saloon. She held his crumpled hat in her hand. Hoss looked at her and then back to me. Then he walked over and tossed my gun belt on the table. That old Dragoon was a chunk of metal and it made a loud "thud" in the deathly quiet saloon.

"Figure you'll be needin' this."

I tried to object but had trouble getting my jaw working. "Hoss let me.... 'splain. We've no need to...."

He cut me off. "Sarah just told me...."

Sissy interrupted. "I told him the truth, Henry, really I did. I don't want anyone to get hurt. I just wanted to get away from Pa and the ranch. I'm so sorry." She sounded like a scairt and repentant school girl.

Hoss looked at her and then turned back to me once again. "She said you had nothin' to do with her runnin'. Is that so?"

I nodded in lieu of a babblin' answer. My jaw was killing me.

"Guess we've got nothing to fight about, then. No hard feelings, Henry?" Hoss gently felt his wounded scalp and looked at Slick, "Or you either, mister?"

We both shook our heads to his satisfaction. Ever'body relaxed a bit and the tension leaked from the room. I noticed Victoria slowly withdrew her right hand from the folds of her dress but kept a wary eye on Hoss.

Sissy walked over to her older brother and gave him his hat. It looked much the worse for wear. Not that it was any great shakes to begin with. He accepted the hat and put it on his head with a wince of pain as it rested on his scalp wound. He faced me and smiled as best he could through his battered lips and shut-up eye.

"Ya fought one helluva fight Henry and you're a lot tougher than I supposed, but don't come back to the Circle K unless you wish to take up where we left off. Sissy will always be my baby sister."

Sissy snapped at him. "Call me Sarah."

All I could do was stare at the floor and keep quiet.

Hoss took a deep breath and continued. "Reckon we'll be heading back home now. Come on.... Sarah."

He turned and walked out the front doors but naturally enough Sissy remained. She walked over and tenderly touched her hand to my cheek. Then she leaned closer and whispered. "You were wonderful, Henry, the way you defended my honor. Now I'm sure you love me. I'll go back home with Hoss but I won't stay. I'll be seeing you real soon." Just like that, the sad little girl had turned into a connivin' Jezebel. It was scary to watch her change and I was speechless.

From out in the street Hoss hollered her name. "Sarah."

Sissy started to answer him then she remembered something and reached into her jeans pocket. She handed me a folded and tattered looking letter. "Someone got your name backward, Henry. It was addressed to Monroe Henry, c/o Gold Hill Café, Virginia City, Nevada Territory. Somehow it got forwarded to our ranch."

From the postmarks, first dated in March 1881, I could tell the letter had been forwarded a couple of times. I had been a hard man to track down. The letter had been handled a lot but was still unopened. I looked at the return address and as luck would have it, the sender's last name was smeared by a water spot.

Sissy went on to explain. "It came before you left but I never got around to giving it to you. I thought it was from an old girlfriend.... that "Taylor" person.... looks like a girl's handwriting to me." She made no attempt to conceal her jealousy or her anger.

Then, quick as a wink, she batted those green eyes at me again and lightly kissed my cheek. As she backed away, she gave me a look that would melt a block of ice in a blizzard. Finally, she tossed back her hair, turned with a whirl and sashayed through the doors. "Comin', Hoss."

Pa always said it was a pure pleasure to raise a little girl until the day she woke up a woman and turned into a passel of folks you'd never known before. Now I think I understood what he meant.

Well, the show was over and folks drifted out of the saloon to return to their own business on this fine morning. With the exception of two rusty cowhands standing at the bar and the girls, we were left pretty much to ourselves. Slick and I were doing better and Victoria coldly dismissed the girls. "Marigold, Conchita, that will be quite enough.

Marigold, or Goldie, hesitated a bit and drew another hard look from Victoria. Slick slapped her bottom as she left and got that same hard look. I considered opening my letter but decided to stuff it in my shirt pocket.

"Aren't you going read your letter?" Victoria was trying to seem casually disinterested.

"Cain't focus enough to read anything right now. It was mailed a year ago so I reckon she'll keep."

They looked at each other and then back to me but Victoria couldn't conceal her curiosity. "So.... Taylor is an old girlfriend?"

"Nah, she's my baby sister." I began to fidget.

I gave my beer another try and fussed with my jaw to slow down the direction of the conversation. Then I got a bright idea and turned toward Slick while extending my right hand. "I figure you saved my bacon out there and I'm beholdin'."

Slick was caught off guard and wasn't sure what to say. "Sure thing. Glad to help. You did the same and more for me last night. Anyway, that big ox blind-sided me and I wanted to return the favor."

"You were doing so well for a while." Victoria leaned forward and went fishing for information once again. "I do believe that you've had some formal training as a boxer. Am I correct?"

I just shrugged a bit and fidgeted some more. I wasn't sure just how much I should say but she kept prying.

"What happened, did you get careless?"

"Yeah, figured I had him whupped." I had to laugh at myself.

The conversation continued friendly and general in nature as we passed an hour or so. Slick went back to blowing smoke rings from his cigar and Victoria kept going on about nothing in particular. Around noon, Bud brought over soup and cold beef sandwiches for us. After eating we got down to the matters at hand.

Victoria served coffee and then sat down. All of a sudden like, she was all business. "Slick and I may have a proposition for you, Mister Monroe. Is it James or Henry?"

"James or Jim.... Henry is my middle name and I use it sometimes."

"I see." That seemed to satisfy Victoria but I could almost hear Slick thinking, James Henry Monroe? He was still unable to put it together but he was getting closer. If he thought of Grasshopper Flats, he'd remember quick enough.

"Might you be interested, Jim?" She persisted, like a nanny goat after a rosebud.

I couldn't imagine what she had in mind but figured I'd play along. "Well, I guess, but I'm just a driftin' cowboy. What possible use could I be? I don't know a thing about the gamblin' and drinkin' business. I'm not much good at either. 'Specially the drinkin'."

Victoria ran out of patience and put her hand up to stop my babblin'. "No Jim, we have another job in mind for you. I'd better explain."

She leaned closer so only Slick and I could hear. "As you know, Animas City is shutting down but I have an offer for 'The Farley House' and I fully intend to sell and get out as soon as I can. While I was checking through some old paperwork to find the deed on this property, I found some things that require further.... initiative on my part. I..." she looked at Slick and sighed. "...We have talked this over and think you can help us."

She sat back to gauge my interest. As usual, I didn't know what to say or do. She had told me nothing of what she wanted, but any kind of paperwork was way beyond me. I could barely read and write. "Sounds like you need a lawyer or maybe a detective fella like one of those Pinkertons."

Victoria shook her head. "No, I'll have nothing at all to do with the Pinkerton agency. I'm sure you will be quite capable of handling everything." Her face flushed as she fought to control herself. She was looking right through me again and I started to sweat. "Will you hear me out?"

I nodded and grabbed for my coffee since my mouth was suddenly as dry as a bleached bone in the desert.

Victoria started to speak but thought better of it. Then she looked at Slick and placed her hand on his arm. "This next part will have to be between Mister Monroe and myself. Why don't you give us a few minutes? Go upstairs and change those dirty clothes."

Slick didn't like it but knew from experience Miss Victoria was bound to get her way and resistance was futile. He smiled and nodded and then excused hisself. Victoria's eyes followed him as he walked away from the table and climbed up the stairs. I also noticed that Goldie was watching for him from the second floor balcony. Any fool could smell trouble brewin' in that coffee pot.

"Slick is a fine boy.... man.... but this must be kept between us. You do understand?"

I nodded like I did but I didn't. Miss Victoria had made me very uncomfortable once again. Reckon I'd rather scrap with Hoss than set and talk with her.

"I want you to pretend to be my son."

Talk about a wild right hook to the jaw. I put down my coffee cup lest I drop it. "Your.... what?"

"Maybe I should start at the beginning... " She continued teasing and tempting me while trying to judge my reaction.

"It all started with my late husband, Charles Upton Farley." She looked fondly at his painting. "Take a good look, Jim. You do favor Charlie. Same coloring, same deep blue eyes and that Farley cleft in your chin. That's why I'm telling you all this."

For the first time, I really studied the painting. She was right; I did share most of his features. It made me wonder what kind of man could tame a woman like Victoria. Then I began noticing his clothes and the furnishings around him in the painting. Leaning up against the desk behind him was a Henry rifle. It looked a lot like mine.

"The man who painted that was a fine painter but a lousy poker player. We let him do the portrait in payment for his gambling debts. Charlie sat for that painting just a week before he left Chicago. He never saw it finished. It's a good likeness but I think his eyes were a sight bluer. More like yours."

She was fluttering her eyes at me and I was sweatin' again. Why did her attention bother me so? Her stare gave a man no place to hide.

"He was quite a man, my Charlie. He was born the bastard son of a wealthy southern family, the 'Uptons' of Charleston, South Carolina. It was said they could trace their lineage all the way back to the Jamestown settlement in the sixteen hundreds.

"His mother was surely a blue blood but his father was nothing more than a drifting Creole gambler. Her family disowned her when she took up with him. She died during childbirth so Charlie was raised by his father. He grew up on the road and spent time in gambling parlors, whorehouses, and honky-tonks. For two years he even lived aboard a paddle wheeler that steamed up and down the Mississippi River. He learned all there was to know about gambling; the legal and the not so legal. He knew all the tricks and on top of it all, he was lucky.

"I met Charlie at a cotillion in Mobile during the spring of 1859." She smiled, remembering, and flushed a bright pink. "He swept me off my feet. I was just seventeen and he was almost thirty, but age didn't matter to us. We fell madly in love.

"It did, however, matter to my father. We were middling folks and Daddy hoped I'd marry up. He considered Charlie too old for me and too poor for him. Besides which, Charlie was way too handy with cards for his own good. After my father lost a large sum of money to him in a poker game, he forbade me to see Charlie again. So naturally, Charlie and I ran off."

Miss Victoria seemed to be reliving her past as she was speaking and her whole nature seemed to change. I think she was enjoying the memory and paused to sip her coffee. Her face softened, her voice went some higher and her eyes widened. Then in a flash, the old fire came back.

"My father bid us good riddance and we ran off to New Orleans. We had a wonderful time until the war started in April of '61. Then everything changed.

"Out of the blue, Charlie received a letter from the esteemed Upton family. Seems that one of his uncles died in the yellow fever epidemic that swept Charleston in 1858 and his other uncle was killed in the early days of the fighting at Bull Run. Suddenly his grandmother, the Widow Upton, had no heir who could pass on her bloodline or inherit her estate.

"Charlie wanted nothing to do with Abigail Upton but she persisted. She hired those damn Pinkertons to track us down and somehow, they found out I was expecting a child. Abigail contracted with them to bring us to Charleston where I would be forced to deliver our baby to her. Instead, we left with what little we had and lit out. We snuck through the Union lines near Vicksburg and made our way north to Chicago."

She paused again while she refilled our coffee cups from the sterling silver coffee urn. My eyes wandered to the painting again as she continued. I was trying to imagine the man.

"At first, we had no money, no friends, and no place to stay. Charlie hit the streets running three card Monte and dice games. He made enough to keep us clothed and fed until our son was born. Finally, he got the break we were hoping for."

I tried to keep a stone face while I listened and watched her reminiscing.

"Charlie conned his way into the biggest card game in the history of Chicago. It was held at the Stock Yard Inn and that game was attended by some of the wealthiest men in the country. Millionaire businessmen, pompous politicians, slimy lawyers, grouchy old judges, and more than a few professional gamblers were there. The game lasted two and half days and, wouldn't you know, Charlie came out the big winner. Besides a large amount of cash, he walked away from the game with IOU's, stocks and bonds, property deeds, mining claims, and even some expensive jewelry."

She was fingering a gold locket hanging from a gold chain round her neck. "Charlie won the deed to our gambling house in Chicago, two silver claims in Nevada, a gold mine in California and even this property here in Animas City."

By now, I was hanging on ever' word she said. I forgot about my sore jaw and ran my coffee cup right into it, spilling some coffee in the process. Victoria just smiled and continued.

"It was just our luck the Pinkerton main office was in Chicago, over on Fifth Avenue. Naturally they heard about Charlie winning that big game. When Superintendent Warner found out we had a month old son, he bribed a judge and got him to issue a bench warrant. The Pinkertons wanted custody of our baby. They claimed we were unfit parents since Charlie was a professional gambler and I was a whore!"

Victoria was full of rage and out of breath. I could tell she really wanted me to believe her story and take her side of it. "That's the way they said it. Right there on the court order. It's true I was managing the girls in our house but I was never a whore. Never." Some parts of her story were fuzzy but that last part was perfectly clear.

Now she was dang near yellin' at me. "They intended to take our son away and give him to his great grandmother, Abigail Upton. Even in the middle of the Civil War, her money and power could move mountains. That old bitch tried to steal my son."

Victoria gradually regained control of herself. "She had us in a tight squeeze without anyone able to help. We really had little choice. Charlie left me to manage our Chicago businesses and he headed west with our son. He hoped to get established out here and then send for me. I was to sell all the Chicago properties and be ready to join him. At the time, the most important thing to both of us was to keep our son away from those awful Pinkertons."

She paused again and I could just about figure what was coming next. The tears were few but they were there.

"Charlie was with a large wagon train traveling the Santa Fe Trail. For some unknown reason, his wagon and a few others lit out of Santa Fe heading due west rather than staying on the trail that went to the northwest. They must'a had something in mind but I know Charlie didn't figure on running into Indians. Their small group of wagons was attacked and everyone was massacred.... butchered, actually. Men, women and even the little children, none were spared. They were so badly mutilated it was difficult to identify anyone and it took some time before the army could notify the next of kin."

Victoria seemed on the edge of breaking down but managed to choke it back. She was determined to finish her story.

"Some months later I received a package with Charlie's personal effects. There was no trace of our son but the army figured his remains went unidentified or the Indians took him away. They were

Navajo, I believe. Either way, my son has been dead to me all these years."

Victoria looked around at the nearly empty saloon. "You can see why this has to remain between us. My relationship with Slick can only stand so much honesty. A girl is entitled to some secrets, don't you agree?"

She dabbed at her eyes with a silk hankie and I tried to figure what was comin' next. I was about the right age and general description of her son but for what purpose?

She took a deep breath and tried to recover her composure. "I suppose you're wondering what this all has to do with you?"

I nodded and awaited her response. She was back in control of the conversation and I was apprehensive as hell. I looked around for a way out but couldn't seem to think of any.

"While looking up that deed, I found a leather bound briefcase that held some old financial papers from Chicago. After all these years, I'd forgotten all about them. Among other things, I found several hundred shares of Union Pacific Railroad stock. I think Charlie won them from the General Manager of the Union Pacific, Thomas C. Durant. That man always played fast and loose with the railroad's money.

"Anyway, the stocks are very valuable today and exactly what I need. I am so very sick of the wild, wild West. I intend to return to New Orleans and I prefer to return in style. The money from those stocks will allow me to do so."

Now she had me leaning forward in my chair. What could all this possibly have to do with me? I knew nothing of railroad stocks.

"This is where you come in, Mister Monroe. The stocks are made out in my name and my son's name. It takes both signatures for them to be cashed in. My attorney has assured me I could get my son declared legally dead but that would take time and money, which I don't have. However, if my son.... was to show up and sign the stocks over to me, I could leave this God-forsaken place and go back home."

Well, it all seemed simple enough. I was to pretend to be her son, sign some stock certificates over to her that are rightfully hers anyway and be done with it. There had to be a catch but what the hell was it? And what was in it for me?

Then the plot thickened. "You'll have to prove you are my son and that might cause a few problems. If you were to just turn up out of the blue, there would be some that would doubt your identity and that could mean another legal matter. However, I think I've thought of a better way to go about it. Can you play-act?"

What in the Sam Hill was I getting myself into? "I reckon. What would I have to do?"

"I want you to go to the Pinkerton Agency and ask them to find out who you are. Claim to be a white child raised by the Indians who wishes to find his family. They have hundreds of open files on lost children and I'm sure they'll have one on my son. Abigail Upton would have seen to that. I'll give you some personal things of ours to show them so they can do their detecting work and find out your identity. Their word will be sufficient in any court. It'll be fast, cheap and foolproof."

Things were getting clearer. "Where would I have to go?"

"The closest Pinkerton office is in Denver but I think we should avoid that one. Their Denver office is a first rate operation with six full time resident agents. Their senior agent, a Mr. Finch, is supposed to be one of their very best. He might be trouble. Our little plan can't stand too much examination."

She paused as if considering her options. "But, they have just hired a part time agent down in Arizona. It's in a little town they're calling Flagstaff. Do you know it?" I nodded that I did. "Besides, Flagstaff is much closer to the Navajo reservation where my son would have been taken. It would make better sense for him to show up there.

"You'll have to ride to Flagstaff and look up that part-time agent and convince him to contact the home office in Chicago. They'll have all the files. When they figure out who you are they'll be right proud of themselves. You come back here with the paper work and we'll be all set."

It sounded simple enough but I was still wary and I really wondered what my part of all this might be worth. Victoria seemed to read my mind. "Now, I suppose you'd like to know what you get out of all this?"

She reached into her skirt pocket, pulled out a legal looking document and placed it on the table in front of her. Reading upside-down, I could see it was a land grant deed for property somewhere in Arizona.

Then she tossed me a small leather pouch. "This is for traveling money and just enough extra to start the Pinkertons working for you. Spend it wisely." It held ten gold eagles, one hundred dollars.

Then she waved the paper at me. "When we cash in the stocks, I'll sign this deed over to you. I won't have any use of this land when I'm back home in Louisiana. I believe there's enough acreage here for a fair sized ranch. A drifting cowboy could become a real rancher with land like this. I believe you mentioned something about that."

She reckoned right. Wouldn't you know? She actually listened to our casual conversations earlier. I wondered what else I'd run on about?

I reached for the deed but she pulled it back. "Will you do it? Will you convince them you're my son? There's little time to waste."

I was thinking as fast as I could. Then something hit me. "What about that Abigail Upton. Won't she find out about me, too? What if she comes lookin' for her great grandson?"

It seems Victoria had thought of that already as she answered casually, "You can deal with her however you want. Maybe she'll wish to take you back to South Carolina and give you her whole damn plantation."

Now she really had me hooked. What could I say? If the stocks were rightfully hers anyway then we weren't doing anything illegal. If that deed was for real, I could be set up for life with a place of my own. Wouldn't Pa be proud of me?

"Why not? It sounds like a good deal all round. May I see that deed now?"

She folded the deed and put it back in her skirt pocket. "All in good time, Mister Monroe, all in good time."

She pulled out another small leather sack decorated with Navajo beadwork. It looked a lot like the ammunition pouch Cleetis had given me but it was most likely a medicine pouch that Injuns often wore 'round their necks. As I understood it, the purpose was to ward off evil spirits and bring them good fortune in battle.

Victoria poured its contents on the table. There were two bear claws, a gold stick pin, an arrowhead, a small wad of tobacco, a used matchbook, a tiny gold locket and chain like a child might wear and a lock of hair tied up with a red ribbon.

Next, she sorted through the contents with her fingers and hand-ed me the gold stickpin. It was a simple lookin' pin but on the back I could see the initials C. U. F. were lightly engraved on it. She tossed the matchbook to me and I could see it was from "The Farley House, Chicago." Finally, she opened the gold locket to show me a small picture of a young woman but it was not just any young woman. The picture was a likeness of Miss Victoria herself, taken some years ago.

I examined each item closely and tried to imagine what a trained Pinkerton detective might think of them. Victoria had planned well. It would be a simple thing for the Pinkertons to follow these clues. I looked at the picture for a minute and tried to imagine Victoria at that age. She was a real beauty, then and now.

Victoria was impatient for my opinion of her Navajo medi-cine pouch. "Well, what do you think? Will they believe all this is yours?"

"I'm no expert but it sure looks good." I held up the lock of hair. "Is this your hair?"

"Yes, of course. It's not really important but a nice touch, I thought." She picked up the items and replaced them in the pouch. After a moment's reflection, she handed it to me. "Can you leave tomorrow morning?"

"Hell, I'm ready to go right now."

"I'd hoped you'd have dinner with us. I like the idea of having a grown son. I'd like to get to know you better.... Jim."

There she was again, leaning towards me with that teasing, seductive look and all that cleavage. Maybe she just couldn't help herself. I started to ask about the deed again but we were interrupted by the sound of riders pulling-up outside.

Bud rushed over to the swinging doors to see about the commotion. He turned around, pale as a ghost, and stammered. "It's Mack McDonald and a bunch of their riders. Looks like they're loaded for bear."

Victoria sprung into action. She called upstairs to Slick and the girls. "Everyone, get down here, now."

There was a ruckus upstairs as everyone scurried around and headed down the stairs. I couldn't help but notice Slick and Goldie came from the same room and even after all this time, Slick was still putting on his clothes.

Bud ran back behind the bar and pulled out a double-barreled shotgun. He took a quick nip from his flask and laid the old scattergun on the bar, facing the front doors.

Following Victoria's direction, the girls hurriedly formed a greeting line and as usual, they were damn near undressed for business. Victoria led Slick to the back of the saloon and started the player piano. She was giving him what for and he was giving it back but the piano covered the sound of their voices. Ever'one seemed to have forgotten me so I just sat and waited. My gun belt was still lying on the table with the butt of the Dragoon facing me.

From outside, I could hear random gunfire and someone shoutin' orders. There was lots of general yellin' and hollerin' from the town folks too. Horses were racing up and down the street, doors were slamming and I heard the sound of glass breaking. I'd heard about towns being treed but I never figured to see it.

Mack MacDonald walked through the swinging doors of the saloon with his gun already drawn. Following close behind him were four of his riders with their guns drawn. Before they could act, a signal from Victoria sent the girls flouncin' up to them. The riders came in hunting trouble and were caught off guard by the overtly friendly females. They had no idea how to handle the seductive nature of the girls.

Goldie rushed up to Mack MacDonald and started to wrap herself around him as the rest of the girls approached the other riders. Three of them seemed to welcome the attention, but the fourth one, a scar-faced man with a worn checkered shirt and bowler hat, was having none of it. He quickly pushed Conchita and another girl out of his way. I couldn't help but notice that the scar ran from his forehead, over his left eye, down his cheek and across his mouth. It was easily the worst lookin' scar I'd ever seen.

Distracted as he was, Mack finally shed hisself of Goldie but his momentary loss of concentration cost him dearly. When she fell to the floor beside him, he leveled his gun at Slick and shouted. "You're gonna die for killing my bro..."

Mack's threat was halted by a blast from Slick's sleeve gun. Like his brother the night before, Mack never saw it comin' and the slug hit him just above his belt buckle. He stared in disbelief at the hole in his stomach and the spreading bloodstain. The girls screamed and all hell broke loose. Bodies flew in every direction.

Mack almost collapsed from the shock but staggered a bit and then regained his balance. He was determined to get off a shot at Slick. Goldie was just as determined that he wouldn't. She clung to him as he tried to push her away. As he raised his gun a second time, Goldie pulled his arm off target and the gun swung around to point directly at her. Then, it just seemed to go off of it's own accord and the bullet struck Goldie right in the forehead. Her face contorted in agony as she released her grip and settled on the floor.

At about the same time, Bud discharged both barrels full of birdshot from that old shotgun and played hob with two of the riders. They hit the floor screaming and cursing in the same breath.

Old Scarface in the checkered shirt shot Slick and sent him spinning to the floor. Victoria produced the Baby Patterson from her skirt pocket and fired point blank into that checkered shirt. He must have been pretty fit as he took five shots of .28 caliber, one right after another, in his chest pocket before he fell to the floor. The girls, in full panic, were still screaming and running ever' which way.

The last rider had been watching rather than shooting and figured to be young and scairt. When he finally pulled his pistol, I dragged out my tired old Dragoon and tried to shoot it from his hand. What with all the excitement and him jittering around so much, my bullet went clear through his right wrist instead. He dropped the gun and screamed in agony. After staring at his mangled wrist in disbelief, he rushed out the doors shouting that Mack MacDonald was dead. I could hear a lot of shoutin' and arguin' outside but finally the rest of the riders mounted up and rode out. I'm sure the whole town heaved a collective sigh of relief. Animas City wasn't much but it was all they had.

So much had happened so fast, I had to take a deep breath and look about. The acrid smell and thick haze of gun smoke filled the saloon. Everyone seemed to be in shock and were moving real slow and cautious-like.

Mack had fallen to his knees and was just staring at Goldie who was staring up at him through her newly created third eye. His shirt and jeans were rapidly turning red with his blood. He looked down at the floor and then pitched forward on it. His pistol slid across the floor as it fell from his dead hand.

Victoria was still pointing her little revolver at Scarface and pulling the trigger but it had run out of bullets. Scarface, on the other hand, had run out of life.

Slick lay on his side in a pool of blood. The two riders who absorbed Bud's shotgun blasts were still alive and rollin' about in agony. The girls were getting up off the floor and coming out from behind tipped over tables. So much had happened so quickly.

Conchita rushed over to Goldie's body as Victoria knelt beside Slick. Bud was behind the bar trying to empty his flask in one long pull. I returned the Dragoon to my holster and moved over to the doors to watch the last of MacDonald's riders disappear down the road.

Victoria yelled at Bud and the girls to get hot water and bandages. She scared Bud so bad he dropped his flask. I walked back to Victoria and Slick. He was alive and conscious but he must have been out of his head as he kept asking Victoria about Goldie.

Victoria gave him a look that could have finished him off. He was hit low on the right side and was losing a lot of blood and whether he lived or died was up to her.

I asked quietly. "How bad is it?"

Victoria commanded. "Someone get the doc, now."

One of the bystanders who had wandered in turned on a dime and ran back out the doors. The rest of the bystanders just gawked at the bodies and started to fuss over the wounded riders. Bud had aimed low and they weren't about to die although they might wish to. Each had bird shot wounds a-plenty south of their gun belts and might have to pee sitting down for the rest of their lives. That really had to hurt.

Doc Walters must have been close by or on his way here for he appeared as if by magic. He started to help the two wounded riders and then he saw Slick. One hard look from Victoria and he reconsidered. Her expression changed his mind and he rushed over to treat the wounded gambler. I got out of his way and moved over to the bar where Bud was busy with hot water and towels for bandages. He looked at me and muttered. "I'm too old for this shit. Too old, I tell you."

Reb Hopkins came in on little cat's feet and moseyed over to where I was standing. His eyes were wide with excitement and he was taking it all in. "That must have been some shindig in here. Those MacDonald riders figured to burn the whole town down. Did Slick and Mack shoot 'er out?"

I nodded in response as I watched Doc work on Slick. I'd seen enough gunshot wounds to figure with a little luck he would probably make it. Of course, you could never tell about gunshot wounds and great loss of blood. One thing was certain; he'd certainly get all the care he needed if Victoria had anything to say about it.

Old Reb was a fountain of news and information. "Heard old Angus MacDonald was agin' this and told his boys to stay to home. That Jameson there," he pointed to Scarface, "has been itching to tear this place down and prodded Mack into comin'. The other boys knew they were going agin' the old man and that's why they lit out once Mack and Jameson bit the dust. This here is gonna hit old Angus pretty hard. He's got a bum ticker, ya know."

The rest of the afternoon and the early evening were spent tending to Slick and cleaning up the mess. We carried him to a room upstairs where Victoria and some of the girls took turns watching over him. Doc Walters worked on the two wounded riders and then we pitched them in the back of his buckboard so he could cart them back to the MacDonald ranch. There wasn't much Doc could do for them, other than pick some of the bird shot out of their thighs and private parts. He removed what he could and left the rest for time and nature. That old scattergun, even loaded with bird shot, was a fearsome weapon.

Hours later, when Miss Victoria finally came down to join me for supper, she looked tuckered out. For the first time, she really showed some age as her hair and make up lacked her usual attention. Neither of us was in much of a mood for eating or talking but we did the best we could.

"Is Slick gonna make it?"

Victoria sighed. "Doc Walters thinks so. He lost a lot of blood but he's strong." Then her face tightened and she looked like she was fixing to explode. "That scar faced bastard, Jameson, he caused all the trouble today. This was all his doing. Mack MacDonald was a hotheaded young fool but he would have stayed at home if not for Jameson. That awful scar made an animal of that man. He was nothing but pure hatred. Last year, he shot his own horse right out there in the street when it accidentally stepped on his foot. I hope he rots in hell."

Victoria paced back and forth as she talked to relieve her stress and worry. "None of our girls would have anything to do with Jameson and when Slick busted him at the poker table, he swore he'd burn this place to the ground. The business with Colin just gave him the excuse he was waiting for. I feel so sorry for Angus. He's a proud old Scotsman and losing two sons in two days might be more than he can take."

I tried to change the subject. "Well, for a dying town, this place sure has been alive these last two days. I reckon I'll lite out first thing tomorrow morning before it gets any more exciting."

Victoria suddenly remembered our earlier conversation. "Then you'll go to Flagstaff and see the new Pinkerton man?"

"Sure thing. A deal's a deal.... Ma."

For the first time, I was testing her reaction. She was taken aback at first but then she smiled like sunshine. "I've always wished to hear someone say that.... and mean it."

We had finished eating so Victoria excused herself and went upstairs to check on Slick and get freshened up. Soon enough, the saloon was open for business once more and the crowd had started to wander in. Bud, and the other bartender, Lou, had just finished mopping up the floor. You'd hardly know that just a few hours before; three people had died in there. I guess no matter what, the show must go on.

The sun was jus' about set when I wandered outside and saw Bobby and his ma locking up the Café. I crossed the street and asked if they might have any carrots or other vegetable scraps for Goner. I'd suddenly realized he'd been saddled-up since this morning and I'd need a treat or two to get back in his good graces.

They obliged me with a bag of scraps and we talked about the gunplay. Bobby tried to keep us talking longer but his poor ma was just too tired. I was thankful. Bobby was forever shopping for a new daddy but I wasn't in the market for the job.

When I got to the livery, the hostler was gone but the stable hand was mucking out a stall as I walked past. Goner snorted and stamped a few times but we made up and talked some. The carrots helped. I promised him that we'd head out next morning then I stripped his saddle and gave him a good rubdown. After all that, we were friends again.

I could see where someone had tried to burn the livery down. There were charred support poles and timbers and the place smelled like burnt hay. Guess the whole town came real close to burning down after all.

When I creaked open the hotel door, Doby seemed wide-awake and alert for a change. "If you need a place for tonight, Mr. Monroe, you got your choice of rooms. After all the doings this afternoon, the hotel is empty." He pointed at the full rack of room keys. "That young woman had to leave but I guess you know all about that."

He was angling for information but I was beyond small talk and tossed him a silver dollar. "Room number two will be just fine. Thanks, Doby."

As I started up the stairs, he commented. "You know them MacDonald riders tried to burn us out today but we fought 'em off. Animas City may be dying but we're not dead yet. No sir."

I had to agree with him. "Not by a long shot."

As I stretched out on the bed and tried to get to sleep, I couldn't help but remember another town that was too tough to die without a fight. That town was Bodie, California.

Chapter V

"Goodbye God I'm going to Bodie"

MARCH 1879

When I finally said good-by to my Cornish friends and left Virginia City, I don't know if I had gold fever or not but I sure had most of the symptoms. I was hell bound for California. Rumors had it the next big bonanza would be in the little town of Bodie, just across the Nevada border. It was only a couple of days' ride south from Virginia City.

Goner and I arrived there in late March 1879. The town had enjoyed an early spring and the weather was mild. The quick thaw had left the streets a foot deep in mud but in spite of the muck, folks were glad to see sunshine. It had been pretty bleak and dim over the winter months. Residents claimed they had "the worst climate out of doors" because of their extremely harsh winters. Along with bitter cold and heavy snowfall, they had winds that cut like a shaving knife. I hoped to be long gone before the next winter.

Bodie was one of a kind. The town was named for "Waterman S. Body" who discovered gold thereabouts in 1859, but they changed the spelling so folks would pronounce it correctly. Whereas most boomtowns tried to maintain at least some fashion of law and order, Bodie did no such thing. It seemed to thrive on its' reputation for murder, robbery, holdups and general lawlessness. The fire bell tolled the age of each new victim when they were being buried and on many days that old bell rang long and loud.

The gold strike came just about the time mining operations were declining along the eastern slope of the Sierra Nevada Mountains. Bodie grew from almost nothing to over ten thousand folks in just a few years and like so many western boomtowns, the influx of people far outstripped the available goods and services. Whiskey was the only staple that wasn't in short supply. Every other building on its mile long main street was a saloon and there were sixty-five all together.

A popular story of the time told of one seven-year-old girl who, upon hearing her family was relocating there, wrote in her diary. "Good-bye, God, I'm going to Bodie." That simple sentence was repeated all over the West.

As I rode in, that infamous fire bell pealed thirty-two times for some poor miner who lost an argument with a gambler. "Judge Colt" settled the matter as he often did. Legend held one such unfortunate miner was about to be buried when his drunken mourners found gold tracings in his grave-site and proceeded to dig up the entire cemetery while leaving him above ground. Life was cheap in Bodie and death was everywhere.

I spent a few days getting the feel of the town and listening to the wild tales of fortunes and failures. The saloons were full of the usual dreamers and schemers. Thieves, cutthroats and murderers were aplenty but most of the lawless were simply small time swindlers, footpads, and sneak thieves. All sorts of scams and con games were going on at the same time.

Foolish and impatient newcomers often bought "salted", worthless or nonexistent claims. Heartless merchants charged starving men double for food and dishonest gamblers cheated miners out of their hard earned money. Down-and-out miners begged for grubstakes while flesh peddlers and rotgut whiskey were ever'where.

The human predators listened intently for word of a new strike or a careless miner sporting a full poke. Some would rush out to jump his claim while others waited till he was drunk so they could jump him on his way back to it. The sound of screams and gunshots could be heard around the main street at all hours.

The wide-eyed newcomers comprised most of the prospectors invading the West. They came from all professions and backgrounds with only one thing in common; they knew little or nothing about prospecting for gold. Farmers had been known to dig for gold with their pitchforks. Some would work long and hard while others would just talk about it while straddling a brass bar rail. Folks called the straddlers "bar-side miners". They usually wandered from strike to strike till they ran out of money, health or both.

Those infected with gold fever said they wanted to "see the elephant." This popular expression began with a cartoon depicting gold fever as a dancing elephant. The reference was to a story of a farmer back East who dreamed of seeing the circus and a real live elephant. He drove his wagon full of perishable produce toward town and was run off the road by a circus wagon that was pulled by an elephant. Although he'd lost ever'thing, he didn't mind cuz he'd finally "seen the elephant" which was after all, his dream. It was that way for most gold seekers. They often lost ever'thing, up to and including their lives, just for the chance to find gold.

Folks came from all over the world to strike it rich in the "Golden State." Few were ever successful and when they were, they usually drank away their small bonanzas or sold out cheap and simply moved on to the next strike. They were eternally optimistic and certain there was more gold to be found "yonder." Even the fabled John Augustus Sutter of forty-niner fame ended up a broke drunk. All in all, they were a sorry lot.

Men with money also followed the boomtowns. They bought up all the claims that were thought profitable and then hired the failed prospectors to work for them as miners at minimal wages. Once they got the operation organized and provided the necessary equipment, the mine would really pay off and they made the big money. Many went on to become millionaires.

I figured I knew better. With my youthful confidence and Cornish training, I intended to find a rich claim, work it for a while and then sell out for a good price before I moved on. I needed a large stake to buy my own cattle ranch but I wasn't about to sweat my life away in no mineshaft to get it. I longed for fresh air, open spaces and a horse between my knees.

My first few weeks in Bodie were spent seeking and not finding. All the likely areas were already staked out. I used a muckstick and gold pan here and there but found no color to speak of. After eighteen-hour days of trying, I usually had to fight for a place to sleep. Most of the prospectors slept right at their claims after a night of drinkin' or gamblin'. Tents and various forms of lean-to were common. I was running out of eating money and patience when the solution to both tripped over me in the middle of the night. His name was "Patch" McCartney.

Patch was sixty if he was a day. He was short of stature and needle thin. His face wore a sour look that made you wonder if he'd been weaned on a pickle. Having lost one eye in a mining accident, Patch got along with his one good eye unless it was dark and he was drunk. Since it was and he was, we met with him fallin' atop me while I was fast asleep. We scrapped a bit and then called a truce as he passed out and I went back to sleep. As it turned out, I'd accidentally trespassed on his claim when I bedded down for the night

The next morning, he greeted me with *Hallo, dere neebr*. Then we shared a biscuit and likker breakfast and became partners in the "M&M Mine."

Old Patch had a tartan swatch with a rawhide strap over his right eye, which proudly proclaimed his Scottish heritage. He was three years from Aberdeen in the Highlands of Scotland but still talked with a brogue so thick you could cut it with a butter knife and slather it on a biscuit. I seldom understood him when he was sober, but as luck would have it, I seldom saw him sober. When he was drunk, he spoke the Kings English like a Shakespearean actor. He truly had "the gift of *gob*", as he said it, and was given to great gestures and proclamations. He often entertained the other miners with his silliness.

Patch was working his small claim of about ten by forty feet along a small stream running down a steep hillside. Farther up the hill was claimed by a stern, bacon-fed Dutchman, name of Van Der Schaaf. The "Dutchman" was a sullen, hog-like man with more than ample weight to fight off starvation. While working, he sweated profusely and was forever using his bandana for a towel as he cursed the summer-like heat.

While Patch only panned enough dust to get drinking money for the evening, Klaus Van Der Schaaf worked with a religious fervor. He labored from sun-up to dark-out and rarely stopped, even for food or drink. His oft repeated dream was to return to *Nieuw Nederland,* as he referred to New York City, a rich and successful man. He wanted to live in an area known as the "Bronx", which he said was named for a fellow Dutchman named Jonas Bronck. Klaus had nothing but contempt for his lackadaisical Scottish neighbor.

Since Patch only had a small lean-to on his campsite, the first thing I did was build a larger shelter and move in my outfit. Most of the prospectors had tents or temporary wooden shelters, which were fine for summer but worthless come cold weather. Only the Dutchman had what you could call a cabin but it was not really fit for the brutal winters either. I boarded Goner at the local livery, as there wasn't room for a horse on our small claim.

While Patch swirled away with his gold pan, I watched the nearby prospectors to see how they were doing. Most were working their small claims with naught but the basic tools, a tin pan and a muckstick. They'd shovel gravel and dirt into the pan and swirl it underwater to settle the heavier metals like gold and then rinse away the worthless residue or gangue as they called it. Some worked harder than others, but gold panning was miserable hard work with small chance of success. The hours were long and their futures bleak as few made more than expenses.

Those who catered to the miners hit the real bonanza in any boomtown. First were the freighters who carried the prospectors and their equipment to the new strike. They brazenly charged double or triple for their services knowing full well the desperate gold seekers would pay.

Then came the merchants and saloon owners who supplied the basics of mining life and controlled the flow to increase the demand. Food, alcohol and women were always kept in short supply so the men were forced to pay dearly for them. The charge was whatever the market would bear and the market "beared" a lot.

Levi Strauss made his fortune selling canvas and denim jeans. Phillip Armour started out as a ditch digger in Placerville and then opened a butcher shop that would make him rich. John Studebaker got his start by building wheelbarrows for miners and went on to building fancy carriages. Numerous hardware and grocery merchants, not to mention saloon owners, became wealthy on the profits derived from the hapless prospectors and miners.

From what I could tell, Van Der Schaaf seemed like he was doing the best of the lot but was it his work efforts or did he just have the better claim? He was the only one around us who used a wooden sluice box. It was about twelve feet long and allowed him to process much more dirt and gravel than any of the others. He was forever digging tiny gold flakes out of his box. Some nights I'd see him working at it by candlelight.

Using my recently acquired mining knowledge, I figured the gold nuggets and dust that most of the miners were panning from their claims came from a vein that ran up and under the Dutchman's claim. I wondered if he knew about underground mining or was just lucky.

I tried to explain it all to Patch but he wasn't interested. His only ambition was to get drunk and stay that way. Panning for gold gave him the opportunity. After losing his family in a fire, Patch had left his beloved Scotland for America. He was only here a short time when an accident with a pick cost him an eye. After that, he saw little use in life and was just living it out day to day. He might get to funnin' on the outside but he was forever cryin' on the inside. The old sot ate only when reminded and was careless with his tools and gear.

Why Patch wanted a partner was simple enough. He needed someone to *hunker doon* and work the claim so he could concentrate on his drinking. He figured after he died, his partner could have the claim all to hisself. He told me as much most ever' night as he drank to our good health.

Since I was young and eager to prove myself, the take from our claim increased. First off, I built a crude wooden cradle. It wasn't pert but it did the job. I "rocked" that cradle as hard as I could to separate out any gold from the sand and gravel. I worked near as many hours as the Dutchman. Patch was content to let me work as hard as I wished, for as long as I wished, as long as he got his share for drinking money. What with the extra money, he stayed drunker longer and was soon no help around the claim at all.

Once, in one of his curious drunken moods, he designed a business crest for our "M&M" mining company. He drew a large thistle between two "M's" with a motto underneath, *Nemo me impune lacessit.* He said it was Scottish for "No one harms me without punishment." He no longer wished to work for his money, but he damn sure intended to keep what he had.

Patch carried a fancy knife he called a *Skean Dhu,* which had the same thistle on the hilt. He said the thistle was supposed to be purple and was some kind of Scottish national symbol. He mentioned something about a battle with Norsemen a long time ago but I never got the whole gist of it.

After seven months of backbreaking labor, spring and summer had drifted into fall and I amassed a fair stake of color in my poke. Not real high grade ore but it would do. I was splitting ever'thing with Patch so I was working twice as hard to make half as much. But after all, as he was want to remind me, it was his claim.

Patch was generally pickled and no bother one way or another. He took to buying a bottle and returning to the claim just to watch me work. He was forever urging me on with "atta boy, laddie buck" and "aye, that's a good lad." His favorite saying was *Whits fur ye'll no gin by ye.* Guess it meant I'd get what was coming to me. I always figured he meant the claim would be mine after he died.

One day, when I was fretting over where I could safely store my small stash of gold, it made me think about the Dutchman. What did he do with all of his gold? For safekeeping, had he taken it to one of the new banks that were opening or maybe the Wells Fargo office? I didn't reckon so. He would'a had little or no faith in the honesty of the local bankers or even Wells Fargo when it came to safeguarding his gold.

Come to think of it, I couldn't recall him ever leavin' the area. He was always working his claim or fussing around the cabin. I'd even seen him hire young boys to run errands for him and get his supplies. Missus O'Brien even picked-up and delivered his laundry.

That must be it. He was sitting on that pile of gold. It had to be right in or around his cabin. If I could figure it, then so could others. Klaus Van Der Schaaf looked to be a fat chicken roosting in a hen house surrounded by foxes.

Later that evening, while Klaus and I were the only ones still at work, I walked over to have a talk with him. We had done little but exchange nods and glances but I felt like I knew him by his labor. I figured he must at least have a grudging respect for my efforts, too. I saw him checking the design of my cradle when I first made it.

"Good evening sir, may I have a word with you?" I was as respectful as though he were a sheriff or a preacher man.

The fat Dutchman looked around suspiciously to see if anyone else was watching or listening to our conversation. He had been cleaning out his sluice box with a careful eye for stray flakes hidden in the riffles and looked to be about done for the evening. "Vat ya vant? I'm busy."

"That you are, I've tried to outwork ya but I can't seem to do it. A good measure of a man is the work he does and I have a fine appreciation for a man who puts in a full day."

"So? Now, vat ya vant?"

This conversation figured to be a short one unless I got to the point quick-like. I looked around again for any "big ears" and lowered my voice. "Last night, when old Patch was reciting Shakespeare to the men, I heard some talk about you and your claim. I thought you should know."

That got his attention. He stopped fussing with his sluice box and moved closer. "Yah? Vat goes vid dat?"

"Old man winter's coming most any day now. You can smell it in the air. The old timers say all the mining will stop for months once the snow flies. Most of the men around here aren't prepared to stick it out and they'll need money to get away. Some figure you've got enough gold to stake them all and they plan to have it."

"Vell, they can't have it. It's mine.... and I plan to keep every ounce of it!" His pale blue eyes were glinting with anger.

I had heard no such conversation, but that didn't mean it hadn't taken place. No one could deny winter was almost upon us and the miners were restless indeed. Few had any use for the grumpy old Dutchman.

"There are some who don't care one whit about who owns what. They only see what's in it for them. They'd gladly kill a man for a small portion of what you've taken out of your claim here. You know the type of men I'm talking about. The town is filling up with 'em." I spoke like we wuz in it together.

His face exploded with anger. "Vat's mine ist mine and vill stay mine."

Then he rifled through his extra bedding and mining gear until he pulled out an old Colt Revolving Shotgun. I'd never seen one but I'd heard plenty. They were a fearsome scattergun that held five rounds of ten-gauge buckshot and were known to leave an oozy corpse.

He waved it under my nose. "I got a shotgun they can have.... and I vill give it to them.... one shot at a time."

This wasn't the time to talk business so I let him be. I had wished to discuss combining our holdings so we could defend them together but now, it would have to wait. Whatever else the Dutchman was, he certainly was no coward and any claim jumpers or thieves would pay dearly for anything they took from him. He would take a lot of killing and they would prob'ly have to pry whatever they stole from his cold dead hands.

As I predicted, the thievin' polecats finally came the night of the first snow. I was soundly asleep after yet another eighteen hours of rockin' the cradle and pannin' gravel. The sound of the Dutchman's shotgun going off, once, twice, and then a third time, stirred me urgently from my warm blankets. I fetched my old Dragoon and hurried, sock feet and all, over to his claim.

In the moonlit darkness, I could make out the Dutchman fighting with two or three men and several others ransacking his camp. I lit into the sackers with a blind fury. I hit the first on the skull with that heavy old Dragoon and likely split his head wide open. He fell in a heap, awash in his own blood. The second turned on me with a skinning knife in his right hand. I had no wish to kill him but he left me little choice. I fired and missed as he lunged at me but a second round from my Dragoon spun him off balance and he landed hard on his own knife. The third man tried to run off but I managed to tackle him from behind. When I rolled him over, I sat on his chest and "read to him from the good book" as my pa used to say. His face took an awful beating, since I didn't stop hittin' it till he stopped strugglin'.

In the midst of all the excitement I heard a fourth shotgun blast, a wild scream of pain and then a fifth blast. I turned to see the Dutchman wrestling with the last attacker. His shotgun was out of rounds but not out of wood so he swung it butt first and stove in the head of his last assailant. As Klaus stood there all alone, I saw a knife hilt sticking out of his chest and blood spreading all over his wool night shirt. He struggled to remove the knife and finally pulled it out and tossed it aside. As the Dutchman staggered a bit, he looked at me and mumbled. "Obliged". His face became ghostly white and his eyes rolled up in his head. Then he fell backward into the stream with a huge splash.

By now, all the noise had awakened the entire encampment and miners were scurrying in from ever' direction. Even old Patch managed to rise up and take a look-see. He appraised my efforts and gave me a knowing grin. "You'll do, laddie buck, you'll do just fine."

Someone went for a doctor and soon enough the Dutchman was spread out on his blankets; getting the best care they could give him. The knife wound was deep but then so was Klaus. The knife seemed to have hit nothing vital. If his wound didn't poison he would most likely survive but with winter comin' an all, he was in no shape to work his claim until next spring. It set me to thinking how I might be able to help him and myself at the same time.

Of the seven attackers, four were put to bed with a pick and shovel and the other three were hung later the next day. Justice, when it was served, came swiftly and surely in Bodie. Once again, that fire bell rang loud and long.

I located and safeguarded the Dutchman's hidden gold stash until we rounded up a Wells Fargo agent to write him a draft for the full amount. It came to almost twenty-three thousand dollars. Klaus seemed mighty thankful when he woke to find that piece of paper. He was laid up in his cabin and a couple of us took turns looking in on him.

All the men knew the Dutchman was in no shape to work his claim and wouldn't be for some time. Left unattended, it would surely be taken over by claim jumpers. Klaus knew what would happen as well. When he was conscious and mindful, we spoke of it and agreed I would buy out his claim for the twelve hundred dollars in gold I'd saved. His claim was worth thousands more but he had little choice seein' that I had so little money.

Since Patch and I were already partners, I agreed to buy the Dutchman's claim and register it as part of the "M&M" property. Patch seemed to care less for all that was going on but he did take the signed paperwork to the claim office.

Winter was coming on with a vengeance and I struggled day and night to keep our claims secure. The weather was bitter cold and windy but I worked as much as possible to get what I could from the nearly frozen earth. The Dutchman recovered enough to travel and hired a wagon to carry him to San Francisco. The teamsters he hired to freight him were a shaggy lot but once again, he had little choice. I'll always wonder if he made it back to his *Nieuw Nederland.*

When winter with all its fury finally engulfed Bodie, temperatures plunged to a low of forty degrees below zero and winds gusted to one hundred miles an hour. The weather lived up to its reputation for being the worst on God's green earth. Miners huddled in makeshift shelters around pitifully small fires and some of 'em actually froze to death when the fires went out.

Luckily for Patch, I'd mined enough for us to stay indoors at the "Golden State Boarding House." However, our poke was thin and I had to cut off all his drinking money. Patch took it all right at first but each day thereafter, he grew more sullen and resentful. With winter only half over and the snow massed over a man's head, there was little else either of us could do.

Each morning, no matter how bad the weather, I went out to our claims to make sure no one else was messin' with 'em. What with the cold and snow, it was a certain bet few would brave the elements and try to dig through the frozen earth to steal our gold. Still, a man never knew and I tried to keep a watchful eye.

One bright February morning, I was shocked to find brand-new claim stakes driven through the snow and into the frozen ground around our claims. They stated the claims were now the property of Langley Mining and Mineral Co. I couldn't believe my eyes. In a fit of anger I tore the stakes from the ground and raced back to the boarding house to tell Patch.

When I couldn't find him in our room, I was directed to the "Five Star Emporium". I knew it to be a short distance away on Main Street. It was one the few saloons that had managed to stay open for business during the winter and was always full of men trying to get warm. Since few had any money for drinkin' or gamblin', they got tossed out on the frozen street. I couldn't imagine what Patch would be doing there since I knew he had no money and would have been warmer at the boarding house.

The "Five Star" was only a couple of hundred yards from our boarding house so I ran all the way. I found it hard to catch my breath in the cold air but I was anger driven and didn't care.

When I pushed my way through the crowd at the door, there he was, standing at the bar with a bottle in front of him and a full glass in his hand. Suddenly I took sick inside.

I was still out of breath but I managed to shout at him. "What are you doin'?" I ripped the bottle from his grasp. "Where did you get the money for this? What have you done?"

Some of the crowd backed off but others edged closer to watch. Patch just looked from the glass of whiskey, to me, and back to the whiskey again. He was just drunk enough for me to understand his words. "Whiskey in the hand is always better than whiskey on the wing, laddie."

Then he downed the drink slowly, seeming to savor ever' last drop. Next, he reached over and grabbed the neck of the bottle I was holding. We had a brief tug of war over the bottle to keep him from refilling his glass but I finally pulled the bottle back and confronted him again.

"No more till you tell me what you did."

Patch stopped grasping for the bottle and looked me eye to eyes and said. "I sold the claims.... both of 'em. Now give back me whiskey."

The crowd cheered for no particular reason and I glared at several of them. They seemed to be enjoying my frustration. "They warn't yours to sell. I was your partner and I never agreed to sell."

Patch pried the bottle from my hand and poured yet another drink. Then he pointed a bony finger at my nose and sneered. "You were my partner in name only, laddie buck. On paper, all the claims were mine alone. You see, my full name is Michael McCartney. The "M&M" crest is mine, laddie buck, not ours."

He downed the full glass of whiskey while I tried to absorb what he'd said. "What do you mean we're not partners? I paid for the Dutchman's claim with my own gold."

He interrupted. "With gold you took from my claim. You had no claim of your own, laddie-buck. Your name is nowhere on the registry. You used my gold to buy his claim so that makes his claim....

mine!" He chuckled at his own cleverness and the damned crowd cheered again.

It finally sank in. He had just used me from the very beginning. I even supposed he'd tripped over me a'purpose on that first night we met. Had I not bought the Dutchman's claim, Patch prob'ly had figured out some other way to get the gold I'd worked so hard to get.

I was a fool to think I could trust Patch or any man when it came to gold dealings. Just the smell of gold could turn ordinary men into crazed animals who fought viciously to possess the precious metal. I'd only lost twelve hundred dollars and most of a year's labor but I knew of many men murdered for much less.

Patch turned his back on me and continued with his drinking. It seemed he had ever' legal right to sell his claims no matter how unfair or immoral it was of him. I'd just learned a hard lesson that would stay with me forever. It was clear I couldn't change what happened but I just had to know. "How much did ya get? And, who's Langley?"

From behind me came a commanding voice. "I'm Sampson Langley and I paid Mister McCartney five thousand in gold for his claims. I figure they were worth every ounce." He laughed out loud and was joined by several of the men around him.

Patch and I turned to see a menacing figure in the doorway surrounded by a group of thugs. When Patch turned back to face me, I couldn't resist telling him the truth.

"You old fool. Those claims were worth ten times what you got for 'em. He played you like a cheap fiddle."

Patch looked past me to Langley and muttered, "But...but you said..."

Langley countered. "I said what I'd give you, not what I figured the claims were worth. This young man is correct. You are an old fool. How does that saying go? A fool and his gold are soon parted." Now almost every man in the bar was laughing.

Patch looked like he was frozen in place. I could only imagine what was going through his addled mind. He suddenly realized he'd squandered a fortune jus' to scratch his likker itch.

I turned around to confront Sampson Langley. He was a huge man in height as well as girth with black hair trimmed to his shoulders. I judged him to be several inches taller than my six feet two and at least a hundred pounds heavier than my two hundred. He wore a fancy top hat, a brand spankin' new broadcloth suit and the fanciest silver-toed black boots I'd ever seen. His black hair framed a face chiseled from granite, a trim mustache, coal black eyes and a jaw an iron pipe might not break. Langley also wore a gold chain hanging cross his vest that was linked to a solid gold pocket watch he held in his hand. It was a big watch but looked like a child's toy cuz his hands were huge and well used. He looked to be a wealthy and ruthless man. That was always a bad combination.

The men crowded around were certainly working for Langley. They were well scrubbed and dressed up but figured to be a tough lot just the same. I couldn't see any guns but I could feel 'em and it was a sure bet they were earning fighting wages. I wondered why a man like Langley would need 'em around but before I could say anything he spoke to me.

"You'll have to excuse me young man." He looked to his gold watch. "I have a previous engagement, but...." He turned back to look at me again as he was walking away. "Tell you what.... since you seem to know his claims so well, I'll hire you to work them for me. If you're interested, I'll gladly pay you foreman's wages. See Zimmerman here." He indicated the man standing next to him. "He's managing all my gold claims that I have in Bodie."

Langley walked off laughing to hisself and Zimmerman pushed his way closer so he might size me up. He was a short, stocky, hard-bit German with a face like a mule. With his wide-set brown eyes and a large oft-broke nose he didn't look like the cheerful type. His mud brown suit was several sizes too small for his wide, muscular body and he was stretching ever' seam. I figured his personality would match his looks so I turned back to Patch and tried to pay him no mind.

Suddenly, a meaty hand grabbed my shoulder and spun me around. Zimmerman was staring up at me with a cherry-red face.

"Don't never turn your back on me, boy. Now, do ya vant the job or no?"

I looked at him and the others at his side and decided to pass up the opportunity. I shook my head and mumbled. "Nah, I figure to get away from here as fast as I can."

After glaring at me for a few long seconds, he just moseyed on down the bar with his companions. For some reason, he was on his good behavior. Maybe the suit was new and he didn't want to get my blood on it.

Patch was silent for a change and was just staring at the back bar. Finally he put the cork in his bottle and turned the glass over. Then he peered up at me with his one bloodshot eye. "Ten times, ya say?"

I almost felt sorry for him. "At least ten times. Might be a sight more. Depends on how much mining Langley's prepared to pay for. He'd have to hire a full crew and start digging shafts and tunnels but if that drift runs the whole claim, it could pay out millions like the Comstock."

Patch was finally coming to understand. His poor whiskey-soaked brains were finally working. "Then I was a complete fool."

Then I really let him have it. "A fool and a thief. The way I see it, you stole my share of the claims and then let Langley steal the whole kit and caboodle from you. Now I ask ya, what kind of man does that to a friend?"

I started to go but I had to leave him with his own words. *Whits fur ye'll no gin by ye.* He had gotten his due.

As I walked out the door I heard him issue his own curse. *Nemo me impune lacessit.*

I figured he wasn't swearing at me so I kept on going. I couldn't decide whether to laugh or cry. I had been foolish to trust but Patch had been downright stupid for the sake of greed and whiskey. He would have to live with what he did and I would have to learn from it. Trust and gold never went together. I wouldn't make that mistake again. Life was teaching me again and it seemed a sure thing I had more hard lessons a' comin'.

I went to our room in the boarding house and waited for several hours while deciding what best to do. When I finally decided to lite out and got all my gear packed for traveling, it was too late in the day. I had to be content with leaving' the next morning.

I didn't sleep much that night and Patch never did return. I didn't figure he would. He couldn't drink enough to forget what he'd done and I knew, deep down, he bore an awful guilt about how he'd treated me.

Next morning I was up with the roosters and eager to be on my way. I wished to put Bodie and all that had happened far behind me. I could feel another storm coming and didn't want to be here when it arrived. Heading south seemed a good choice since it had to be warmer.

When I got to the livery the stable boy told me my board bill for Goner was paid and I owed them nothing. He said "old one-eye" paid it sometime last night. That seemed a strange thing for Patch to do but since I'd barely enough to pay the bill, it was good news. Now I'd have a small traveling stake and I was thankful.

Goner was stampin' and snortin' when I got to his stall. He was usually road-eager but I think he could feel the storm a'comin', too. In spite of his fussin', I was all saddled up and ready to go when the hostler came from the tack room.

"Hey there... Monroe? I got something for ya." He produced an old weather beaten leather satchel. "That one-eyed Scottie left this for you when he paid your bill. He sure was a strange old buzzard."

He handed me the satchel and I was taken aback by the weight of it. "What is it? Did he say?"

The old man scratched his bald head. "He tried to make himself known but who could understand him? He had to point at your horse three times before we knew who's board bill he was trying to pay. In gold-dust no less."

I remember thinking if they couldn't understand him, Patch must have sobered up before he came here. What the hell was he up to?

It suddenly occurred to the hostler. "Say.... you don't suppose there's gold dust in that bag do ya?"

I tugged open the flap but kept the contents from his sight. One look told me it was gold dust all right, along with a bait of oats on top. "No such luck. Just some special feed for my horse. Patch loved old Goner here."

He gave me a fish-eyed look but didn't challenge what I'd said. He was still muttering to hisself as he walked back toward the tack room. I mounted Goner and was about to ride out when another thought came to mind. "What did you mean... was... an old buzzard?"

The hostler looked at me as if I had three heads. "Cain't you hear that there ringing?" I was suddenly aware the fire bell had been clanging for some time. "That's him they're ringing for. Got his-self kilt down at the Emporium last night. Right after he left here, I reckon."

"Patch, dead? How?"

"Heard he got beat to death. Some German fella, Zimmer or Zimberly did it, I don't rightly recall. They say some of the boys held the old man and the German hit him till he wasn't fit for dog-meat. Was that old Scot kin of yourn?"

I paused a minute and replied. "No, just a old mining partner. He didn't say nuthin' else, did he?"

The hostler scratched his head again and commented, "Couldn't understand him very well, like I said. But I think he said something about gin. Didn't make much sense to me. Maybe he needed a drink."

That was it. He was making sure I got what was coming to me. The satchel probably had my half of the gold he received. He was going after Sampson Langley and wanted to square things between us before he did.

I thought about going down to the Emporium, but to what end? I couldn't bring Patch back and Langley would still own our claims. As for Zimmerman, well he'd probably just get his boys to back a claim of self-defense. I was certain none of his crowd would testify against him. It was hopeless and foolish to try to avenge Patch under those circumstances. I had a gut feelin' I'd be running into Langley and Zimmerman on another day when the odds would be better. I gave Goner a nudge and we headed south. The fire bell finally stopped ringing for Patch and then with little pause, started the toll for some other poor soul. The first flakes of a furious blizzard were falling on Goner's flouncin' mane as I rode out of Bodie.

Chapter VI
"Alias Navajo Kid"

SPRING 1882

Animas City had turned out to be a very eventful place. My head was full of the day's happenings and any sleep I got was light and fitful. Somewhere around midnight, my tossing and turning was interrupted by a soft knock on my door. With Dragoon in hand, I cautiously opened the door a crack and was pleasantly surprised to find Conchita in the hallway. She was dressed for work and, if anything, she was more beautiful than I remembered. I eagerly opened the door all the way to let her enter.

In broken English, she said after all the shooting, things were slow at the Farley House and Victoria figured I might like some company. Now didn't that beat all? I felt like a kid on Christmas morning who was about to unwrap his present. In my view, it would be a shame to waste such a fine bed since it figured to be a while before I saw another, so.... we didn't. Her ability to pleasure a man was more than I could have imagined. Whatever men normally paid for Conchita's company, she was worth double.

When I finally rolled out of bed in the gray before dawn, Conchita was already gone. I left the hotel out the back once again and snuck around behind the buildings to get to the livery. I was determined to get away without seeing anybody else.

The livery was shy of folks so Goner and I were saddled-up and on our way in minutes. I left a silver dollar in the hostler's office to pay for the extra night. A couple of dogs barked and a rooster crowed as we rode out of town heading south. It shaped up to be a bright sunny day with the morning air clean and cool as an icy creek.

I couldn't help thinking how things had changed in the last two days. I'd ridden into Animas City without knowing anybody at all. My plan was to stay the night, catch breakfast and keep working my way back toward Grasshopper Flats. I guess even the best laid plans have a way of goin' goofy.

Now, as it turns out, instead of me going to the Flats, the Flats had come to me. Good old Slick, who was so involved with all my troubles there, was here in Animas City and he didn't even recognize me. Maybe I'd been frettin' over nothing.

Next thing ya know, Sissy and Hoss catch up with me and we have to get that mess settled. Then Victoria pays me to go where I was already going and promises me a ranch of my own if I can pull off a little play-acting. Throw in two shoot-outs, a fistfight, and a night with an angel and there you have it. Good old Animas City.

After leavin' town I followed the "river of lost souls" southward into New Mexico Territory and the small town of Junction City. It was situated at the confluence of three rivers, the La Plata, the Animas, and the San Juan. The sorry little "city" was settled in the 1870s by pioneers from Animas City. It had a general store, a livery, one small café and three saloons. I was lucky to pick up supplies and fresh water. Both were getting hard to come by in that barren and unsettled country. It was still springtime but the weather was already turning hot and dry and many of the seasonal water tanks were already dried up.

From Junction City, the trail headed straight west and I followed the setting sun for three weeks. We passed through Ute and Zuni territories, went around the Hopi hunting grounds and finally rode onto the Navajo reservation. By traveling mostly at night and off the known trails, I avoided encounters with any Injuns. I saw lots'a

Injun tracks and trails and was just plain lucky none of them Injuns ever saw me.

Game was plentiful at first and I was grateful. Antelope, prairie grouse and jackass rabbits were added to my grub line. We saw several herds of wild horses and Goner had a hard time controllin' his urges. I reckon there's no changing the heart of a stallion. Their tracks were plentiful as were those of unshod Injun ponies. The Major taught me to tell the difference by the manure. Wild horses stopped and formed a pile while Injun ponies kept on moving and left a manure trail. It was a good thing to know.

We found just enough water to keep us going. Much of it was so alkali you had to chew it before ya swallered but it tasted mighty good when you were thirstin'. Once we passed Monument Valley and got through Marsh Pass, we staggered into Mormons' Well. Goner and I were both walkin' by the time. Thankfully, the water was cool and the grass was green. We stayed put for two days to recover and that made Goner happy. In the desert, a happy horse can be the difference 'tween life and death.

We skirted Black Mesa and passed by Thief Rock on our way to Tuba City. It was located on the edge of the Painted Desert. Tuba City was really little more than an adobe trading post set up by some Mormons years before. It was named for a Hopi chief that guided them though the area. By the time we got there, I had run out of just about everything, including my patience. That trading post was surely a welcome sight.

The cost of goods was double but I was loath to argue the point. Supplies can be worth their weight in gold anywhere but specially near any kind of desert. Most places, a man could live off the land what with game and water a'plenty but the desert, well it had its own ways and gave comfort grudgingly. Canny men could live off the desert but I never took to it nor cared to learn.

Upon leavin' Tuba City, I aimed right for the San Francisco Peaks. They were over twelve thousand feet high and could be seen everywhere in Northern Arizona. Pa told us the early Franciscan monks that lived with the Hopi named them for Saint Francis of Assisi. The

Peaks were sacred to many Injun tribes including the Hopi who considered them to be the winter home of their Kachina gods that lived in the clouds. The Hopi called the Peaks *"Nuvatukaovi"*, meaning the place with snow on the very top. By heading toward the Peaks and keeping the Echo Cliffs on our right, we crossed the Painted Desert without getting lost. It was a land of endless sand dunes and lava beds with rock pinnacles rising up to form rough sculptures. Though it was truly beautiful, it was a harsh land just the same. Very little lived there and even less survived passin' through. It was with grateful hearts we crossed the Little Colorado River and entered the ponderosa pine country of Flagstaff.

From a distance, Flag didn't look much different than the first time I saw 'er when it was more of a crossroads than a town. In those days there were just a bunch of sheep ranchers settled 'round Antelope Springs. Now it was squattin' right on the dusty wagon trail that ran from Santa Fe to the *Pueblo of Los Angeles*. We used to drive some of our cattle to Flag twice a year so Pa could sell beef to the settlers.

Flagstaff actually got its' name following a Centennial celebration held on July the 4[th,] 1876. Some traveling folks from Boston lopped all the branches off a tall ol' pine tree and ran up an American flag. They were celebrating the first hundred years of our country's history. That flag was up there so high you could see it waving for miles and miles. Travelers used it as a guidepost to keep on the right trail. "Head for the flag staff" was the only directions necessary.

Now that the railroad had gotten to Flagstaff, the town was setting-up to provide for the railroad workers. Ever'thing was re-organizing around the railroad station. Fresh water was always a problem but folks in Flag were able to get what they needed from McMillan Spring at the base of Mars Hill.

I found a livery stable for Goner and got him set up for rest and relaxation. A young Navajo stable boy seemed eager to tend to him. He could tell Goner was a good horse and certainly earned his keep.

I checked into the Beaver Street Hotel. It had just been built and smelled of new wood, fresh paint and varnish. A young redheaded desk clerk was standing behind the counter and seemed primed for action. He was sportin' a new cap and uniform and looked proud as a pup with a new collar. Displayed proudly on his chest was a fancy name badge which read "Kenny." The young man snapped to attention as I came through the door.

"Good day to you, sir, and welcome to the brand new Beaver Street Hotel. It's the newest and finest establishment of its kind, west of Santa Fe. We'll make it our business to see your stay with us is a pleasure."

Well, that was surely a mouthful. His boss had him wound tighter than a two-dollar watch. I couldn't help but smile. "Relax partner, I'm just a cowboy looking for a clean room."

"Yes sir, and it will be the...."

I cut him off short. "Yes, I'm sure it will. Could I have a room key, please?"

He was still full of bluster but he swallered it and handed me a key. "We'd be pleased to have you sign our guest book. See? We're still on the first page."

Just like that it hit me. Who the hell was I now? What name was I gonna sign? Why hadn't I thought of this? I had to have a name to tell the Pinkertons and it had to make some kind of sense. I signed the first thing that came to my mind. "Navajo Kid."

Kenny turned the book around and read what I had written. Then he looked at my Dragoon and the Henry rifle and he got downright nervous and went to stammering. "On... ah... behalf of the management, I'd like to.... ah.... welcome you.... Mister.... Kid?" His face was flushed and his eyes widened. "Are you famous, should I have heard of you?"

I had to laugh. The "Navajo Kid" did sound like some kind of gunfighter's name and I was sporting two firearms. Flagstaff was just civilized enough so most men didn't wear open guns anymore. They still had 'em but they were under cover of clothes.

"No Kenny. I told ya. I'm just a drifting cowboy. The Navajo raised me after they killed my folks. I never really had a given name so I just made one up." Now that last part was the Gods' honest truth.

He nodded his head and settled down. I figured our little conversation was good practice for the tall stories I'd have to tell later. I headed up the stairs to my room with a whole new set of problems to consider.

After bathing and eating a quick supper in my room, I relaxed on the bed and thought about what I had to do the following morning. First off, I had to find the part time Pinkerton man. Then I had to convince him that I was the "Navajo Kid" and was looking to find any family I might have. That could be simply done unless he started asking too many questions.

What would I say if he asked where and when was I taken? Where did I grow up? What was my Navajo name? Did I speak Navajo, and if not, why not? How and when did I get away from them? What had I been doing since I got away from them? This was fixing up to be anything but simple. I had to get some "facts" straight.

I worried on the answers to those questions for a couple of hours then I hit the streets to see some of the town. I went from saloon to saloon keeping my ears open and my mouth shut. A fella could pick-up a lot of good information that way.

Many Irish customers in the local saloons were still toasting John L. Sullivan, the World Heavyweight Boxing Champion. They called him the "Boston Strong Boy" and he was a national hero. The papers said he knocked out someone named Paddy Ryan in the ninth round to win the championship and it all took place somewhere down in Mississippi. Folks said the boxers fought bare knuckle until one got knocked off his feet. Then they started all over again. The match ended when one of 'em couldn't toe the line after a knockdown. It took a real man to earn that championship.

I also heard all about current events and the latest news concerning the railroad. I got caught up on current cattle prices, range conditions, the spring weather, and all the local outlaws.

The other big news of the day was the death of the famous out-law, Jesse James. He was back-shot on April 3. Some other outlaw named Robert Ford dry-gulched him in his own front room. Shot him fairly and squarely.... fairly sudden and squarely in the back of the head. Five thousand dollars reward is what they said. I know of plenty'a men would have kilt him for less.

As usual, there were some for and some agin' the killin'. Some said good riddance and others wanted Ford charged with murder. The James Boys still continued to cause such arguments and pas-sions. I couldn't help but think of my old friends, Mal and Josh, the other "James Boys."

The big social event of the season was a marriage of a local cat-tleman's daughter to some mining big shot from out of town. They planned some big doings next month. Other than that, there were the normal and natural births and deaths to keep folks talking.

I was relieved I didn't see anyone I knew. I heard nothing about my family and didn't ask. I had to take one thing at a time and first things first. I'd get this play-acting over with and then go back home. The last thing I needed was to be recognized by an old friend or fam-ily member while pretending to be the Navajo Kid. There was no way to explain what I was doing.

Sunrise found me up and eager in my hotel room. I shaved, bathed and donned my cleanest dirty shirt. That's when I found the letter from Taylor. I had changed shirts when I lit out of Animas City and forgotten all about her letter. I opened it and read the short message.

Dearest Monroe,   3 - 4 - 1881
Whenever and wherever you get this letter, please hurry back home. There has been a terrible accident and we need you on the ranch. I am praying this letter finds you alive and well. We all miss you so much.

Love, Taylor

I couldn't imagine what kind of accident could happen that would mean they needed me to come back home. Taylor had Pa and three older brothers to take care of her and the ranch. Maybe one of them had an accident. I wish she'd written more. Her short letter asked more questions than it answered.

Whatever happened, it was over a year ago and probably taken care of by now. Either way, I planned to return to the ranch as soon as I was done with my business. It amazed me that little Taylor could write a letter like that all by herself.

I put her letter away and finished getting dressed. At first, I considered not strapping on the Dragoon but found I felt plumb naked without it. I knew times were changing but I was kind of old fashioned when it came to my pistol. Flagstaff, and the whole West for that matter, was bound to become more civilized but for now, I preferred to be safe rather than sorry.

When I got to the hotel dining room, a pert young waitress, named Glory, took my order and then scurried about her rounds. She was a real cute little blonde but none too friendly. She seemed to have her sights set for a dude and had no time for a poorly dressed cowboy.

There were several travelers coming and goin' as the morning train was about to depart. Some of the locals walked in and sat down at tables to share breakfast and gossip. Just based on their clothing and manner, I'd say Flag was starting to prosper.

I heard a woman's voice coming from the front door and was shocked to see another ghost from my past. There she was, big as life, that pretty girl I'd seen in Grasshopper Flats. She was a bit older and a mite prettier but she was certainly the same girl. She was accompanied by an older man I surely hoped was her father. Sure 'nuff, the Flats was coming to me again.

APRIL 7, 1878

Once again, I recalled every lurid detail. I was drunk enough for two young fools when I staggered out the swinging doors of the "Rainbow's End" and saw her waiting in a buckboard. She was beyond beautiful. I could hardly believe my bloodshot eyes. Since she was waiting for somebody, I figured it might as well be me. It was certainly worth a try.

Next thing you know, I slipped off the board sidewalk as I was approaching her and fell face-flat in the dirt. The commotion drew a crowd so I rose up and gallantly tried to introduce myself properly. Once the laughter died, however, she turned away and pretended I wasn't there. The crowd started to giggle and snicker so I figured she was just playing hard to get. I managed to swing up under the hitching rail and greet her close up. So there we were, damn near nose to nose.

Well, the good thing was, she no longer ignored me. The bad thing was she hauled off and slapped me hard enough to cripple my grandchildren. I spun all the way round, tripped on the hitching post and hit the ground again. When I regained my senses, the crowd was cheering her as she rode off in the buckboard with some old man. Meanwhile, I was eating dirt and trying to figure which way was up.

I lay in the street until some of the "good old boys" from the saloon came out to find where I'd gone. They threw me in the horse trough to sober me up. The evening was still young and I wasn't quite through providing entertainment for folks in the Flats.

SPRING 1882

The girl of my dreams and her escort took a table to my right and I tried my best not to stare. Our eyes met a few times but her mind was elsewhere and I quickly looked away. She wore a pale green dress that really favored her orange-red hair and emerald green eyes. They were just out of earshot but I could hear enough to know they were arguing about something. She was doing most of the arguing and he was doing most of the listening. If he was her father, she was showing him little respect. Wouldn't you know, the madder she got, the prettier she got.

Glory brought my eggs, sausage and biscuits, so I tried to concentrate on breakfast. I had to attend to first things first. I decided to put off skirt chasing and concentrate on the matter at hand. I finished breakfast and left the hotel without any further contact but could imagine her eyes on my back as I walked out. It sure would have been nice to catch her name.

The sign over the battered door read "Cecil Abernathy, Solicitor-at-law and Justice of the Peace." Underneath, in fresh new paint, it read "Pinkerton National Detective Agency", with a big eyeball and the words "We Never Sleep." I remembered Pa warning all of us to keep skunks and lawyers at a distance but I knocked on the door anyway. After waiting a few moments, I heard some scuffling about and a voice muttered, "Come on in."

The tiny office was bleak and not at all what I expected. It was empty 'cept for an old worn out desk fronted by two spindly chairs. There were several sheepskins hangin' on the wall that bore Cecil's name. The glass in the single window was cracked and seemed to be held in place by the dirt that was caked on both sides of it.

Cecil stood up behind his desk but was still mostly concealed by it. He was really short and thin with a moth-worn suit, a bowler hat and thick spectacles. I'm not sure just what I'd expected, but he wasn't it.

I introduced myself as the "Navajo Kid" and he didn't even bat an eye. When I told him my sad tale and intention to seek my long lost family, he listened intently but withheld any direct comments. When I finished up, he started in with his questions.

"Are you able to pay for our services today or are you hoping your new found relations will provide?"

I assured him I had money and would get more as needed.

With that important matter out of the way, Cecil continued. "So, you claim to be a "sagebrush orphan"... a white child taken captive by the Indians?" I nodded in agreement but said nothing.

"Now tell me again, Mister "Kid", when and where do you contend this abduction took place?"

He might not have looked like much, but he sure as shootin' sounded like a real lawyer. "I was too young to know for sure but I figure it was about twenty years ago, somewhere in New Mexico territory." I paused as if to recollect the details of my childhood.

"I grew up around Junction City but we moved around an awful lot. I remember we spent some time near Monument Valley." I was recalling my recent trip through that area and the various places I'd passed through.

"Were you raised as a Navajo child?"

I was really ready for this question and feigned anger and resentment. "No, I was raised as a slave and treated worse than their camp dogs! I kept running off till they got sick of comin' after and just let me be."

My sudden outburst startled him and he was taken aback. "Then how did you...?"

"I survived by luck and wits. I begged, stole and borrowed whatever I needed. I worked at jobs I was old enough for and some I wasn't. I finally got enough money saved up to find my real family and that's what I aim to do."

That did it. I really wasn't upset but surely sounded like I was. Cecil was through asking questions but wasn't quite convinced. It was time I played my ace in the hole, the Navajo medicine bag. I explained what it was and told him he could search it for any clues it might provide. He poured the contents on his desk and we went through them one by one.

I explained the bear claws and arrowheads as being my Navajo toys. The tobacco I claimed as not being of any importance and I denied any knowin' of the gold locket, the stickpin, the matchbook or the lock of hair with the red bow.

Cecil got right to work with his "detecting." He opened the locket and saw the picture of a young Victoria and looked at the lock of hair. Next, he examined the stickpin and wrote down the initials. He was looking over the matchbook when I got up to leave.

Cecil finally remembered the first order of business. "I'll need forty dollars to get things started."

I paid Cecil his retainer in gold coins and he wrote out a receipt. He went back to his "detecting" so I left his office and headed back to the hotel. When I entered the lobby, Kenny was nowhere in sight and the guest register was open on the counter. Right off I found what I was lookin' for. Her signature read Mrs. Megan Black and her home address was given as the S Diamond Ranch. She had taken a single room by herself. The name below hers was poorly written but seemed to say "Trace Cummings." The word "foreman" was printed after the name.

That last part seemed simple enough. The older man wasn't her father but her foreman. But then it hit me. Megan was married.

What the hell did I expect? A woman her age was past her prime if she wasn't married. Where was her husband? Why was she staying by herself at the hotel and for how long? Where was the S Diamond Ranch? The more I found out, the less I knew.

Instead of going up to my room, I decided to walk around and see more of the sights. It afforded me another chance to listen and learn. The town was alive with folks doing this and that, going about their daily lives. Business was brisk in all the stores and shops. For a little while, I stood around and just watched the construction work at the new railroad depot. I even spotted Cecil heading into the telegraph office.

When I passed Goldman and Son Dry Goods Store, I thought I heard a familiar voice. Sure enough, lookin' through the plate glass window, I could see Megan Black. She seemed to be busy shopping and her foreman was chasing after her like a lost puppy.

Trace Cummings was a big man and well built with a red mustache and burnsides. He reminded me of pictures I'd seen of the old Vikings. Megan had him toting a bunch of hat boxes and paying the clerk as she continued to browse. Trace figured to be a top hand and I bet he'd rather stuff a polecat down a gopher hole than follow her around like that. I felt truly sorry for him.

I loitered around in front of the store but stayed out of sight. I wished to meet Megan but I figured there'd probably be a better time. When they left the store, it was a fifty-fifty chance but they turned the other way and didn't see me. I went right in to speak with the shopkeeper, Jonah Goldman.

Jonah looked to be around fifty years old. He was a roly-poly man with thinnin' gray hair and a bushy mustache. He had a quick smile and twinkle in his eye for a paying customer but had neither for me. As I approached, he picked up some clothing and busied himself putting it back on the shelves.

"Was that big red-headed fella Trace Cummings? You know, the 'honcho' of the S Diamond ranch."

Jonah stopped his stockin' but didn't answer.

"I'm hunting a job and some fellers over to the saloon said the S Diamond was short a hand or two."

Jonah still didn't answer but he did turn around to size me up. I could see he wasn't impressed by my clothes or my old six-shooter and was trying to decide if I was worth his attention.

"Yes, that was Mr Cummings.....and his employer. I think I did hear something about them being shorthanded. When he's done playing errand boy for his boss-lady, you'll most likely find him at the Kaibab Saloon." He pointed in the general direction and went back to his stock work.

I figured I'd best buy something if I was to get any more information out of Jonah so I fetched a box of .44 rimfire ammunition off the shelf and tossed a gold eagle on the counter.

Now I got to see the smile and the twinkle. Being an honest merchant, he pointed out that the .44 rimfire was a rare caliber and wouldn't fit my old Dragoon. I told him it was for my Henry rifle.

As he made change he commented, "A Henry's a good rifle. You don't see 'em much anymore. I keep the ammo in stock for a good customer of mine. Lives on a ranch out east of here. He's got an old Henry he uses mostly for hunting."

I forgot who I was supposed to be for a moment. "Say, that wouldn't be the Box H ranch would it?"

He was taken aback by the comment. "How would you know that young fella?"

I had to think fast. "I'm hunting any job I can do from horseback. The Box H is another name I heard mentioned. They said the man to see was named Porter Henry and he favored a Henry rifle."

Jonah chewed on my answer for a moment and then leaned closer to keep his voice down. "Folks talk too much. Porter's a good man. He runs a family ranch and didn't used to hire out but since the shooting a year ago, I hear he's taken on a hand here and there."

"Shooting, what shooting?" I was certain Taylor's letter had used the word "accident" and not "shooting."

Before Jonah could answer, we were interrupted by a high-pitched voice coming from a dowdy old woman racing toward the counter. "Mister Goldman, I simply must see your catalogs. Where was that divine pink bonnet I wished to get for the wedding?"

Jonah looked to the ceiling for assistance but, upon receiving none, lowered his eyes and took a deep breath. "What can I do for you, Miz Harrison?"

She spoke with great impatience and started pacing up and down in front of the counter. "My bonnet. You remember. It's the pink one. I need to order it in time for the wedding. Where is it?"

Jonah took another deep breath, reached down and pulled up two dog-eared catalogs. He gently placed them on the counter in front of her. "Here are the catalogs Emily. Why don't you take them home, pick out whatever you want and come back? There's still plenty of time to order."

Mrs. Harrison started to protest but thought better of it and picked up the catalogs. As she turned to leave, Jonah commented, "That wedding sure has our women folk in a lather. It's been a hellacious bother but it's been good for business. Why, the "Black Widow" spent most of a hundred dollars just this morning."

"Who's wedding?"

He looked like I was addled. "Why hers, of course. The Widow Black has staked out her next victim." He laughed at his witty remark and "winked" at me.

My befuddled look led him to explain. "Miss Megan is the beautiful but somewhat spoiled daughter of Clayton Shaw. He owned the largest cattle ranch in northern Arizona. Their ranch, the S Diamond, is just south of here near the head of Oak Creek Canyon. Since she was an only child, Megan grew up as "daddy's little girl" and got whatever she wanted whenever she wanted it. That treatment has spoiled her for the real world. No young man can ever hope to keep her in the style to which she had become accustomed."

All that talking must have been tiring cuz Jonah pulled up a stool and sat down.

"Until he passed, good old Clayton was lobbying to be appointed as the new Arizona Territorial Governor. The term of our current governor, John C. Fremont, is about to expire and Fremont isn't about to serve another term."

Jonah looked around to make sure no one was listening and leaned closer. "What with her orange-red hair, ghost-white skin and that....well...bodacious body, Megan commands attention wherever she goes. Her life has been one continuous social whirl and let me tell you she's played the game. With all that beauty, wealth and social position, she has had her pick of all the eligible young men in the area and has certainly taken her own sweet time making a matrimonial choice."

Jonah paused to collect himself.

"She manipulates young men for her own pleasure. Many were the times her suitors competed and fought with each other for her favor. She always pretended not to notice, but she was well aware of everything that went on. Why she even brazenly claims to have refused seven marriage proposals and had at least one affair with a prominent married gentleman."

I was taken aback by Jonahs' comments. I chose not to think of Megan that way. All I could think was that Megan was a Widow woman. Even if she were about to get remarried, that changed ever'thing.

I started to ask what the hell he meant by "the shooting" when the front door opened and a family with five or six children came into the store. Kids went ever' direction and all were racin', chasin' and hollerin'. While the mother tried to round up her brood and the father gathered up merchandise, a young couple came in and were followed by an old man with a limp. Now the store was packed and Jonah was bound to be busy, so I decided to let my questions go unanswered for the time being.

As I left the store, I looked across the street at a freight wagon that was tied up in front of the "Feed and Tack" store. There was a young mother sitting on the bench seat holding her baby and a little boy in the back playing with the sacks and boxes. That wagon and the team of horses sure looked familiar. If memory served, they looked just like ours at the ranch. Since I didn't know the woman, I figured Pa must have sold this team and wagon and bought another.

Just then, a girl dressed like a cowboy came out of the "Feed and Tack" and slung a large bag of feed into the back of the wagon. She stopped to say something to the woman and went back inside.

I was stopped dead in my tracks. That girl was a real natural beauty. She wore saddle polished jeans and a yellow print shirt that was doing its best to contain her. Under her battered hat, I could see dark brown eyes and long hair all took up in back. She moved with a strength and coordination that befitted a tomboy rather than a young lady.

I crossed the street and passed the wagon. It sure was our old freight wagon. I could see where I had carved my initials when I was eleven years old. The woman and boy paid me no mind as I walked down the street. I was disappointed that the girl didn't come out again but figured to leave well enough alone. I already had Megan Black to fret about.

My next stop was the Kaibab Saloon. It was probably the oldest building in Flagstaff. You could almost imagine the two whiskey barrels and long wooden plank it sprung from. Being early in the day, only a few crusty customers were there along with a surly bartender. I ordered a beer, sat at a table in the back to watch and wait.

Since good old Cecil was hard at work and wouldn't be getting back to me by tomorrow at the earliest, I could spend the day figuring out what the wedding fuss was all about. And, what was it Jonah said about a shooting? I'd have to chase that story down too. Then I thought of the pretty tomboy, damn, this was getting to be an interesting day.

Two beers and three hours later, I was about to call it quits when Trace Cummings finally walked in. He was chawin' on his bit and in bad need of a drink. He called for a bottle of rye and the barkeep obliged. With bottle and glass in hand, he went to a table and sat down by hisself. After he gulped down two drinks, I went over to join him.

He looked like a man clouding up to storm but I was all sunshine. "I'm huntin' work and I hear you're the man to see."

Trace wasted neither time nor words. "Sit.... drink." He poured some of his rye whiskey in my beer glass and refilled his own. "If ya want a job you can have it. Ever ride herd on a filly?"

"You mean a young woman?"

He shook his head. "Yup. The Black Widder lady needs a chaperone for a couple of days and I've had it." Then he gulped down his third drink.

I had to ask. "You don't believe that Black Widow nonsense...?"

He paused as he was refilling his glass. "Let's just say I've become watchful for snakes, I check my cinch every time I mount up and I get real careful whenever I'm cleaning my six gun."

I had no idea what he meant and wasn't sure what to say. "I was just hunting a job pushing cows around...."

"And you'll have it. Bring her back to the ranch when she's ready and I'll set ya up."

"What would she have me do?"

He swallowed his fourth drink and loaded up number five. "Just do whatever she says. Help her with shopping mostly. Take her out for meals and just watch over her."

Well, this was surely a way to get to know the lady and what was going on with the wedding so I agreed. "When do I start? Should I meet her first to see if...?"

"Join us for supper at the Beaver Street Hotel around seven."

Once again, I figured to leave well enough alone and rose to leave.

"They call me the Navajo Kid. I'll see you at seven."

He grabbed my left sleeve. "Hey Kid.... You didn't drink your drink."

Not wishing to offend, I downed the "boilermaker" and excused myself. He just laughed to hisself and bottomed number five. His mood had improved considerable but I was relieved to be on my way. I headed back to my room to let the liquor settle and collect my wits. Flagstaff was getting almost as crazy as Animas City.

If I got the job, I could find out all I wanted to know about Megan and get to know her in the process. I could at least hang around until Cecil and the Pinkertons got through with their investigation.

If need be, I could take off and go back to Animas City, take care of my business with Miss Victoria, and then return. If I had my own ranch maybe, just maybe, I could talk Megan out of this marriage business and convince her to give me a chance. It was surely worth a try.

On the way to the hotel, I passed by Goldman & Son and thought about getting some new clothes. I had outgrown much of what I owned and the rest was worn beyond repair. I really wanted to make a good impression when I had supper with Megan. Expecting Jonah, I was surprised to meet his son.

Marty Goldman was a younger version of his father only with darker hair and more of it. His bulbous cherry-red nose said he had more than a passing acquaintance with old John Barleycorn. He did, however, have his father's practiced smile and twinkle. It surely ran in the family.

I picked out several wool shirts and two new pairs of jeans. Even sprung for a new broad cloth suit in charcoal gray. I looked at some new boots but mine were still holding up and the money was better spent elsewhere.

I was able to get all the clothes I needed but not all the information. Marty said he hadn't heard anything about the Box H shooting Jonah had mentioned. He did, however, know all of the gossip involving Megan, or as he called her, the "Black Widow." When I questioned the name, he patiently explained the word play.

"The female black widow spider kills the male after they mate."

When I still didn't get it, Marty told me the whole story of the "Widow Black."

"A year or so ago, two of Megan's suitors got in a gunfight and one of 'em was killed. She wore a mourning dress for about a day or two before going back to her usual ways. Then, after a few months, her whole world started to unravel. Her "daddy", the rich and powerful Clayton Shaw, was bitten by a rattlesnake and died from it. One of the strangest things I'd ever heard of. He was bitten while sitting right on his own front porch.

Since she couldn't manage the ranch all by herself, Megan arranged a business marriage to her fathers' old friend and attorney, James Alcott Black. Being almost her father's age, old lawyer Black was extremely flattered by Megan's attentions. The marriage brought him a beautiful young wife while Megan had someone to run her business affairs while she handled all her personal ones. If you know what I mean."

Marty was really getting into the story telling.

"That arrangement served them well for three months until her new husband somehow got himself trampled to death in a stampede. There seemed to be no earthly reason for the stampede or for him to be involved in the first place, but there he was, trampled flatter'n a dried out cow chip. Most folks figured it was just a case of the wrong place and wrong time but it did cause some talk.

Megan's troubles continued when her ranch foreman, Tucker Morrison, found some way to shoot himself right between the eyes while cleaning his six-gun. They found him on the floor of the bunkhouse with his pistol still in his hand and his cleaning supplies laid out on the table. Whoever heard of a man cleaning his gun with a live round in the cylinder?"

I was trying to keep it all straight but his story was getting a might confusing.

"Next thing you know, the latest of her young suitors, Jake Lawson, took a bad fall off his horse when he was leaving her ranch. He was laid up for several months with a twisted wrist, a dislocated shoulder, a broken leg and various cuts and bruises. Now I thought every rider checked the set-up of his saddle before he mounted but I guess Jake didn't. Maybe he was still mooning over Megan but somehow his horse got spooked and took to bucking something fierce. The cinch strap broke and young Jake, saddle and all, took a real nasty spill. That really set tongues to wagging."

To help me keep track, Marty held up his hand and indicated a finger for each incident.

"First, the death of the first suitor and then her father were just considered bad luck. When Black died there was a lot of talk about coincidence but Morrison's death and Lawson's injuries were too much for most folks. After that, they took to calling Megan the "Black Widow" rather than the Widow Black. Like the female spider, she seemed to be killing her mates. Megan was furious but there was little she could do. In less than a year, she descended from the top rung on the social ladder to the very bottom. She's still young, rich and beautiful but few wish to be the next man in her life. Reckon she found someone who hasn't heard all the stories."

Marty claimed not to believe in superstitious gossip but he was amazed that any man would dare to court Megan. Even after all I'd heard, I was amazed any man wouldn't. She certainly was young, rich and beautiful. As I was leaving the shop, Marty added one last comment.

"Oh, I just remembered... that first boyfriend that got shot was shot by his own brother. His own twin brother...just like Cain and Abel."

That sent a chill down my spine. The only twins I'd ever known were my brothers and I was certain that no woman could come between them.

Dressed in my brand new Sunday best, I got to the dining room a little early and shocked Glory. All of a sudden, I was the center of her attention. I guess clothes do make the man. When I told her I was meeting Megan and Trace, she started to warn me about the Black Widow. I thanked her but said I was only looking for a job, nothing more, and had heard all the stories. She hinted she was off at eight if I was interested in seeing Flagstaff by starlight.

Missus Megan Black arrived with her ranch foreman, Trace Cummings, at the specified time. She was very stiff and formal like our supper was a business meeting. The only time she smiled was when she heard my name. Trace, on the other hand, seemed to get a big kick out of the whole affair. He made a fuss over my new clothes and assured Megan I came highly recommended and was quite trustworthy. All the while he was laughing behind his moustache. He didn't know or care how trustworthy I was. All he wanted was to get out of Flagstaff and I was his best way out.

We ate while discussing range conditions, cattle prices, the railroad, and of course, the late Jesse James. I tried to get the conversation around to the big wedding but Trace warned me off with a look that said "shut-up" in no uncertain terms. Megan capped the evening with a discourse on the clothes she bought during the day. I agreed to meet with them over breakfast the next morning and Trace figured to leave right after and I would take over as her companion.

It was almost eight when we finished and I thought about waiting around for Glory to get off work. Then, I thought again. What was I thinking? Didn't I have enough to worry about?

The morning dawned bright and sunny and I was out early to check in with Cecil. He wasn't in his office but I ran into him on his way back from the telegraph office. He held up a telegram and said he had some news from the Chicago office and would report to me later in the day. I explained my new work situation and he just snickered. Seems the Widow Black and her troubles were well known.

In the hotel diningroom, Glory served breakfast with little or no comment. I reckon she was put out that I hadn't stayed around the night before. She was all business and had a hard piercin' look for me.

Trace only had coffee, as he was eager to get back to the ranch. When he left, Missus Megan Black magically turned into Megan, the pretty girl from Grasshopper Flats. Right off, she started calling me "Kid" and seemed quite pleased with our new arrangement. Guess she was as sick of Trace as he was of her.

No matter, from that moment on, we had a wonderful time just wandering around Flagstaff and taking in the sights. I must'a seen the inside of a dozen different stores. Megan shopped whenever the mood struck.

Megan was a truly beautiful woman. She was everything I expected and more. She was very intelligent and well educated and the two don't always go together. She didn't seem to know too much about her own cattle business so I did my best to explain some of the details to her. Later on, it occurred to me that she might have been playing dumb to see how much I knew. If it was a test, I'm sure I passed.

When we were enjoying supper at the hotel, Megan brought up the business about her being the "Black Widow." I could see how much it distressed her. She related the same stories with most of the same details as Marty but with no names. We were just finishing supper when Cecil entered the hotel lobby and motioned for me to have a word with him. I excused myself and followed him outside.

Cecil waved a hand full of telegrams at me and said excitedly. "We know who you are. The home office has everything. You've been a priority case since...."

"Who the hell am I?" I got a little excited.

"Charles Ulysses Farley."

I was so caught up in the play-acting that I believed him. "What kind of name is that?"

"It's your name and it's an important one, I'm thinking. The head man from our Denver office, Arthur L. Finch, got on a train today and will be here day after tomorrow. They wanted to present their findings in person. Oh," he handed me back my two gold eagles, "he said there was to be no charge for the service. They were plumb tickled just to find you."

I thanked Cecil and went back to rejoin Megan. I could sense she was curious but she didn't ask about our conversation. In a town as small as Flagstaff, she probably knew Cecil and his many occupations.

Later on, I saw her to her room and got a notion she might wish to ask me in. Maybe it was just my imagination or my male ego working overtime but either way, I didn't sleep much that night. In my head, I kept relivin' that awful day in Grasshopper Flats

My second day with Megan was even more enjoyable than the first. We were getting to know each other better and I was feelin' pretty good about my chances. Megan had a way of making a fella feel important. Walking around with her made me feel ten feet tall.

I saw Cecil once but he just waved from across the street. We went back in Goldman & Son again when both Jonah and Marty were working. They both seemed amused at the turn of events. As Megan browsed around the store, Jonah "winked" at me several times and Marty just stood there and grinned like a town gossip with a new secret.

Megan sure could spend money. Near as I could tell, she went through another three hundred dollars in the two days I was with her. I had no idea weddings could be so costly.

During our long conversations, she talked in general about the wedding but seldom mentioned her fiancee. It was clear that "Sam", as she called him, had plenty of money and they would be able to live high on the hog after the wedding. I wondered if she was marrying the man or his money.

After a wonderful dinner, we went back to her room and spent another hour sharing each others company. I was careful not to get ahead of my relationship with her although I felt she might wish to. She hugged me and kissed my cheek as I left.

My third day as chaperone started with a quick breakfast of coffee and a buttermilk donut. By now, Megan and I were getting quite friendly and Glory had little to say to either of us. I excused myself after slurping the coffee and rushed over to the Pinkerton office.

On the way, I got the strangest feeling I was being followed but I couldn't see anybody except an old Injun loafing by the livery. It bothered me some but I had other things to worry about. I could hear the morning train pullin' out and figured the "big shot" from Denver was already in town.

The door to Cecil's office was open so I walked right in and met up with Arthur L. Finch, Senior Pinkerton agent from the Denver office. Victoria had warned me about him so I was edgy as a long-tailed cat in a room of rockin' chairs.

Agent Finch had the look of retired military about him. He was just about my height with a slim build and stood as straight and solid as an oak tree. His clothes were smartly tailored and his boots were spit-shined. His graying hair and mustache were trimmed to perfection. He had a stone-cold look about him that made me shiver a little. When he introduced himself, he shook my hand with an iron grip. Cecil just sat down and shut up so I took the last chair and waited for the show to begin.

Finch got right down to brass tacks. "Well, today the Navajo Kid becomes Charles Ulysses Farley. It is a great day for you, sir, and our agency. Your case," he passed me a thick file folder, "has been open for more than twenty years and we can finally claim success for all concerned."

He paused as I opened the file. "Go ahead and read it.... You can read can't you?"

I looked up but didn't answer. Of course I could read. Did he think I was raised up by Injuns? Wait a minute.... he did think I was raised up by Injuns. I had to remember I was play-acting.

I took my time and looked through all the papers. The first thing I noticed was there was no mention of the Upton family. None whatsoever. That seemed mighty strange since I thought they had been the ones to open the file in the first place. I did see Miss Victoria mentioned a couple of times as well as Charles, but no Uptons.

As I read farther, I got more confused. If I was reading right, Victoria had opened the file with a letter requesting they find her lost son. Then there was another letter from a Mr. Smith of Santa Fe that said much the same. They both mentioned the same wagon train that had traveled from Missouri to Santa Fe in September of 1861. There had to be some mistake.

Finch finally interrupted my reading. "There can be no doubt as to who you are, sir. Your age and description are a match and the items from your".... he held the pouch in his hand...."medicine pouch make it certain. *Res ipsa loquitur*."

I knew that last little bit was Latin for "the case speaks for itself." Finch meant it as a private joke to be shared only with Cecil. The funny thing is it was one of the few phrases of Latin that I knew. Pa picked 'em up somewhere along the line and used 'em when they applied. My favorite was *Carpe diem*.

Finch held up the gold locket. "The lady in this picture is your mother. It was taken twenty years ago, of course. Her letter is in your file." He put down the locket and held up the stickpin. "This was your father's. Those are his initials, C. U. F., Charles Upton Farley."

"And this," He held up the used matchbook. " is from their gambling hall in Chicago. I'll bet this lock of hair is your mother's too. As I said, case closed."

Agent Finch produced a thinner file and handed it to me. "Here is a legally notarized copy of your birth certificate. Signed and witnessed in Chicago in front of a Federal judge."

He waited as I looked over the certificate. "On the second page, you'll see how to get in contact with your mother. She currently resides in Animas City, Colorado, and is most anxious to meet you. As you can see from the copy of a telegram she sent us, she was very grateful we found you."

I read Victoria's telegram. It was honey-sweet and just like her. I almost laughed out loud as I read it. At the same time I wondered why she'd lied about the Upton Family. And didn't she say she would have nothing at all to do with the Pinkerton Agency? There was also a Mister Smith from Santa Fe to consider.

Pa always said, if you don't know.... ask.... so I did. "Who's this Smith fella?"

My question caught agent Finch off guard. Maybe he thought I'd skip over the name. "Well.... he's a person with some connection to that wagon train massacre. He wished only to be informed if and when you were located and we have done so."

I knew from the letter that wasn't exactly the truth but I let it go. I wanted to know more about Mr. Smith but I was more interested in what came next. What else did agent Finch have up his tailored sleeve?

Finch reached in his coat pocket and handed me a train ticket. It was a one-way ticket to Durango. "Your mother paid for this ticket so you could proceed to Durango immediately. I'll be on the same train. It leaves at three o'clock this afternoon. I trust you'll be able to join me."

Boy, things were moving fast and damn near perfectly. Taking the train would get me there and back in just a few days. Megan would still be single and I might have land enough for my own ranch. I'd no longer be just a homeless drifter with nothing to offer.

I thanked agent Finch and assured him I would be at the station in time for the train to Durango. I even thanked Cecil for all his help. Then I excused myself by saying "*Carpe diem*, gentleman.... Seize the day." The look on their faces was priceless.

As I left the office, I heard Finch say something to Cecil about getting larger and better quarters. I guess solving this case was going to put the Flagstaff office on a full time basis.

It was just after nine o'clock in the morning so I had six hours to get Megan back to her ranch and return to catch the train. The S Diamond was only an hour away so I should be able to make it easily.

When I got back to the hotel, Megan was almost ready to go. She seemed eager to get back to the S Diamond. Trace had rented a buckboard at the livery so I went to get it. As I was hitching up the horses, I got that funny feeling of being watched again and as before, I saw no one out of place. The old Injun had moved inside the livery but looked to be fast asleep in one of the back stalls.

I loaded all Megan's purchases for transport. She had more than I could have imagined. The bed of the buckboard was full of boxes, cases and shopping bags. It was after ten before we finally rode out of town heading south to the S Diamond.

I would have rather ridden Goner to the ranch but sitting next to Megan in the buckboard had its advantages too. I was really relieved she never connected me with that drunken fool in Grasshopper Flats. We sat close to each other on the buckboard seat and she clutched my arm for a good part of the ride.

As we traveled to the S Diamond, I told her of my dream to have my own cattle ranch. I also let slip some of what was going on between the Pinkertons and me. I didn't tell her ever'thing but just enough to hold her interest. I wanted her to know that because of my "inheritance", I would likely have my own place in just a few days. I neglected to mention I had to con the Pinkerton Detective Agency to pull it off.

The S Diamond Ranch must have covered more than twenty thousand acres of hills and valleys with good grass and ample water. It was well set up and sectioned off. I saw large herds of cattle grazing in three different locations as we approached the ranch house. There must have been more than two thousand head in those herds alone. Trace saw us coming and rode over to welcome Megan and help me unload all the boxes and cases.

Right off, Megan explained to Trace that I would have to be gone for a week or so but would return to work on the ranch. Trace heard what she said and looked at me through different eyes than he had before. He knew Megan well enough to know something had happened between us in the last two days. Her mood was relaxed and her manner was open and friendly. Whatever happened, he surely didn't wish to know. I just figured we got to know each other a little and became friends. I had much to learn about Miss Megan.

When we finished unloading the buckboard, Trace went back to the bunkhouse and Megan and I were left alone to say our goodbyes. We stood close and I took her hands in mine. Then I stared into those beautiful emerald green eyes and prayed for the right words.

"Please wait for me.... to get back."

Megan teased. "Maybe I will and, maybe I won't. I am so very sick of this Black Widow nonsense I just want to get married and get it all done with."

"But if you don't love him...."

Megan laughed in my face. "You silly boy, what's love got to do with it? I certainly don't love Sam and I doubt very much that he loves me. This is a business deal for both of us. He gets a wife with a big ranch, which is what he's always wanted. I get his name, a lofty social position and the security that I need. Did I tell you he might even get himself an appointment as Territorial Governor? That was my daddy's dream."

Then she paused, stared into my eyes and put her hands on my chest. "Things might be different with you, Kid.... if you could afford me. I am sure Sam can afford me and that's all that matters to me right now."

She must have seen the disappointment on my face. "Look, just because I marry Sam doesn't mean we can't still be.... friends. You'll be right here on the ranch and Sam travels a lot, so.... we can see each other."

I put my fingers to her lips to keep her from saying anymore. I was so stunned to hear her talk that way I had no words. Megan would certainly be nobody's blushing bride.

"Does that shock you, Kid?"

I pulled away and got in the buckboard. "Reckon I'll have to hurry up and get back before the wedding."

As I turned the team around and headed down the road, Megan called out. "You do that Kid.... get back here before I get married and become Missus Sampson Langley."

My heart almost stopped. I was glad my back was turned so she couldn't see my face. "Sam" was short for Sampson? Could there be two men with that same name? How well I remembered him and his Mining and Mineral Company.

It was an hour's ride back to Flag and I had a lot of thinking to do. I knew Sampson Langley to be a rich and powerful man who was used to getting his way. I also knew he would stop at nothing to get it. If he was moving into ranching then he was fixing to get even more powerful and he would have his hired killers around to make sure no one tried to interfere. How could Megan even consider marrying such a man? What was it she said... it was just a business deal for both of them? That had to be the reason. Now all my hopes and dreams seemed to be like dust a'blowin' in the wind

Chapter VII

"California at last"

I returned the buckboard to the livery and got to the train station with an hour to spare so I walked out on the platform and sat down on the wooden bench. It was a warm sunny afternoon and the platform and bench had the smell of brand spankin' new lumber so I didn't mind waiting. Actually, it gave me time to think about things.

I paid a week in advance at the livery so Goner would be taken care of and left my saddlebags and rifle at the hotel desk so they wouldn't be in the way on the train. I packed a small carpetbag with just enough clothes and supplies to last a few days.

I was eager to get going and finish with all the play-acting. Should I confront Miss Victoria with her hiring of the Pinkertons? Did she know about the man named "Smith? And, what about Abigail Upton? Was she still involved? If I didn't want the deed to that land so much....

I didn't know what to think about the change in Megan and I was really worried about Sampson Langley but Agent Finch and the Pinkerton Agency were my first concern. If they found out about our little deception, I would get nothing and might even land in jail. I figured it was worth the risk but just barely.

Part of me wanted to ride to the Box H. I had to find out about the shooting or accident but since it happened over a year ago, I reasoned that there was no particular hurry. I couldn't change what happened but a quick trip back home would have to come first when I returned from Animas City.

That said, I couldn't forget Sampson Langley and his Mining and Mineral Company. He ended my mining hopes in Bodie and his man Zimmerman killed old Patch. In Calico, his men killed my partners and forced the sale of my claim. I chose to leave both towns before I had any head-on trouble with him. Was I afraid or just using good judgment? I had a flood of mixed memories when I thought about the round-about way I went from Bodie to Calico.

FEBRUARY 1880

I lit out of Bodie on a gray day about the middle of February. The Sierra's were just about to get hit with a full-blown blizzard. I got out just in time as I heard later they had their harshest winter yet and that was saying something for Bodie. Rumors were the wind was so cold it could freeze a man's gonads rock hard.

Goner and I made our way the best we could through blinding snow and fearsome winds. The weather was so harsh we finally had to seek refuge in an old abandoned cabin. It was pure luck we found it at all since it was almost buried by the blowin' snow. I had run out of options and Goner was about done in.

The "tight" little cabin was built into a hillside and was sheltered on the south by a stand of pine trees. In spite of a hard-packed dirt floor, stonewalls and pole roof, it looked like a royal palace in the middle of that snowstorm. I brought Goner right in with me and we made ourselves at home. There was no grub or wood for a fire but we didn't mind. Anywhere out of that storm was fine with me and I could tell Goner felt the same.

After three days, what little food we had was gone. The storm had let up and it was time to make a run for it. I forced open the door and faced three feet of snow that had drifted up. The drifting was even higher in some places and travel seemed hopeless but we had no other choice but to git. With grim determination born of sheer desperation, we were able to make our way through the waist-high snow and down the mountain toward the Owens Valley.

Even under a foot of snow, the valley was beautiful. We followed the froze-up Owens River as it meandered southward. I was warned to be on the lookout for Paiutes but they seemed content to wait out the storms in their lodges. Majestic Mount Whitney loomed off to the southwest and served as my guidepost.

Somewhere I heard the Owens Valley got its name from Richard Owens, a member of John C. Fremont's party who passed through the area in 1845 but that mattered little to me. As pretty and as peaceful as it was, I was only interested in getting to Bishop Creek. Folks figured they had about three hundred residents and all the comforts of a growing community. I'd already had enough High Sierra winter and hoped for nothing less than a warm bed and hot meals.

When we finally reached Bishop Creek I found that warm bed in the Valley View Hotel. They even had a stable out back where Goner could feel right at home. A young Mexican boy named Chico promised to give Goner the best of care, which he surely deserved. It took a special kind of animal to make the trip down that mountain and I'd be forever grateful.

I stayed put in Bishop Creek and waited for the weather to warm up. The cold and snow had the town shut up tight and folks were getting on each other's nerves. Since I was a stranger, they generally ignored me and I stayed pretty much to myself. I spent the time getting all my gear in shape. Right off I cleaned and oiled my weapons and got my clothes washed and mended. I even got my old saddle repaired at the Clark & Dunlap Harness Shop. I knew Goner would appreciate that cuz it had been riding rough on him.

The grub was hot and the bed was warm but after a week, I had to get back to moving. Bishop Creek was in cattle country where there would be no jobs for several months and I was running out of spending money.

Of course, I had that satchel of gold dust Patch left me but I figured to invest it in some sort of business. It should weigh out about twenty-five hundred dollars but that wasn't enough to buy my own ranch. I'd have to partner-up with someone and find some way to make it grow. Mining, cattle or sheep, it didn't matter. That dust was gonna buy me a piece of tomorrow.

So, after my week of lollygaggin', I headed south once more. We passed through the towns of Independence and Lone Pine as we skirted the Alabama Mountains. A fella at the saloon in Lone Pine told me local Southern sympathizers named those mountains after a Confederate cruiser of Civil War fame. Bet the local Yankees loved that.

I spent the last of my cash on grub for me and feed for Goner since there was still too much snow for him to graze his way south. We were bound for Southern California where I hoped the weather would be warm and the grass green and plentiful. Wasn't California, after all, the promised land of the Bible? I believe Exodus three verse eight said it was "flowing in milk and honey."

Our long journey ended as we passed through Lytle Creek on the way down the mountains to the San Bernardino Valley. I saw neither milk nor honey but I did see willow trees, cottonwoods, sycamores and wild mustard growing on the hillsides. Water was plentiful from all the mountain run-off.

When I finally got to the valley, the trail led right into San Bernardino itself. It was a sleepy little adobe town built by the Mormons in the 1850s. I noticed a little cattle and sheep ranching as well as some small mining operations when I rode in. Another bunch of farmers were planting tiny orange and lemon trees in huge orchards or groves. With all the goings-on, it figured I could find a job and a place to stay.

When a man wanted work, he usually went where he could find it. That meant the local saloons. At the "Gem Saloon", I heard about a local freight company that needed a man to drive stagecoaches and freight wagons. I'd handled a team for Pa and figured a stagecoach would be about the same. Folks said they paid their drivers well and it seemed to me to be a good way to see the country.

The company was "Hughes Freight and Storage." Their loading station was a fairly new building just off the main trail into town.

When I got there, it was full of passengers comin' and goin'. I was told to see Grady Hughes, the station master and I found him out back in the workshop pounding horseshoes on a blacksmith's forge.

Grady, at about forty years of age, was a man of average height but more than ample girth. As with any blacksmith, the weight was mostly muscle and his forearms were huge. He was decked out in coveralls over red long johns and wore a rumpled hat that had fallen in the fire a time or two. He had a big smile and friendly way about him I liked right off. After about two minutes of jawing, he sized me up and offered me the job. He even advanced me a gold eagle to tide me over to my first payday.

When Grady shook my hand to seal the deal, he almost lifted me off the ground. "I like to get to know a man when I give him a job. What do I call you?"

There it was again, that naggin' question. Who was I now? I left home as Monroe Henry. I became Henry Monroe on the trail drive and then Henry James in Virginia City. I switched to James Monroe and became "Jimmy" to my Cornish friends in the gold mines. In Bodie, I was plain ol' Jim Monroe. Grady had asked a good question and he asked it the right way. He didn't ask for my name, only what to call me.

"Henry Monroe."

Grady could sense my hesitation and grinned. "All right. Henry it is."

When I asked about places to stay, he said I could hole-up in the workshop until I could find a place. There was plenty of room for Goner since the station had its own stable and corrals.

Grady warned me ever' once in a while there would be shooting trouble along the line and I'd better be ready. I assured him I would be. Then he looked at my old Dragoon and asked, "Does that old boat anchor still work?"

I suddenly felt out of time and place with that big old percussion pistol. "Yup. On occasion it has also made a pretty fair hammer and a mighty fine Billy club."

Grady chuckled at my explanation. "Well, get yourself a cartridge gun like a Peacemaker when you can. I'll provide the ammunition."

He held up an old scattergun. "I also provide a twelve gauge double-barrel shotgun for the drivers when they're riding alone. We run extra shotgun guards when there's something 'special' on the coach."

"Special?"

"You know.... payroll shipments, bank boxes, ore deposits... 'Special' means something worth stealing."

I took Goner to the stable and rubbed him down. There was plenty of feed as well as other supplies for the horses. I could see that Hughes Freight and Storage had good stock and meant to keep 'em that way. Goner never had it so good and he caused quite a stir with some of the mares, which was to be expected. I'd have to make sure he was well tied or he might get to courtin'.

I brought my outfit to the shop and settled in. I found a loose board in the feed bin and stashed my satchel of gold dust deep in the shadows behind it. I would have to get along on what I made working for Grady. That gold was to be my future.

Grady said he wanted me ready to roll the next morning so I planned to bed down early but instead, I gave him a hand with his metal bending and we shared a couple of beers as the sun went down. Then, agin' my better judgment, we stayed up late. Grady was a talker.

During our ramblin' conversation, Grady told me he was partners with two men from Oklahoma but he ran the business day to day. His partners were investors only and rarely came out west. They had a contract with the Wells Fargo to provide mail and passenger service from San Bernardino to the *Pueblo de Los Angeles*. Since the railroad had taken away the majority of the stagecoach business, freight transportation was now a big part of their operation. Storage was a sideline but took little effort and was pretty easy to keep track of.

Produce, namely fruits and vegetables, was the bulk of the freight business. I was to deliver to markets in and around Los Angeles and *Rancho La Brea*. Then I'd bring back commercial loads of goods for local merchants and ranchers by special order. Grady said it was a good steady business but nobody was getting rich at it.

The stagecoaches normally ran three days a week but were doubled up whenever the trains broke down or got way behind schedule. We took detours to smaller stations to provide service to those the railroad usually by-passed. Mostly, we followed the old Santa Fe Trail right out to the Pacific Ocean at Santa Monica Bay. I couldn't wait to see the Pacific Ocean and was finally gonna get the chance.

The next morning began with first light as Grady had me up with the roosters. We rounded up the horses and got them hitched to the coach. It was an old Concord coach but still in pretty good shape. Normally it used four horses but we could always hitch six for heavy loads or more speed. After two cups of Grady's coffee and some hard tack biscuits, I was ready to roll.

First off, I'd heeded Grady's warning about my old Dragoon and switched guns. When I climbed up into the boot, I was sporting Mal's Silver Star gun belt and the engraved Colt Peacemaker. I'd almost forgotten how great the Colt looked and felt. When Grady saw it, he let out a long low whistle but made no comment.

The coach was full up with eight passengers. Some carried little luggage and kept it with 'em while others stashed what they had in the rear boot. There were five men, two women and a little Mexican girl who was traveling with the younger of the two women. The men had the look of drummers and none were too talky that early in the morning. We had a small mail sack and some extra packages and boxes but nothing "special." It figured to be an easy run for my first day.

Grady gave me written instructions that outlined where and when to stop. It was pretty straightforward. All stops were for team changes but some were also for dropping off and picking up passengers. I noted the stop at the San Gabriel Mission included a short rest and time for grub. The food was never as important as the down

time. Passengers needed to get out of the coach to stretch and un-
wind. Traveling by stagecoach wasn't for everyone. It was endured
rather than enjoyed and could be hard on the very old and the very
young. With all the little detours, it figured to take six hours to get to
the coast, give or take. Given a quick turnabout, I could be back just
about sunset if all went as planned. I figured there was slim chance
of that.

We got no further than our second stop, the Mountain View Inn
in Upland, when trouble started brewing. Our first stop and team
change in Colton had been fast and smooth but that second stop in
Upland included the boarding of two unscheduled passengers. Since
the coach was already crowded, they were forced to ride on top with
me. They were Mexican fellas dressed like *vaqueros* and carried
no luggage. They both, however, were wearing pistols and skinnin'
knives. They weren't the friendly type and acted like they might be
trouble.

About five miles out of the station we came upon a man laid
out face down on the road ahead. From where we were sitting, it
was hard to judge what was wrong with him but he wasn't movin'.
Being suspicious by nature, I pulled the coach up about ten yards
short of the man and checked the trail ahead and behind. I couldn't
see anything but I could feel it comin'.... something was wrong. A
few of the passengers started to get out but I chased 'em back inside.
The two new passengers on top seemed to pay little attention to the
matter.

The *hombre* who was lying on the road seemed unconscious,
but was he? I slowly nudged the team toward him and when the
lead horses got kissing close, he cursed in Spanish and rolled out of
the way. Under him, he had a six-shooter in his hand and was about
to use it. Suddenly, the two men on top made their move but I was
ready for 'em. I jumped the horses with a crack of the whip and the
stage suddenly lurched forward. Both men lost their balance. One
fell off the back of the coach and landed in a heap while the other
slipped to his knees and hung on to the rail for dear life.

The *hombre* on the road fired in haste at the passing stage and missed me but hit his partner. The bullet ripped through his ribs and came out his chest. He lost his grip on the rail and slid down the side of the stage as we careened down the road. The stage ran over his body with a "thump" but he was surely dead before he hit the ground. Two more shots screamed overhead as I drove the stage out of range.

Up ahead about a hundred yards or so, two more would-be stage-coach robbers were blocking the trail. They waited with guns drawn as we bore down on them at full speed. If they thought they had a greenhorn kid driving the stage, they'd made a fatal mistake. When they raised their guns, I shot first and the Colt worked to perfection. I fired four times but two would have been plenty. I don't know if they were already dead as we passed but they sure were lead heavy. The stage kept going and we never looked back.

Well, wouldn't ya' know the passengers couldn't stop talking about what happened. At every stop, those who got off told those who got on and all of 'em held his or her opinion. Everyone stared at me with a combination of fear and awe, specially the young woman with the little Mexican girl. The two of them finally got off at the San Gabriel Mission.

For some reason, that young woman made me feel all "itchy" and uncomfortable. I was sure I'd done the right thing but she made me feel like I hadn't. What would she have had me do different? Maybe she thought I could'a talked 'em out of robbin' us.

I knew right away all the talk would mean trouble for me and eventually for Grady. Once again, the Majors' words came back to haunt me.... "You could be too good for your own good."

We finally made it to the end of the line near *Rancho Malibu* and I got my chance to see the Pacific Ocean for the first time. I walked in the sand, smelt the salt air and watched the sea gulls. I wished for more time to explore the coast but the horses were changed and return passengers boarded before I knew it. They'd all heard about our eventful trip, however, and I was the subject of their hushed conversations. Some were glad for what I'd done and some were agin' the shootings but all were impressed with my gunfightin' skills.

For my part, I was trying to figure out why those men had attempted to hold up the stage. We weren't carrying anything valuable unless one of the passengers was carrying something "special." Maybe it was one of the passengers they were after. Otherwise, it made no sense to me. At least three men had died and for what?

The Wells Fargo station manager in Santa Monica, a salty and sullen feller named Clyde, didn't wish to know anything 'bout the shooting and said so. It was none of his affair as long as the company had suffered no loss. He just wished me luck on the way back and waved us off.

The ride back to San Bernardino went off without incident. I never even saw an indication there'd been any trouble along the way. I guess the *banditos* picked up their dead and lit out. It was just after sundown when we finally got back to the Hughes Freight Station. We were right on schedule.

Grady came out and helped me unhitch the team. If he'd heard anything 'bout the shooting, he wasn't saying. We talked in general about the trip and how the horses handled, the trail conditions and so forth. He did thank me for a job well done but I just wished I could go back to sleep and start the whole day over again.

The following day, and in fact, the whole next week, passed by without any problems. I went back to carrying the old Dragoon, which didn't attract undue attention. The "Daily Times" newspaper in San Bernardino ran a column on what happened but just referred to me as "the new driver." I'm sure I had Grady to thank for that. The last thing I needed was another "gunfighter" reputation to live down.

When I wasn't working for Grady, I usually hung around the station. I cared for Goner and took him on some short rides but I was wary of meeting-up with any strangers. After all the gunplay, it didn't seem possible it could be over and done with. I remained vigilant at all times and kept a watchful eye on my backside.

One afternoon, Sheriff Towne came by and talked with Grady. They looked my direction a couple of times but he didn't bother to question me. Since they seemed to part on friendly terms, I relaxed just a little. Grady had yet to say a word to me about the shooting and I was thankful.

The next afternoon, when I returned with a freight wagon full of oranges from *Rancho de Cucamonga*, I saw a group of people standing by the workshop talking with Grady. I recognized the young woman and little girl that had been on the stage. They were waiting with a group of *vaqueros* and an older gentleman. Judging by his fancy attire, he figured to be a man of considerable wealth.

What they wanted, I could not imagine. As I stepped down and started to unhitch the team, I heard a familiar voice behind me.

"*Què pasa*, Henry? It's been a long time, *amigo*."

It was Carlos Delgado from the cattle drive.

"Carlos. It's so good to see you."

We shook hands and embraced like the old friends we were. All of the other *vaqueros* gathered round to be introduced. The older gentleman, the young woman and the little girl waited with Grady.

Carlos led me over to them and introduced the older man as his *patròn*, Juan Carlos de Estrada. He said Juan Carlos owned the vast holdings known as the *Rancho de Estrada*. Carlos claimed the old man could trace his ancestors back to Alfonso de Estrada who came to Mexico in 1524 with Cortez. With obvious pride, Carlos boasted that both his father and grandfather had worked for Juan Carlos and he'd been named for him.

Juan Carlos was very polite and formal as we shook hands. "*Buenas tardes, señor.*" His riding outfit, boots and hat were the finest quality I'd ever seen. The boots were heavily decorated with silver *conchos* and colorful stitching. Age was catching up to the old man and it showed here and there but he still had a forceful handshake and regal manner. His gray eyes studied me intently and I felt fully measured.

Carlos dropped to his knee to introduce little Elena. She was the *nieta* or granddaughter of Juan Carlos. She was only six years old but was already a beautiful child with black hair and dark haunting eyes. Carlos explained that Apaches killed her parents and she was being raised by her grandfather on the *Estrada Rancho*.

The young woman with them was introduced as her tutor and nanny. Carlos called her Miss Robinson. She seemed very stiff and formal but I could sense another spirit inside. She might even be pert if she weren't so prim and proper.

Carlos went on to say Elena was the only family old Juan Carlos had and the failed stage robbery was really an attempt to kidnap her for ransom. One of the men killed in the robbery attempt worked on the *rancho*. When he went missing from work, they were able to piece out the details. The other four were relatives or friends he recruited to help him with his plan. The two that got away had fled back to Old Mexico.

Carlos saw my reaction to that news and chuckled. "Don't worry. The old man has many friends in Old Mexico. They will not flee for long, *amigo*."

Little Elena, with nudgin' from Miss Robinson, stepped forward and spoke in practiced but perfect English. "Thank you for saving our lives. We will always be in your debt, *Señor* Henry".

I knelt down and said in my very limited "Spanglish." "*De nada, Señorita*, it was my pleasure." Elena broke into a big smile and looked up at Miss Robinson. Then she spoke excitedly in Spanish. Carlos laughed behind me and leaned forward to translate. "She says you are a gentleman and not *el Diablo* after all."

Miss Robinson flushed crimson and Juan Carlos seemed quite amused. Carlos continued to explain as we walked over to the station. "Miss Robinson thought you were too cruel and violent to be any kind of gentleman. She is from back East and doesn't understand the ways of the West. In time, she will."

We held a celebration of sorts in the station house. Juan Carlos brought wine, cheese and fresh fruits from his *rancho* while Grady provided cold meats, *tortillas* and cigars.

As we finished eating, two of the *vaqueros* brought in an incredible saddle. It was coal black and completely hand tooled with sterling silver *concho* trimmings and fancy *tapaderas*. I'd never seen the like of it.

When Juan Carlos indicated the saddle was a gift for me, I was dumb struck. He spoke to me in Spanish and Carlos translated. "He is most grateful for your protection of his young granddaughter. He wishes to express his thanks with the gift of this saddle. I remembered your old beat-up saddle and told him you could use a new one."

I had to agree with Carlos. "You're sure right about my old saddle." Everyone laughed and cheered as I just stared at the incredible saddle before me. It was so beautiful I was almost afraid to touch it let alone ride on it. Goner was gonna think he died and went to hoss heaven.

There was a lot of handshakin' and backslappin' and then the party continued. Everyone seemed to have a good time except for Miss Robinson. She barely touched her food and wanted none of the wine. She sat by herself and seemed to go out of her way to ignore me. Little Elena tried to get her involved in the festivities but to no avail. I'd never seen anyone work so hard at not having a good time.

Finally, in late afternoon, Juan Carlos and his party packed up and got ready to return to his *rancho*. I promised I'd ride over, on my new saddle, as soon as possible. Grady and I watched them ride off into the setting sun.

"Mighty nice folks.... good customers too." Grady commented as we headed back to the workshop. "They do a lot of freight business with us during harvest season. I'd say old Juan Carlos thinks the world of you. It was a fine thing you did, saving his granddaughter."

"Sure, but that Miss Robinson doesn't think much of me. She hates me."

"Well, she ain't no part of his family so what she thinks don't count for squat. She's just another greenhorn from back East and don't know no better. She'll learn or she'll git."

As I hoisted my new saddle and headed for the stable, Grady grabbed me by the arm. "Good judgment comes from experience,

Henry, and most experience comes from makin' bad judgments. You've got the makings of a good man.... you just need seasoning."

"Thanks...." For a moment there, Grady sounded just like my Pa and his words almost brought me to tears.

Goner wasn't as excited as I hoped but I fit the new saddle on him and went for a ride in the foothills anyway. As I rode out of town, I noticed a real big feller decked out like a common cowhand. He showed no pistol but was toting a Winchester rifle and watching me with more than casual interest as I rode past. It was probably nothing. Anyway, I was having entirely too much fun breaking in my new saddle.

Two more weeks went by without incident. I drove the stage-coaches and freight wagons and generally earned my keep. Grady let me stay in the workshop permanently so I was always "around and available" as he put it. I found time to ride over to the *Rancho de Estrada* and had a great time with Carlos and Elena. Miss Robinson stayed away from me again and it was starting to rub agin' my grain. Guess it wouldn't have mattered if she weren't so durn pretty.

Time and again I saw the big cowboy with the rifle hanging around town but he seemed to pay me no mind. I did take notice of just how big he really was and how well made. He had to be six inches taller than my six foot two with broader shoulders, a thick muscled chest and slim hips. He was fit enough to hunt griz with a hickory switch. His huge hands gripped his Winchester rifle like it was a pistol. There was something familiar about him but I was sure I'd never seen anyone like him before. His manner was calm and relaxed but he was watching ever'body and ever'thing while saying very little.

I normally stayed around the workshop at night and fought shy of the local bars. But one night, Carlos came to visit and decided we had to make the rounds of the local *cantinas* to check out the pretty *señoritas*. I did my best to remain sober but it wasn't always pos-sible around Carlos. He was forever chasing the worm at the bottom of the tequila bottle. The music was loud, the *señoritas* were pretty and the tequila went down easy.

We finally landed in Rosita's *Cantina* and got down to some serious drinkin'. Then, before I knew it, Carlos was in a death dance with another *vaquero*. They circled the bar with their knives drawn. They snarled back and forth in Spanish but I couldn't understand any of it. The crowd was alive with blood lust and tightly encircled them as the tension rose.

Carlos struck first with a quick feint and a thrust to the stomach. His victim squealed like a pig caught in a barn door and fell to his knees. Suddenly, two *vaqueros* from the crowd moved in to help their friend. One of 'em hit Carlos from behind and knocked him to the floor. Drunk or sober, he was in big trouble and I had to help. I grabbed the second one from behind and tried to choke him into giving up while Carlos grappled with the first one. The last thing I remember was a woman screaming, the sound of glass breaking and my face hitting the floor.

I woke up on my makeshift cot in Grady's workshop. I had a knot on my head and a headache that roared in my ears like a wounded buffalo. Carlos was sitting on the workbench grinnin' at me. His left arm was in a bloody sling and his shirt was cut to doll rags.

He got up and walked to the hearth where the coffee was brewing in my old pot. "So *amigo*, you finally wake up. You sleep like a *niño*."

I struggled to sit up but my balance was shot. "What happened?"

He poured two cups of coffee. "You don't remember?"

I accepted the cup of coffee and tried to unscramble my brains. "I remember the fight starting, then.... nothing."

Carlos laughed. "The little *mesera* hit you with a bottle of tequila. You were choking her boyfriend. You fell like an oak tree in a *Santana* wind.... boom." He laughed again and sat down on the bench.

I finally sat upright and tried the coffee. It was hot and strong, just what I needed. "Then how did we get back here? You must have lost a lot of blood. "

Carlos looked at his arm and sneered. "Bah, it is nothing. I've been cut much worse by the barbed-wire." Then he pointed towards the station. "It was your *amigo grande*. He stopped the fight and carried us both back here. He is *muy hombre*.... much man."

"You mean Grady?"

"No, the big one they call the *gringo grande*.... the tall one."

I could finally focus enough to see Grady talking to that big cowboy I'd seen around town. He actually made Grady seem small. It was amazing, the size of 'im.

They walked over and Grady was grinnin' like a weasel in a henhouse.

He pushed his hat back on his head and put his boot on the bench. "So which is it? Henry Monroe or Henry James? Stage driver or gunfighter?"

Carlos started to laugh and I didn't rightly know what to say.

"This fella says he's your brother.... Zackariah James."

Now wasn't that something? That huge cowboy I'd seen around town was the older brother of Mal and Josh. He stepped forward, shook my hand and almost yanked my arm from my shoulder. He seemed very happy to meet me but the size of him left me speechless. I started to introduce Carlos but they had already met.

Zack explained he'd heard about the attempted stage robbery all the way down in Yuma. My description and fancy gun belt matched the description he had of Henry James, the gunfighter, so he hightailed it up here for a look-see. He'd been searching San Bernardino trying to find me.

Zack said his family was still trying to make sense of his brothers' killings. He'd traveled all the way to Virginia City to find their graves and even talked with Major Wilkes at the Gold Hill Café but it was me he needed to talk to. It was good to hear the Major and Jenny were still sparkin'.

We had a long talk and I related all the details as well as I could remember. Zack seemed relieved to finally hear exactly how the shootings happened. I left out the part about Mal's drinking but I was sure he'd already guessed that.

I got out Mal's gun and holster rig and tried to give 'em to Zack. He thanked me for the offer but said I was better suited to 'em than he was and should wear 'em with a sense of pride.

I tried to thank him for pulling us out of the fight but he just smiled and said it was something any man would do for a brother. He was right. We shook hands and from that moment on, we were brothers. The James family lost two sons but gained another in return. I would always be a part of their family and got a permanent invite to visit whenever I wished.

After Zackariah left to return to Yuma, I had to deal with old Grady and he was riding roughshod on me. "When were you gonna tell me you were Henry James, the Virginia City gunfighter? And what were you doing getting in a fight down in the *cantinas*? Don't you know better? Men get cut there every night. Sheriff Towne don't even bother with 'em unless there's a shooting. You and Carlos could have been stuck like bulls full of *bandilleras*."

I apologized and promised to stay out of the *cantinas*. Grady just grinned at me, wrapped his big arm around my shoulders and lead me to the workshop. Then he told me to get back to work. Carlos was able to ride so he headed home and I ended up freightin' lemons to the railroad spur.

For the next week or two, we had some young bucks sniffin' around the freight station and asking after Henry James but I was able to stay out of sight and therefore, out of trouble. Driving stagecoach and freight wagons kept me on the road a lot and made me a lot harder to find. Finally the talk died down and I was able to come and go as I pleased. I answered to Henry Monroe but when I wore that fancy Colt and gun belt, I would always be Henry James.

The next six months flew by. I was having the time of my life. I toiled long and hard for the freight company but had time to myself, too. My days off were spent exploring southern California. I spent a lot of time in the *Pueblo de Los Angeles*, getting' to know the town and its people.

Often as not, Carlos would meet me at Buffum's Saloon and Gambling Hall and we would go out and explore the *pueblo* together. I saw the very worst and the very best Los Angeles had to offer. We roamed from the *Calle De Los Negroes* to *Rancho Rodeo De Las Aguas*. Once, we visited the Pico House, *El Ranchito*, and met the former Spanish Provincial Governor, Pio Pico. Some nights, we just watched the sun set into the Pacific Ocean and slept on the beach. We even camped out high in the majestic San Bernardino Mountains. Mount Baldy was over ten thousand feet high and snow capped most of the year. I found California to be a beautiful and bountiful land with some of the nicest people I'd ever known.

I made new friends and visited old ones on the *Rancho de Estrada*. After a time, I even got a mite friendlier with Miss Robinson. I found friendly words from her were harder to come by than hen's teeth but well worth the effort. She was a kind and gentle soul who saw the world as it should be and not how it really was.

Turns out her given name was Katrina and she was from upstate New York around Albany. I made a point to tell her my folks hailed from an Albany, too, only their Albany was in Wisconsin. After her parents died, she answered an advertisement for a nanny position and moved from one employer to another until coming west to work for Juan Carlos. At 22 years of age, Katrina was over the hill by western standards but ever' ounce a lady. She was well educated and strong of mind and body. We went on several picnics and I was content to listen to hear read poetry and speak of life in Boston and New York. It was a world I knew little of but one she desperately longed for.

For a time I thought she might be the right woman for me but in the end, she could never feel the same as I do about too many things. Her upbringing didn't allow for an acceptance of me or the western way of life. To her, any killing was murder, no matter how necessary for self-defense. It was the gentle side of her I loved but it kept her from truly loving me. I hoped we would always remain friends.

We were creeping up on the holiday season but you couldn't tell it from the weather. Ever' day was bright and sunny. The nights were starting to cool off but nothing you could rightly call winter. It was plain to see why so many folks were arriving here from back East. California was bound to get real crowded, real soon.

Just as I was getting used to the idea of staying put, fate sent me out on the road again. One afternoon in early December, Grady showed me a telegram from his Oklahoma partners saying they'd sold the station, lock, stock, and stagecoach to the Wells Fargo Company. Wells Fargo was buying up their contract stations and putting in their own men to run them. Grady would get a share from the sale but as of that moment, we were both out of a job.

I helped Grady pack all his belongings in one of the freight wagons. Everything I owned fit in my saddle bags. When we were finished, there was nothing else to do but stay up late drinkin' and yarnin'. The next morning found us going our separate ways. Grady was returning to his hometown of Lubbock, Texas and I was bound for the *Rancho de Estrada*. Carlos always said I could work on the ranch if I got tired of hauling freight. I was sure gonna miss Grady and told him so.

I was welcomed with open arms at the *rancho* and really enjoyed working for Juan Carlos. The days were long and hard but I was doing what I loved. Goner and I got all our cattle skills back and then some. Although I could never keep up with Carlos and the other *vaqueros*, I was a bunch better than the average cattle pusher. I got a pair of Mexican spurs with the big rowels favored by the *Californios* but I never could get used to their sixty-foot *riatas.*

The only problem on the *rancho* was my future. I had none if I continued to work for someone else. Monthly wages kept a man fit and fed but didn't provide any extra for savin'. I had to have my own spread. I needed to prove myself to Pa and my older brothers. Somehow, I had to grow my small savings and buy an existing ranch, or start a new one.

After our big Christmas celebration and the New Year's *fandango*, I was ready to drift once again. On the fifth of January, I was up early and packed to leave. I said another sorrowful good-by to Juan Carlos and Elena over breakfast and rode out with Carlos. He bid me "*Vaya Con Dios*" as we parted at the front gate and I headed east into the rising sun.

Katrina was nowhere in sight and just as well. Pa always said when I found myself in a hole; the first thing to do was to stop digging. That's how it was with me and Katrina. I was just digging deeper and getting nowhere. It was time to move out and move on.

SPRING 1882

I was suddenly aware of a train coming into the station. Lord almighty but it made an awful racket. I'd been daydreaming on the bench and was unaware of all that was going on around me. Passengers were scurrying about and the station master was directing the loading crew.

I got up just in time to greet Agent Finch as he came out on the platform. Cecil was trailing behind with his luggage.

Arthur L. Finch was all business. "Well hello, Mister.... Farley.... isn't it? Glad you could make this train. It'll be a pleasure to have someone to talk to on the ride. We can get to know each other better."

I wasn't up for any questions and answers session with a Pinkerton detective. Did he suspect something or was he just being friendly? I certainly wasn't the least bit interested in getting to know him. "Perhaps we will. Right now I'm of a mind to get some shut-eye."

I picked up my carpetbag and walked around the two of 'em and up the stairs to the train. They were both staring up at me as I entered the passenger car and my impish nature got the better of my good sense. I quoted the last of my fathers' Latin phrases, "*Pax vobiscum*, gentlemen."

The passenger car was only half full so I sat by a window and tossed my bag in the seat beside me. I scrunched down in the seat and put my hat over my face as if to sleep. I heard Finch enter and sit down behind me. I wasn't about to go to sleep but this way; maybe, I could avoid any of his embarrassing questions. I wasn't any great shakes as a play-actor.

I started to think over my situation again. First, I had to finish this short trip to Durango. Then I'd meet with Miss Victoria to cash in her railroad stocks before I collected the deed to my ranch and hurried back to Flagstaff.

Next, I had to make the short trip to the Box H to see my family and find out about the shooting or accident that happened a year ago. Then, the tricky part, scurry back to Flag and convince Megan not to marry that murdering bastard, Sampson Langley.

Lastly, I had to convince Megan to marry me. It was simple. What could go wrong.... besides ever' damned thing?

The train jolted forward with two shrill blasts from the whistle, and a loud clank from the wheels and couplings. Steam filled the air and clouded the platform. I could barely make out Cecil waving good-by.

The conductor in his rumpled uniform and squared-off cap was coming through the car to collect tickets when I noticed an old newspaper left by some previous passenger. It was a copy of the "Arizona Free Press" out of Yuma, dated two weeks earlier. It reminded me of the James family and my adopted brother, Zackariah.

On page two, right below the banner, was an article about Sampson Langley and his Mining and Mineral Company. It said he was taking over some mine holdings and was having some legal trouble. There were also reports of beatings and at least one murder. It was Bodie all over again.... and Calico. How I regretted most of my time in Calico. Well, it was too late for re-hashin' the past, or was it?

JANUARY 1881

When I left the *Rancho de Estrada*, I headed north and east toward the little town of Calico. It was yet another boomtown built around newly discovered silver mines. Located in the God-forsaken high desert of central California, it offered nothing to mankind except what mineral treasures it might yield. At the very least, Calico figured to be a warmer and drier version of Bodie. With only twenty-two saloons to service its five hundred miners, however, it prob'ly wouldn't be as rowdy.

My plan was to use my mining knowledge and limited savings to buy into a few small claims and help 'em to become bigger claims. If my experience in Bodie taught me anything, it was clear the real money came in developing the claims after they were discovered. I was content to let the prospectors do the hard work of prospecting. Mining still seemed to be the quickest way to grow my small stake into a ranch of my own. It never occurred to me that it was also the quickest way to lose it.

My route of travel took us back into the San Bernardino Mountains and through the Cajon Pass into the Mojave Desert. It was the first time I'd traveled on a toll road. The winding mountain road was privately owned and maintained. The toll was twenty-five cents for Goner and me but going any other way would have cost much more in time and energy.

After the long uphill ride, Goner and I were ready for a rest when we came upon a broken down wagon along the trail. One of their wheels had come apart and a group of folks were trying to get the old hub off and a new wheel back on. Since I was ready to stop anyway, I thought I might as well lend a hand.

First thing I noticed was this wagon was quite different than any wagon I'd ever seen. It was built real tall with wooden sides, a high arching roof and a real door on the back. They'd painted it with many bright colors and put in tiny windows of tinted glass. There was a crate holding three chickens strapped to the side and a goat tied up behind. The wagon was pulled by a pair of the largest and most beautiful horses I'd ever seen. They were black and white like a pinto but much larger. I could make out two men, a woman and a young girl. Their two mongrel dogs spotted me before I could speak and set off an awful racket.

The folks were skittish of me at first but by the time we got the wheel on the wagon we'd become old friends. The older couple, Rye and Lucerna, were gypsies or as they said it, *Romani*. They were nomadic people that lived in their *Vardo* or caravan wagon. The huge spotted draft horses were known as *Vanners*.

The other fella was their driver who went by the name of "Banjo Billy." He was an out of work cowpoke that needed a job and transportation so he hooked up with 'em. The little girl was an Injun half-breed they picked up along the way and sort of adopted. She was about ten years old and didn't speak much. They named her "Syeira", which made her their little "princess."

After the exhaustion of putting on the new wheel, we made camp and got to work on supper. Lucerna and Syeira rustled up some grub as Billy and I got a fire going. As we gathered more firewood, he filled me in on all the details of their group or *Kumpania*, as they called it.

Rye and Lucerna came to the United States in 1860. Slavery had been abolished in their homeland of Romania in 1856 and the *Romani*, who were former slaves, were finally allowed to leave the country for the first time. They were members of the gypsy nation known as *Ursari*. Their tribe was the *Linguari* who were known as singers and poets. They made their living by entertaining folks as they traveled around. Since Billy played the banjo, he fit right in.

The supper was great. Along with beefsteak and taters, they served eggs fresh from the chickens and real goat's milk. The coffee was easily the best I'd ever tasted. Afterward, Billy played his banjo and Rye favored us with a few songs. It was the most pleasant evening I'd had in a long time.

Morning found me stuffing my face again. Lucerna was a great cook and she made delicious buttermilk biscuits. I still couldn't get over her coffee. She must'a added some secret spice to it. I'd almost forgotten 'bout Goner but he was busy cropping grass with his new friends, the *Vanners*, so I let him be.

Rye told me their route would take them right past Calico so it made good sense that we travel together. At their slower pace, it would take some extra time but I was in no particular hurry. The Mohave Desert had been described as "hell without the fires" but it wasn't too harsh in the middle of winter. I could only imagine what it was like in the heat of summer.

Banjo Billy and I became fast friends. Like my old friend, "the Major", he'd been around a lot and had a heap of stories to tell. Rye was easy going and friendly but Lucerna only seemed to tolerate our presence. To her, we would always be *Gaje*, or non-gypsies, and could never be accepted as true members of their *Kumpania*. Little Syeira and the mongrel dogs paid us no mind.

When we arrived in Calico, Rye set up his wagon just outside town and was soon overrun with miners. He sang while Billy played his banjo and Lucerna danced. They passed the hat after each song and the entertainment-starved miners gladly paid the piper. I bid them Godspeed and went into town to check out the local saloons.

As I made my way around, I was amazed ever'one of the twenty-two saloons were full of drinkers. I wondered who was mining the mines. All the small shops lining the dirt streets seemed busy and the streets were full of wagons and riders. Would-be prospectors of all ages, races and backgrounds were parading up and down the dusty streets. The newly built mercantile, which sold mining supplies, had a long line of customers waiting out front. Calico was really boomin'.

I was looking for able prospectors to grubstake. Not just any prospectors, but those who had the look of honest and hard-working men. A proper grubstake could entitle me to a third ownership in any silver they might find. I'd heard tell of a fella in Leadville Colorado, name of Horace Tabor, who wound up a millionaire after "staking" the right men.

I stayed at the Calico Hotel for a few days and bided my time. I watched men come and go and tried to judge the best of the lot. After all, I only had twenty-five hundred dollars to invest and had to be careful. I finally settled on three men who were mining together and really workin' hard.

Their leader, Manfred Becker, was a German immigrant from the coal-mining district called the "Rhineland." He grew up in the mines as his father and grandfather before him but wanted a better life for his family. He had the thick, stocky build of a hard ore miner and worked like a beaver building a dam. He was saving his money to bring his wife and three children to America.

The brains of the group, Morris Pulaski, was right off the boat from Poland where he'd taught metallurgy at Cracow University of Technology. He wished to prove his theory about finding silver deposits in a bluish tinted lead ore called "Galena." He'd set up a crude laboratory so he could analyze the ore. He kept a detailed journal of the results so he could publish his findings.

The last member was the dreamer, Jackson Whitehorse, a young Mojave Indian. His old grandfather had trained him in the art of silver smithin'. He left his village to work in the white man's world but yearned to return with enough money to help his people.

Somehow, these three men developed a common language and pooled their respective skills and energies. Best of all, they kept each other around their claim and out of the saloons. They hadn't hit any real payin' dirt yet but I was certain they would. At the moment, however, they'd run out of store credit and had no eating money.

I offered to pay up their debts and keep them stocked in food and supplies for at least three more months. I wanted a third of their claim but after some hagglin', we agreed on a four-way split. We called our mine the "Four Square", in honor of our new partnership.

It cost me three hundred dollars to get our partnership started and I figured it would take another hundred a month thereafter. With that done, I set out to buy into some existing claims.

The "Blue Belle" and the "Silver Lady" were my choices. These claims were well staked and legally filed with the claim office. Both mines were producing a fair amount of ore but needed capital to expand their operations. I invested a thousand dollars in each for a ten percent ownership. I made sure the papers were properly filed, as I wanted no future problems about my ownership percentage or my proper name. I used James Monroe Henry on all documents.

That pretty much used up my stash of gold dust. Ever'thing I had in the world was on the line but I was sure I'd done the right thing. Then came the hardest part, the waiting.

For the next few weeks, I kept daily watch on the "Blue Belle" and "Silver Lady" and felt assured things were running smoothly. At the "Four Square", my three partners, Manny, Mo, and Jackson, were still struggling but I had faith in them, too. That said, the waiting was killing me.

The winter weather was mild by any standard but included many days of heavy rains, which turned the streets of Calico to mud roads and the claims into sink holes. Bitterness and depression took over some of the miners and trouble was brewing in every corner. The rain had to end soon or the town would explode from the tension.

At the same time, I noticed a change in the newcomers. There were few regular prospectors and more camp followers. Gamblers, footpads and gunmen were starting to show up and so were the sportin' girls. I recognized some of them as being fresh off the trail from Bodie.

One particular group of gun slicks was following a cocky young fella calling hisself "Kid Coyote". He had the "look" all right; a thin, wiry build, sunken yellow eyes, beak nose and rotten teeth. He always had a jaw full of chewin' tobacco and spit whenever and wherever he pleased. There was twisted grain in the wood of that man. You could see it in his face and his movements. He reminded me of a rattlesnake who was shedding his skin cuz that's when they're poison mean and ready to strike without warning. He spent his days drinkin' and gamblin' but I could tell he was waiting on something or someone.

His little band of followers were trouble hunters looking for a leader and he was it. I remembered two of them from Bodie. The one called "Turner" was a hired gun and I think "Hutch" was a sneak thief. All the others were new to me but I knew their type and gave 'em a wide berth.

February and March flew by and I was running out of money. The heavy rains were over but they had slowed all the mining operations. Some of the tunnels had flooded while others collapsed completely. The "Silver Lady" declared a small dividend, which netted me two hundred dollars and I spent half of that re-supplying my three partners. Now the waiting was really getting on my nerves. Maybe I wasn't cut out to be a businessman.

April first brought a real live April fool to Calico. Fresh off the noon stage came my old friend, Sampson Langley. When he got off the coach, you could see him sizing up the town and it's unhappy residents. Somehow, he knew what was going on in Calico and had come to take advantage. Langley was dressed for success and knew exactly where to go to find it. His first stop was the "Last Chance Saloon."

First thing he did was order a "tin-roof "drink. A drink on the house always got ever'body's attention. Next, he made it clear he was in town to buy-up claims and was doing so with gold and not mining stock as was the custom. In almost no time at all, the bunch quitters started lining up to sell and Langley was taking names and claim numbers.

I stayed out of sight but continued to watch and wouldn't you know it? Who should stand right next to Langley at the bar, like an attack dog on a leash, but "Kid Coyote?" He didn't take an active part in the dealing but ever'one that had a question about "how much" or "how soon" found themselves staring the "Kid" in the face. He answered all of their questions without saying a word. He just spit tobacco in their general direction and waited for them to reconsider, which they generally did.

I hurried away to warn my partners and tell them to be extra careful. Kid Coyote and his pack of wild dogs were not to be trifled with. 'Specially if they were taking their marchin' orders from Sampson Langley.

The following morning, I got one of the biggest shocks of my life. I was handed a flyer that informed me the Langley Mining and Mineral had purchased controlling interest in five claims and were temporarily shutting 'em down. The "Blue Belle" and the "Silver Lady" were two of the five they were closing.

It was an old trick in a minin' town. The majority owner could shut down the operation and wait out the minority owners. When the small investors ran out of money or patience, the majority owner would offer to buy their shares at pennies on the dollar and end up owning the whole she-bang. With that done, he could start 'em up again and have all the profits to hisself. It was a cutthroat way to do business but legal and many a fortune had been made in just that fashion. Without success at the "Four Square", Langley would have me over his barrel like the other investors.

Sampson continued to stir the pot but it was Kid Coyote that brought it to a boil. Whenever someone challenged the low price offered for his claim, he suddenly had a fallin' down accident or worse. One miner was found with a broke neck at the bottom of his own mine shaft and another, name of Harper, got hisself shot in a bar fight. He was gunned down by Abe Turner, one of the Kid's pack. Some said Harper was unarmed but Turner had three witnesses who swore the old miner was not only armed but had actually drawn first. There was no real law in Calico to settle the question so nothin' was done.

In the middle of all the tension and strife, we struck a bonanza. Morris came to me with a sample of the ore, which assayed at several thousand dollars per ton. It figured to be the richest strike in the whole damn town. He was certain we'd struck the mother lode. It would be hard to keep the secret that we were gonna be rich.

As it turned out, it wasn't our secret for long. The big mouth assay clerk was shouting it from the rooftops before an hour was up. At the "Fore Square", we barely had enough time to share a champagne toast when the assault began. Would-be miners and claim jumpers came from all directions but the four of us stood our ground and defended our mine. There was some scufflin' and shoutin' but I ended it for a while with a salutation from "Colonel Colt". We established an uneasy truce and went back to work.

Now that we'd found our bonanza, could we hang on to it?

That was the question two days later when Sampson Langley approached us. He gave me a hard look when we met but didn't seem to recognize me from Bodie, which was just as well. The four of us had been fighting off the claim jumpers for forty-eight hours straight and were bone tired.

I had to admit his points were well considered. How could we work our claim and defend it at the same time? We couldn't afford to hire guards or more miners to get the job done but he could. If we would sell out at his price, we could leave Calico as relatively rich men and need not worry about the mine any longer.

We took a vote and it was four to none agin' selling. Sampson accepted our decision with a knowing smile and wished us well. In a pig's eye. The attacks on our claim became more threatning and more frequent. Rifle shots whizzed over our heads and some of our spare shoring timbers were set afire. It was crystal clear to all of us Sampson Langley was behind all the turmoil but we couldn't prove it. He was used to getting what he wanted and wasn't about to take "no" for an answer.

After an exhausting week of little sleep and less mining, things started to return to normal. Other mines in the immediate area were hitting hi-grade veins and it looked like we were off the hook, or so we thought. A man like Langley had too much greed and pride to let us be.

The harsh reality of our situation became clear when three men jumped Jackson on his way back to the mine after picking-up supplies. They beat him to within an inch of his life. He was found unconscious with a serious concussion and several broke ribs. His face was stomped-on so badly that his nose was smashed, several teeth were knocked out and his left eye was damned near torn from its socket. Old Doc Edwards said even if Jackson recovered, he'd never be able to see out of that eye again. All he had going for him was his young age and his Injun toughness. I guess it was a small miracle he even survived the attack. The three men got clean away but a good guess would have been Kid Coyote and two from his pack'a jackals.

The doc kept Jackson at his place and we took turns guarding him. He never came to his senses so we never found out if he knew who'd attacked him. Two days later, the shack next to the doc's place caught fire and seven buildings burned down before the volunteer firefighters could put it out. Jackson was burned alive and so was

Morris, who'd been on guard at the time. The doc said Mo might have been dead before the fire but his body was so badly burned he couldn't tell for certain.

Well, Manny and I knew for certain. Langley was bound to have his way, one way or the other. We both wished to fight to the end but we knew it was hopeless. I knew Manny was in it for his family so I signed over my quarter share to him so he could sell the complete claim to Sampson and git. I still had my ten percent of the "Blue Belle" and "Silver Lady" and the hope they would pay off someday.

That was the second time I'd backed away from a confrontation with Sampson Langley. Was it my fear of the man or just good old common sense? Either way, it stuck in my craw. I left Calico the next day aiming for Leadville, Colorado. It was another boomtown awash in the agony and ecstasy of instant fortune and I figured to give mining one more try.

After a long and sobering ride, Goner and I arrived in Leadville. We found a town that was livin' and dyin' all at the same time. It had originally been called "Cloud City" because of its elevation of over ten thousand feet. By actual count, it had eighty-two saloons, thirty-five bawdy houses, seven churches and one school to service some twenty thousand residents. It had fancy buildings like the Grand Hotel and the Tabor Opera House but it also had thousands of shacks and tents where life and death were at odds with one another.

Leadville was a testament to the adage that where you found gold, you found trouble. What little law they had was the law of fang and claw. Might was always right. It wasn't quite as bad as Bodie but a lot worse than Calico. There were a hundred homicides before they had their first trial and conviction. Then, they had a double hanging and ten thousand folks showed up for the show. It was just another boomtown built on the combination of lawlessness and get-rich fever.

The deplorable livin' and workin' conditions in Leadville finally made it clear that mining was never gonna work for me. I had to get back to something stable, something I knew so I decided to leave the day I arrived, July 15, 1881. I'll always remember the talk of the town was the death of the outlaw Billy the Kid. Rumor had it he was shot in New Mexico, the day before, by Sheriff Pat Garrett. Billy was another outlaw that was a hero to some. Buffalo Bill, Oscar Wilde and Susan B. Anthony visited Leadville in its heyday but the folks were more apt to remember the visits of the James Boys and Doc Holliday.

I had nowhere to go and nothing to do but as luck would have it, I rode out of Leadville and ran smack into Banjo Billy. Fate had brought us together once again. He sure was a sight for sore eyes. Seems that after leaving the gypsy caravan, he'd taken a job nurse-maidin' cows at a local ranch called the Circle K. He assured me that they were still short-handed and I could find work on the ranch.

The next morning he took me to their round-up and I showed 'em my recently acquired riding and roping skills. I was a perfect fit and was hired on the spot. It would be good to be working off the back of a horse again.

After a few months of normal ranch work, winter came upon us in a hurry. Everyone bedded down and I ended up in a line shack till spring. I saw Billy and some of the other hands when they stopped by or brought me supplies. Good old Sissy came by with special treats once in a while too. I had plenty of time to read the outdated papers they brought me.

September of 1881 saw the death of President Garfield and the ascension of Chester Arthur to be the twenty-first President of the United States. That sure set tongues to waggin'. The biggest news of the year, however, came on October 26th when the Earp Brothers and Doc Holliday shot it out with the Clantons and the McLaurys at the O.K. Corral in Tombstone, Arizona. For weeks, it was the subject of almost every conversation west of the Mississippi River. Folks argued about the shootout and those involved.

My tattered and worn out copy of the "Tombstone Epitaph" seemed to say it all with the headline, "Three Men Hurled Into Eternity". They were referring to Billy Clanton, and the McLaury brothers, Tom and Frank. As with most ever'thing in life, folks held strong opinions about the Earps. They were either heroes or villains depending on the point of view.

It was awful cold and lonesome in that shack but I had time to think things through. I finally decided it was time, even past time, that I go back home and face-up to my fears. When spring arrived, I was ready.

Chapter VIII
"Alias Charles Ulysses Farley"

SPRING 1882

The train was running smoothly and the gentle swaying of the rail car was about to put me to sleep. The newspaper article about Langley included a list of his holdings and mentioned Bodie and Calico along with Virginia City, Denver and Santa Fe. He was a rich and powerful man who looked to be more so. I wondered if he'd ever reopened the "Blue Belle" or the "Silver Lady". Did he know I was a minority owner? Would he remember me from Bodie? He was a ruthless man operating beyond the law and totally without conscience. What would happen if I challenged him over Megan? Ah, Megan. I fell asleep hoping to see her in my dreams.

When I awoke, the train had stopped for water and most of the passengers were outside stretching their legs. Since agent Finch was still sitting behind me, I decided to strike up a conversation. He was friendly enough and at first, we kept our comments short and to the point. I figured we might as well try to get along since we still had a long ride ahead of us.

The more we spoke, the easier it became. I sure was relieved when Finch just wanted to converse in general terms and not ask any questions. I guess he'd bought my story and wasn't concerned with my case any longer. He said he looked forward to meeting Miss Victoria, as she was well known even in Denver. He referred to the picture in the gold locket and wondered what she looked like today since she had to be getting on in years.

I almost forgot myself and told him how good she looked now and that was a rude wake up call for me. Finch might be relaxed and friendly but he was first and last a sharp detective. Wasn't their motto "We Never Sleep?" Maybe he was still working and not just talking. I'd have to be careful and remember who I was pretending to be. I had to continue being the Navajo Kid for a little while longer.

Finch did ask what I would like to do now that I'd located my family and I found myself telling him the God's honest truth. I wanted a ranch of my own. He said he understood my feelings and wished me well. After that, we seemed to get along fine and I wasn't aware of any "loaded" questions.

Since we had nothing but time, and Finch loved to hear hisself talk, I got to hear all about Allan Pinkerton and his National Detective Agency.

Pinkerton had been a deputy sheriff in Chicago until he opened his detective agency in 1852. He became famous after solving a series of train robberies. Following the election of 1860, he was given the task of guarding President-elect, Abraham Lincoln. On the way to Lincoln's first inauguration in 1861, Pinkerton uncovered and foiled an assassination attempt on the new president.

At the start of the Civil War, Pinkerton helped form a spy network that was to eventually become the U.S. Secret Service. Young Arthur Finch was one of his first recruits. Finch said he spent most of the war years as a personal bodyguard to President Lincoln. He made it perfectly clear, however, that Edwin Stanton, Secretary of War, and Colonel Lafayette Baker were responsible for presidential security on April 14, 1865. That, of course, was the night John Wilkes Booth murdered Mr. Lincoln at Ford's Theater. Pinkerton and Finch were back at work in Chicago at the time. Finch said he was absolutely positive that he would have prevented the assassination.

The façade of their three-story Chicago headquarters bore the damned logo, "We Never Sleep", with a huge black and white eyeball, which became their trademark. Because of this, their detectives were called "private eyes." I mentioned I'd seen the logo on Cecil's door and Finch predicted they would be opening a proper office for Cecil in the near future.

The train pulled into Durango as the sun was rising in the east. The day was clear and cool with the scent of pine in the air. We were all awakened by the metallic screeching of the brakes as the train shuttered to a halt. When we got off the train there she was, "Mom."

Miss Victoria was all smiles when she met us. She wore a lilac-colored dress cinched up to overflowing with a matching hat, shoes and parasol. Bud, the bartender stood at her side. She must have known Finch would be with me, and Bud must'a been told about our little scheme since they both greeted me like I was a stranger.

Then, Victoria made a big fuss over finally seeing her long lost son. There was huggin' and kissin' aplenty. She laughed and cried in equal measure as I tried to keep a straight face. Finch was so taken by Victoria, as were most men, he probably wouldn't have noticed if I'd laughed out loud.

Agent Finch walked Miss Victoria to the other end of the plat-form and concluded their business out of earshot. He gave her some papers and she gave him an envelope, which I took to be payment for services rendered. Bud just gave me a knowing "wink" and whistled a little tune. I think he was enjoying the charade. I wanted to ask 'bout Slick but figured I'd find out soon enough.

With their business complete, Finch bid us good-by and got back on the train. We waved as the train pulled out and sighed a collective sigh of relief as it lumbered out of sight. Victoria was all smiles and threw her arms around my neck.

"You did it." She waved the legal papers Finch had given her. "This is all we need."

"It went just like ya said it would."

We got in the buckboard and headed down the main street. Miss Victoria was chattering away about the current value of the stocks. She said the railroad was buying up their outstanding stock at a premium price and a lawyer right here in Durango would act as their agent.

I was thinking how things hadn't gone exactly as she said. Abigail Upton was not mentioned in the report. Victoria was the one who hired the Pinkertons to find me. They were working for her all along. And there was some guy named Smith who was somehow involved. Did Victoria even know about Mister Smith?

Before leaving Durango, we pulled up in front of the Law Office of Sparks and Donovan. Miss Victoria and I went in and met with Attorney Edgar Sparks while Bud tied up the horses and joined us after a few minutes. The office had the feel of a courtroom and lawyer Sparks certainly looked like a judge. He was expecting us and got right down to business.

We hovered like hawks above a gopher hole as he looked over the legal papers Victoria got from agent Finch. After giving them considerable attention, he finally seemed satisfied that ever'thing was in order.

First off, I signed over the U.P. Railroad stocks. I noticed right away they were only made out to Charles U. Farley. Victoria's name was nowhere to be seen. She'd lied to me about that, too. Victoria didn't need to sign a damned thing.

When Sparks wrote out a bank draft for just over thirty-eight thousand dollars, it was made out the same way, Charles U. Farley. At Victoria's urging, I signed the draft over to her with lawyer Sparks and Bud acting as witnesses. This whole deal started smellin' like a polecat under the porch, but I didn't know how to stop it.

We quickly left the attorney's office and headed toward Animas City again. Victoria's double dealin' bothered me but it was already too late to do anything about it. Anyway, it was a short ride on a beautiful spring morning.

I was reunited with my old friend Slick when we got to The Farley House. This time, Victoria introduced him as Mister Sylvester Glick. He was to be her escort and traveling companion back to Louisiana. Now, at least, I knew how Slick got his nickname, as today he looked a lot more like a "Sylvester" than a Slick. It'd been over a month since he was shot but it seemed like he got his spirit shot along with his body. He was moving about with the help of a cane and seemed to have lost a lot of weight. His face was gaunt and his eyes were sunken. It made me wonder if Goldie's death had anything to do with it. The color of his face reminded me of a unhealthy corpse. He said he was getting better but I wasn't so sure.

The Farley House hadn't opened for business yet so we had the place pretty much to ourselves. We sat at a table and Victoria showed Slick the bank draft. They both seemed to get excited as they looked it over. Bud brought a bottle of Champagne to the table and we toasted to our futures. It was early for me to be drinking so I went real easy on the toast. I would have been much happier with a home-style breakfast like Bobby and his mother served-up across the street.

Victoria brought out the land deed and handed it to me wrapped in a red bow, just like the lock of hair in my medicine pouch.

"Thank you, Mom."

I opened the deed and looked it over. It was for six thousand acres in Northern Arizona. The legal description and location meant nothing to me but I figured the directions could come later. I stuffed the deed in my shirt pocket and rose as if to leave but Victoria put her hand on my arm and gave me that "look."

"Now son, don't be in such a hurry. Wouldn't you like something to eat, or drink or... anything else?" She casually looked toward the stairs.

I followed her eyes and looked up to see Conchita, slowly sashayin' down the staircase, smiling at me. She was truly beautiful and dressed to kill but her entrance felt like a planned event. Warning bells started going off in my head. From the reflection in the mirror, I could see Bud move to the far end of the bar behind me and to my right. I could sense the jaws of a trap closing down on me.

I backed up a little and tried to say just the right thing. "I sure thank ya for the kind offer, but I would really rather...."

Out of the corner of my eye, I caught Slick, as bad off as he was, extending his right arm down his side so his sleeve gun could slide into his hand. Before he could get off a shot, I drew my Dragoon and laid the barrel across his forehead. He went head over heels and took the table and chair with him. His face was covered with blood and he didn't move after he hit the floor.

Suddenly, Conchita screamed and I turned just in time to see Bud pointing his double-barreled shotgun in my direction. I aimed for his shooting arm but he moved as I fired and my bullet caught him in the throat. The scattergun went off into the chandelier and crystal glass showered all over us. Bud was dead before he hit the floor and the gun slid across the bar, fell off the end and knocked over a brass spittoon.

When I turned around, I was facing Miss Victoria and her Baby Patterson revolver. She had me dead to rights, so reluctantly; I let the Dragoon slide down to the floor.

"That's a hell of a way to treat your long lost son."

Victoria seemed like a whole other person. Her face was beet red like an expectant boil and she was mad beyond reason. She looked down at Slick and screamed at him. "Can't you do anything right?"

Now, Slick might have already been dead for all I could tell but Victoria took the guesswork out of it. She put a bullet in his chest just to make sure.

"That's for Goldie, you bastard. Did you think I didn't know?"

Suddenly, Victoria stopped her screamin' at Slick and regained control of herself.

"And now!" Her voice was as cold as ice as she turned the gun toward me. "It's your turn to die."

I dove for the overturned table and her reaction time was a bit slow. Her first shot grazed my right arm and burned its way across my back. With her second shot, her aim was no better and the small caliber bullet dug into the solid oak table but didn't pass through.

Then a much louder shot went off and Victoria froze. I turned and saw the silhouette of a man standing inside the front doors with the morning light at his back. I couldn't make out his features but he was a tall man and well dressed in a white suit and wide plantation hat. He held a Remington Frontier .44 revolver pointed at the ceiling and seemed to be staring at Miss Victoria.

Anger and fear rendered Victoria temporarily mute but she finally got back half her voice and gasped. "You?"

The man laughed at her hoarse voice. "Yes, my love, after all these years. Now drop your little toy gun or I'll put a large ugly hole in that beautiful body of yours.... and that would be such a waste."

Victoria collapsed in a dead faint. The Patterson fell on the floor and the man walked over to pick it up. Reckon he knew her pretty well since he never took his eyes off 'er while he did it. Then he looked at me and smiled. "Well.... good morning, son. Should I call you Charlie or Chuck?"

I was taken aback and merely mumbled "Charlie" as I looked from the man to the picture on the wall and back again. No doubt about it, he was some twenty years older but it was him all right, Charles Upton Farley.

I got to my feet as he righted the table and sat in one of the chairs. I felt the burning of my wounds and winced as I sat down at the table. Lou, the other bartender, and the rest of the girls were peering over the balcony or coming down the stairs. Charles directed Conchita to tend to my wounds and ordered Lou to fetch a bucket of river water special for Miss Victoria.

Folks were crowding around outside the front doors to see what the shooting was about but Lou shut the doors to keep the onlookers at bay. He told the crowd something about a drummer showing off his new guns. That would hold 'em for a while but sooner or later somebody would have to explain two dead bodies.

Charles looked over all the paperwork from the Pinkertons, folded the bank draft and put it in his jacket pocket. "Well from here on the Navajo Kid is dead. You're my son, Charles Ulysses Farley. Reckon I will just call you Charlie. That sounds better than Chuck don't you think?" I nodded agreement.

He was about my height and weight and filled out his fine white suit through the shoulders and arms. He looked ever' bit the southern gentleman. Being in his mid-fifties, his hair and mustache were going gray but his eyes were still a deep blue. Victoria actually told the truth about that.

Conchita bathed my arm and back with hot water and tried to apologize for her part in the distraction. Whether intentional or not, her scream alerted me to Bud's bushwhack attempt so I figured we were about even. I could never stay mad at her anyway. After all, she made bandages for me from her petticoat.

When Lou arrived with the bucket of ice-cold river water, Charles took it from him and dowsed Victoria. Now I'd never seen a wet wildcat but I got a good idea what one might sound like. Miss Victoria screamed and swore worse than a mule skinner forced to take a spring bath. It took a full minute before she stopped her tantrum and settled down.

Victoria glared at Charles but he just grinned back at her as she spoke through clenched teeth. "You've been alive all these years and you let me think you were dead?"

"It was a small miracle I survived the Indian attack and I figured it was best to leave it that way." He was playing with the Baby Patterson revolver. "The last time I saw you, you tried to kill me with this little toy pistol. Do you remember?"

Miss Victoria was regaining her composure and seductive nature. "It was wrong and stupid of me to do that. But you cheated on me and I was so much in love...."

Charles laughed out loud. "Vicki, you haven't changed one bit. You're still the same lying whore you used to be."

In a blind rage, Victoria rose to strike him but he hit her first with a backhand that sent her spinning to the floor once again. She lay there in a heap just blubberin' and cursin'.

"Should have left you passed out. Just like a player piano, if you're not upright, you're grand." Charles laughed again at his joke.

After watching Victoria for a few moments, Charles called for a bottle of brandy and poured a glass for each of us. He said it would ease the pain of my wounds. Then he proceeded to tell me the real story about him and Vicki, as he called her. It sure was a different version from the one I'd heard.

First off, his middle name was Ulster and not Upton. He knew nothing of any family from Carolina named Upton. He reckoned Victoria must'a made all that up. Charles' Irish parents named him for their homeland. They emigrated from Londonderry, in Ulster County.

Secondly, Victoria's real name was Vicki Bodine. When Charles met her, she was a sportin' girl in a New Orleans brothel with a five-month-old "whorehouse bastard" to take care of. She'd been raised in the swamps and was obsessed with leaving them and her baby son far behind. Charles was a gambler down on his luck and Vicki was a bayou girl with big city dreams. They partnered up and started drugging her customers so he could lift their wallets. They got caught by a suddenly sober deputy constable and were forced to flee New Orleans and head out for Chicago in 1860, long before the war started. Charles was adamant they were business partners and sometimes lovers but never married.

Charles did admit to winning that big poker game and all the money like Victoria said, but she neglected to mention he was living with a young cleaning girl named Lacy. Lacy, like Cinderella in the Charles Perrault fairy tale, was forced to care for her older "sisters" and never allowed to go out. Well, good old Charles played the part of Prince Charming and got her pregnant. Ultimately, she bore him a son on July 23rd, 1861 and died during childbirth. The boy, Charles Ulysses Farley, was born strong and healthy but Victoria was so angry and embarrassed by the birth she tried to kill both Charles and his son. She hired a private nurse to strangle the baby and planned to shoot Charles herself.

The plan failed when the nurse couldn't bring herself to kill the baby and Victoria couldn't shoot straight. Charles escaped with his life and his son.

Soon after, Charles left Chicago with his month-old baby and joined up with a wagon train heading west by way of the Santa Fe

Trail. That's when Victoria hired the Pinkertons to track them down, claiming to be the boy's mother.

By the time the wagon train reached Santa Fe, Charles had tired of driving his own wagon and hired a teamster to handle it from there. They left the main train and headed due west with five other wagons. When they were a week out of Santa Fe, the Navajos attacked and everyone was massacred. The teamster's mutilated body was mistaken for Charles, who'd been off hunting with his Sharps rifle when the attack came. He returned to find ever'one dead and his son missing. Still in shock, he made his way back to Santa Fe and has lived there ever since.

I was trying to decide who or what I could believe. Victoria had made up an elaborate story but it wasn't holding water. She sat on the floor and listened as Charles related his version. Her silence spoke volumes.

As Charles paused, I asked. "So, I reckon you're Mr. Smith?"

He looked mildly surprised and chuckled. "So the Pinks told you about me. I wanted to know whatever she knew whenever she knew it. You are my son, not hers. Those U.P. Railroad stocks were meant for you. That's why she tried to kill you. I knew she'd try to get her delicate little hands on that money."

Suddenly it hit me; he really thought I was his son. He believed the report of the Pinkerton Agency. I had to figure out what to do next. Should I tell him the truth? What would Victoria say if I did? Who else besides Slick and Bud knew what was going on? Charles had the bank draft but what about the land deed in my shirt pocket? Things were getting out of control.

One hour and several glasses of brandy later, my wounds had gotten a sight better or at least I certainly thought so. I was watching a subdued Victoria listening as Charles read to her from the book of reason. She held a cold compress agin' her swollen cheek and sullenly paid attention.

He offered her ten thousand dollars if she would pack up and leave at once. The afternoon train to Denver left at four o'clock and she was to be on it. The money would get her back home and be enough to start up whatever business ventures she had in mind.

The alternative was to stay around and get nothing. She could pursue him legally or otherwise but Charles said he'd see the money burn in a bonfire before he gave her a cent. Her choice was pretty clear and being a "reasonable" person, Miss Victoria wisely accepted his offer.

He forced her to sign over The Farley House to Lou, Conchita and the other girls. They could run it or sell out as they saw fit. This insured their silence concerning the morning's shootings. Otherwise, Victoria could go to jail for Slick's murder and we'd have to find a way to explain Bud's death.

The girls helped Victoria pack her belongings and Charles and I finished off the brandy. He informed me that my middle name, Ulysses, did not honor that damned Yankee general and U.S. President, but the Homeric hero of the Iliad and the Odyssey. He rambled on and on about some wandering hero who slew dragons and rescued fair damsels but I had no idea what the hell he was talking about.

I still didn't know what to tell him. So far, Victoria had kept our little secret a secret and I figured she'd continue. There was no telling how he'd take knowing I was an imposter. It was in her best interest not to tip over the apple cart so she could collect her money and leave. I was mostly concerned with the deed to the land and decided to ask Charles about it.

I took the deed from my pocket, unrolled it and slid it over to him. "Victoria gave this to me. I reckon it's yours."

He glanced at it and chuckled. "I bet she did. It would be mine if it was real but it's only a copy. The original deed bore the notary seal from the Federal Court in Chicago. It was part of my winnings in that poker game. I had two copies made so I could stash the original in a safe place. Victoria had one copy and I had the second hidden in your cradle. I suppose it got burned up with the wagons."

"So this deed.... or copy.... is worthless?"

"Yup. She gave you a handful of air, son. I was planning to settle on that ranch land and that's why we left the main wagon train to head west with the others. We were bound for northern Arizona. That land is somewhere near the new town they're calling Flagstaff."

"Do you have the original deed?"

"No, I don't. I'm afraid it was lost along with the wagons. Without it, we have no real legal claim to the land. This copy tells you the legal boundaries but I'll bet some squatters have settled on it after all this time."

Well, so much for my big plans. My ranch was gone and with it, any chance I had to marry Megan. Charles returned the deed and I put it back in my pocket.

Charles could see my letdown and tried to cheer me up. "You'll still have most of the bank draft, about twenty-eight thousand dollars. That money will buy a lot of land most places and stock it, too. If that's what you have in mind."

In my brandy-clouded mind, I'd forgotten about the rest of the money because I'd been so focused on the deed. But the money wasn't mine. I wasn't his son.... and I had to tell him.

Before I could speak, Conchita started to fuss over my wounds again and distracted my attention. She was very good at that. She made an excellent nurse as she had a gentle and loving touch. Charles went to make sure Victoria was getting packed to go.

Conchita whispered in my ear. "Please. *Señor* Henry, do not tell him you're not his son. We will all lose."

Well, that answered my question about who else knew the truth. I guess there were few secrets in a bawdy house. If Conchita knew, I guess they all did. And if Charles were told the truth, I would end up with nothing. Once he knew Victoria "conned" the Pinkertons, she would be left without any money and the rest of 'em wouldn't get The Farley House.

Seductively, Conchita's loving touch was wandering from my wounds. "If you have the time, we could go upstairs...."

As tempting as that offer was, I wasn't interested. Conchita was just fighting for her future with the weapons at her disposal and she was well heeled. I decided to keep my mouth shut until Victoria was on the train. When Charles and I were out of Animas City, I could tell him the truth.

Victoria packed up all of her belongings and we loaded the buckboard full of suitcases and shipping boxes. She should'a been dressed for traveling but she was dressed for hunting, with herself as bait. Her burgundy and white traveling outfit concealed little and offered a lot. Like Charles said, it would really be a shame to shoot that body.

Charles and I accompanied her to the First National Bank of Durango. They figured to be the only place around that could cash the bank draft for us. Luckily, they did have enough cash on hand and we left with a full carpetbag containing almost thirty-eight thousand dollars. We continued to the train station since we had only a half hour to spare before the last train to Denver pulled out. Charles gave Victoria her share of the money and we waited with her for the train to board. We hadn't planned on running into agent Finch.

So there we were, the three of us, sitting together on a bench in the train station with a carpetbag full of money and up he walks, proud as a peacock.

He tipped his hat and greeted us. "Good afternoon, folks. I thought I might find you all together. A family reunion perhaps?"

Charles was the first to speak. "Yes, of course, and we have you to thank, agent Finch. I didn't know you knew about.... Mister Smith."

"Let's just say I had my suspicions. I decided to stay around and take a later train so I could witness the final chapter of the Farley case."

Victoria just couldn't keep her mouth shut. "We saw you get on the train this morning."

"Yes but you didn't see me get off before the train left the station and follow you to your place of business. You've had a very busy day and a rather noisy one. I heard four pistol shots and something that sounded like a double-barreled scattergun going off. Yes sir, lots of noise."

Charles and I looked at each other, wondering what he was up to. Except for the shootings, which could be justified, we'd broken no laws. If Finch still believed I was their son, then he should have no further interest in us.

While we were ponderin', Victoria was taking action. She started toward Finch and then feigned a fall. He had little choice but to reach out to catch her but it was agent Finch who got caught. He got a close-up eyeful of Miss Victoria and his resolve turned to mush.

Judging by his wide-eyed reaction, Victoria went in for the kill. "Well, I can assure you that nobody in The Farley House got anything they didn't rightly deserve. You can be sure of that, Arthur, is it all right that I call you Arthur?"

Finch's mind was definitely adrift. "Yes.... yes... please call me Arthur."

Now she had him. "Are you married, Arthur?"

She tucked her left arm around his right arm and pressed it against her bosom. Then she turned him around as neat as ya please. Before he knew what happened, they were walking arm in arm toward the train. Victoria held her right hand by her side with four fingers extended. It appeared to be a casual act but, knowing Victoria, I suspected it was done with purpose.

As they boarded the train, we helped the porters load all of her luggage. I was relieved to see 'em leave but I think Charles was already missing her just a little.

He watched the train disappear down the tracks and sighed. "Some things never change and Vicki is one of 'em. She's still the same ol' whore she always was. Did you see her right hand.... with the four fingers held out? Well, that's an old whorehouse signal for an all-nighter. One finger was for a "quickie". Two was for a half hour and three meant a full hour. The girls would signal the madam so she would know when they would be available again. Vicki was telling us that she just hooked an all-nighter."

After all that happened, I think we both wished her well and God-speed to Louisiana. With a stake of ten thousand dollars and her looks, she'd probably do a lot better than "well."

Charles and I went back to The Farley House and made plans to stay the night. Our train to Flagstaff wasn't till the next morning and we were getting along as father and son. I felt guilty as hell but didn't know how to tell him the truth. I kept diggin' myself deeper and deeper into that hole of deception.

Lou was running the bar when we got back. He'd worked for Charles in Chicago and was the slow and steady type. He was more accountant than gambler and could surely manage the business. Charles held a short business meeting with Lou and Conchita and then gave them three thousand dollars to make repairs and keep the saloon going.

Slick and Bud were taken out by someone and buried somewhere. I didn't know who and didn't want to know where. The whole place was spotless so the entire crew must have been hard at work while we were gone. The only evidence of the ruckus was the busted chandelier and that would take some special fixin'.

From what I could tell, Conchita was managing the girls. Guess they got that straightened out after we left. They still needed someone to run the gambling' operation since Slick was no longer available and Conchita hinted I could have the job. I was flattered and tempted with her offer but politely refused since I had other places to go and lotsa things to do. Besides, how could I do the job. All I knew of gamblin' was how to lose.

Charles and I had supper with Bobby and his ma at the Rocky Mountain Café. She sure set a fine table. We both had seconds of her crumb crust cherry pie. Bobby was unusually busy with customers and we didn't have much time to speak. Local folks drifted in and out but didn't pay any attention to us. We heard some talk about the goin's on at The Farley House but no one seemed to have much information yet. Knowing folks, I was sure they would know ever'thing in a day or two.

During and after supper I let Charles do most of the talking. He told me he was in Denver, on business, when he got the news about his son being found. A telegram from the Pinkerton Agency was forwarded to him from Santa Fe. He caught the first train to Durango because he figured correctly that I would be traveling here to meet with Victoria. He had kept a watchful eye on her and The Farley House ever since she'd opened it.

Charles got into Durango the night before I arrived. The next morning, he got to the saloon just after we did and waited outside for us. He was still waiting when he heard the first shots. He rushed to my defense and made it just in time.

Bobby and his Mom were about to close up the café and we were about to leave when wouldn't you know it, old Reb Hopkins came stumbling in. Luckily, he had a snoot full and didn't recognize me. I tossed a quarter on the counter and told Bobby to give him some of their leftovers. Upon hearing that, old Reb stood at attention and saluted us as we left. Charles found that very amusing.

Back at The Farley House, Charles and I drank a little, played a few hands of gin rummy and generally had a good time. He was an easy man to like. With his southern charm and knowin' ways, he was never at a loss for words. He told me of his life in Santa Fe and how he longed to share it with his son. I reminded him I had business in Flagstaff and wasn't sure what I intended to do afterward. He wasn't one to take "no" for an answer so he decided to accompany me on the train even though it was out of his way. I could tell he was making future plans for both of us. My conscience was killing me but what could I do? I could not figure any other way out of the mess I was in.

Charles continued to reminisce. "After losing my wagons, supplies and cash money in that Navajo raid, I ended up flat broke in Santa Fe. Starting from scratch, I hustled my way from street gambler, to house gambler and then saloon owner. Finally, I had enough money to build my own bar and gambling hall. I called it "Saint Charles Place."

I asked about the name and he laughed. He'd gotten the idea from a joint in New Orleans. Since he had to change his name to avoid the "Pinks", as he called 'em, he just reversed his name from Charles Farley to Farley Charles. So, "Saint Charles Place" wasn't much of a stretch. He said "reversing" was the easiest way to change names. Since I'd done the same several times, I had to agree.

The burn on the back of my right arm was healing pretty good but the furrow across my back was still raw and tender. Noticing my discomfort, Conchita came over and volunteered to have another go at bathing and dressing my wounds. She gave Charles a long sultry look and he got the "message". He excused himself and went looking for a card game. We retired to the privacy of her room.

As the new madam, Conchita had literally taken over ever'thing. Her new room was Miss Victoria's old *boudoir* that took up most of the third floor. I'd never seen such a set-up. It was designed and furnished to entertain politicians, tycoons and royalty so I felt way out of place. There was a fine leather sofa, a solid oak desk, lace curtains on the windows and a large hand woven rug on the floor but the bed was the centerpiece. It was a huge four-poster canopy bed that was two feet off the ground. It had a thick down comforter and a canopy with overhead mirrors. I just stood and stared until Conchita started to giggle.

She took off my shirt and started to examine my wounds and then we sort of toppled onto that fancy bed. Then, using her most professional bedside manner, Conchita quickly changed from nurse to lover. Her passion seemed limitless and overpowered us both. She lowered the kerosene lamps and gave me the best treatment any patient could wish for. We'd been together before, but this was different. It was a special night for both of us. Now, she was the madam in charge and with me because she wanted to be. I could tell the difference.

The first gray light of the morning found me sitting at the oak desk and gazing out at the La Plata Mountains. From the third floor it sure promised be a beautiful sunrise. Mostly out of boredom, I looked through the papers on the desk. Victoria left in such a hurry that the papers were scattered all about. I was sure she had taken anything of any importance but I looked around anyway. In one of the drawers, I found a crumpled envelope addressed to her in Chicago. The postmark was dated, November 1863. The return address included that damned Pinkerton eyeball and was from their Chicago office. I started to look at the letter inside when Conchita called me back to bed. I hid the letter in my boot and did as I was told.

Conchita confided to me that the previous evening was the first time she'd slept with a man because she wanted to. It was a good feeling and she liked it. I told her I was right partial to the feeling myself.

We talked some and tried to get to know one another better as the sun was peeking over the horizon. One of the other girls brought us hot coffee and buttered pastries and I got to feeling like a big frog in a little pond. I didn't have much to say about myself but Conchita had quite a story to tell and tears filled her eyes as she told it.

"My real name is Consuelo Maria Vargas. I grew up near Sonora in old Mexico and was the oldest of seven children. On my thirteenth birthday, my parents sold me to a *gringo* miner named Matheson. He had gold to trade and my poor parents desperately needed food for my brothers and sisters. My life was bartered for beans, rice and corn *tortillas*. Slavery in old Mexico, especially of children, was frowned upon but never formally outlawed. My parents broke no laws but they surely broke my heart."

I was amazed at how well she could speak English when it suited her. She described Matheson as a disgusting man with the appearance and the habits of a feral pig. Conchita was forced to do for him for almost three years. She was expected to cook, carry and fetch for him all day and then warm his bed at night. They traveled from one mining town to another as Matheson tried to strike it rich. Her life was so dismal that inside, little Consuelo wanted to die.

Two years ago, Matheson lost her in a poker game. The winners, and her new owners, turned out to be Slick and Victoria. While still fifteen, she went from slave to prostitute in the wink of a one-eyed jack.

Slick set her buy-out price at five hundred dollars and she'd been saving what she could to eventually purchase her own freedom. For two years she'd put up with drunken miners, hell-bent cowboys and impotent businessmen and had succeeded in saving only sixty-two dollars.

I told her with Slick dead and Victoria gone, she could leave anytime she wished. She was almost eighteen and had a brand new chance at life. Consuelo could go back home and Conchita could rest in peace.

Then suddenly, she changed right before my eyes. Conchita replaced Consuelo and laughed in my face. "Leave.... now? Are you *loco*? You have given me part ownership of The Farley House. Even with Animas City drying up, I can make a fortune here. Why would I want to go back to the poverty and desperation of my family?"

Conchita may have taken over for Victoria but in some ways, she also became Victoria. Poor little Consuelo never had a chance.

I knew it was time to quit diggin' again and climb out of another hole. I wondered which girl I'd slept with, Consuelo or Conchita. I guess men were never meant to understand women. I finished my coffee and got out of bed, as it was past time for me to leave.

Conchita offered me Slick's old job again and made it perfectly clear I would receive all the fringe benefits along with a share of the winnings. I was more certain than ever the gambling business was not right for me. I slipped the envelope in my shirt pocket, grabbed my boots and hat and scrambled down two flights of stairs.

Charles was up and waiting when I reached the first floor. We shook hands with Lou and wished him well. Conchita waved good-by from the top of the stairs and we were almost on our way.

As we got in the buckboard, Doby ran out from the hotel waving a telegram at us. The message was for me and was from Banjo Billy. It had been sent from Leadville and received five days earlier when I was still in Flagstaff. Sissy must'a told him where I was staying. The wording was short and to the point.

"Trouble coming, dressed in black".

I couldn't be sure what that meant but I had a good idea. That old man had followed my trail to Leadville and was coming back this way. Well, that was another good reason to get out of Animas City as quick as I could. I told Charles it was a joke but he knew better.

The train pulled out on time and we settled back to enjoy the return trip to Flagstaff. I caught just a glimpse of a tall rider pulling up to the station as we got up a head of steam. He looked like he was riding a black horse with a white blaze. I think he was also dressed all in black but from a distance I couldn't be sure. It was probably just a coincidence since lots of fellas dress in black and the whole thing might've been my imagination. But if that feller was that old man Doby warned me about then he'd have to wait for another day.

Chapter IX

"It's good to be back home again"

After riding a few hours, our small talk got tiresome. I knew all I wanted to know about Charles and I'd certainly told him all I dared about me. The rolling motion of the train and the monotonous chugging of the engine was enough to put anyone out, so finally, we both nodded off. Several hours later, something woke me but Charles was still snoring.

I pulled out the phony deed and looked it over again. It recorded the transfer of the ranch property to Charles U. Farley. The land was described as six thousand acres, but the location was written in legal terms. Why couldn't the deed just say the property started three miles north of the old oak tree, ran east to the big rocks, south to the old fence posts and then west to the bend in the creek?

Along with the deed, I found the envelope I'd removed from Victoria's desk. The letter inside was a follow-up report from a Pinkerton agent in Chicago:

"To Mrs. Victoria Farley;
November 22, 1863
We regret to report we have no new verifiable information regarding the disappearance of your son. We do, however, have a statement from an Indian on the Navajo reservation claiming that a white baby was taken from a Navajo village by a Hopi raiding party

a short time after the wagon train massacre. Without additional con-
firmation, we cannot verify this statement. As per our agreement, we
are informing you because it is a possible lead. We will, of course,
attempt to follow this lead to its resolution.

The Pinkerton Detective Agency."

That report was as much of a disappointment to me now as it
must have been to Victoria some twenty years ago. I wondered why
she kept it all these years. Maybe it was just a stray envelope that got
lost in the mess on her desk.

I was bored so I looked around for a magazine or paper to read
and wouldn't you know, on the seat across from me was another
edition of the "Arizona Free Press." It was only a week old and was
likely to have another article about Sampson Langley.

It didn't take long to find what I was looking for. The bold
headline read: "Ranchers Battle Miners Over Disputed Land." The
article went on to detail a series of shootouts and fist fights between
local ranchers and the Langley Company miners. According to the
reporter, the miners were squattin' on grazing land and the ranchers banded together to run 'em off. Several men on both sides were
wounded or killed. No arrests had been made as the sheriff was still
rounding up all the evidence and eyewitness reports.

The story mentioned several names I didn't recognize but
"Moses James" was one I did. I was certain Zackariah told me his
father's name was Moses. How many "Moses James" could there be
in Yuma? The paper said Moses was badly beaten but was expected
to recover. It was quite a coincidence my adopted family in Yuma
had a run-in with Sampson Langley before I did.

When we arrived in Flagstaff, Charles and I went right to the
telegraph office so I could send a wire to Zackariah. I wanted to
know his father's condition and let him know Langley was headed
to Flag. At twenty-five cents a word, I kept my message short and to
the point. I knew Zack would understand.

"Hope father well. (stop). Langley coming to Flag.(stop). Will advise.... Henry."

When Charles and I checked in at the Beaver Street Hotel, Kenny was his usual energetic self and greeted me as the Navajo Kid. Not wishing to cause any more confusion or loose talk, I signed the guest book as "The Kid." Charles laughed and signed it "Farley Charles." He said "the Kid" was a perfect name for me. I wondered if anyone ever signed his real name in a hotel register.

As soon as we got settled in our rooms, I was eager to head for the Box H. I told Charles I had some old business to attend to and I'd be back in a few days. He wanted to go with me but I assured him he would be better off staying put in Flagstaff. He was a born gambler who could get along most anywhere and Flag looked to be his kind of town.

I left Charles to his own devices and hurried to the livery so I could renew my relationship with Goner. He stamped and blew some when I approached him but after two carrots and a small crab apple, he seemed to forgive me for leaving him behind. I figured life in the stable was pretty easy and he should thank me but horses don't seem to think thataway.

I saddled up and we got on the road in a hurry. Since we both remembered the way home and Goner was dying to run, we made a fast trip of it. Along the way, memories came at me from every direction.

First off, there was Mount Humphrey. I'd admired that mountain ever'day of my life as I was growing up. In 1873, some scallywag changed the name to honor a retired Brigadier General but we always called it "old snow top."

The rest of the mountains, the many different kinds of trees and the trail itself were like old friends. I saw three good-sized herds of elk, several smaller herds of deer, a bunch of wild turkeys, two coyotes and a stub-tailed bobcat. A flock of geese landed on a small pond as we passed and I heard a cougar yowlin' in the distance. All the sights and smells were right. It was mighty good to be home.

As I rode across the open range to the ranch house, I could feel something was wrong. Call it premonition or "the gift" but all of a sudden, I had it. All I could think of were the words "accident" and "shooting."

It was getting on to dark and I couldn't make out the ranch house till I got close-up but right off, I noticed a new addition. A three, maybe four, room addition had been added to the east side. Something little, maybe a dog or a small child, was out front and scurried inside when I rode up.

I hitched Goner to the rail and started for the house as folks came at me from all directions. G.W. came out of the addition with a woman beside him and a young boy holding his hand. Pa came out of the barn, dropped the pitchfork and ran toward me. Then a girl, a beautiful girl, came running from the main house and threw her arms around my neck.

The excited girl wrapped herself around me and was shouting my name and crying all in the same breath. Pa rushed over to shake my hand over and over and I did my best to remain standing. G.W. stayed where he was, waiting for the ruckus to quiet down.

I tried to remove the young lady from around my neck and find out who she was. "It's me," she said. "Taylor.... don't you recognize your very own baby sister?"

Well, I sure as hell didn't recognize her and it wasn't just the poor light. Little Taylor wasn't so little any more. She was full growed and all woman. I couldn't believe it.

For his part, Pa looked the same but seemed a lot older than I remembered. He also seemed shorter. I'd plumb forgotten my late growth spurt. I was four inches shorter when I left. Pa couldn't stop saying how glad he was I'd finally come home.

In some ways, G.W. was the biggest surprise of all. He would always be my "big brother" but now I towered over him. Physically he hadn't changed but he'd gotten married and become a daddy twice over. That made me an uncle twice over. I couldn't believe that, either.

His little boy, Franklin, was at his side and his baby girl, Miriam, was inside in her crib. I figured his daughter was named for Ma but I had to consider his son's name. Finally it hit me, Franklin Pierce Henry. If the four of us Henry boys continued breeding, we'd surely run out of dead presidents to name our kids after.

G.W. introduced me to his wife Susanna and we went inside to see little Miriam who was fast asleep. She was so small and fragile looking she didn't seem real. Susanna said the baby was doing just fine.

When we came back outside, I noticed the hitch wagon on the far side of the barn. Suddenly it all made sense. The wagon I saw in Flagstaff was still our wagon. It was Susanna, Franklin and little Miriam I saw. That meant the pert tomboy in the feed store was.... Taylor. I was excited and ashamed at the same time. She was my baby sister. Taylor and Susanna went to fussing in the kitchen. I stabled Goner in the barn and then joined Pa and G.W. on the porch along with my little nephew, Franklin. It had been a long time since I played with a youngster and the first chance I had to play with my very own nephew.

Pa was full of questions and he wasn't shy about asking.

"Why did you leave? Where did you go? What have you been doing? Do you intend to stay put this time?"

I had questions of my own but I had to bide my time to ask 'em. I figured Pa would look a bit older when I got home but he looked a lot older. His hair was whiter and thinner, his step slower and his temper shorter. Why had he aged so much?

To satisfy his curiosity, I repeated the tired line about still seeking my fortune when Taylor called out from the kitchen to say she wanted to hear ever' word so I should hold my stories for the supper table. That ended the interrogation for awhile.

G.W. started to talk about his young family when it occurred to me the twins were nowhere about. There was no sign of 'em anywhere.

"Hey, where are the twins? Are they out gallivantin'?"

My questions were answered by a stony silence. I looked at G.W. and he looked at Pa who just looked at the stars and spoke in a hollow voice.

"Your brothers are dead, Monroe. Nothing to be done and 'nuff said. Ashes to ashes and dust to dust." The tone of Pa's voice left little room for further discussion but the words "accident" and "shooting" were ringing in my ears. I had to know the truth but this wasn't gonna be the time. G.W. just took a deep breath and pretended to count the nails in the porch floor.

Since Pa made it clear that subject was closed, I started talking about the ranch. I got to rough-housin' with Franklin as we discussed range conditions, cattle prices and the like. We were arguing about fencing the south pasture when the supper bell rang.

I caught the smell of home cookin' and suddenly remembered I'd forgotten to eat all day. I was almost numb from hunger. Taylor and Susanna outdid themselves on such short notice and I was truly impressed. They prepared elk steaks, a beef roast along with boiled potatoes and gravy, green beans and sourdough biscuits. I had three helpings of ever'thing as I regaled them with the stories of my wanderin'.

Not wishing to cause too much concern, I omitted some details about my travels, glossed over others and added a few I'd only heard about. They were amazed, amused and horrified by my wild adventures. I made a point to tell Pa I finally had my very own Henry rifle.

Pa listened along with the others but I could see he was reading betwixt the lines. He'd been around and knew life in the West wasn't as safe and simple as I made it out to be. As usual, he said little but listened a lot. His pipe tobacco sure smelled like home.

Taylor wanted to know about the fancy ladies. "What are the latest styles? What are they wearin'? Have you seen any operas or plays? Have you met any famous people? Did you get to see the Pacific Ocean?" She was chuck full of questions and bursting with excitement. News of the world was a scarce thing on the ranch and I had a load of it.

I was surprised to find out G.W. and Susanna seemed real interested in California. They'd heard all the stories 'bout the warm weather, fertile soil and land free for the taking. "Is it really the land of milk and honey like everybody says? Could a family make a living as farmers? Would it be a safe place to raise our kids?"

Little Franklin, being three years old, just wished to hear 'bout the cowboys, Injuns, and outlaws. "Did'ja ever see Billy the Kid or Jesse James? Did'ja have to fight any wild Injuns? How many outlaws did you shoot?"

I mentioned my run-ins with the Paiutes and the Utes and told 'em what I'd heard about General Crook and the Apache uprising in southern Arizona. I also mentioned I knew some "James Boys" but not Frank or Jessie.

After two large pieces of Susanna's gooseberry pie, I was too stuffed to talk. As Taylor cleared the table and Susanna fussed over Miriam, G.W. went out to the barn to check out my fancy saddle and took Franklin with him. I failed to mention the Silver Star gun belt and engraved Colt in my saddlebags. They might have heard a description of "Henry James" and I didn't wish to explain.

So there we were, Pa and me, with so much to say and unable to say it. As was his want, Pa excused himself and retired to his room. I got up to follow but Taylor motioned me to follow her out on the porch. She was still so excited about all the news that she hugged my neck and kept going on about how happy she was to see me. She was so much a woman I had to remind myself over and over that she was my little sister.

We sat in the rocking chairs on the porch and stared at the nighttime sky as she told me all about my twin brothers, John and Thomas.

"They got involved with that brazen hussy, Megan Shaw."

I swallered hard but tried to hold my water. Were they the twins that Marty mentioned?

Taylor leaned closer and kept her voice low. "Megan changed them from loving brothers to Cain and Abel. As you know, in many ways they were just like Cain and Abel. John was the quiet brother like Abel while Thomas was brash like Cain. They looked to be two peas in a pod but were actually as different as rain and shine. Megan seduced Thomas first and then threw him over for John."

I didn't want to hear what was coming but there was no stopping Taylor once she got started. I stood and started to pace just to ease my apprehension..

"Turning twins against one another seemed to offer that harlot the ultimate challenge. I heard she told her girl friends she could get the twins to fight over her and she was right. First they fought a war of words, which only made matters worse. Before long, they weren't speaking at all and wouldn't even eat supper together.

Next came a horrible fistfight in the barn. Pa stopped them but not before Thomas had almost beaten John to a pulp. It didn't do him no good cuz Megan chose to nurse John and berate Thomas for whipping his brother. We tried to get Thomas to back off but he couldn't or wouldn't let it go. He refused to believe Megan could prefer John to him."

I could guess what happened next.

Taylor took a deep breath and continued. "Everything came to a head in Grasshopper Flats. Evidently Thomas spent the entire day drinking in the Rainbow's End and got goaded into action by some of the local misfits. We heard they taunted and teased him just for the sport of it. Soon enough he was on the street hunting trouble."

Taylor paused to get her emotions under control. I could tell she was barely holding back a flood of tears. I took both her hands in mine and she went on with her story.

"Awash in alcohol and jealously, Thomas finally found John walking hand in hand with Megan in front of the livery and angrily challenged him to settle things once and for all. The local riffraff quickly gathered around and urged them on. The talking and the scrapping were over and neither one had much of a choice. The stupid code of the West demanded each of them stand their ground or be branded a coward. The gunfight neither really wanted was upon them. John had to prove his manhood and courage to Megan while Thomas was desperately trying to win her back."

At this point, Taylor broke down and cried for a minute or two. I sat next to her and tried to be a comfort but she was determined to finish.

"John never saw the day he was a match for Thomas with a six-gun. His attempt to draw was pathetically slow and he was gunned down right there in the street. I guess Thomas stood in silence over him like a man awakening from a horrible dream. Folks said he seemed unable to comprehend what he had done. Finally, he actually started crying and that's when the crowd turned on him. Their cheers turned to jeers.

Megan's reaction was to rush to John and put on a great display of grief and sorrow. Then she screamed at Thomas and called him a murderer. The crowd seemed to agree with her. His loudest critics were those who had teased and taunted him into the street in the first place. Thomas was left alone in the middle of the street. Later, when he brought John's body to the ranch, Pa also turned him away. Neither his family nor his friends wished to listen to his side or hear how sorry he was."

I was up and pacing once again. This time, I was fighting back the tears.

"That evening, Megan and her father made it quite clear Thomas would never be welcome at their ranch either. I heard that Clayton chased him away with the threat of a scattergun. Megan's vicious charade was finally over."

Taylor felt no sympathy for Megan or her part in the awful love triangle. She had given me the background and details as best she knew 'em. She finished by saying no one had heard of or seen hide nor hair of Thomas in more than a year. She and G.W. didn't agree with Pa concerning Thomas, but their opinions on the matter carried little weight.

As she spoke, all the pieces of the Megan puzzle fell into place for me. The story I'd heard about Megan and the twin brothers was true. The "shooting" Jonah mentioned and the black widow comparisons were also true. Sadly, for all concerned, it all made sense now. Megan, the pretty girl I'd fallen in love with four years ago in

Grasshopper Flats, was responsible for John's death and Thomas' exile. She was all they said she was and more. Right there and then, I lost any feelin' I might have had for her.

Since I was well acquainted with Megan and her seductive ways, I understood exactly what had happened. As I saw it, John and Thomas were both wrong but that was water over the damn. Thomas was still my brother and I had to find him and help him get past his guilt. Later on, we could deal with Pa.

Taylor and I lit candles and we went to visit the burial mound behind the house. It was snuggled in a peaceful spot amongst the towering ponderosa pines and junipers. There we faced the four markers and mourned our loved ones.

The first marker was for young James Madison Henry. He died from small pox during the trip west and his little body was actually buried along the wagon trail somewhere in southwestern Kansas. A marker was placed here so future members of our family would never forget him. The marker read, "Born January 8, 1860, Died September 27, 1861."

Andrew Jackson Henry was next. He was born on October 5, 1866 and died one month later on November 8th. "A.J." was yet another infant victim of cholera or prairie fever. No matter what you called it, the fever, dysentery, diarrhea or cholera, once a small child got it, there was little that could be done. The very young, the very old and the physically weak were the usual victims of the deadly disease. No one knew the cause or how it was spread but spread it did. The fever was known to wipe out complete wagon trains as well as small towns and Indian villages. It struck like some dusty phantom of death, took its share of victims and vanished from whence it came.

The third marker was for Ma, Miriam Anne Henry. She was buried beside her two small sons. She died of the same mysterious fever on January 9, 1867, two months after young "A.J." passed. Ma was only twenty-seven when she died, having been born in November 1839.

The fourth and newest marker was for John Adams Henry. He was only twenty-two years old when he died. Such a waste and what a tragedy for the whole family.

Suddenly, Taylor started to tell me all about John's funeral and what I'd missed.

"The weather that day was gray skies and a cold drizzle with no relief in sight. It seemed stuck somewhere betwixt winter and spring and gave us the worst of both. But friends and family gathered here in spite of the impending storm. The miserable weather mirrored what we were all feeling."

Taylor closed her eyes and seemed to relive ever' moment of it.

"As you well know, Pa's never been an overly religious man but on this occasion, he felt the need to speak long and loud from the "Good Book." He seemed to be overcome by opposing emotions. Mostly, he showed great sadness but he was also driven by a seething anger. Pa controlled those emotions best he could but I could tell. He started out with the twenty-third psalm and ended one full hour later with the fourth chapter of Genesis. In verses one through twelve, he talked about the conflict between Cain and Abel. He repeated, several times, the last line in verse twelve, "A fugitive and a vagabond shalt thou be in the earth."

Thomas wasn't allowed to attend the funeral but in a real sense, he was buried right along with John. When Pa turned him away, he declared that Thomas Jefferson Henry was no longer his son.

For weeks after, Pa prayed every night and questioned God about all that happened. Guess he wondered what he'd ever done to deserve all this? Finally, he just sat in his room and waited for answers that never came."

Taylor was silent for awhile and then bitterly added. "In the very back of the mourners stood that awful Megan Shaw. Dressed all in black, she went through all the motions of the funeral without any of the emotions. No one spoke of it but everyone knew the shoot-out and John's death were all her doing."

I asked Taylor if our old friend, Hopi Joe, was there and she was quick to respond. "No. He only came around once last year and spent all his time with Pa. We barely knew he was here."

That didn't sound like Joe. He usually came by several times a year and he always spent time with each of us. Something had to be wrong with him, but what?

I spent the next two days getting reacquainted with the ranch and the members of my family. Funny how ever'thing on the ranch was smaller than I'd remembered. Sometimes I rode with G.W. and other times with Taylor. We had some mighty long conversations and I got to know each of them a lot better.

G.W. was a man in conflict with himself. He loved and respected our father but also understood the actions of our brother, Thomas. He prayed time would heal the wounds but knew better. Pa was too stubborn and prideful to ever forgive or forget. G.W. had suddenly lost two of his brothers and was struggling to hang on to his father.

Being the oldest son at twenty-four, G.W. had started his own family but he continued to live on the Box H. Being of medium height with a stocky build and dark features, he favored Pa in both looks as well as in personality. Always the dutiful son, now a husband and father himself, he was nothing if not dependable and predictable. All his choices in life had been made for him but he never rebelled nor complained. He just seemed to trudge through life one day at a time always carrying his own freight. I respected and felt sorry for him at the same time.

G.W. confided in me that he rode to Grasshopper Flats on the morning of the fourth day following the funeral and found Thomas passed out on the floor of The Rainbows End. He was awash in his own vomit and urine. How long he'd been like that was hard to tell. Deke, the bartender, was cleaning up the saloon but seemed to pay him no mind. G.W. drug Thomas outside and threw him in the horse trough. Thomas splashed and swore in a drunken fit as he struggled to get out of the trough. When he finally did get out, he collapsed face first in the street and passed out again. He was a pitiful sight. The town folks walked by without question or comment.

Finally, G.W. had to hoist Thomas over his shoulder and carried him to the livery. He set him down in a stall and covered him with an old horse blanket. He tossed a twenty-dollar gold piece to the Mexican stable hand with instructions to bed and board Thomas until he was able to do for himself. It was the best he could do. G.W. returned to the ranch but never told Pa or Taylor how he'd found Thomas.

That was the last time any of the family saw Thomas. He rode out two days later and left little trace. G.W. asked around but no one could provide any further information on his whereabouts.

Taylor was tall for a girl and rapidly maturing from a tomboy into a beautiful young woman. Like the twins, she favored our mother rather than her father. All three had lighter complexions and finer features than either Porter or G.W. I guess I was somewhere in between.

Taylor and the twins were real outgoing and fun loving folks so it was certain none of them would stay hitched to the Box H for too long. The stifling daily routine of ranch life suited G.W., but not them.

Having just turned seventeen, Taylor longed to experience life away from the Box H but felt forever bound to the ranch and her family. Her worldly knowledge came mostly from books or the occasional visitor to the ranch. Books were a way for her to escape from the ranch routine if only for a little while. She said she favored the classic works of William Shakespeare and Sir Walter Scott and dreamt of great adventures and wild romances.

To Taylor, big cities were home to all the things she dreamed of. How she envied me cuz I had gone off and seen the world. I repeated that I'd only seen a little but to her it was a bunch. She longed to know all about my travels. Since I hadn't written in two years, Pa had feared for my safety but Taylor was always certain I was all right and would surely come back home. After the funeral, she even wrote that short letter requesting my quick return to the ranch.

Whenever I went riding, Goner had a good old time and wanted to race with the wind. Taylor and her horse, Domino, were always up for the challenge if not the race. We beat her ever'time but never by much. That girl could surely ride like a man and look like a woman while she was doing it.

The ranch itself was pretty much the same but the livestock had doubled in the last four years and they were having water and grass problems. They needed range management, which was a fancy term that meant the cows needed to be moved from one pasture to another before they wore out the grass. Herd rotation was the answer and G.W. and I had a long talk about it.

Ever'where I looked, there was something that needed fixin'. The old barn sorely needed paint and a new roof but we were shy the materials and manpower. It might have to last another few years before we got to it.

There were fences to be mended and corrals to be built but, as Pa would say, the fences had to be horse-high, pig-tight, and bull-strong and that would take a heap of work. The windmill was falling down and the irrigation ditches needed clearing, but who had the extra time?

We decided the first thing to be done was round up all the old cattle and drive 'em to market. That would bring in needed cash money to fix some of the problems but with just Pa and G.W. pulling the load, nothing else would get done. They had all they could do to keep the place from falling apart let alone building 'er back up.

Taylor, no matter how growed up, was still a tomboy at heart when it came to working 'round the ranch and handling cattle. She had the instincts of a wild mustang but lived the life of a plow horse. Her daily chores included all the cooking, mending and housework so there was little time left over. Susanna had all she could do to manage her own household while she tended to G.W. and the kids.

Pa had no money to hire extra hands and no extra hands to help 'im get any money. Taylor was right, with the twins gone, they desperately needed my help and I intended to provide it as soon as I returned from Flagstaff.

I planned to go back to Flag, take care of whatever business I had with Charles and get back to the ranch as quickly as possible. I was no longer interested in Megan or the job at the S Diamond but Charles was another fence that needed mending.

On my third night home, I finally got up enough nerve to corner Pa in his room. Strangely, he seemed quite willing to talk. The only problem was, he wanted to talk about the past and not the present or the future.

He rambled on about the long trip west and James' death along the way. Then he described how they saved Hopi Joe and survived the first winter. He finally got around to the death of Ma and little A.J. He kept repeatin' what a good woman Ma was and what a shame she died so young after bearing him six children.

I almost corrected him since I counted seven children but I thought better of it and kept quiet. Finally, Pa started crying. Whatever was eating at him had broke his spirit.

As a child growing up, I never realized how hard Ma's death hit him. Taylor had mentioned his long talks at the grave site and now I understood. The death of John and the loss of Thomas had just sucked the air out of him. He was stumblin' through life without purpose or direction.

Attempting to change his mood, I pulled out the copy of the deed Victoria gave me. I handed it to him and asked if he could tell where the property was located.

Pa fetched his reading spectacles and turned up the kerosene lamp so he could study what it said. After only a few seconds, he took off his glasses, sat back in his chair and let loose with a deep sigh. The phony deed slipped from his fingers to the floor and neither of us spoke for a few seconds.

"Pa, what's wrong?"

"Where did you get this deed? How long have you known?"

I was taken aback. "I got the deed a week ago in Animas City and I don't know.... nothin'."

"You didn't get it from your Ma's cedar chest in the attic?"

"I haven't seen that chest or been to the attic in four years. What are ya talking about?"

I rose from my chair and towered over Pa. I was confused and angry and I could see fear in his eyes. When he didn't answer, I turned away and started to pace back and forth.

"I was given that deed for services rendered by a Miss Victoria Farley from Animas City. I thought it was a true deed and the key to my future. Turns out it's only a copy of the real thing and of no value. I just wanted to know where the ranch was located and thought you could figure out from the legal description. That's all."

Then I sat down and waited for him to speak. He looked at me with his eyes all teared-up. "The property mentioned in this deed is our ranch. There's another copy just like this one up in that old cedar chest. We've never had no legal right to it.... only squatters' rights. I've been waiting on the day when someone would bring a legal claim against us. For twenty years I've been a'feard."

Once he got started, Pa rambled on for almost an hour. He spoke with solemn feeling and chose ever' word carefully. I listened in disbelief.

His story began the day he and Ma saved Hopi Joe. All us kids thought we'd heard the hows and whys of those days but there was more to the story than we knew. Much more.

After months of misery and heartache, the family's wagons were some two hundred miles east of the current Box H ranch, in Navajo territory, when they came upon a young "Hopi Joe." His bleeding body was staked out awaiting the pleasure of the circling buzzards and stalking coyotes. His small band of Hopi had lost a fierce battle with a Navajo war party. Although badly wounded, Joe was the only Hopi left alive. Out of pure meanness, the Navajo didn't kill him right off but staked him out to die slowly. Such was their hatred for the Hopi. It was the circling of those buzzards that brought the family to his rescue. Pa and Ma treated his wounds and transported him to his village. After that kindness, Hopi Joe felt forever in their debt.

A week or two later, when Joe had recovered enough to travel, he tracked the wagons as they moved westward. He felt honor-bound to repay them for saving his life so he hung around and watched to see how he could help. When the folks finally did settle down, Joe was there to lend a hand with our first ranch house. He and Pa became blood brothers. Now I got to hear the rest of the story.

"Joe came bearing the gift of a white boy baby to replace the son we'd lost along the trail. His people had taken the baby during a raid on a Navajo village. He'd sensed Ma's great sorrow over losing James Madison and figured replacing her lost son was the best way for him to repay his debt. He gave us a life for a life."

Conflicting notions filled my head. I was afraid to hear what came next. Was Pa telling me he wasn't my real father? Was he right when he said Ma had bore him only six children?

Thankfully, Pa relieved my fears.

"The baby was sickly and died after only a couple of days at the ranch. We buried his body under the marker for James Madison.

Hopi Joe brought the baby on an old cradleboard that was wrapped in a Navajo blanket. Ma found a copy of the deed and several double eagles sewn inside the cradle's lining. At first, I thought the deed was real. It figured that if the parents of the baby were dead, no one would be the wiser if we settled on the land. I took the gold coins for found money and bought my Henry rifle with 'em. It wasn't broke wagons or hard weather that caused us to stop here, it was the notion that the land was free for the taking. That's my shameful secret. I eventually found the deed was a phony and had to face the truth. All we have is squatters' rights to the ranch."

That's what he had been trying so hard not to tell me.

All of a sudden, I remembered the Pinkerton report that I found in Victoria's desk. It said a white child was taken from the Navajo about the same time. Now ever'thing made sense. Based on what Pa said, the baby Hopi Joe brought them figured to be that child. Given the deed they found, the baby was surely Charles' son.

The Box H wasn't really our ranch since it still belonged to Charles. Now I knew the reason G.W. was so interested in California. Pa told him the truth after John died and he knew he'd have to leave or live with that secret hanging over his head. He and Susanna had been making plans to move out before someone came to claim the ranch.

Pa said a year ago, right after John's funeral, he'd ridden with Hopi Joe to the site of the wagon train massacre and looked for any sign of the attack. After all the years he knew it was hopeless but he was trying to make peace with his broken family. He was a'feard I'd never come back and he wouldn't be able to set things straight with me. Joe told him I would return and he had to tell me the truth.

When Pa finished speaking, we both sat there like headstones in a graveyard. I could feel the pain in his words and the ache in his heart. He'd carried a guilty burden long enough. I didn't explain how but I told him I could get the deed legally changed to his name. That meant G.W., as the eldest son, could stay on the ranch when he passed. I also neglected to tell him I knew Charles or that I was pretendin' to be his son.

By now, I had tears in my eyes and a lump in my throat. I gave Pa hug and then we walked out to the knoll behind the house and explained ever'thing to Ma. We came in when it started to rain.

The next morning I talked with G.W. and made it clear he could stay on the Box H. I told him the ranch was to be his even though Pa's deed was a phony. I assured him I could get a real deed signed over to Pa but I never said how. He was confused but relieved. Turned out he wasn't as interested in California as I thought.

I needed time to think before heading back to Flagstaff so Goner and I took to the hills the next morning. It was a bright sunny day and the hills were alive with the sounds of critters.

Overhead, a red-tailed hawk announced his presence and in the distance I could hear the mournful howl of a lonesome coyote. All around me I heard the chirpin' of early birds out after worms and recognized yellow warblers, a pair of vermilion flycatchers and a summer tanager. Ma was partial to bird watching and left us several books on the subject.

I spied a small pack of timber wolves stalking a herd of deer and a huge old brown bear rooting around some deadfalls for grubs and mites. When I came upon an elk herd, I put my Henry rifle to use and brought down a big buck. I cut out the choice parts and left the carcass for the wolves and coyotes. They'd have to hurry for there were a couple of turkey buzzards keeping a sharp eye from above.

I was heading back to the ranch when I ran into Taylor. We rode toward home together and she told me how interested she was in finding Thomas. I promised I'd help her when I got back from Flagstaff. She asked what was so important in Flag that couldn't wait and I couldn't tell her about Charles so without thinking, I said "a girl". Well, little sister didn't like any part of my answer. She gave the spurs to Domino and lit out for the ranch. Goner and I tried to catch them but, for the first time, she actually beat me and was pretty smug about it.

I provided fresh elk for supper and we had a "beast feast", which included venison, turkey and rabbit as well as elk. The family was in rare form and ever'one but Taylor seemed in the best of spirits. G.W. and Susanna had forgotten all about California and were talking about the garden they were gonna have. Little Franklin wanted to go hunting with me but I had to tell him he would have to wait a few more years. Pa looked a lot better since our little talk but he hadn't spoken to Taylor yet and she knew she was missing something. Little sister was polite but didn't eat much and kept her comments short. What was the matter with her?

I left the next morning after a quickie breakfast of coffee and biscuits. Pa and G.W. were off to work and Susanna was fussing with Franklin and little Miriam. Taylor said sarcastically that she'd ride along but I assured her it wasn't necessary. I was afraid I might run into real trouble and I didn't want my little sister in harm's way. I had the feeling even if Megan weren't involved, Sampson Langley and I were meant to butt heads sooner or later.

Goner and I made good time and got back into Flagstaff late in the afternoon. I left Goner at the livery and made sure he got rubbed down and fed. I noticed the stable was almost full of horses as were the corrals out back. Something was going on. There were a lot more folks in town than last week and I couldn't imagine why.

Chapter X

"Live by the gun die by the gun"

The streets of Flagstaff seemed uncommonly busy for so late in the afternoon. I couldn't recall any holidays or celebrations at this time of year but folks seemed in a festive mood and the town was filling up for some reason. It felt a little like a *fandango* in the *Pueblo de Los Angeles*.

Before returning to the hotel, I stopped off at the barbershop to get a shave and haircut as I was in dire need of both. I found "Pepe", the barber, to be chuck full of information and eager to share. He informed me folks were in town for the big wedding the very next day.

That meant Megan's wedding had been moved up and Sampson Langley was prob'ly here in Flag already. Pepe also said that rumors had it Langley closed some big deal in San Francisco ahead of time and rushed here so they could get married right away. Balderdash. Hadn't anybody else in Flagstaff read the Yuma newspaper?

When I got to the hotel, the lobby was really crowded with folks comin' and goin'. Kenny was hopping around like a frog in a frying pan. He tossed me my room key and shouted something about Mister Charles being at some saloon. That figured.

I took a hot bath and a short nap before donnin' my new suit. I forsook my old Dragoon, as I wanted to appear a modern young gentleman. I figured it might be my last night in Flag for a long while and I wanted to do it up right. Charles and I could light up the town.

Since Pa told me about the white baby and the deed, I saw Charles in a different light. A week ago, I just wanted to be shed of him, but now, I wasn't sure how I felt. Seeing as how his son was buried on our ranch almost made him part of the family.

It also occurred to me he had almost twenty-five thousand dollars he meant to give his son. Before, it would have been like stealing to accept his money but now.... well, I'd have to see. After all, Pa could sure use some of that money around the ranch and I'd still have enough left for a spread of my own. Since Charles wanted a son more'n anything, there would be winners all around. But no matter what good could come from lying, I had to tell hin the truth. Charles could never be my father but he could be a Dutch uncle like Hopi Joe.

I set out to find Charles and started with the hotel dining room. It was early for supper but with Charles you could never tell. Wouldn't you know? In the lobby, I ran smack into Megan and her betrothed, Sampson Langley.

They were both dressed like they were bound for a ball. Sampson resembled a stuffed penguin but Megan was absolutely stunnin' in her pale blue gown. Ever'thing about her was visually perfect but as tall and well proportioned as she was, next to Langley, she looked short and thin. His bulk was barely contained in his black suit and his collar looked about to burst from the pressure of it.

Megan gave me her very best practiced smile. "Sam, may I present the 'Navajo Kid'?"

Sampson gave me a hearty handshake which I returned in kind. He had a smile on his face but a questioning look in his beady black eyes. He knew we'd met afore but he couldn't quite recall who I was or where we'd met. Since I was all cleaned up and decked out in my Sunday go-to-meetin' clothes, it was small wonder he couldn't place me. In both Bodie and Calico I'd been just another scruffy miner to him. I'd been someone to take advantage of but never really ac-knowledge or remember. I enjoyed the advantage.

"I'm proud to meet you and congratulations on your upcomin' marriage."

Megan casually explained to Sampson that I worked for her on the S Diamond and had been away on a personal matter. Then she boasted to me that her "Sam" was a businessman, financier and in the running to replace Frederick Tritle as our next territorial Governor. I wondered if she really believed that hogwash or was just trying to convince herself. Deep down she had to be wondering if she was doing the right thing by marrying him.

Then, out of the blue, Megan invited me to a reception being held that very night, instead of after their wedding ceremony. They were having it in the hotel dining room at eight o'clock. I accepted her kind invitation and excused myself. I could see Langley was still in a fog as I turned to leave so I stretched my luck.

"How are things going at the Blue Belle and Silver Lady mines in Calico?"

He seemed at a total loss for words so I nudged his memory.

"I'm a minority shareholder in both mines and am simply curious as to their current operational status."

His face flushed and a look of pure hatred crossed his face. He knew me now. "I'll try to find out...'bout...." He could barely contain his anger so I let him off the hook.

"There's no need to hurry. I'll be seeing you later....at the reception."

Langley was embarrassed, frustrated and almost wild with anger. Megan, on the other hand, was wild with curiosity. I could see it in her eyes. Woman's curiosity always gave men an advantage if they knew how to exploit it. She was wondering who the Navajo Kid really was and what sort of relationship I had with Sampson.

After seeing 'em together, I wasn't sure how I felt. There was some kinda feeling but was it anger, envy, or jealously? I honestly couldn't tell. Two things were for certain; I had no love left for her and the two of them certainly deserved each other.

Searching the saloons in Flagstaff for Charles was like trying to locate a cross-eyed tadpole in a murky frog pond. Ever' place in town was packed with customers doing some pre-marital celebrating. Many of 'em were getting a head start on the formal festivities. I finally found him playing poker at the Kaibab Saloon of all places.

No sooner had I spotted Charles than I ran across Trace Cummings. Like everyone else, he was in town to attend the wedding. I joined him at the bar and ordered a beer. Trace was just starting on his bottle and was delighted to find a friend to share it with. He turned my beer into a boilermaker as he went on and on about his plans for the S Diamond while I kept my eye on the poker game.

The saloon was packed with customers clamoring for alcohol and entertainment. Cigar and cigarette smoke filled the air with a blue-gray haze and a player piano filled my ears with honky-tonk music. Charles looked like a king sitting on his throne. He had a dancehall girl on his arm, an unlit cigar in his mouth and a drink in his left hand. In front of him, he had a stack of poker chips large enough to choke a horse. Charles was a pure gambler and born to the life.

I could hear Charles overdoing his southern accent for the sake of the crowd. It had a soothing effect on most westerners and it certainly went along with his white suit and plantation hat. I remembered Victoria saying he was so good at poker that he didn't need to cheat. I wondered if the other players in the game appreciated his skill.

I didn't have to wonder for long. Charles was sweeping in another big pile of chips when angry words were exchanged and a man with his back to me stood up, threw his cards at Charles and shouted,

"You're a God-damn cheat!"

Before anyone else could make a move, the man drew his gun and had Charles dead to rights. The saloon girl was quick to move away but Charles just kept gnawin' on his unlit cigar and smiling up at the man. He was trying to calm things by not reacting to the threat. Just when it looked like the heat of the moment had passed, the bastard shot Charles point blank in the chest.

Charles lost his cigar and stared in disbelief at his assailant for a moment. Then he pitched face first on the table and rolled off onto the floor. He was covered with blood. Poker chips and drinks flew in every direction. The other players scrambled to gather up their chips while the gunman slowly turned to face the bar. It was none other than Kid Coyote with a snarl on his lips and a look of triumph in his eyes. His final despicable act was to look down on Charles and spit tobacco juice in his face.

The customers moved in several directions at the same time. Some ducked for cover, some suddenly decided to leave the bar and still others edged closer to get a better view. After looking around to make sure no one objected to the shooting, Kid Coyote holstered his gun and joined the scramble for the chips.

I pushed my way closer to the table to see if Charles was beyond my help. The Kid had drawn down on him so fast that Charles never even went for his gun. If he was dead, the shooting was nothing but cold-blooded murder. I was so mad I could barely breathe.

The next thing I noticed was that Turner and Hutch were two of the other players at the table. That certainly figured since they were running buddies of the Kid in Calico. It was a good bet his whole pack of cutthroats were here. They were surely in town for the big wedding.

Charles was alive but badly hurt and losing a lot of blood. The green felt table had turned a dark maroon color. I was torn between helping Charles and avenging him when I suddenly remembered I wasn't heeled. Both of my guns were back in my hotel room. I had dressed so fashionably I was defenseless. I vowed to never let that happen again.

With help from Trace, I carried Charles out of the Kaibab and down the street to the doc's office. It was a recently converted coffee house but Doc Lewis seemed to know his business. He went to work on Charles and I went to get my guns. True to the western tradition of "in for a penny, in for a pound", Trace was siding me all the way.

The crowd in the hotel lobby was in a frenzy. They heard the shot and were trying to find out the "who" and "why" of it. While ignoring their questions, I made a bull rush through the crowd and raced up the stairs to my room. I strapped on my gunfighter belt and stuck the Dragoon in my waistband, just in case. I went out huntin' a coyote.

As I pushed and shoved my way back through the crowd in the lobby, I heard Kenny shout something about a big fella asking after me. My mind flashed to the "man in black." Perfect, that was all I needed right now, a Bible-toting gunman looking for Henry James.

Trace was waiting outside the Hotel and took immediate notice of my Silver Star gun belt and fancy Colt Peacemaker.

"Now ya' look like the Navajo Kid."

I looked toward the Kaibab and saw that Kid Coyote and his two buddies had left the bar and were about to mount up. I fired a shot in the air to get their attention and it did. They cautiously spread out as we approached.

Beaver Street looked like a stomped-on anthill. Folks were scurryin' in all directions at once. Some wanted to hide and some wanted to watch but all wanted out of the line of fire.

Kid Coyote had a wry smile on his face. He lived for these moments. Like any natural born predator, he had tasted blood and yearned for more. It never once occurred to him it might be his own blood he'd be tastin'. He spat tobacco juice in our general direction and motioned to his pack to fan out on either side of him.

Turner and Hutch weren't certain they wanted hands in this game but, as always, they were willing to follow his lead. As we got closer, I whispered to Trace.

"Take the one on the right."

Hutch was a thief and not known as a gunman. I would take the Kid and his buddy, Abe Turner. It was easier to swing my gun from right to left in a single motion and I was aimin' to start with the Kid.

I was consumed with righteous anger and bound to avenge the cold-blooded shooting of my friend Charles. I'd gotten so caught up in the play-acting that for the moment, I felt like he was my father. I was also remembering Calico. Although never proven, these three men were probably responsible for the deaths of my mining partners, Morris and Jackson.

No words were spoken or necessary. With each step we took the tension grew. Anger over-road fear and I was set to face the devil hisself. The fact that I was going up agin' two men and might not survive never even entered my mind.

Our pace slowed as we got closer until Hutch lost his water and went for his gun. Tensed and ready as they were, Kid Coyote and Turner followed his lead and slapped leather, too.

The Kid was lightning fast but this time he was a little too fast. His aim was low and his first shot hammered the dirt at my feet as my first shot bore a hole clear through his belly and out his backside. I fanned a second and third shot at Turner as he was just clearing leather and he took 'em both in the chest. He'd followed the wrong man to the wrong place at the wrong time and paid dear. His errant shot just pounded the dirt 'neath the water trough.

The Kid managed a second shot which knocked the Colt clean out of my hand. As he staggered and tried to get off a third, I cross-drew my old Dragoon with my left hand and shot him dead center in his rotten teeth. His face burst wide open with blood and tobacco juice sprayin' ever'where. He slowly spun to the ground, shuddered a few times and finally lay still.

An eerie quiet settled over the street. The many gunshots echoed in the distance. Trace had exchanged several shots with Hutch and both were wounded. Trace was grazed on the left hip but was still standing and ready. Hutch was on his knees with bullet wounds in his right thigh and left shoulder. His gun lay in the dirt and he was through shooting. All the gunplay had taken no more than five seconds.

My right hand was tinglin' with a thousand little needles but was otherwise all right. The Kid's bullet had struck the cylinder of the Colt and caved in one of the chambers. It also bent the cylinder pin.

I picked up the broke Colt and slipped it in my holster. It would take a heap of fixin' before I could use it again.

Trace wore a satisfied smile but I don't think he knew he was hit yet. I pointed at his hip and he knew it then. A bloodstain was running down his leg. Folks came out from under cover and the street went from pin-drop quiet to a celebration. They were cheering and hollering to beat the band. They'd gotten a twofer. They came to town for a wedding and got to witness a real life western shoot-out. Once common enough, they were rare in Flagstaff these days.

Trace headed towards the doc's office and I was about to follow when Zimmerman, of all people, blocked my way. I'd a'known that "mule-face" anywhere and he was wearing the same brown suit he'd worn in Bodie. I had no idea he was even in Flagstaff but it figured. All of Langley's stooges were surely here for the wedding.

When I saw Megan and Sampson in the crowd behind him, I could guess the rest. Judging by the angry glare Sampson gave me, he'd finally remembered exactly who I was. Megan seemed excited by the shooting but he looked mad enough to chew up nails and spit out tacks. It was a sure thing Zimmerman was marching to his tune.

Distracted as I was, I didn't see Zimmerman's right fist coming at me until it was almost too late. I turned my face as he hit me, which lessened its power to that of a glancing blow but my quick turn threw me off balance and I landed on my back. As I tried to get my bearings, Zimmerman shed his jacket exposing his shoulder holster and pistol. He removed the holster since he preferred fists to guns. It reminded me old Patch had been beaten to death and not shot. Now I was honor-bound to avenge another friend.

I feigned dizziness and stood up slowly. Then I unbuckled my gun belt and removed the Dragoon from my waistband while Zimmerman glared at me. When I tossed the guns aside, he lunged at me in a surprise move that surprised no one. I ducked out of the way but stuck my leg in his path. He tripped over it and went face first in the dirt.

The gunfight crowd "crowded" 'round us shouting encourage-ment and insults in a rabid frenzy. Nothing fired up some folks like a fistfight. In a rare moment of fair play, I let the fallen German get up and set hisself.

Zimmerman's instincts were those of a brawler and he came at me with his head down and both arms swinging wildly. I slipped his punches easily and jabbed his nose flatter than it already was. He took a half dozen jabs on his beak and a right cross to the eye before he backed off and circled around. His wide nose was broke once again and bleeding freely. His lower lip was split and puffy and his left cheek was rosy red. I was feeling strong and confident.

The crowd roared its approval of my fighting skills and even Zimmerman took notice. "Gut, gut, you haff training. Ve can fight like gentlemen."

The stocky German assumed an upright boxing stance and came at me with fists held high. It was plain to see he'd had some training, too. I knew prize fighting was popular all over Europe at the time and it was plain to see that Zimmerman had noticed too.

For the first time in a real fight, I was looking at the business end of a hard left jab and I didn't cotton to it at all. I went back to duckin' and feintin'. We danced around in the street as the crowd cheered and jeered. All the while I was thanking Chip O'Leary for my "dance" lessons.

My height and reach advantage allowed me to hit the short-er German while staying just beyond his reach. I stuck him with ever'thing I had and he either took 'em or slipped 'em without too much effect. His face was full of blood and his eyes were closing but he was a patient and powerful fighter. He was waiting for one knockout punch and I was trying my best to avoid it.

Suddenly, Zimmerman went into a crouch and cut me off as I danced around. The folks in the crowd were a bloodthirsty lot and clamoring for action. Zimmerman dropped his left hand as he jabbed and suckered me into unloading my right hook. He slipped inside the hook and came up at me with a left uppercut, a right cross and a groin kick that damn near crippled the twins. I landed on my back and lost my wind. As I tried to open my left eye and clear the fog, he charged and kicked at my head. I rolled back and forth trying to stay away from his boots. Finally, he jumped atop me and we rasseled in the dirt. We punched and gouged and bit as the crowd cheered. So much for fighting like gentlemen.

Despite all the yellin' and cheerin', I heard Langley's voice loud and clear above the crowd, "Ya got him, now kill 'im, kill 'im!"

It was suddenly clear to me that I was in a fight to the death. This wasn't just a knuckle and skull scrap till one man was whupped. I realized one of us wasn't gonna walk away from this fight and Zimmerman knew it, too.

I finally got my leg across his neck, yanked him off me and we both scrambled to our feet. We exchanged wild swings at each other which had little effect and only tired us out. Then, when I missed and slipped to one knee, Zimmerman tried a straight hard kick at my head. I leaned back and caught his foot at the top of the kick. Then I stood up and twisted his ankle, which flipped him flat on his face. Before he could recover his bearings, I stepped forward and stomped my left boot on the back of his neck and it was over.

As I stood over his body I remembered old Patch and said under my breath, "*Nemo me impune lacessit.*" Zimmerman paid for his part in killing Patch.

The sound of his neck bones breaking had silenced the crowd. I was dripping blood and sweat as I gasped for breath. I'd never killed a man with my bare hands and sure hadn't wanted to but Sampson left me little choice.

As I reached for my gun belt, someone hit me hard from behind. I fell face flat in the dirt and heard Langley roar. "I'll kill ya for that. I'll stomp ya into dust."

I braced for another assault but none came. The crowd had started up with the cheerin' but suddenly got silent again. I rolled over and looked at Langley out of my one good eye. He was froze in place, just staring at someone or something behind me. I heard him ask. "Who the hell are you.... his big brother?"

I rolled over half-expecting to see G.W. standing there but I was in for a shock. The setting sun was at his back and I couldn't see his face but the man standing behind me was much, much bigger than G.W. It could only be Zackariah James.

I heard his deep bass voice loud and clear. "You might say so." Then he looked down at me. "Got here as quick as I could, Henry. Mind if I take over?"

I started to wish him well but I had no words. It didn't really matter cuz he was already taking over. Zack stepped over my body and strode right up in Sampson's face. Now, Sampson Langley was a mighty big man but he'd never fought a man who was bigger, stronger and faster then he was. Zackariah James was all of that and more.

They stood toe to toe and went at it but Sampson couldn't match the pace. Zack lit into him like a griz-bear takes to a beehive. He just flat tore 'im apart.

Giving credit where it was due, I'll have to admit old Sampson sure could take a punch. In fact, he took a bunch. Zack hit him over and over with both hands but Sampson stubbornly refused to fall. His nose was flattened, his lips were split, both eyes were down to slits and he was spittin' teeth. Given the way his jaw was hanging, it was surely broke, too. It might have been Zimmerman who beat Moses James down in Yuma but it was Langley who paid the tab for it in Flagstaff.

Finally, beaten to a bloody pulp, Sampson went to his knees and pitched forward on his face in the street. He didn't figure to get back up, not that he didn't try. There was no dog in the man. Megan rushed over and knelt by his side and Zack came over to help me to my feet.

With almost no effort, Zack lifted me up from the ground with one hand and brushed dirt from my backside with the other. "You're a hard man to find, Henry. I've been asking around town for you since I got here yesterday."

Well that was a piece of good news. It wasn't that old man in black that was looking for me. It was Zack.

From the corner of my eye, I saw the movement of Megan's blue dress. While lying on his back, Langley pushed her out the way and was desperately trying to get his holdout gun from his jacket pocket.

It just wasn't his day. The hammer caught in the lining of his fancy jacket and he couldn't get it out. He swore in frustration, gasped for air and then seemed to pass out. Megan was sitting on her backside in the street covered with dirt. They made a likely pair.

I offered Megan my hand but she cursed and turned away. She was embarrassed beyond her wildest dreams. All her plannin' and schemin' had come to this. She was the laughing stock of Flagstaff on the day before her wedding. It made me wonder if there would even be a wedding.

"Am I still invited to the reception tonight? Eight o'clock, I believe ya said."

If looks could kill, I would have been a dead man twice over and this time, Megan didn't get prettier as she got mad. She was squealin' like a stuck pig as Zack and I headed for the doc's office. The last thing I heard was Megan pleading for someone to get the sheriff. I could hardly hear her over all the laughing from the crowd.

Doc Lewis was still busy with Charles when we entered his office. Trace had his jeans half down and was fussing over the bloody furrow on his hip. The doc told him to clean it with alcohol and put on a clean bandage. Trace claimed it weren't nothing but I could see the hurtin' of it in his eyes.

Zack and I tended to our hands, as they were cut-up and bloody. Other than that, Zack didn't even look like he'd even been in a fight. On the other hand, I was a mess. My left eye was almost shut and my lip was swole-up and split. My new suit was covered with dirt and blood and the seam was ripped across my right shoulder. The breast pocket was almost torn off along with several buttons. I wondered if they had a tailor somewhere about but plumb forgot to ask.

Trace had watched the fight from the doc's office and couldn't get over how Zack had man-handled Sampson Langley. He said folks would be talking about their fight for months. I asked about the law and he said there was no need to worry. The only law Flagstaff had was an old washed-up sheriff and he was just putting in his time. Besides, all of the fighting was fair and legal in the eyes of the law and we had more than ample witnesses.

That evening, I treated Zackariah to supper in the hotel dining room. Glory waited on us and had big eyes for ol' Zack. She barely acknowledged I was at the table after she got finished teasing me about my blackened eye and busted lip. I was a' might put-out but not many men could stand next to Zackariah James and be noticed.

Over supper, Zack and I caught up on old times. It'd been almost two years since we'd met in San Bernardino. First off he told me that his father was getting better and would fully recover from the beating he took from Zimmerman. Then, he thanked me for killing the German as it saved him the bother. Seems I avenged two wrongs instead of one.

Zack confirmed what they reported in the Yuma paper. The ranchers down there had gotten together and rode Langley and his hoodlums out of town. I told him about my run-ins with them in Bodie and Calico. He'd witnessed the shootout so he already knew about Kid Coyote.

On the personal side, Zack said his sister, Ester, finally got married off. She was almost nineteen and he worried for her. He said she wasn't the best looking filly in the herd but she worked hard and could cook up a storm. That brought to mind my sister, Taylor. She was pushing eighteen and still unmarried.

For his part, Zack usually worked around his father's ranch but took some time for wandering, too. He did a little prospecting here and there and even went chasing after camels a time or two.

Now most everyone knew the stories of Beale's camels but Zack had made a study of them. Just before the Civil War, the United States Army tried an experiment with camels in the Southwest. A Navy Lieutenant name of Edward Beale was in charge of the project and thought they'd work out real good as pack animals. The camels carried four times what a mule could and had four times the stamina, but they scared the horses and mules and took to spitting at folks so the army give up on 'em. The government sold some to zoos and circuses and let he others loose to run wild in the desert.

That was twenty years ago but ever so often, someone would report spyin' one of those ugly critters around. Zack said chasing them was like trying to find a lost gold mine. They were out there somewhere but always beyond the horizon. As for myself, I'd never even seen a camel.

We finished supper and went back to the doc's office to check in on his patients. Trace was up and gone. Prob'ly back at the Kaibab Saloon telling and retelling his version of the day's events.

Charles was still in some danger and would require rest and attention for some time before he was fit again. His "good luck" continued as the bullet seemed to miss his heart and lungs but he'd lost a lot of blood and was semi-conscious at best. An inch either way and we'd 'a been fittin' him for a wooden overcoat.

Hutch was patched up and fast asleep. He'd think long and hard before he followed another fool into hell. I was glad he was alive. No sense in all of 'em dyin'.

Doc Lewis said Sampson Langley refused any treatment and was carted off to his hotel room. The bodies of Kid Coyote, Turner and Zimmerman were thrown in a manure wagon and taken to boot hill. The doc was tuckered but still kept a watchful eye on his patients.

Zack and I went to our rooms. He was staying two doors down from me at the Beaver Street Hotel. Being his business was complete, Zack intended to head back to Yuma the following morning. I invited him to visit the Box H but he declined. He wanted to get home to check on his pa's condition and take charge of their ranch. I made him promise to come back and stay with us another time. We agreed to meet for breakfast so I thanked him again and went off to bed.

When I tried to get to sleep, the events of the day kept coming back to me. As the Major warned me years before, I had a special gift with a six-gun that was also a curse. After what happened tonight, Henry James would be back on the list with Clay Allison,

Luke Short, Ben Thompson, Cullen Baker, and all the rest. I'd have to leave tomorrow to avoid meeting another Preacher Daniels.

I had an early breakfast with Zack since he was eager to get on the road. Glory went from sunshine to cloudy when she heard he was leaving. The poor girl was having no luck with men at all. As we were finishing our coffee, Kenny ran into the dining room to tell us the big news. "The big wedding is off. Sampson Langley is dead!"

I could see the news bothered Zack as he figured to be the cause but Kenny wasn't finished with the news. "Mr. Langley was snake bit. Right there in his hotel room. Somehow, a rattlesnake got in and bit him. How do you figure that?"

Well, that really was news. The same thing happened to Megan's father 'cept he was on his own front porch when he got bit. Snakebite wasn't uncommon but where those two were, when they got bit, was. A man figured to be safe from rattlesnakes in a hotel room or on his front porch. Sampson's death was sure to fuel the stories about Megan being the Black Widow and she was likely to have a hard time of it.

Speaking of the devil, who should walk in the dining room right then but the Black Widow herself. She didn't look fit for company. Her hair, clothes and make-up were a mess and she had a sour look on her face that could curdle fresh milk. When she saw us at the table, she rushed over screamin'. "It's all your fault Sampson's dead. What happens to me now? What am I to do?"

Poor Zach didn't know what to say and tried to apologize. "I sure am sorry but your man left me no choice."

Megan hadn't heard a word he said. She was saving all her fury for me. "You were jealous. You wanted me and you killed Sampson so I wouldn't get married. I hate you!"

Now I did feel kinda sorry for her, but she made me laugh. "I haven't wanted you for quite a spell and I didn't kill your Mister Langley. Maybe all those stories about you being the Black Widow are true."

I could'a put that a whole lot better but she also made me mad. As I saw it, she made her own bed and could damn well sleep in it. Folks around the dining room started to snicker and whisper and Megan was fixin' to explode. In a purple rage, she whirled and stomped out of the dining room to a chorus of hoots and hollers from the onlookers. Glory was cheering the loudest of all.

As Zack and I got up to leave, Glory came over to the table and brushed past me with the devil in her eye and on her tongue. "Since you don't want her anymore, who do you want?"

Zack swallered a chuckle and I turned red to the ears. Glory was surely a caution. She set her cap for me again now that Zack was leaving town. I had no answer for her so I rushed out of the dining room and jumped from the frying pan right into the fire. Megan was in the hotel lobby with a six-shooter pointed at my nose.

The beautiful girl of my dreams turned into a crazed animal right before my eyes. More termagant than princess, she had the look of a varmint caught in a steel trap. She was mad as hell and scairt to death at the same time. Her hands were shaking as she held the pistol. Megan was trying to speak but the words came out sideways and made no sense. Zack and I slowly spread apart so she had to swing the gun wider from right to left to cover us both. Folks were crowding around the lobby, just holding their breath and waiting to see what happened next.

I had no intention of drawing my gun on her but it suddenly came to me that the Colt in my holster was broke and useless. I'd gone and left my old Dragoon in my room and was unarmed once again.

I didn't think she'd shoot but I didn't want to take a chance. I could see Zack was thinking the same thing as we continued to slowly spread farther apart to flank her. Now she had to swing the gun in a wider arc and was having trouble holding it steady. I had to find a way to pinch her fuse 'fore she exploded.

Suddenly, someone from the crowd jumped on Megan like she was a branding calf at roundup and sent her sprawling on her face. Her pistol slid across the floor and Zack picked it up. Slick and quick Megan was bound up with piggin' strings and stretched for show. With a wave of her hat to the cheering crowd Taylor whirled around and said triumphantly. "How's that, big brother?"

The crowd continued to cheer as Taylor stood with one boot planted on Megan's rump and raised her hat like a calf roper in a rodeo. Glory raised Taylor's other arm like they did after a prizefight. Megan was struggling on the floor and was fit to be tied.

Trace Cummings hobbled his way through the crowd and knelt over his hog-tied employer. I guess the morning after had found his hip hurting more than he figured. She was cursin' and screamin' at the same time and he seemed hesitant to untie her. His was a tough job.

Zack and I escorted Taylor out to the street as the crowd dispersed. Then I introduced my sister Taylor, to my brother Zackariah, and assured Taylor I would explain it all later.

Taylor wished to get better acquainted but Zack figured to get while the getting was good so we quickly said our good-byes and he rode off down the road. Taylor and I stood and watched as he disappeared from sight and I tried my best to explain.

"I was 'saddle partners' with two of his brothers, Mal and Josh. When they were killed, I sort of took their place with his family. They have a cattle ranch down by Fort Yuma. He's already saved my hide on two occasions and I'm mighty beholdin'."

Taylor, as usual, was smart-mouthed. "Well, he sure is our big brother."

"Yeah, they don't grow 'em much bigger than Zack."

I didn't know where to start explaining to Taylor or more importantly, where to stop. So instead, I questioned her. "What are you doing here? I thought we agreed you'd stay at the ranch."

She gave me one of "those looks" and said. "You agreed but I didn't. You might be my big brother but you don't speak for me, Monroe Henry, and don't you ever forget it." I was plumb certain she wouldn't let me.

Taylor turned away and headed for the hotel. "Guess I better take a room if we're staying. We are staying aren't we?"

She caught me off guard with that one. I didn't know what to say. "Yeah, I reckon."

The hotel was running on empty as folks were leaving as fast as they'd come. The big wedding was off and folks were leaving town like rats running from a barn fire. Kenny told Taylor to take any key, as all the rooms were empty and paid up for the night. We went to her room and I tried to explain what had happened since I left the ranch yesterday. The way word spread in Flagstaff, she'd certainly heard some version of it already.

I told her about my friend Charles getting shot by Kid Coyote. Then I hemmed and hawed about the gunfight. I was short on details as I was embarrassed to speak of my gun fighting skills. When I mentioned the fistfight, I made Zimmerman's death sound more like an accident than it really was and stressed how Zack saved me from Sampson Langley. My battered face and hands were proof enough of that.

Langley's death this morning was reason enough for Megan's strange behavior and like everyone else, Taylor was skeptical of the snakebite story. She knew all the Black Widow stories.

Then, I told her I had business with Charles and had to wait for him to recover so we could complete it. Taylor had all the facts of what happened but none of the "whys" or "what-fors." She was about to ask when I excused myself to go check on Charles. She asked to come along but I said she should wait till he was feeling better. The fact was, I wished to talk to Charles alone and as soon as possible.

I tried to sneak through the hotel lobby but Kenny saw me and shouted out. "Are you really Henry James, the gunfighter from Virginia City? Folks are saying you are."

I had no good answer for Kenny so I just waved at him and kept on going. I had to get out of town fast or face the "big-name" hunters. Some would be on their way to Flag as soon as they heard the news.

Charles was unconscious and resting fitfully when I got to Doc Lewis' office. The doc wasn't in very good shape hisself as he stayed

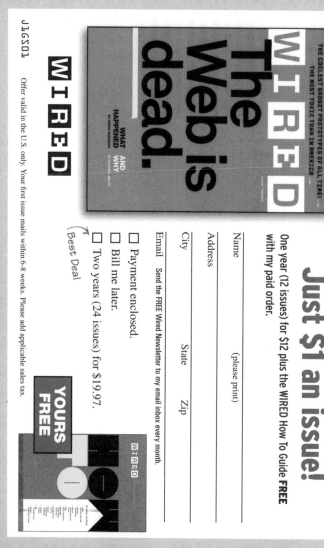

JUST $1 AN ISSUE

www.wired.com

up all night with Charles and Hutch. He looked about to pass out standing upright so I told him to lay down a spell and I'd watch over his patients. It gave me time to think out what I had to say.

Charles surely thought I was his son and thanks to the Pinkertons, in a legal sense, I reckon I was. Of course, according to Pa, Charles' young son actually died on our ranch some twenty years ago and was buried there.

The phony deeds and the original, wherever it was, were made out to Charles U. Farley. That could mean Charles or his son since the middle name wasn't spelled out. One way or the other, I had to get the legal rights to the Box H. I didn't think Charles would care about the ranch either way and it would take a big load off Pa.

Timing was the problem, should I act on my own or wait for Charles to recover? Should I tell either of my "fathers" about the other? How much should I tell Taylor about all this and when? What about the twenty-five thousand dollars Charles was holding for his son? That money could fix up the Box H and leave me enough to start up the ranch I'd always wanted.

The biggest question of all was who was I and who did I wish to be? Four years ago I left home as James Monroe Henry. Right off I became Henry Monroe and then Henry James. Next I tried James Monroe, but it was shortened to Jimmy and finally Jim. I went back to Henry Monroe and then became the Navajo Kid. Now, Charles thinks I'm his son, Charlie Farley, Zachariah thinks I'm Henry Monroe but refers to me as his brother, Henry James, while Taylor and the rest of my family figure I'm still Monroe Henry.

After a couple of hours, I was lost in thought and staring out the window when Charles finally came around. "Charlie, is that you son?"

Well, that answered one big question for the time being, I'd be Charlie Farley for Charles' sake. "Yeah Charles, I'm here. How do you feel?

He coughed and cursed under his breath. "Terrible. I think I've run my last bluff."

I felt his forehead and it was burning hot. He was spittin' blood and gurglin' as he tried to speak. "Son, I...."

I leaned closer as he was having a hard time getting it out. "Is there anything I can do?"

He coughed violently. "Wells Fargo.... I put the money in your name. I'm proud... that.... you're my son."

I felt like I was gut-punched. "And, I'm proud that you're my.... Father."

Charles smiled as best he could. "Wish we had more time together. I never...."

He started coughin' and chokin' again. I woke Doc Lewis and he went to work on Charles. He asked me to step outside so I started to walk away when Charles called to me. "Charlie.... son..."

I knelt by his side and took his outstretched hand. The doc just shook his head in a manner that said it all.

Charles was bound to speak his piece. "I saw a lawyer while you were gone. I made out my Last Will and Testament. I left you everything. I didn't want that old whore to get it." He smiled when he said that. "My saloon, 'Saint Charles Place' in Santa Fe.... and that deeded ranch.... they're yours...."

Tears filled my eyes and cascaded down my cheeks. I was watching Charles die but I was thinking of my own pa and the Box H ranch. "I'll take over the Saint Charles if that's what you want, but the deed to the ranch is no good without the original...."

Charles choked a bit but tried to continue. "Original was..... Henry Staaa..."

He coughed up some frothy blood and gasped his last breath. Charles never finished the name as his hand released its hold on mine and life left his body.

"Henry who? .... Charles...?"

Charles was beyond hearing or answering. The bullet had hit a lung after all and he never had a chance. I wanted to bawl like an orphaned calf but felt like a fool. Charles thought I was his long lost son but to me, he was little more than a friendly stranger. A stranger who just left me twenty-five thousand dollars, a gambling hall in Santa Fe and a copy of the deed to the Box H ranch.

I was glad for Charles' sake I hadn't told him the truth. He died thinking he had a son who would carry on and that was good enough for most men. My guilt would be in accepting his property but as far as I knew, there was no one with a better claim.

I paid Doc Lewis for his service and made arrangements to box up Charles' body so he could be transported to the Box H. They'd pack him in ice and a teamster could bring him out by wagon in a day or two. In death, at least, Charles could lie near his son.

I left the doc's office and headed for the hotel. I figured to get Taylor and leave as soon as we paid a visit to the Wells Fargo office. Passers-by were taking particular notice of my fancy gun belt. I was unsettled by all the attention. Henry James was too well known and his reputation would become a real problem, real soon. Then I remembered I was still totin' a broke Colt and was actually unarmed again. That thought hasten my steps.

Kenny was at the desk when I entered the hotel lobby. He got all excited and lost his composure. "Kid.... Mister James.... there was someone else looking for you. A big old man, dressed all in black. He was carrying a big gun and a Bible." That was just what I needed, once again.

I cut off his stammerin' by telling him Charles had died. I told Kenny to box up any personal stuff Charles left in the room and send it to the Box H. I tossed him a Double Eagle and thanked him in advance for his service. Then, I raced up the stairs to my room.

I knocked on Taylor's door and told her Charles had passed and we were leaving right now. Once I'd gathered up all my gear, I paused at the door and checked the hallway. It was empty till Taylor poked her head out looking for me. We ran down the stairs and out of the hotel as fast as we could. Taylor was laughing like we were playing a game. Only thing was, I wasn't playing. Kenny just stood there staring as we ran past.

Taylor's horse, Domino, was stabled next to Goner in the livery and we were saddled and mounted in no time. Taylor finally realized

I was serious about getting out of town and was dying of curiosity. I told her, any questions she had would have to wait.

We made one stop at the Wells Fargo office so I could see what account Charles opened in my name. Taylor stayed outside with the horses while I went in.

The resident agent, Mr. Quincy, greeted me as the young Mister Farley and I went along. He was eager to show me their records. The money was there, ever' penny. I left twenty-four thousand in the account and took the balance in cash.

Charles left his Last Will and Testament in their care along with two copies of notarized letters. The originals were addressed to his pit boss and the bar manager at Saint Charles Place. Everything seemed in order as the letters instructed them to turn over the Saint Charles to me in case of his death. The instructions also assured them of their current positions for as long as they wished. I noticed by the stationery's letterhead Charles had gone to my old friend, Cecil Abernathy, for the legal papers.

I knew the rest of the money was best left on deposit with Wells Fargo but I took Charles' Will and the letters with me. It looked like a trip to Santa Fe was in my future. I was thankful that Taylor was waiting outside so I wouldn't have to explain about my name or the money. I thanked Mr. Quincy and left his office.

As we were riding out, I saw Trace coming out of the doc's office. He was walking with some discomfort but claimed his wound was nothing more than a scratch. Trace was as tough as aged rawhide and would mend in a hurry. He told us Doc Lewis had given Megan something to calm her down after our earlier encounter. She was still hysterical and madder than a treed cougar. He said I shouldn't plan on taking her up on the job offer. I laughed and told him she could keep her job but he could come by the Box H if he ever needed one. He shook my hand and said he might just take me up on it.

Taylor and I left Flag heading south for a few miles before we doubled back around and headed west. We might not be followed but I wanted to be sure we didn't accidentally bring any gun trouble to the Box H.

Chapter XI
"Grasshopper Flats at last"

Taylor pestered me with questions all the way home. Why did we leave Flagstaff in such a hurry? Who did I think was following us? What happened to Charles and what business did I have with Wells Fargo?

I told her what little I knew about the man in black and why he might be following me. When I mentioned the name Henry James, I could see in her face she'd heard it before. That meant I had to tell her about Mal and Josh and how I came to get that name. When I showed her the busted-up Colt in my holster, she said Pa had some old gun parts at the ranch that might fit.

Explaining 'bout Charles was a trickier thing. I couldn't tell Taylor who Charles really was since Pa never told her 'bout the deed or the baby so I just said he was a friend and partner in the cattle business. I casually mentioned I hoped to bury him at the ranch but I didn't say why.

Next thing, I had to show her the papers I had when I left the Wells Fargo office. I let her see Charles' Will and the letters concerning Saint Charles Place. Taylor was shocked at first and then got real excited about going with me to Santa Fe. I promised to ask Pa if she could.

I couldn't explain the copy of the deed, so I got Taylor off the subject by mentioning Megan. I figured she'd have some thoughts about her and the doin's in Flagstaff. Turned out she had lots of thoughts.

Taylor figured Megan got just what was coming to her and was proud of her small part in it. She never liked Megan before John's death and would never forgive her part in it. She felt the curse of the Black Widow, if there really was one, could be viewed as some measure of justice for all the grief Megan caused.

When we got around to discussing Langley's death, Taylor had a strange memory to share. "Monroe, do you recall how much Thomas used to like snakes? Remember how he used to tease me with 'em? He was forever tossing 'em at me just to hear me scream. He never threw poisonous ones but how was I to know which was which? I really hated it and Pa finally made him quit."

I saw where she was going. "Just like with Clayton Shaw and Sampson Langley? You figure someone threw the snakes at 'em?"

She pulled up her horse and said very seriously. "Not just someone. I think it was Thomas. Think about it, Monroe. Revenge might be all he has to live for. Megan made his life a living hell so he might be doing the same to her. Or... maybe he's just crazed with jealousy and wants to keep anybody else from marrying her. Who knows?"

I couldn't believe it of my brother. "What about the others, her lawyer husband, the ranch foreman or that Lawson fella? They weren't snake-bit."

Taylor sounded like a Pinkerton detective who had the case all figured out. I suspected her reading must have included Edgar Allen Poe and his *Murders in the Rue Morgue* since she sounded a lot like his hero, Auguste Dupin.

She continued in a frenzy. "Her husband might have been snake-bit before the stampede and her foreman, Tucker, might have been shot to cover up another snake bite. Once a fella gets trampled or shot up, who bothers to look for a snakebite? As for Lawson, his horse got spooked by something before the cinch broke and he got bucked off. Why not a snake?"

I had to admit her theories made more sense than all the non-sense about the curse of the Black Widow. Taylor kept on supposin'.

"I think he hangs around somewhere keeping an eye on her and then kills anyone who gets too close."

A chill ran through me as I remembered the times it felt like I was being followed when I was in Flagstaff. I'd been escorting Megan around town and if Taylor was right, Thomas might have been stalking me.

"If you're right, we'll have to find him and put an end to all the killing."

Taylor agreed but added. "We can't tell Pa what we're doing until we know for sure. He banned Thomas from his life but he still holds him in his heart."

"Pa doesn't have to know. We'll make up some excuse and head out to look for him in a couple of days. Got any idea where he'd be?"

"Only one place he'd feel at home.... somewhere 'round Grasshopper Flats."

That figured. One way or the other I was going back to the Flats and there was no way of avoiding it.

It was dark when we got to the ranch. Taylor and I put our horses up in the barn and fed 'em after giving each a good rub down. Goner and Domino were getting along and seemed to enjoy each other's company. Guess mares and stallions always got along.

Supper was long past but Susanna set out fresh coffee and some leftovers for us. I tried to tell Pa and G.W. what I could about my two days in Flag but it wasn't easy. I'd no sooner mentioned Charles' death than Taylor interrupted with the news about Saint Charles Place in Santa Fe. She was burstin' with excitement but Pa and G.W. held reservations. They didn't want either of us leaving the ranch.

Taylor went off with Susanna to plan her upcoming trip to Santa Fe so I could speak freely. I explained that Charles thought of me as his long lost son. I went on to say the original deed to the ranch might never be found but since Charles and his son were both dead, it wouldn't matter. They were disappointed about the original deed but accepted the fact they might never have legal title to the ranch.

256   ROBERT OLIVER BERNHAGEN

I certainly understood how hard it was for 'em to plan for the future without clear and outright ownership of the ranch.

When I told 'em Charles' body was being brought here for burial, Pa started to object so I reminded him Charles could be buried right next to his son. That closed the matter as Pa and G.W. exchanged questioning looks.

Taylor and Susanna came back and I let Taylor tell 'em about Megan and her troubles. She even demonstrated her tacklin' and ropin' skills on poor Susanna. Taylor barely mentioned the gunfight or the fistfights but that didn't get me off the hook with Pa. He'd taken notice of my battered face and hands so I had to explain.

I finished the conversation by telling them Taylor and I would head out for Flagstaff in a few days to order badly needed supplies and building materials for the ranch. I showed 'em the cash I'd taken from the Wells Fargo account and said it was all to go toward making improvements around the Box H. That made ever'body happy and let me get a good night's sleep for a change.

The next two days were spent taking a close look at the ranch and writing down how much of ever'thing was needed. At the top of the list were barbed wire and fence posts but the list went on to include paint, lumber, tools, leather goods and seed corn. Susanna put store by a garden and wished for fresh sweet corn next year. She was also partial to sorghum or as we called it, corn squeezin's.

I searched through Pa's sack of gun parts and found a cylinder and cylinder pin that fit right into my Peacemaker. They weren't fancy like the original parts but they worked just as well. I took off the ivory grips and replaced them with plain wood. Without the gold inlay on the cylinder and the fancy grips, the gun looked pretty much like any other since the rest of the engraving couldn't be seen unless you looked at the gun close-up.

Taylor came up with the idea of removing all the silver stars from my gun belt and replacing them with some well used Navajo conchos from an old belt of hers. With that done, the gun belt no longer attracted unwanted attention and looked as old and worn as the conchos. That would help keep Henry James, the gunfighter, in the past but I still worried 'bout the old man dressed in black.

The next morning, a teamster and his wagon arrived from Flagstaff with Charles' body. We planted him on the mound behind the house, right next to his son. The ceremony was short and bittersweet. I was the only one to speak and had little to say except to thank Charles for leaving me his property. I didn't know how things would turn out in Santa Fe but the money he left was sure welcome around the ranch. I felt thankful and guilty at the same time.

On the third day, Taylor and I rose with the sun and rode back toward Flag. The weather was beautiful and the company was, too. Some women were all flutters and ruffles but Taylor was a true western girl. She could ride, rope and shoot as good as 'most any cowboy and still look beautiful doing it. There was a mighty lucky man somewhere in her future.

Flagstaff had gone back to being a sleepy little town again when we rode in. With all the extra folks gone, the hustle and bustle was back to slow and steady. We left our "want list" with several merchants figuring they could transport ever'thing to the ranch. It would mean hiring several teamsters and wagons but there was no help for it. We left 'em a long list.

Without taking time for lunch, we headed south toward Oak Creek Canyon. Along the way, I showed Taylor where the S Diamond was but we gave it a wide berth. It was a beautiful ranch but held only bad memories for me. I was certain Megan wouldn't be up for company.

The trail ran through grassy meadows surrounded by dense forests of tall ponderosa pines. We saw herds of elk and deer casually grazing the afternoon away. A Golden Eagle soared overhead and jackass rabbits scooted away as we rode past.

When we started going down into the canyon, the beauty of the red rock formations took my breath away. Four years ago, I was too young to really appreciate the sheer cliffs, hundreds of feet tall, that descended from the rim above to the creek below. It was lush and green and smelled of pine and juniper. Since Taylor had been to the Flats many times, she was familiar with the best way to go and took the lead. Our descent was steep and slow going at first and then leveled out. At this point, the trail followed along Oak Creek which was running shallow as it splashed over the rocks and boulders that peppered its path. We even disturbed a big old brown bear that just stood up on his hind legs and stared at us as we rode past. I reckon curiosity is universal to all animals.

I couldn't help but think of my ride through there four years ago. I was such a dumb kid. Thinking I knew it all when I knew almost nothing. I guess it's that way with most kids. I was lucky to have survived the last four years.

We came upon what looked to be a long abandoned cabin by the creek and decided to stop so we could rest the horses. They could drink from the creek and graze on the grass by the bank. The water was cool and clear, and the scenery was almost beautiful beyond description. Taylor unpacked some grub she and Susanna had packed for us and got set up for a picnic. It seemed a perfect spot for one until we heard a salty voice growl at us from the cabin.

"This here's private property. Git off."

We thought the cabin was deserted but it was plain enough we were wrong. The gravelly voice even sounded familiar to me but I couldn't place it.

"We're not staying. We only wished to rest our horses and fix some grub."

Taylor was ahead of me as usual. "Would you like to join us? There's plenty."

Frozen in place, we waited some long seconds until the voice spoke again. "What kinda grub ya got?"

We heard him rustling around inside the cabin and relaxed a' might. It sounded like he was fixin' to join us. Before I saw him, I smelt him. Right off, I remembered that God-awful smell from the Flats. The voice in the cabin belonged to the old bear hunter who beat the snot out of me four years ago. I wondered if he'd remember.

When he came out of the cabin, the barrel of his .56-50 Spencer rifle preceded him and he kept it pointed in our general direction as we talked. He was as I pictured him in my nightmares about the Flats. Tall and thin with a face like a brush broom. It was my bet he was still a tough old blister and a man to fight shy of.

"Said, what's for lunch? "

Taylor opened her saddlebags to show him. "We have beef sandwiches, buttermilk biscuits, canned peaches and fresh coffee."

He seemed interested. "Peaches.... and real coffee?"

Taylor answered quickly. "Yup.... as soon as we get a fire going."

That broke his stubborn resistance. He lowered his rifle and started to help me gather wood for a fire. We had coffee ready in a few minutes and actually enjoyed our little picnic.

The old recluse said his name was Rufus and except for some feller named "Big Jim Thompson," he was the only white settler in the canyon. He said he'd lived here and about for ten years and only wandered over to Grasshopper Flats once or twice a year. Naturally, it had been my great misfortune to run into him on one of those rare trips. It was some small comfort he hadn't recognized me, so far. I was three for three. Slick, Megan and now Rufus had all forgotten what I looked like. Maybe, just maybe, I'd changed so much no one would remember.

Rufus was mighty glad for company and ate like a bear fresh from hibernation. He told us all about his lonely life and tried to help us in our search for Thomas but he didn't know much about the Flats or any of the folks who lived thereabouts.

Old Rufus was a nice enough fella but it was hard to be around him cuz of the stench. I could see it was bothering Taylor and even the horses seemed to notice. When we were ready to leave, a thought crossed my mind. "Would you happen to have yourself a younger brother?"

"Only one I recall was a half-brother, name of Cleetis, short stocky feller. Came out west to trap beaver about.... forty years ago. Haven't heard of him since. He came along with Pa's second wife. Pa's on his fourth now, with twenty-one young-uns in his line so I reckon I've got a whole passel of brothers and sisters, half and otherwise. All of 'em much younger, of course."

"Well, don't shoot anything that looks like a short griz bear until ya see its snout. It might turn out to be your kin."

He was amused. "Sure 'nuff?"

"Yup, last I knew, Cleetis was heading this way with his squaw."

"A squaw? Can she cook?"

"Gets right along.... Lil's a good woman."

"Well, what do ya know.... Cleetis, ya say?"

Taylor and I said our good-byes and promised to stop whenever we passed that way again.

We hadn't gone fifty yards when Taylor was rejoicing in the fresh air. "I wonder if he always smells that bad. You think he's ever had a bath?"

"I imagine not.... he smelt the same way four years ago"

Taylor whirled around in her saddle and glared at me. "You knew him four years ago?"

Since my mouth had outrun my brain again, I figured it was time I told Taylor about my first trip to Grasshopper Flats. It might come up when we got there and she should hear it first from me. I told the story from beginning to end as we rode the winding trail. Taylor laughed at my childish behavior and was amazed I'd met Megan back then but was concerned about my run-in with Rufus. I told her it was a good lesson learned and I was grateful to him now. Some men would have kilt me for what I'd done.

As I retold the story, it came to me I still didn't know anything about the town drunk. The shooting was a blur in my mind but I remembered he ran me out of town. Maybe by going back I could come to terms with that last part of my awful dream.

As we rode into Grasshopper Flats I couldn't help but notice it looked pretty much as I left it. There were a few more tents and makeshift cabins as well as a new storefront or two but some of the old fronts were vacant and others were falling apart. The Flats was a dying town. Only one saloon survived but it was my old favorite, The Rainbow's End.

The sun was just starting to set as we tied up to the hitchin' rail. Since saloons weren't generally too keen on young female customers, Taylor waited with the horses while I went inside. Wouldn't you know it? The first thing I see is good old Deke standing behind the bar like he'd never left it. He was tall, lean and butt-ugly, just like I remembered. That rovin' eye of his still made me uneasy. He showed no sign of recognizing me as he came over to my end of the bar. "Welcome, stranger. What can I get ya?"

I just smiled at him and held his attention for a few seconds before I finally spoke. "I'll take a beer but what I'm really looking for is information."

Deke poured me a beer from a bottle and waited as I quenched my thirst. There were only four other customers in the place. They were sitting at a table in the back playing cards. The rest of the saloon was exactly as I remembered.

"I'm looking for Thomas Jefferson Henry. I hear he used to hang out here."

Deke seemed surprised by the question. "Thomas Henry? I ain't seen hide nor hair of him in more'n a year. He tried to drink hisself to death after he kilt his twin brother. They were in love with the same woman, ya know. Iffin love is blind, then his must have also been deef, dumb and just plain stupid too.

This here saloon became his only refuge. After the shoot out, he spent the next few days marinating hisself in alcohol. He sat all alone at that table right back there and drank. Whenever he finished off a bottle of whiskey, I just brought him another. By noontime ever' day, he was staring down his second bottle and getting sadder and madder. No telling how much he drank. I gave up counting. Ya know, a man cain't never drink hisself out of a hole cuz drinking just dug the hole deeper."

"Didn't anyone try to stop him?"

Deke took out a well-used bar rag and started pushing the dust around on the bar top. "Mostly, customers came and went with little notice taken but I do seem to recollect that his older brother came by once. Ya gotta understand, after Thomas sat here for three days running, he ceased to be a person of interest. Folks figured he'd finally pass out or pass away from all the alcohol. Either way, it was pretty much the same to them. He kilt his own brother in a fair fight, sure enough, but that made no never mind. The law might'a been satisfied but his father and most of the folks in this town weren't. Soon enough he found that even an alcoholic stupor wasn't doing him no good. Don't believe there's enough whiskey in the whole wide world to block out his memories."

"Do you have any idea where he went after he left here?"

"Folks saw him over in Rimrock....that's about 20 miles south'a here. I don't rightly know for sure but I heard he wandered down to Fort Verde and then over by Prescott. Guess he got in some shooting scrapes along the way. Course that's all rumors and gossip. The last time I heard.... he was in that mining camp they call Jerome, I think. But that's been at least six months ago.

I remembered Pa describing Jerome. It was basically a tent and shack community located on Cleopatra Hill, part of the Mingus Mountains. It was some thirty miles northeast of Prescott and twenty-five miles southwest of the "Flats." Jerome was populated by miners, gamblers and outlaws of every breed and nature. Born of mud, blood and beer, it was just setting up for a massive copper mining operation. Thomas would have been drawn to it like a bear to honey.

Deke figured it was time for him to ask the questions. "Why are you hunting him?"

I was enjoying my advantage over Deke so I gave him a riddle to chew on. "The day he killed his brother, he killed my brother, too." I slowly downed the beer and turned to leave. "Much obliged."

Deke was confused. "If he was your brother.... and his brother.... then.... you must be...."

I had to laugh at his bewilderment. "James Monroe Henry, the kid from Grasshopper Flats. Remember?"

Deke turned a whiter shade of pale and stammered. "We were just funning with you back then. We didn't mean no harm."

I let him off the hook. "I know, I know. Anything that doesn't kill a man makes him stronger, right? Remember....if you hear anything about Thomas...."

Deke was relieved I wasn't angry with him. "I'll get word to your ranch.... yes sir.... it's the Box H, ain't it?"

I had one more question I was almost afraid to ask. "Do you remember the town drunk? The one that chased me out'a here with a pistol. Who was he?"

Deke looked like a stoppered soda bottle sitting in the sun. He wanted to answer but something was holding him back. "Yah, I remember but I cain't recall a name. No matter, he ain't around anymore."

He knew more'n he was telling but I was still concerned with finding Thomas. The town drunk from four years ago would have to wait.

Taylor and I lit out for Jerome. There was just enough light to make it before dark if we hurried. Along the way, we rode through the little town of Cottonwood. Taylor said it sprung up about three years earlier. Unlike the Flats, it looked like a real town as it housed many of the miners from Jerome. I noticed they had a sheriff's office and thought maybe he'd be of help if we couldn't find Thomas on our own.

It was full dark when we neared Jerome and we decided to make camp a mile or so from town. Jerome was little more than a tent town, set up for miners to sleep between shifts in the copper mines. It had all the usual vices of a boomtown but none of the fashion. There were few buildings. Even the bars and brothels were run out of tents. It was no fit place for decent folks let alone a young lady like Taylor, 'specially at night.

We got an early start the next morning and asked around about Thomas as we went from mine to mine. Finally, a grizzled old miner named "Cap" had an answer.

"I recollect Thomas Henry. Fancied hisself a card sharp and a gunfighter just like that notorious toothyanker Doc Holliday. Both of 'em had the same death wish. That makes a man hard to figger. When a man ain't afeard of death, he has a powerful edge.

Thomas was always in a black mood which got him to drinking, gambling, fighting and then more drinking. He weren't any great shakes with a sixgun but he was more that a match for the copper miners and working cowboys around here. Heard he kilt two men and wounded some others."

Cap said we should check out a certain old abandoned mine-shaft. He said if we was looking for the "Hermit of Copper Top Mountain", that would be the place to find him. We had no idea what he meant by that but Taylor coaxed him into leading us in the general direction of the shaft so he could continue his story.

"When he got here in Jerome, Thomas got into his usual scrape over a card game but there was no gunplay.....no sir. Before he could draw his six-gun, a group of miners jumped him from behind and took his pistol away. Then they took turns trying to stomp the life out of him. Dying might 'a been an easy thing for a man like Thomas but I bet taking a beating like that weren't in his plans. His mind must'a come unhinged cuz afterwards, he didn't seem too certain what was real and what weren't. He holed-up in that old mineshaft and survived by trapping small animals and scrounging for scraps in the camp garbage. Some claimed he lived on rats and mice. He rarely comes out during daylight and we all generally avoid him when he does. Us miners tend to be kinda superstitious."

Taylor had heard the wild stories about the crazy hermit but never connected them with Thomas. She couldn't believe the "Hermit" was her brother.

From the mouth of the tunnel we called his name but got no response. That meant someone would have to go inside and that someone figured to be me. I fashioned a half-assed torch out of broken branches and old oil rags and ventured into the mountain. The tunnel had several drifts off the main shaft, as the first miners who worked the claim must have been digging by trial and error. None of the drifts went too far and I found no sign of recent activity. There was residue from several old campfires and some animal bones but they looked mighty old, too.

My torch was burning out and I was about to turn track when I saw a sliver of light up ahead. There was a back way out of the tunnel. It figured. No matter how disturbed, Thomas would have provided himself with another way out. Pa always said even a gopher was smart enough to have at least two ways in and out of his hole. I followed the shaft of light to an outside entrance, which was carefully concealed behind a rockslide and natural vegetation. There were fresh tracks around and embers from a recent fire. I went back into the tunnel a ways and found another blind shaft that was far from abandoned. It looked like a den or hideout.

The set up sure looked like Thomas knew what he was doing. He'd built a fine nest in that abandoned tunnel. He had stacked firewood, several cases of canned goods, a bed made of thick animal hides and three large pottery crocks full of fresh water. I could see a beat-up coffee pot and frying pan off to one side and a small stack of candles on the other. Then I heard a rattle.

All of a sudden, the tunnel was alive with rattlesnakes, prob'ly Diamondbacks or Mohave Greens. There had to be at least a dozen of 'em. They were coming at me from several directions all at once. Every hair on my body stood up and I froze in place. I was cut-off from the rear entrance so I leaped in the other direction and made my way back the same way I came in. This time, however, I had no torch to light the way and the light shaft from behind me disappeared as I stumbled along. I tripped over rocks and debris and fell several times. I also ran my head into two low overhangs, which liked to knock me senseless.

I shouted for Taylor so I could follow the sound of her voice through the blackness. At first, her voice seemed far off but thankfully, it kept getting louder. Finally, I got to where I could see the light behind her as she stood in the tunnel entrance. Old "Cap" was still waiting with her.

From my description of the rear entrance, Cap was able to lead us around the mountain to the general area. Thomas' backdoor was so well concealed we were a half-hour finding it. By accident, I happened upon a huge old alligator juniper, which Thomas must have used as a regular hitchin' post. All the grass around was close cropped and there was fresh manure. With some careful study, I was able to backtrack him until I found the entrance. I guess I wasn't the only one listening to Hopi Joe when he told us about survival in the forest. Thomas had listened too.

It was pretty clear Thomas had been using these tunnels as his hideout and created the crazy hermit myth just to keep folks away. The stories of him eating rats and mice were to cover the feeding of his snakes. It sounded silly to say it but my brother was a snake-herder.

If Thomas was responsible for Langley's death, then he'd had plenty of time to return from Flagstaff while we were at the ranch. Considering the snakes he kept, that seemed a sure bet. We could either try to track him down or wait for him to return. We chose to wait.

Cap went back to some tent saloon while Taylor and I hid out and waited. We talked of many things but mostly of Thomas and what he'd become. His tunnel set-up showed cunnin' and long-term plannin'. A crazy man might hide in an old mine but he wouldn't stack firewood and candles or have a case of canned goods. Thomas also kept a horse and found his way around when he stalked Megan. He was crazed but not crazy.

Taylor also spoke at length about her dreams to get away from the ranch and see the big cities of the West. Denver and San Francisco were at the top of her list but she'd recently added Santa Fe. In my travels, the only big city I'd seen was the *Pueblo de Los Angeles*. Big cities were all right to visit, I reckon, but I couldn't imagine wanting to live in one.

Midday passed and it was late afternoon before we saw or heard anything other than the normal sounds of the forest. I was sitting on a lichen-covered rock eating wild raspberries when I noticed the sky was cloudin' up. All of a sudden-like, I could feel the wind whippin' around and the temperature dropped like a stone. That usually signaled a summer monsoon rain was upon us and we'd better beware. Such storms were likely to be very heavy but brief. We got our slickers from our saddlebags and ducked inside the rear entrance to the tunnel. I wasn't about to go in any farther. I had no wish to disturb those damned rattlesnakes again.

The rain came in a raging torrent. It pounded the ground and was whirled about by the violent and twisting winds. At times, the rain moved horizontally and came way in the tunnel.

Through the thunder and fury of the storm, I heard a horse approaching at full gallop. Someone figured to get out of the rain as quick as possible. The horse and rider pulled up to the alligator juniper, which we figured was Thomas' hitchin' tree. The rider dismounted and tied the horse. He pulled his Winchester from its scabbard, grabbed his saddlebags and headed in our direction.

I only got a quick glimpse cuz the rider had his hat pulled down low but it sure didn't look like Thomas. He was Injun dark with his long black hair in braids. His clothes were well worn and he was wearing moccasins. From his general size and description, I would have figured him for a Navajo.

The rider was so intent on getting into the tunnel he never even looked up to see us until he was only a few feet away. Then, he dropped his saddlebags and started to lever his Winchester. Taylor screamed. "Thomas!"

I knocked the rifle from his hands with a large piece of firewood. He reached for the pistol in his waistband but I swung with the log once again and knocked him hard agin' the tunnel wall. Momentarily stunned, he fell to the ground and I grabbed up his guns.

Looking down at him, I couldn't believe the rider was Thomas. Somehow, he'd colored his hair black and his skin was burnt brown from the sun. He was dressed in white man's clothes and looked for all the world to be a reservation Injun. It was small wonder no one had seen him about. He could walk around any town with his head bowed and folks would pay him no mind. I was pretty sure I'd seen him hanging 'round the livery in Flag.

Taylor bent down and fussed over him. "You didn't have to hit him so hard. He's still our brother."

"Brother or no, I didn't figure to let him shoot us." I pulled my pistol and moved off to the side to keep an eye on him. "Careful.... he might not know who we are."

When Thomas regained his senses, he pulled away from Taylor and glared at me. His eyes were wide white and twitchin' back and forth. He didn't seem to hear Taylor talking to him as he stared at me and my gun.

"Thomas! Are you all right? It's me, Taylor.... your sister. This here is our brother, Monroe...."

His face contorted with hate and fear as he shouted at me, "You'll never have Megan. No one will ever have Megan. She's mine."

Panic seemed to come upon him and he looked back and forth for somewhere to run. Since I was standing between him and the rear entrance, his only escape route would mean going back into the tunnels. He leaped to his feet, grabbed Taylor and flung her into me. Then he whirled around and ran for his nest. In the dark, and as panicked as he was, he must have run right into his den and stepped on his snakes. We heard him curse and scream in pain. There was a brief struggle with the sounds of agony echoing through the tunnels. Finally, all was quiet.

Taylor buried her head in my chest and cried for her brother. I tried to console her but was in shock myself. Whoever or whatever ran into those snakes was not my brother. He might have been once, but not any longer.

After the storm had passed, we fashioned some torches and went into the tunnels just far enough to reach Thomas' body and drag it out. Judging by his face, he died a horrible death but there was no help for it. If his life had to end, it seemed fitting that his snakes caused it. We tied him to his horse and trailed down to Cottonwood.

After all the rain, the streets were near empty when we rode in and hitched up in front of the sheriff's office. The sheriff came out and introduced himself as County Sheriff Bradford Mullins. He was a year or two past his prime but wore his badge with pride. There was no nonsense in the man and it was clear he was there to serve the people who paid his salary.

We gave him our names and explained the snake-bit body draped over the horse belonged to our brother, Thomas Jefferson Henry. He made a careful inspection of the body as I went on about the snakes as best I could. He nodded his agreement as to the cause of death. "Why did you bring him to me? This here ain't no business of the law."

I looked at Taylor and she reluctantly told the sheriff of our suspicions and what we'd found in the tunnels. He listened carefully as she spoke and looked at me when she finished to see if I had anything else to add. "Heard about the Henry twins shooting it out over a woman. Terrible thing, that. Minds me of Cain and Abel in the Good Book."

Slowly and respectfully I asked a favor. "Sheriff, I was hoping you could keep our suspicions under your hat since we don't know any of it for sure and either way, Thomas is dead. We just wanted you to know in case you were still investigating any of the cases."

Sheriff Mullins pondered that a moment. "Come in a minute and I'll make a report. You go ahead and sign it for my records and that'll be it. There ain't no punishment for the dead and the rest of your family has surely suffered enough."

I went into the sheriff's office, sat down and watched him write out a short report. As I signed at the bottom of the page, the sheriff leaned across the desk and said in a lowered voice. "Guess you don't remember me from Grasshopper Flats?"

That was so unexpected I was rendered speechless. I couldn't recall anything about any sheriff in the Flats. I looked him straight on and had no memory of him at all. "Ah.... no I don't, Sheriff. Were you there four years ago?"

The sheriff laughed. "Yes, only I wasn't the sheriff then. I was the town drunk.... now do you remember?"

It was a good thing I was already sitting as I might have fallen down as the last part of my dream flashed before my eyes. It was truly ironic that the only one to recognize me from that day was the town drunk. Once again, I was back in Grasshopper Flats and relivin' that fateful day.

APRIL 7, 1878

The fun loving good old boys at Grasshopper Flats woke up the old town drunk named Brad and told him they had a young drunk fixing to take his place. "His place" consisted mainly of sweepin' and swampin' out the bar in return for sleeping in the storeroom and a drink now and then. When or if he ate, no one knew or cared.

When the old drunk was awake and just sober enough to protest the firing, they arranged for the two of us to strap on pistols and settle our differences like real men.

So there we were, two drunken fools standing in the middle of the street facing down each other. I was just drunk enough to think the whole thing was mighty funny until I dropped my pistol while drawing it and the old drunk actually shot at me. He didn't hit anything important but he kept trying as I hightailed it out of town to the hoots and hollers of those good old boys.

That's what bothered me all this time about that day in the Flats. It wasn't the drinkin' or the gamblin' my money away. It wasn't even getting slapped by Megan or beat-up by Rufus. It was that I'd run away. I got scared and didn't stand. I was afraid deep down.... I was a coward. All this time, I'd been afraid of being afraid.

SPRING 1882

I regained my senses and answered the sheriff. "Now I do. What in the world happened? How did you get to become sheriff?"

Sheriff Bradford Mullins sat back in his chair and smiled at me. "In a way, I owe it all to you. I had been a deputy Marshall back in Texas but I accidentally shot a bystander during a shootout and got run out of town on a rail. Then I started to drink so I could forget. After a while, I forgot what I was drinking to forget so I just drank for the hell of it. Now any fool knows you cain't drink yourself out of trouble but for many years I kept trying."

He opened his desk drawer and pulled out a piece of red gingham cut in the rough shape of a star. "The boys at the Rainbows End pinned this on me after you lit out. Said I could be the town sheriff as well as the town drunk. Somehow, this pitiful red star woke me from my long drunken stupor and I stopped drinking, cold turkey. I cleaned-up and got back my self respect. By working odd jobs around the area, I was able to buy some new clothes, a horse, saddle and pistol. I ran for the sheriff's job as soon as there was an opening here in Cottonwood. The good folks elected me and I've been at it for more than a year."

I got up and shook his hand. "Glad I could be a help. That day in the Flats meant a lot to me, too. It taught me a lot about life." I pointed to the report. "Thanks again, Sheriff."

Taylor and I left Cottonwood and headed back toward Grasshopper Flats. We couldn't make it all the way to the ranch so we decided to camp out again. Taylor figured that anywhere in the canyon would be all right as long as we got upwind of Rufus' cabin.

We planned to stop in the Flats just long enough to rest and water our horses. There was a big black gelding with a white blaze tied to the hitchin' rail when we rode up but I was too busy thinking about the events of the day to give it much notice.

Taylor went over to a broke-down boarding house to see if we could get anything to eat. I went in The Rainbows End to get a beer and tell Deke that Thomas was dead. He'd see to it everyone else heard about it. Good news or bad, western gossip traveled like a wind-blown grass fire. Our news should put an end to the questions about Thomas and the tall tales about the crazy Hermit of Copper Top Mountain.

Once inside, I found Deke tending bar and the four card players from yesterday still at the same table as if they'd never left. There was also one large, grouchy old man dressed all in black. Too late, I remembered the black gelding with the white blaze.

Deke rushed over to me with a phony smile and a forebodin' look on his thin face. "Well, if it ain't James Monroe Henry. What can I get ya?"

His loud and deliberate use of my full name told me all I had to know. The old man must have been asking around for Henry James. I ordered a beer and kept my gaze casual. Deke started to break out in a bead sweat and had to wipe his high forehead with a bar rag.

The old man looked to be ever'thing they'd said he was. He had to be a couple of inches taller than I was and maybe fifty pounds heavier. He was dressed all in black and held a glass of water in his right hand and what looked to be a Bible in his left. He sized me up as I walked in and took particular notice of my gun and gun belt. I was thinking how smart it was of Taylor to replace the stars on my gun belt with her old conchos.

The old grim reaper spoke in a powerful and commanding voice. "I'm huntin' a murderin' bastard named Henry James. Been chasing him for almost four years. Do you know of him?"

"Nah, can't say that I do."

He placed the glass of water on the bar without taking his eyes off mine and slowly moved a step or two closer.... "Do you know who I am?"

I tried to remain calm but my temperature was rising. "No sir, I don't believe we've been introduced."

"I am Deacon Daniels, the avenging right arm of God Almighty."

He raised his left hand with the Bible in it and waved it over his head. Out of the corner of my eye, I saw the four card players duck under tables and behind chairs.

I wasn't hunting trouble but I wasn't about to be scared by this fire and brimstone preacher. It was the same situation in the same place as my dream but I wasn't the same person. There was no longer any "back-down" or "run-away" in me.

"Proud to meet ya'. I'm James Monroe...."

The Deacon moved another step closer and interrupted. "I heard what he called you.... but names can be changed.... James Monroe

Henry could become Henry James real easy and you sure fit the description."

I could'a tried to talk him out of it but he had me dead to rights and seemed to know it. Besides, I was sick of being hounded. I decided to show him my hole card.

"All right.... I've been called Henry James but I never claimed it was my name."

He paused as if relishing the moment and pulled his long jacket back to reveal a Walker Colt strapped to his right leg. "You murdered my son four years ago and I'm here to send you straight to perdition. You're bound for eternal damnation and the fires of hell...."

I didn't wait for him to finish his sermon. I drew as fast as I could and fired three times right into the Bible he was waving over his head. It exploded and filled the air with confetti, which fell on him like a Sierra snowstorm.

The enraged Deacon was actually rendered speechless and he slowly lowered his left hand with the remains of the Bible still in it. "You destroyed the word of God." Then he stared at me with the wrath of God in his red-rimmed eyes. He was poised to draw but found himself staring down the barrel of my Colt.

"I just wanted your attention so I could tell ya' I didn't murder your son. Preacher dealt his own hand and played it the best he could but he wasn't fast enough.... and neither are you. My advice is to let it be."

If he still wanted his chance, I was prepared to give it to him. I spun my Colt back into the holster and waited for his move.

I was afraid but I was in control of my fear. Fear itself is a good thing. It makes a man cautious. Controllin' the fear is what separates a hero from a coward. No matter what happened today, I knew I'd never have that awful dream again.

Deacon's anger had him out in front of his good sense and he went for his gun. Not wishing to kill him, I aimed high-left and caught him in the right shoulder. That proved to be a mistake as the impact of the bullet just whirled him full circle and he came up shooting. His momentum threw off his aim and his bullet tore the hat off my head. I placed my last two rounds square in the middle of his big black chest but he still stood his ground.

Like a wounded bear, he growled his defiance and tried to lift the gun in his right hand. With my lead in his shoulder, the weight of that big old Walker Colt was too much and he couldn't raise it. His grip slipped and a second shot ripped into the oak flooring. He looked down at his bloody clothing and the growing red pool at his feet. "Damn you to hell." Then he slowly collapsed on the floor.

I looked down upon his body and slowly reloaded my Colt. "Amen, Deacon.... Amen."

I finished my beer as Deke and the card players came out from under. "Boys, the Deacon here came hunting for Henry James the gunfighter, and found him. I'd be obliged if that's the way ya told it." I tossed a gold eagle on the bar and spoke to Deke. "See his horse gets a good home and bury him as deep as you can. I don't favor him ever being resurrected."

Taylor ran into me as I was going out through the batwing doors. She'd come a'runnin' at the sound of the gunshots. She noticed the hole in my hat but had the good sense not to mention it. I assured her I was all right and we would have no further problem with the old man in black. After all the weeks of not knowing who he was, I still thought of Deacon Daniels that way.

Taylor and I camped out in the canyon that night and avoided old Rufus. We finally got back to the ranch the following afternoon. Wagons had already started to arrive from Flagstaff with some of the supplies and building materials we'd ordered. The ranch was alive with excitement but when we rode in with Thomas' body, we put a halt to all that.

Taylor and I told 'em how Thomas died but not what we suspected. With help from G.W., Taylor and I got Pa to allow us to bury him on the mound back of the house next to John. It was a simple ceremony with only our family attending. Taylor spoke from the Bible of God's love and forgiveness while Pa stood with his eyes closed and his fists clenched. After the ceremony, ever'one went inside as the sky was cloudin' up to storm but I remained on the mound to gather my thoughts. So much had happened in such a short time.

Just a few weeks ago, I was heading home worrying about my past when I ran smack into my future. Now, two of my bothers were dead and so was Charles and our little graveyard was getting crowded. Pa was frettin' over his ownership of the ranch and G.W. was preparing to leave. Taylor and I were bound for Santa Fe to take over the Saint Charles Place. Ever'thing was changing all at once.

At the sound of a horse approaching, I looked up to see Hopi Joe riding in. Somehow, he'd learned of my return to the ranch and got here just as a light rain started to fall. We shared a warm greeting and our great sadness as I explained Thomas' passing. I was telling Joe the highlights of my travels when the rain started to come down in buckets. We rushed to the barn to get out of the downpour. I continued my story telling while Joe tended to his horse. I forked some extra hay for Goner and Domino and spoke to them as Joe finished up. He left for the house and I was about to join him when I thought of the Henry rifle. I had to show it to Joe. He was a great admirer of fine firearms.

While Taylor prepared supper, I sat on the porch with Pa and Joe. The rain finally let up and G.W. was busy with Susanna and the kids. Joe was caressing the Henry rifle and working the action. When he asked about the engraving and initials, I told him I'd never given it too much attention. Joe scooped up some mud from the yard and rubbed it on the receiver. Then he carefully wiped the excess off the receiver with an old rag. The dark mud filled the engraved lines and made them stand out against the brass receiver. What do ya know? There they were, plain as day, the initials, C. U. F.

All I could think of was Charles' stickpin with those same initials. Was it possible? Could this have been Charles' rifle all along or were those initials just some weird coincidence?

What was it Cleetis said? "Old Red Dog took it off a dead 'Pache but judging by the trappin' the 'Pache probably fetched it off some poor Navajo. No telling how far it's come or how long ago. Funny how a gun can get around." Cleetis was righter than he knew.

Then I thought back to Charles' last words about the original deed being left with Henry Staaa.... All along I thought he was trying to speak a name of the teamster he'd hired to drive his wagon but what if he meant the Henry stock? Had he put the deed in the rifle stock for safe keeping?

Hurriedly, I checked the Henry's stock and found the keyhole opening in the metal butt plate. I pried it open and shook the rifle. My excitement was stifled when all that fell out were parts of a old cleaning kit. Joe, however, had another idea and held the rifle to the lantern as he looked at it. The hollow chamber in the stock was a perfect hiding place for a rolled up document and that's where we found it. Rolled up inside was the original deed to our ranch.

I couldn't believe my eyes. I'd been totin' it around all this time and didn't know it. The deed was in perfect condition and bore the notarized stamp that Charles mentioned. It wasn't lost in the fire after all. A Navajo warrior must have fetched the Henry before they set fire to the wagons. Somehow, it got passed to an Apache, and then old Red Dog took it off him.

Just like the copies, the original deed named Charles U. Farley as the rightful owner of the ranch. With Charles' Will and the Pinkerton documents, I could take this deed to Flagstaff and have my old friend Cecil Abernathy transfer ownership over to Porter Henry, free and clear. I showed the deed to Pa and told him he'd never have to worry about losing the ranch again.

Pa put on his spectacles and read the document over and over. Tears trickled down his face as he read. I told him Charles left the ranch to me in his Will. That was mostly the truth. I left out the part about Charles thinking I was truly his son.

Hopi Joe was still fondling the Henry when he spoke to Pa in a low voice. "Now.... you must tell him."

Pa put down his glasses and put the deed on his desk. He was strugglin' with whatever he had to say. "I know you're right but I promised Miriam."

"She would understand. He must know now."

Pa sat down and for the first time, told me the whole truth about my past. "After James Madison died on the trail, Ma caught the pox, too. She was in her fifth month of carrying another child at the time. She eventually recovered but she lost the baby. It was too much grief for her to accept. She rode in the wagon and took care of the older boys but never talked, smiled or laughed at all. I was afraid I'd lost her, too." Tears started to roll down his face.

"When Joe brought us that little baby boy, Ma saw him as her own dead son. She wouldn't hear of it any other way and made me promise never to tell the truth of it."

Pa looked at me with more tears streamin' down his face. "You are that child, Monroe. You came from that wagon train. I reckon that Charles Farley was your real father after all."

Pa broke down again and I just sat there with my thoughts. Things had come full circle. Charles had been so sure I was his son and now it turns out he was right. Had he known the truth all along? Did the Pinkertons find out somehow and tell him? How I wished I could've spoken with him as his son and not some third-rate play actor.

It was hard to believe that Charles Ulysses Farley was my real born name. That meant the Saint Charles Place and all the money were my rightful inheritance all along. I wouldn't have to feel guilty anymore. Pa and G.W. would have the ranch and I could start a new life in Santa Fe.

Then it hit me, Taylor.... what would happen with Taylor? She planned to come with me to Santa Fe but that was when she thought I was her brother. What would she do now that we were...? I had to consider.... what were we.... just friends?

The whole family got together and Pa retold the story from the very beginning. I watched Taylor and G.W. as they finally heard the whole truth. They were sad-faced and silent. Pa repeated that in Ma's mind, I was her son and their brother even if I wasn't really blood kin.

Then I showed 'em the real deed to the ranch and told G.W. that it was his alone after Pa passed. It was meant to be the Henry ranch and not the Farley ranch. I repeated to Taylor that she was welcome to go with me to Santa Fe where my business would give us both a new start in life. With the extra money, Pa could afford to hire men to help run the ranch.

I kept the Wells Fargo bank account to myself, as that was my ace in the hole. If the saloon business didn't work out I could use the money to start up ranching.

After two weeks of helping out around the Box H, Taylor and I finally saddled up and headed out for Santa Fe. We made one short stop in Flag to see good old Cecil and arrange for the deed transfer. I ran into Trace and wouldn't ya know Megan had sent him packin' too. I sent him to the Box H with a note to Pa. Trace had earned his place at our table and was more than welcome. He'd be all the help they'd ever need.

Taylor was a joy to be with and I no longer felt guilty about admiring her as a young lady. She was a pure western woman with a strong sense of who she was and what she wanted of life. Even though we weren't brother and sister anymore, we could still be friends and that would do.... for now.

As for me, I finally knew who I was. I had been born Charles Ulysses Farley but raised as James Monroe Henry. Along the way, I had been known as Henry Monroe, Henry James, James Monroe and the Navajo Kid. But from now on, I would honor both my fathers and be known in Santa Fe as the owner of the Saint Charles Place and the son of the late Farley Charles.... Mister Henry Charles.

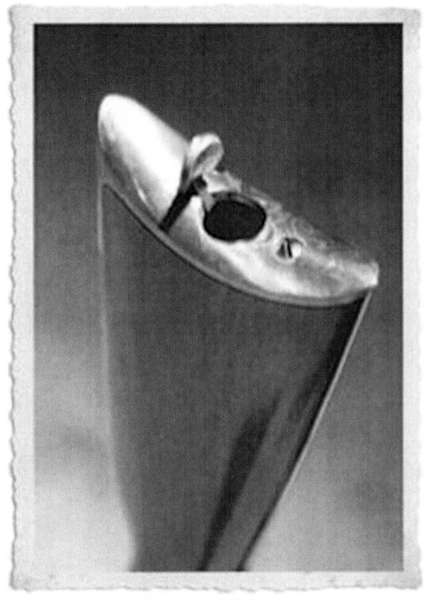

"We checked the Henry's stock and found a keyhole opening in the metal butt plate."